The Corpse Light

Lesley McEvoy was born and bred in Yorkshire and has had a passion for writing in one form or another all her life. The writing took a backseat as Lesley developed her career as a behavioural analyst/profiler and psychotherapist – setting up her own consultancy business and therapy practice. She has written and presented extensively around the world for over twenty-five years, specialising in behavioural profiling and training, with a wide variety of organisations. The corporate world provided unexpected sources of writing material when, as Lesley said, she found more psychopaths in business than in prison! Lesley's work in some of the UK's toughest prisons was where she met people whose lives had been characterised by drugs and violence and whose experiences informed the themes she now writes about. Deciding in 2017 to concentrate on her writing again, Lesley produced her debut novel, *The Murder Mile*. These days she lives in Cheshire with her partner but still manages to lure her two grown-up sons across the Pennines with her other passion – cooking family dinners.

Also by Lesley McEvoy

The Murder Mile
The Killing Song
A Deadly Likeness
The Invisible Dead

The
Corpse
Light

Lesley McEvoy

ZAFFRE

First published in the UK in 2025 by
ZAFFRE
An imprint of Bonnier Books UK
A Bonnier Books UK Company
5th Floor, HYLO, 105 Bunhill Row,
London, EC1Y 8LZ

This is a work of fiction. Names, places, events and
incidents are either the products of the author's
imagination or used fictitiously. Any resemblance to
actual persons, living or dead, or actual
events is purely coincidental.

A CIP catalogue record for this book is
available from the British Library.

ISBN: 9-78180-418-475-2

Also available as an ebook and an audiobook

1 3 5 7 9 10 8 6 4 2

Typeset by IDSUK (Data Connection) Ltd
Printed and bound in Great Britain by Clays Ltd, Elcograf S.p.A.

The authorised representative in the EEA is Bonnier Books
UK (Ireland) Limited.
Registered office address: Floor 3, Block 3, Miesian Plaza,
Dublin 2, D02 Y754, Ireland
compliance@bonnierbooks.ie
www.bonnierbooks.co.uk

To my husband, Ian.
This one is for you.

'Besides this earth, and besides the race of men, there is an invisible world and a kingdom of spirits; that world is around us for it is everywhere.'

Charlotte Brontë, *Jane Eyre*

Chapter One

Yorkshire Moors, Wednesday, 29th January

At any other time, Hayley would have thought the tarn, a remote lake on top of the Yorkshire Moors, was a beautiful spot. But not tonight.

Tonight, all she could think about, as she watched her boyfriend throwing the last of their stuff into the small two-man pop-up tent, was how cold she was.

'I can't feel my feet.'

Lee stood up, brushing soil from his jeans. 'I'll get us a fire going later. You'll be fine.'

'That's later.' She moaned. 'What about now? I'm bloody freezing.'

Her boyfriend was distracted, pulling the expensive Sky-Master binoculars from his rucksack.

'Get in a sleeping bag then.'

Hayley hugged herself, hopping from one foot to the other. 'Why do we have to come up here in flippin' January? Wouldn't mind so much in summer.'

'I told you, it's a dark-sky site – no light pollution, and winter is the observing season. The air's clearer and it gets dark early, so we don't have to wait as long.' He began setting up a tripod. 'It's a new moon tonight, so there's no light to wash out the fainter stars.'

The young blonde tilted her head back, looking up into the inky blackness, already dotted with bright stars. 'I can't see a moon.'

He grinned at her, shaking his head. 'That's what "new moon" means . . . there isn't one.'

'Well, that's daft. They should call it a "no moon" then.'

She watched him set the tripod on top of the grassy slope that ran down to the tarn.

This was a desolate place, even in summer. Over an hour's hike from the Tarn Hill Tavern, where they'd left the car, across the windswept landscape of wild moorland and tufted heather, to the legendary Wytch's Tarn. A place only frequented by serious hikers, who didn't mind the rough terrain and steep inclines. Many of them attempting the 268 miles of the Pennine Way, usually between May and September.

But there would be no 'Way' walkers at this time of year.

Hayley didn't mind the distance, or the tough landscape. She was a keen hiker. Her and Lee walked most weekends. But that was in daylight – not pitch black like this.

An owl screeched somewhere in the distance and she hugged herself tighter.

'This place gives me the creeps.' She muttered quietly, straining to look across the still, dark water of the tarn. But the view was fading to blackness as the night deepened.

Lee had his back to the lake, staring through the binoculars into the inky sky.

'You can see the Milky Way,' he said enthusiastically. 'Even without the binocs.' He pointed above his head. 'Look, Hales . . . isn't that beautiful?'

Hayley *was* looking. But not at the sky.

She stood, transfixed . . . staring at a small ball of light on the surface of the water moving slowly towards them.

'Lee!'

'I know.' He didn't take his eyes from the binoculars. 'Amazing, isn't it?'

'What's that?' Hayley's voice went up an octave.

'What?'

Her whole arm trembled as she pointed across the water. '*That*.'

He swivelled round to look at the amber-coloured glow, which seemed to stop near the middle of the lake.

'Bloody hell.' He breathed. 'Dunno.'

He walked to the edge of the grassy slope, straining to see.

'Come away, Lee.' She couldn't keep the fear out of her voice. But, as usual, he was doing the opposite – scrambling down the muddy slope to the water's edge.

'I want to see,' he called over his shoulder, staring at the small, flickering flame on the water.

'Pass me the binoculars, Hales.' He reached his arm back without taking his eyes off the light.

But she was frozen to the spot, slowly shaking her head.

'Come back, Lee . . . I'm scared. What the hell is it?'

He turned back, as the light began to move away across the water. 'We're going to lose it—'

'Good!' Her whole body was shaking so hard she could hardly stand up. 'Lee, for God's sake, come back up here. Now!'

Something in her voice finally shook him out of it and he started up the slippery bank. He'd only gone a step when his feet slid in the mud and he stumbled backwards.

'Shit!' He threw out his arms, only just managing to stay on his feet, but he was almost up to his waist in ice-cold water. Quickly, he turned to look for the light, but it was gone.

'Frightened it off,' he said with a nervous laugh, turning back to look up at his girlfriend.

But she wasn't looking at him.

Her face was drained of colour, her eyes wide with terror. Staring at something behind him.

'Hales?'

He felt the water stirring slightly, as ripples swirled around his legs.

Something glistened white as it broke the surface of the water and brushed against his leg.

That's when Hayley's piercing, primeval scream of horror shattered the night.

Chapter Two

Tarn Hill Tavern, Thursday, 30th January

Every time I came to the Tarn Hill Tavern, I remembered how much I loved it. And every time that happened, I vowed to come more often, but life had always been too busy, until now.

As a freelance consultant, it went against the grain to turn down work. Always worried that the present job might be the last. Realistically, though, there wasn't much chance of that in my particular line.

As a forensic psychologist and criminologist, my diary had always been full.

Psychiatric assessments for the courts or offender profiling for solicitors' clients and parole boards kept me occupied – every minute of every day.

Then on top of that there was the police consultancy. In theory, only a small part of what I did, but in recent years, an all-consuming part. Both professionally and personally.

I looked at the man sitting opposite. Detective Chief Inspector, Callum Ferguson. The person responsible for getting me involved in his world, when he'd asked me to advise on a case a few years before, and now undeniably part of my personal life.

I watched him tuck into his roast dinner, like a man who hadn't eaten in a month.

'Is it good?'

'Amazing.' His barely discernible Scottish accent muffled, as he wiped his mouth with a napkin. 'If I'd known the food was this good, I'd have come here sooner.'

He glanced around the seventeenth-century inn, nodding approvingly.

Whitewashed walls, exposed beams and Yorkshire stone floors, with roaring log fires that, in centuries past, welcomed local farmers and drovers moving livestock across the Pennines. Now, frequented by muddy walkers, crossing the bleak moorland, or people like us, driving miles to sample the award-winning food.

'Thanks for suggesting it, Jo.' He raised his pint in a silent toast.

'Doing things like this makes a change for me too. Especially midweek,' I said, pushing my plate away.

'Jen letting you off for the day?' He smiled. 'Must be getting soft in her old age.'

'Don't let her hear you say that.' I thought about my friend and PA, who worked with me at the farmhouse most days. 'She's only ten years older than me.'

That boyish grin. 'Exactly.'

I playfully kicked him under the table.

'She still clucking round you like a mother hen?' He was only half joking as he glanced at my left wrist – the livid, purple scar, still visible from where I'd had to have it surgically repaired six months previously.

We'd both been injured attempting to catch a killer. Forcing me, at least, to take the last few months away from work. Not Callum though. He'd been back at his desk after just two weeks – as a senior investigating officer (SIO), on West Yorkshire Police's Homicide and Major Enquiry Team (HMET).

'She's been brilliant,' I had to admit. 'Making me take more time out . . . no bad thing really.'

'Getting any easier?' he asked, quietly. Startling blue eyes studying me, in that way he had that made me feel he could see my very thoughts.

'Yeah.' I smiled, flexing my fingers. 'Off the painkillers now. All good.'

He ran his fingers through thick grey hair, which I knew he'd had since he was a teenager. An unusual feature for a man in his forties – one that had earned him the 'silver fox' tag, from the women at Fordley nick, though never to his face.

A gust of wind slapped horizontal rain against the window next to me. The weather forecast was for more rain, which on these uplands would probably turn to snow. The last few weeks had seen torrential rainstorms, which had flooded the lower valleys. I stared out into the mist, not really seeing what was beyond the window.

The past months had allowed me to focus on my most recent book. The latest in a series I'd written about my work, profiling some of the most depraved offenders in the British criminal justice system. But more than that, it had given me time to take stock.

'Penny for them?' Callum's quiet voice tugged at my attention.

'Just contemplating whether I really *want* to go back to the day-to-day.'

He nodded slowly into his pint. 'Know what you mean.'

He didn't. Not really. He was a copper to his core. He'd never think of giving it up. Not for a minute. Not even when, on occasion, it had nearly cost him his life. For him, work *was* his life.

No wife . . . no kids. Just the job. Occasionally a woman would enter his life – causing me an irrational pang of jealousy and regret over what might have been for us. But they never seemed to stay for long. Or rather, Callum never wanted to have them in his life for long. And then they'd leave and it would be us again.

Whatever 'us' meant.

Not a relationship in the normal sense of the word.

An undeniable physical attraction that pulled us together and a volatile mix of personalities that would, almost inevitably, force us apart again.

7

For now, we were in our usual on/off state. More than friends; occasional lovers, with a reluctance to commit to more. Especially me.

'I suppose the longer you're away from it,' he was saying, 'the harder it might be to go back.' He glanced at me over the rim of his glass. 'I hope you don't decide to just write your books though.' He smiled. 'We need all the help we can get these days.'

'Busy?'

He nodded. 'Always. It never ceases to amaze me the inventive ways people will find to kill, maim or disfigure someone else.'

'Tell me about it,' I said with a wry smile. 'I usually only get to see the weird ones.'

'Latest one isn't a weird MO – more like a strange location,' he said, staring outside.

But my interest was piqued. 'Oh?'

'Body found at Keelham Hill landfill site.'

Keelham Hill was just a few miles from the village of Kingsberry, where I lived, in a converted farmhouse on the moors above Fordley.

'I hadn't heard anything about a body.' Remote as my farmhouse was, the moorland communities were small and big news like that travelled fast.

'It only came through in the early hours.' He leaned back to ease knotted shoulders. 'We've asked the press to keep a lid on it for now – until we get a positive ID and can inform the family . . . if there is one.'

I thought of all the stories I'd heard about body parts turning up at landfill sites. 'Why so strange?' I asked.

Callum took a sip of his pint. 'What do you mean?'

'It's not uncommon for body parts to turn up, is it? I mean, rough sleepers taking shelter inside industrial bins at the back of shops. Especially the ones for cardboard. Warm and off the streets. Then waking up as they get tipped into the back of the bin lorry being crushed.'

He shook his head, wiping froth from his top lip.

'Not parts . . . a whole body. Looks like he was killed by a blow to the back of the head.'

'Was he an employee at the site?' I couldn't help myself.

'Nope. That's the thing. No one knows what he was doing in there. Members of the public can't just wander in. Looks like he broke in through the perimeter fence sometime during the night and got himself killed.'

'Why would anyone want to break into a landfill site?'

Callum shrugged. 'That's one question. The other one is why would he get murdered once he was in there?'

I was about to ask what made him think it was murder rather than an accident when we were interrupted by the young waitress coming to take our plates. I was contemplating treating myself to another glass of red when the door opened behind me, bringing with it an icy blast.

'Blimey, Owen,' the landlord called to the soaked farmer who stood in the doorway. 'Put wood back in the 'ole. Heat's getting out.'

A regular at the bar glanced over his shoulder. 'Aye, Owen, you know how tight Stan is . . . wood an' coal cost money.'

There was a ripple of laughter around the pub as the farmer slammed the door shut, before going to stand with his back to the fire.

'You're late,' the landlord said. 'Thought you must be sickening.'

'Nah.' Owen clasped his hands behind his back, warming them against the fire. 'Had a drama up at farm . . . early hours. Made me run late this morning.'

Stan was already pulling Owen a pint of his usual. 'Drama?'

'Young kids, camping up at Wytch's Tarn. Stargazers or summat. Got a scare. Came banging on our door early hours to be let in. Young lass were in a right state. Took a while to get any sense out of either of 'em.'

'Oh aye.' Stan was interested now. 'What kind of scare, then?'

Owen shrugged out of his oilskin, draping it on the back of a chair near the fire. 'Said they'd seen a strange light on the water . . . moving over the tarn. Then young fella slipped and fell in.'

'And that's what shook him up?' Stan placed Owen's pint on the bar.

'Not as much as seeing a skeleton's hand, coming out of the lake.' Owen gratefully took a sip of his pint.

'You're kiddin'?' Stan took payment for the pint.

'That's what the lad claimed.' Owen wiped the froth from his top lip. 'Lass saw it too. Hand – all bone – rising out of the tarn.'

'Jesus.' The landlord gave a low whistle. 'Then what?'

'What do you think? They scarpered.' Owen took his pint glass back to the fireplace. 'Left all their stuff and legged it.'

'What? In the dark?' Stan was leaning forward, interested now, elbows on the bar.

'Aye.' Owen nodded. 'Ours was first place they came to, being only half a mile from the tarn.'

'Bloody lucky they didn't stray into the bogs,' Stan said, shaking his head. 'Pitch black last night.'

'New moon.' A gravelly voice from the corner of the room made everyone turn to see who'd spoken.

I recognised the old man. Tommy Earnshaw, a retired shepherd.

'That's when they come out . . . .' he said quietly.

Chapter Three

Tarn Hill Tavern, Thursday Lunchtime

There was a long silence, before someone in the pub took the bait.

'What comes out?' A man sitting with a group of walkers, who were obviously not locals.

'Corpse lights,' Tommy said, as if that explained everything.

Across the table, Callum shot me a glance and raised his eyebrows in a silent question.

I just smiled, not wanting to steal Tommy's thunder.

I'd heard these tales since childhood. Spun on wintery nights, in front of the fire. A mix of local folklore and superstition that explained the sights and sounds on the moor which had haunted those who'd witnessed them for generations.

Tommy, with his wealth of knowledge about local legends, was, without a doubt, a good storyteller.

Living and working on the moors all his life. Now retired, he spent his afternoons perched on the chair reserved specially for him, at the corner of the bar, nursing a pint and engaging in the latest gossip.

'What?' the walker asked.

Tommy stared into his empty glass. 'Man's not a camel.'

'Excuse me?' The walker frowned.

Stan took the empty glass from Tommy. 'He means he can't go that long without a drink.'

The penny dropped. 'Oh yes, of course.' The walker left his friends at the table and came to the bar. 'Whatever this gentleman is having.' He paid for Tommy's pint and leaned his elbow on the bar. 'So,' he asked the old shepherd, 'these lights . . . ?'

'Spirits of the dead,' Tommy said, before taking a sip of his pint. 'Wandering the moors to lead travellers off the safe paths.'

One of the walkers, sitting at the table, stifled a short laugh. 'Don't leave the road.' He mimicked the line from the film *An American Werewolf in London*, followed by a theatrical howl at an imaginary moon.

Tommy never missed a beat.

'You can scoff, lad,' he said, his voice quiet and low. 'But many a walker's been lured into the bogs or off the cliff edges, following those lights at night.' He looked at the walkers, his thick brows drawn down. 'Death omens – that's what they are. Appear in places where there's been a tragedy . . . or when there's about to be one.'

'Has there been a tragedy up at the tarn?' a woman sitting with the group asked. She was looking intently at the old shepherd, taking this far more seriously than her companions.

'Aye, more than one,' Tommy said, taking a long pull on his pint. Eking out the moment for dramatic effect. 'Most famous was back in the sixteen hundreds. Old Mother Hewitt, local midwife – lived alone on the edge of the moors. Accused of being a witch. They had a trial and she were taken up to the tarn, bound ankles to wrists, and chucked in. If she floated, it proved she were a witch and she would've been burned at the stake.' Another mouthful of beer, taking his time.

'Luckily for Ma Hewitt, she sank – so they knew she were innocent. Trouble was, by the time they'd pulled her out she was dead as a doornail. Drowned.'

'Oh God,' the young woman breathed. 'That's awful.'

'Ever since then,' Tommy went on, 'corpse lights are seen at the tarn . . . and flitting across the moors. An omen of death . . . or trouble for some unfortunate. I've worked on these moors all my life. Seen corpse lights many a time and always before summat bad. Tragedy follows . . . always.'

A stillness fell over the pub. The quiet only broken by the crackling of burning logs in the fireplace. Surprisingly, it was Callum who broke the silence.

'And this skeletal hand?' His voice sounded too loud, almost irreverent in the hush. 'That been seen before?'

Tommy slowly shook his head. 'Not that I know of.'

'Don't suppose the young lad held on to it . . . the hand?' Callum didn't even try to hide his scepticism.

'You kidding.' It was Owen, the farmer. 'Nearly crapped himself. Couldn't get out of the water fast enough. When he looked back, it'd disappeared.'

'Of course it had.' Callum smiled, taking a sip of his pint. 'Did they report it?' he asked no one in particular.

'The lad called the police this morning, after we'd given them breakfast. Bobbies said they'd make a note of it.' Owen rolled his eyes. 'Can't imagine they'll be in a rush to come gallivantin' over the moors on the word of a couple of scared kids.'

'Got my shed broken into last summer,' Stan said. 'Couldn't be bothered coming out for that. Just gave us a crime number.'

Owen nodded in sympathy. 'They asked the kids if they'd been drinking or taking drugs. Don't think they believed a word of it.'

'What about you?' Stan asked.

Owen shrugged. 'Went up there this morning on the quad bike, to collect the kids' tent and stuff. They were too scared to go back. I had a quick look round the edge of the tarn . . . didn't see nothing.'

'Can't imagine they did, either,' Callum muttered into his pint.

Slowly the hum of quiet conversation resumed. People discussing the latest in hushed tones.

'You don't believe it?' I asked with a half-smile.

Callum glanced at me, raising that one expressive eyebrow of his. 'What? Corpse lights and skeletal hands, rising out of the water, like the Lady of the Lake? What's not to believe?'

'I've seen them,' I said, watching for his reaction.

He looked more surprised than interested. 'Skeletal hands?'

'No.' I laughed. 'Lights, across the moors.'

He sat back in his chair. 'And what do *you* think they are?'

'Will-o'-the-wisps. My dad showed them to me when I was a kid. He said the flames were formed by marsh gases, from rotting vegetation. That's why they're usually seen near bogs. The natural methane ignites spontaneously, forming these little standing flames.'

'Explains why people who see them walk into the marshes,' he said. 'Not *lured away* by ghosts. Just happen to be near them anyway.'

I smiled. 'Ahh, but that's not as entertaining as Tommy's version, is it?'

'Suppose not.'

We sat in companiable silence for a minute, until I brought him back to the topic that interested me.

'So, this body at the landfill . . . what makes you think it's a murder?'

He stretched back. 'Early days yet, but paramedics attending pronounced life extinct. Only injury they could see was to the back of his head.'

'Enough to be the cause of death?'

He nodded. 'Obviously we'll know for sure after the post-mortem, but looks like it. There was nothing to suggest he'd hit his head in a fall. No objects around him that could explain the wound. Just a body, lying in open ground, with his head caved in.'

I finished the last of my wine. 'Who's doing the post-mortem?'

'Your mate, Dr Richardson. She was Home Office pathologist on call.'

'That's good.' Elle Richardson was the best and I didn't just think so because she was one of my closest friends.

Tommy slid off his stool by the bar and shrugged on his jacket. Calling his 'goodbyes' to the table of walkers and Stan behind the bar. He paused as he came past our table.

'Not seen you in a while, Jo.'

'No . . . been too busy, until recently.' I smiled.

'And you'd be her copper friend?' He looked at Callum. 'That's been keeping her so occupied.'

'And how would you know that?' Callum's tone was friendly enough, but the smile didn't quite reach his eyes.

'Oh, not much gets past folk round here.' Tommy pulled on his flat cap, then turned back to me, his expression suddenly more serious.

He jerked his head towards the group of walkers. 'Them city types can make fun, but you're a local lass and you know those corpse lights are a warning. You be careful, living up on the moors on yer own.'

'Of what?' Something about the old man's demeanour sent the hairs prickling across my scalp.

'Evil, lass. It'll be visiting someone round here soon, mark my words.'

Chapter Four

Kingsberry Farm, Friday Morning, 31st January

I looked at the blank page of manuscript that stared back accusingly from my laptop and rubbed my eyes for the umpteenth time.

It was no good. Whatever inspiration I was hoping for was playing hard to get.

The silence in my office was broken by the dulcet tones of Harvey, my boxer dog, snoring contentedly on the rug and Jen, at her desk across the room, tapping the keys of her computer.

I swung my chair round to gaze out of the arched window behind me, which overlooked my garden. Usually, I could distract myself by watching the birds and squirrels fighting for a place on the birdfeeders. But today even they weren't playing.

I couldn't blame them. The weather had been foul for days. High winds, sweeping across open moorland, pushing sleeting rain ahead of it that cut to the bone. Some of the heaviest rain we'd suffered in years.

'Writer's block?' Jen's voice tugged my attention.

'Something like that,' I said, still looking out of the window.

'Fancy a brew?'

She knew me so well – this woman who'd thankfully come into my life so many years ago. She was more than my PA. A best friend, confidante and invaluable colleague.

Ordinarily, I never turned down tea. But I felt sluggish and restless. I looked out at the weather. For now, there was a lull in the relentless downpour.

'Maybe later. Might go for a walk, while there's a break in the rain.'

Harvey stretched and got up from the rug, coming over to nudge my hand with his wet nose. I ruffled his silky ears and he sat beside my chair, gazing out of the window with me.

'Come on,' I said, finally. 'Not getting anything done here.'

Never needing to be told twice, he was already padding to my office door, nosing it open to trot down the glass corridor that connected my office to the main house.

'You get off if you want, Jen. Not much doing here today.'

She nodded, distracted by whatever she was doing. 'I'll finish up here first. If you're not back, I'll lock up. Take your key.'

'OK.'

I followed Harvey down to the kitchen, reassuringly warm from the constant heat of the Aga, and into the porch where I kept coats and boots.

Harvey leaped around, impatient to be off, as he watched me pull on boots and the old Barbour jacket that lived on a hook by the heavy oak door.

As soon as I opened it, he shot out in a pent-up tangle of muscle and energy, skittering down the gravel drive and through the opening in the hedge, which lead onto the moors.

I didn't hurry, knowing he would eventually stop and wait for me to catch up.

Thankfully the wind had dropped, though it was still bitingly cold. I pulled up the collar of my jacket and dug my hands into my pockets. My boots crunched across frozen tufts of stiff moorland grass and dried heather, crusted with sparkling ice crystals.

Thirty yards ahead, Harvey stopped and glanced back, then carried on sniffing. His nose to the track. Long white-tipped tail whipping in excitement as he picked up the scent of elusive wildlife.

The day was dull. Pewter skies robbing me of the usually spectacular views across the Dales, to the hills in the far distance. The path was getting steeper as I walked towards the high point, known to locals as 'The Mountain', though in reality it wasn't high enough to qualify.

The top was shrouded in mist and I realised I'd lost sight of Harvey.

I called him and waited, but he didn't appear.

Probably off chasing a rabbit.

I picked up the pace – my heavy breathing suspended in white plumes, as I panted with the effort. A reminder, if one were needed, that I wasn't as fit as I should be. A familiar dull ache began to spread through my left thigh and into my groin, making me curse as I pulled up the steep incline.

Several years earlier, I'd been attacked and stabbed in the leg. The injury had severed the femoral artery, leaving me with an ugly scar to add to my collection. It ached when it was over-worked and gave me a slight limp on really bad days.

'Harvey!'

Nothing.

It wasn't like him not to come when I called.

As I reached the top of the hill, visibility was reduced to just a few feet. The track seeming to melt into hazy swirls of fog that drifted across the moor.

I stopped and listened, but all I could hear was my own laboured breathing and the rush of blood in my ears.

'Harvey!'

My voice seemed to echo back to me from the void.

I took a moment to catch my breath, not moving.

Something caught my attention . . . a half-heard sound.

I tilted my head, trying to work out where it had come from.

Snatches of my conversation with Tommy, in the pub, began scrolling, unbidden, through my mind.

'*. . . those corpse lights are a warning. You be careful . . . up on the moors on yer own.*'

There . . . a voice – calling out.

I took a few steps further down the track. 'Hello?'

'Over here.' A woman's voice, clearer now.

As I went down the track, I could make out the dark shape of a figure, close to the ground.

Then Harvey bounded out of the mist towards me, stopped and ran back towards the figure.

It was a young girl, sitting on a rock. A rucksack that looked bigger than she was leaning against it.

'He's beautiful.' She laughed, fussing Harvey, who danced around her, loving all the attention.

My heart rate returned to normal, and I took a relieved breath.

Harvey reluctantly returned to my side, looking suitably sheepish. 'So that's why you didn't come when I called?'

The girl swept a dark ponytail over her shoulders. 'To be fair—' she smiled '—I was finishing a bit of pork pie when he ran up to me. Giving him the crust might have been a big distraction.'

'Hmm.' I gave him a fuss. 'Don't suppose I can compete with pork pie, can I, boy?'

It was then I noticed she had her boots and one sock off.

She followed the direction of my eyes. 'Blisters,' she said simply. 'I stopped for a brew while there was a break in the rain. Decided to treat my feet before I pushed on.'

I sat on another rock on the opposite side of the track, as Harvey went back to his new friend, sniffing hopefully at the rucksack.

'You walking the Pennine Way?' I asked.

'Yep. The whole thing. Edale to Scotland – didn't pick the right weather for it though, did I?'

I stuffed my hands deeper into my jacket pockets and glanced down the half-visible track. 'Brave, taking it on in January.'

She was already applying padded plasters to her heel, replying without looking up. 'Only time I can do it this year. Starting a new job next month so got a few weeks off.' She pulled on a thick woollen sock.

I watched as she started lacing up her boots.

'You on your own?'

She nodded. 'Prefer it that way.' She looked up and smiled, the expression transforming her face, and I realised how pretty she was, despite the bedraggled hair.

'Can set my own pace, you know? Stop off to see things I'm interested in . . . . don't have to accommodate anyone else.'

'Still, it's pretty desolate along some parts. Not sure I'd have tackled it on my own at your age.'

She was packing stuff into her rucksack. 'You sound like my mum.' She laughed.

'I have a son, not much older than you.' I smiled at the thought. 'Hope you check in more often than he does with me?'

'I try. When I stop off for the night usually. I'm Rachel, by the way.'

'Pleased to meet you. I'm Jo.'

Harvey barked, not wanting to be left out.

'Oh, and your new best friend here is Harvey.'

She got up and bent over my dog, nuzzling her cheek against his. 'Do you live round here?'

I nodded in the general direction of the farmhouse. 'Just down the hill.'

'Great.' She pulled a map out of the front pocket of her waterproof poncho. 'Then maybe you can give me a pointer? Think I've gone wrong in the fog.'

I stood beside her, looking at the route, marked in red.

'I'm heading for Hebden Bridge – detouring to Top Withens. They say the farmhouse there was Emily Brontë's inspiration for the Earnshaws' house in *Wuthering Heights*.'

'Don't be too disappointed,' I said, still looking at the map. 'It's nothing but a ruin now.' I traced the map with my finger.

'You should have gone left, across the stile at the bottom of the hill. It's about an hour and a half from there.'

She nodded. 'Great . . . thanks.'

'Then where to?'

'Ickornshaw. Staying there tomorrow night.'

'A lot to cover in a day. Might want to reconsider going to the Withens in this weather.' I could hear myself trying not to dampen her enthusiasm too much.

She folded the map and hefted the rucksack over one shoulder, glancing round to make sure she hadn't forgotten anything.

'Planning to camp out tonight, then I've booked a B & B at Ickornshaw. I'll be fine.'

'Well, good luck, Rachel. You take care.'

Harvey whined softly as we watched Rachel stride off down the track, waving as she vanished into the mist.

'Sorry, boy, no more pork pie.'

I stood, listening to the silence, then turned to walk back the way we'd come.

Just as we reached the bottom of the hill, my phone shrieked.

'McCready,' I answered distractedly.

'Jo, it's me.' Callum's voice.

I could already tell from his tone this wasn't a social call. 'What's up?'

'Remember I told you about our body at the landfill site?'

'Guy with his head bashed in?'

'Turns out he was in the system. So, when we ran his prints, we got an ID.'

'OK. Not sadistic or deviant – so why are you calling me?'

'Because he's a friend of yours.'

Chapter Five

Kingsberry Farm, Friday, 31st January

'I'd hardly call him a friend,' I was saying, cradling the phone under my chin as I pulled my boots off in the porch, back at the house.

'You *did* know him, though?'

'As a client, when he was serving time in Armley prison.'

I hung my coat on the hook and went into the kitchen. Grateful for the welcoming warmth, after the freezing conditions on the moor.

'Red had learning difficulties,' I said, filling the kettle and flipping the lid on the Aga hotplate. 'Typical case of someone who needed treatment, not prison. His solicitor arranged for him to be assessed by a psychologist.'

'Which is where you met him?'

'Yes. After the assessment, we managed to get him transferred off the wing to a psychiatric unit.'

As I prepared the teapot, I thought back to my first meetings with 'Red' – real name Jimmy Wilcox – whose shock of ginger hair earned him his nickname.

I couldn't help feeling a wave of sadness that he was dead . . . apparently murdered. Whatever he'd been involved in, the man I knew didn't deserve to end like that.

I said as much to Callum.

'He was a member of an organised crime group.' Callum didn't sound in the least sympathetic. 'Anyone who spends his life working for Chris McGarry and his crew is hardly a saint.'

'True,' I conceded. 'But as far as I knew, once he was released, he went back to stay with his mum . . . was living a quiet life.'

Red's mother, Audrey, was in her eighties. Severely handicapped, she'd relied on her only son to provide for them both since his teenage years.

Schoolfriends, Chris McGarry and his brothers had been only too happy to take the six-foot-six gentle giant under their wing and employ him in their fledgling criminal activities. All of them doing time in young offender institutions and eventually adult prison. But Red had always been 'looked after' and was fiercely loyal to his gangland family.

Chris had used him as a courier and general gofer in the family business – drugs and arms dealing – which secured the 'firm's' place as a major force to be reckoned with. Making the McGarrys one of the wealthiest and most feared gangs in the North of England.

It could all have come to a deadly end a couple of years earlier, when Chris had been sentenced to life in prison for the brutal murder of two rival drug suppliers. Shooting them in the back of the head at point-blank range – execution style.

His legal team had tried to say that the balance of his mind had been affected at the time of the shooting and asked me to do a psychological assessment. But their client hadn't wanted to plead diminished responsibility and, inevitably, had to serve his sentence in a prison.

Chris wasn't about to relinquish his hard-won empire that easily. He had prison officers and – according to those in the know – police officers on the payroll and I was reliably informed that he was conducting business as usual from inside his high-security prison cell at HMP Wakefield, known colloquially as 'The Monster Mansion'.

The OCG – Organised Crime Group – was intact and running under the supervision of Chris's trusted associates on the outside.

'How's his mother taken the news?' I knew Audrey's world would have effectively fallen apart.

'I wasn't the one who delivered the death notice.' Callum was matter-of-fact. 'But I imagine, like any other mother. Even if her son *was* a gangster.'

My breath left me in a frustrated gust. 'He *wasn't* like that, Cal. I know you find it hard to imagine, but Red was a decent sort.'

'We'll have to agree to differ.'

I could imagine him raking long fingers through his hair in that way he had when he was frustrated or tired.

'Then look at his record,' I persisted.

'Already have.'

'So, you'll know – no violent offences . . . never hurt anyone.'

'True,' he finally admitted. 'But didn't exactly earn an honest crust either. No sign of regular employment. Being on McGarry's payroll is all I need to know about where his income was coming from.'

This wasn't getting us anywhere, so I shifted the topic. 'Any idea what he was doing at the landfill site?'

I could almost see him shake his head. 'No. That's why I'm calling. Wondered if you knew anything?'

I poured tea into a mug and took it over to my long-pine kitchen table. 'Why would I? Last time I saw him was when he was in the psychiatric unit – almost two years ago.'

'What about his solicitor?' I heard him shuffling papers. 'Joshua Weston? You spoken to him recently?'

Joshua had been a well-respected solicitor on the northern circuit when I'd first set up my private practice, years ago. He'd referred cases to me and I'd acted as an expert witness for him, on more occasions than I cared to count.

We'd built up a good working relationship that had become a friendship over the years and brought me into contact with characters like Chris McGarry and Red.

Despite Chris's reputation, I couldn't help but like him. He had a boyish charm and undoubted good looks that somehow made you forget, when you were with him, what he did for a living.

Callum knew that I was on good terms with Chris and his solicitor, and didn't hide the fact that he didn't approve. Which was maybe why this conversation was starting to feel uncomfortably like an interview.

'No. He hasn't referred any cases to me for a while now.'

'I meant, have you spoken to him about McGarry... or Red?'

There was something about his tone that was putting me on edge. A subliminal instinct – maybe an inevitable feeling, when being questioned by a cop? Or maybe my own guilty conscience?

'I told you... no.'

An unnerving pause, then, 'OK. Just thought I'd ask... as you knew him. Have to cover all the bases.' And with that, he was gone.

*　*　*

I tried to go back to work, but my mind was occupied with thoughts of Red and more sadly, Audrey, his poor mother.

Jen had left by the time we got back from our walk on the moors so I was alone at the house.

I'd just shut down my laptop and turned off the lamps in my office, when the landline rang.

'McCready?'

'Sweet pea?' Elle Richardson's voice was a welcome surprise. 'Why you calling the landline?'

She exhaled loudly and I knew she was smoking. A surprising vice for a doctor and pathologist, but one she refused to relinquish, along with all the other decadent pleasures she enjoyed.

25

Elle was a sybarite – enjoying life to the full – perhaps *because* of the job she did, rather than despite it.

'Because I thought you'd have your nose to the grindstone, darling.'

That made me feel suddenly guilty.

'I should have . . . but not achieving anything, so I'm knocking off early.'

'Wonderful. I was ringing to invite you out for lunch. I've just finished in court – got the afternoon off.'

'Oh, go on then – if you twist my arm.'

'I'll pick you up in an hour.'

Chapter Six

McNamara's Pub, Fordley, Friday, 31st January

McNamara's was an Irish pub in the centre of Fordley, owned and run by my late father's best friend and my godfather – the eponymous Finn McNamara.

Sunday lunches were a family tradition here and I had many fond memories as a child, of being entertained by Finn and his family.

Now, it was a favourite place to meet with Elle, whenever we were both in the city.

It was close to the courts, police station and hospital. Places that marked a regular circuit in both our working lives.

Elle was first through the door and greeted by Finn's booming voice.

'It's herself . . . and I hope you've brought my girl with you?'

Elle's laugh sounded like the tinkling of ice in a crystal glass. 'Of course.'

I followed her through the door, glad for the blast of warm air, which smelled of beer, coffee and comfort food.

Finn McNamara strode over, this bear of a man, with a smile as wide as the ocean.

'Here, ladies,' he gushed, as he took our coats and ushered us to a cosy corner table. 'Let's get yer settled by the fire.'

I was squeezed in one final bear hug before he gallantly pulled out our chairs.

'Menus are on the table. Will it be your usual to drink, while you wait?'

At my nod, he beamed then was gone. Sharing friendly banter with his customers as he weaved through the tables, back to his place behind the bar.

Typically, Finn's giant personality and gregarious welcome left me feeling slightly breathless. The regulars in the bar slowly turned their attention away from these two women who'd had such a fanfare of an entrance, back to their own conversations.

'What a character.' Elle watched him go and smiled as she swept long auburn tresses over her shoulders.

I marvelled, not for the first time, at an effortless elegance, I'd never been blessed with.

This willowy-tall woman, a young-looking forty-something, with supermodel looks and a scientific brain. The kind of woman who knew a dozen different ways to put her hair up using a paper clip and make it look stylish. Unlike me, who always looked like I'd left the house in a rush.

Since her colleague and predecessor, Doctor Tom Llewellyn, had retired, Elle had taken over as Home Office pathologist, at the local teaching hospital, which was where we'd met, decades before – called to give evidence at various criminal proceedings.

With an intellect I admired and a warm personality that was a welcome plus in my life, an unexpected bond had grown between us. Forging careers in male-dominated environments. Supporters and allies, who had become close friends.

Elle distractedly glanced over the menu. I already knew what I wanted. When it came to eating at McNamara's, I was boringly predictable.

The waitress arrived, carrying a tray of tea – with teapot and milk jug – just the way I liked it, and Elle's usual cappuccino. She smiled as I waved away the menu.

'Don't need to look.' I smiled. 'Colcannon and rashers, please.'

'Giant Yorkshire pudding for me,' Elle said. 'Filled with sausages and onion gravy.'

It never ceased to amaze me how Elle could eat the way she did and stay so slim. Though I knew that when she was working, she lived on coffee and cigarettes.

'Your metabolism runs like a greyhound on crack,' I said, stirring the teapot.

'Eat when I get the chance. You know how it is at the mortuary.' She took a sip of frothy coffee. 'Barely get time to go for a pee, never mind a proper meal.'

'Busy?'

'Always.' She sounded weary. 'No shortages of sudden deaths in this city, are there?'

I'd considered various ways of introducing the subject of Red's sudden death but couldn't come up with any that didn't sound contrived. I wasn't involved in an official capacity but couldn't help being interested. So, I just asked.

'Callum called me earlier about a case he said you were dealing with. It's someone I know . . . well, knew.'

Her shrewd green eyes suddenly looked concerned. 'Oh God, I'm sorry.'

I shrugged, taking a sip of tea. 'Not a friend . . . ex-client actually. Which was why Callum asked me about him.'

She watched me, waiting in silence for me to fill in the gaps.

'Guy called Jimmy Wilcox?'

'Oh yes. File said he went by an alias – Red?'

She stopped as the food arrived. We both waited until the waitress was out of earshot.

'The results aren't all in yet,' she continued, spreading a napkin across her lap. 'But on initial examination, looks like he died from a massive blow to the back of the head.'

I concentrated on my plate, suddenly feeling much hungrier. 'Nothing apart from that? I mean, no defence wounds or anything?'

She shook her head, chewing thoughtfully. 'Nothing obvious. A slight cut on the back of his right hand. More a scratch than a serious wound. Fresh – so it happened the same night he died, I'd say, but I can't give you more than that at the moment.'

'Any signs of a fight?'

'Doesn't look like it. Apart from some serious cuts and grazes to both of his knees.'

I stopped with the fork halfway to my mouth, struggling to come up with an explanation for that.

'He was on his knees when he was hit?'

She shook her head. 'I'd say he fell on his knees after being bashed on the head.'

I ran that image through my mind. 'But surely, dropping to your knees, then presumably falling face down after a blow like that wouldn't cause serious grazes, would it?'

'Unless he was moving, at speed. After being felled by the blow. The momentum would scuff his knees, as he fell down and forward . . . that would be consistent with what I found.'

She attacked her sausages. 'Why's the Boy Scout getting you involved? It's pretty straightforward, isn't it?'

'Boy Scout' was Elle's pejorative term for Callum.

I'd long ago stopped trying to change her opinion of him, which had been pretty much fixed when he'd cheated on me, over a year before.

'I'm not involved . . . officially.' I shrugged. 'Just mentioned it to me because I knew Red, I suppose.'

'Further examinations booked for tomorrow. Toxicology and blood work should be back then.'

'The Red I knew never touched drugs . . . or drink. I'd be surprised if anything like that shows up.'

She lifted her shoulders in a light shrug. 'You never know . . . stranger things have happened.' She paused and took a sip of water. 'Speaking of strange – what's all this about ghostly goings-on up at Wytch's Tarn?'

'How did you hear about that?'

'Apparently it's gone viral on social media.'

'Thought you'd rather stick a fork in your eye than go on social media.'

She laughed. 'I would, but Rina's all over it.'

Rina – a counsellor at Fordley's drug rehab centre – was Elle's long-term partner. They lived together in a beautiful farmhouse in a remote part of the Dales and were completely devoted to one another.

Fifteen years younger and about as different to Elle as it was possible to get, Rina had a passion for motorbikes and sported a purple buzz cut. The archetypal 'odd couple' – but it seemed to work for them.

'Apparently two sky-watchers, camping up there, saw a will-o'-the-wisp. Freaked them out.' I just gave the edited highlights.

'Hmm, I heard a skeleton was in on the act too.'

'Not a whole one.' I laughed. 'Just a hand. But whether that's what they *actually* saw . . .' I let the thought trail off.

'Well, it's gone viral on *Insta-Face* or whatever.'

'Instagram . . . or Facebook?' I shook my head in mock bemusement. 'Thought I was the technophobe round here.'

'Well, whatever. Rina says the moors are inundated with ghost hunters and New Age types – trying to catch a sighting.'

'The local pubs and B & Bs need the business,' I said. 'Anything that brings tourists here off-season is a good thing.'

If only I'd known what was to come, I might have been more careful about what I wished for.

Chapter Seven

Kingsberry Farm, Saturday, 1st February

Nursing a mug of tea, I swivelled my office chair and stared out of the window.

The weather matched my mood. Horizontal rain, howling across the open moorland, to batter my remote farmhouse – pushed along by a roaring wind, described as 'wuthering', in Yorkshire.

The two-foot-thick stone walls had held against the storms here for over two centuries, but at times it sounded as though they might be breached.

Even though I'd been in the office all morning, I wasn't being productive. Hadn't been for weeks. My writing had stalled and I couldn't find the motivation to continue. At least for now.

Jen was, as ever, sympathetic and supportive. Telling me the last twelve months had been tough ones and maybe I just needed a break. That I should practise the self-care I often preached to others, but never found the time to give myself.

Perhaps she was right.

Just as my thoughts were turning to the possibility of booking a holiday somewhere with sun and sandy beaches, the office phone rang.

'McCready.'

'Jo.' It was Elle. 'Thought I'd find you in the office.'

'Physically, maybe.'

'What does that mean?' She exhaled loudly as she smoked.

'Just not getting anything done.'

'Well, good job one of us is, then.' I could tell she was smiling. 'Just ringing with some more info on your ex-client, Red.'

'Go on.'

'As you predicted, toxicology shows no sign of drugs or alcohol in his system.'

'OK.'

'Cause of death, definitely the blow to the back of the head. Crushed the skull, causing traumatic brain injury. Death would have been instant.'

'Any other injuries?'

I could sense her shaking her head. 'None. Apart from the abrasion to the back of his right hand and the scuffs on his knees that I told you about. Police found the perimeter fence wire at the landfill had been cut. They think that's how he gained entry. Forensics found traces of blood and tissue on the sharp edges of the chain-link fencing. It's a match for the cuts on his hand.'

'So, it proves he cut through the fence to break into the site. But we have no idea why he would?'

'Not my department, sweet pea.' She exhaled again. 'But what I *can* tell you is that I can't see any innocent way he could have sustained the head injury. Crime scene photographs, show him lying in open ground. Nothing close enough that he could have hit his head on after a slip or trip. Wound was caused by a heavy object. Like a metal bar or tool of some kind. If he'd fallen, hitting his head on the ground, it wouldn't have caused an injury like this. And before you ask, Forensics have examined all the vehicles in the compound. No sign of blood or tissue on any of them. So, he didn't hit his head on anything there either.'

'So, whatever caused that injury has been removed from the scene?'

'Correct. Which leads us to *your* area of expertise.'

'A killer.'

Chapter Eight

Kingsberry Farm, Saturday, 1st February

After Elle's call, I stayed in the office, staring out of the window, going over everything she'd said.

Red had been murdered.

The thought saddened me – for all kinds of reasons.

Red had been a part of an organised crime group – working with Chris McGarry – but he wasn't the same as the others.

I'd spent enough time assessing Red while he was in Armley prison to know that he was about as non-violent an offender as it was possible to be. The 'outbursts' that had landed him in trouble with prison staff had been caused by frustration and worry for his mother on the outside. Compounded by his neurodiversity. Not by any inherent violent tendencies.

He'd trashed his cell – or banged his head against the walls – causing harm to himself, never to anyone else.

Even when he worked with the crime gang, he'd been Chris's driver, his gofer, not an enforcer.

It might be a cliché, but 'gentle giant' was the best way to describe the forty-year-old man, with learning difficulties, that I'd come to know during our sessions.

I was sad too, for his mother. The person who'd campaigned tirelessly for her son to be moved to a clinical environment, knowing he wouldn't survive for long on the prison wing.

Ironic then, that he'd been killed on the outside.

Maybe if he'd stayed in prison he would still be alive?

I pinched the bridge of my nose, suddenly feeling exhausted. Not physically, but mentally. Worn down by the relentless nature of the work I'd done for the last twenty-odd years. Mental torment – anguish and cruelty. The things that typified the cases I dealt with.

Finally, I got up and stretched. Tea. I needed tea and a change of mood.

I was halfway down the corridor to the kitchen when my mobile rang. I fished it out of the back pocket of my jeans.

Caller ID said 'Callum'.

'Hi.'

'You OK to talk?' He sounded distracted.

'Yep – just making a brew. Want one?'

'I wish. Can't think of anything I'd rather be doing than curling up on the sofa in front of your log fire with a nice cuppa right now.'

I flipped the lid on the Aga, putting the heavy-bottomed kettle on the hotplate. 'Instead of doing what?'

'Working ... what else?' I could hear him shuffling paper and imagined him sitting at his desk in the CID office of HMET, West Yorkshire Police's Homicide and Major Enquiry Team.

'Got a bit more info on your mate, Red.'

'He wasn't my ma—'

'Remember we couldn't think why anyone would break into a landfill site?'

'Hmm.' Still annoyed at his insistence on referring to an ex-client as a friend.

'Frank went to see the site manager yesterday.'

Frank Heslopp – Callum's DI. A gnarled, old-school cop who'd transferred from the Met. A dinosaur in many ways, but highly rated by the team, who despite his unfashionable attitudes still managed to get results.

'And?'

'The site's had a spate of break-ins recently. People stealing diesel from the vehicles.'

'Stealing fuel? Can't see Red being involved in that.' I didn't even try to hide my scepticism.

'Why not? It's criminal . . . and lucrative.'

'Still—'

'We're not talking about kids siphoning the odd litre here and there,' he ploughed on. 'They've been nicking up to a thousand litres at a time.'

'Blimey. How do they carry that much away?'

'Quad bikes, or flat-bed trucks,' he said simply. 'Carrying IBC cubes.'

'Which are what . . . exactly?'

'Intermediate Bulk Containers – for carrying liquids. Chemicals mostly, but in this case, white diesel. At current market prices, each robbery is netting the thieves two to three grand a time.'

'Not to be sneezed at,' I had to admit.

'Considering your mate, Red—'

'For the last time—'

'Started his criminal career lifting milk bottles from neighbourhood doorsteps, I'd say this is hardly beneath him these days.'

I poured boiling water into the teapot.

'You can't use what he did as a kid as evidence of what he might be doing now. Besides, he was a driver for Chris, not a thief.'

'Well, he's not driving McGarry these days, is he?' He wasn't about to let it go. 'At least I hope not, seeing as he's banged up in a supermax prison. Maybe Red's had to find another way to make ends meet now that his boss is off the grid?'

'Hmm.'

'Forensics put him at the perimeter fence,' he went on. 'Injured his hand cutting through it. So we know he broke in there.'

That was my cue to tell him I already knew. That I'd spoken to Elle about it. But for some reason I didn't feel inclined to share.

'His four-by-four – the Ford Ranger – was found parked in a copse near the perimeter.'

'With one of these cube things in it . . . for the fuel?'

'No.' He sounded disappointed. 'But it doesn't mean he wasn't involved in the thefts.'

'Did the site lose any fuel that night?'

'No.' Again, that disappointed tone. 'Working hypothesis: he was killed before he could carry out whatever he was there for.' His breath left him in a long sigh. 'Maybe not fuel, maybe some of the heavy plant machinery.'

I stirred the teapot. 'I've been thinking about his mother. I'd like to go and see her . . . if you don't have any objections?'

'Depends on the reason.'

'Common decency,' I said simply. 'She's a lovely woman and she's just lost her only son. The person she relies on the most. Got to know her quite well, when I was working on getting Red transferred. I feel sorry for her, that's all. Want to pay my respects.'

'As long as you make it clear you're not there as part of the police investigation, fine by me.'

'Of course.'

'But while you're with her . . . if you pick up on anything, pass it on – OK?'

I was about to say, *Of course I will*, but his double standards were so blatantly obvious, I couldn't let it pass. 'Oh, so you want me to make it clear to Audrey that I'm *not* part of your investigation, while at the same time, looking out for anything that might help that very same investigation? Great way to get me working for free.'

'I didn't mean it like—'

37

'Bye, Cal.'

* * *

It was almost midnight.

An unproductive day had slipped by and I felt frustrated and upset, for lots of reasons that I didn't want to brood over. The sooner this day was over, the sooner I could start again, hopefully in a better mood.

I'd just turned off the lights and was about to go upstairs, when my mobile rang.

The blue glow from my phone's screen bathed me in an eerie light in my darkened kitchen.

Caller ID was a number I didn't recognise. For a second, I debated rejecting the call, but instinct urged me not to.

'McCready.'

'Monster Mansion calling.'

A familiar voice and the last person I expected to hear from.

Suddenly my mouth was dry and the hair stood up on the back of my neck.

Chris McGarry.

Chapter Nine

Kingsberry Farm, Saturday, 1st February

'Sorry for the late hour.' He laughed softly. 'Safer to call at night.'

It didn't take a genius to work out that he must have an illegal burner phone, smuggled into the prison, so he could conduct business, as usual.

'This isn't a social call then?'

'Unfortunately not.' He was speaking quietly, but there was no mistaking his tone. Gone was the usual ebullient banter that had endeared me to him when we'd first met.

'You're taking a hell of a chance, Chris.'

'Worth taking.' There was a slight pause, then . . . 'It's Red.'

'I know.' It was out of my mouth before I could check myself. Being tired and strung out had a lot to answer for.

'Good. Saves me having to explain why I'm calling then, doesn't it?'

His tone wasn't friendly. Whatever cordial relationship we'd had in the past wasn't being carried over into the credit column now.

This call was trouble – I could feel it coming.

I moved to sit at the kitchen table – still in pitch darkness, except for the glow of the phone. Somehow it felt appropriate to be having this conversation in the dark.

I frowned. 'Not really.' I found myself speaking as quietly as he was – conspiratorial in hushed tones.

'Come on, Jo.' He wasn't trying to hide his impatience. 'You know what Red meant to me . . . to my family?'

'Of course, but that doesn't explain why you're calling *me*?'

'It hasn't been reported in the media, yet. So if you know what's happened this soon, you found out from your . . . er, what should I call him? Boyfriend? Lover . . .?'

'Cut the crap, Chris.' I was in no mood to play games. 'Yes, Callum told me and no, he's not my boyfriend.'

God, I hated that term. At my age, it felt somehow tacky to have a *boyfriend*.

'Lover then?' His laugh was snide, devoid of humour. 'Whatever you two have going on these days. You're on the inside and that's what I need right now.'

'I'm *not* on the inside.'

It was an effort to keep my tone level, knowing that any display of irritation on my part would feed the anger I could hear in his voice. And, banged up or not, it wouldn't be wise to antagonise the likes of Chris McGarry.

'I'm a forensic profiler, Chris, not a cop.'

'So what? You've been involved in Ferguson's investigations before, and I have it on good authority that he's the SIO on this one.'

'Yes,' I conceded, 'he's the senior investigating officer and if you "have it on good authority" then you've probably got a serving cop in your pocket.'

Chris had told me often enough that he had cops, lawyers and certainly prison officers on the payroll.

'You told me once that Fordley nick had more leaks in it than a sieve, so why the hell do you need me?'

His frustrated breath gusted down the phone. 'As it goes, I haven't got anyone close enough to his team. The ACU – Anti-Corruption Unit – cleaned out HMET.' He rode that fact for just a heartbeat, before adding quietly, 'Which was down to a favour I did for *you*, if memory serves me right?'

My stomach dropped.

I'd been dreading this. The day Chris would call in a favour for a debt that he believed I owed.

'I never asked you to do that.' I was whispering now. Irrationally fearful that if I spoke too loudly, my dreaded secret could be overheard – carried on the wind that howled across the moors.

'I killed a man . . . for you, Jo.'

'I didn't ask—'

'You *knew*!' The volume increased as much as he dare. 'Exactly what was going to happen. We *never* spell these things out in so many words. I knew what you wanted – needed – to happen and I took care of it.'

'I didn't ask you to.'

'You didn't tell me *not* to, either.' His voice hissed down the phone, sending the hairs prickling across my scalp. 'You're not that naive. Not now and certainly not then.'

I washed a hand across my face – heart pounding against my ribs, robbing me of breath. I took a lungful of air, trying to compose myself.

If we were adding up the columns of a perceived debt then I had to play what cards I held too.

'I got you transferred to a prison closer to home.' I was glad we were doing this over the phone and I couldn't see his eyes. 'When your son was ill and you were in Belmarsh.' He took a breath to interrupt, so I spoke faster, unwilling to concede. 'So that Sarah and the boys could visit. I pulled strings for you too, Chris, so we're even.'

'That's not the same as murder, Jo.'

'For the last time, I never said—'

'Yes, Mikey was ill and Sarah was going out of her mind,' he was saying. 'I was grateful for what you did for her then, still am. But I could have been transferred nearer without it being here. The "Monster Mansion" of all places.' His short laugh dripped with sarcasm. 'Very convenient for you, wasn't it? That message was loud and clear. I knew what you wanted to happen, and it did.'

My mouth had gone dry and my tongue felt heavy, thickening my speech.

41

'I didn't have the pull to get you transferred specifically to the Monster Mansion,' I lied. 'That was down to the prison service.'

'Not what Joshua said.'

At the mention of his solicitor, my system delivered a shot of adrenaline that sent electricity through my entire body.

'Joshua . . . He knows what you did?' The thought that others might know brought me close to abject panic.

'No,' he snapped. 'I'm not stupid. It stays between the two of us – for now.' He let the inference dangle and it terrified me. 'Joshua told me how much influence you had with the referral team. Coming here was no coincidence and we both know it, so stop bullshitting before I *really* lose patience with you, Jo.'

'You wouldn't . . .' I struggled for the words. To say out loud what we both knew he was threatening me with. 'Accuse me? I mean, it would affect you too.'

'You think?' He snorted. 'I'm serving life for double murder. They've thrown away the key. One more isn't going to make much difference to me now, is it? You, on the other hand . . .'

'Please don't do this to me, Chris.' I could hear the tremor in my voice and hated myself for the weakness of it. But I was struggling for a foothold, anything that could change his mind and pull us both back from the edge of this impossible abyss. 'I thought we were friends . . .'

'We are,' he said softly. 'But Red was a friend too . . . *my* friend. For over forty years, Jo.'

'I know.' My throat constricted as I thought of the young Jimmy Wilcox that I'd become fond of.

'And some bastard saw fit to cave his head in and leave him for dead. In a fucking rubbish dump, for Christ's sake.'

'Oh, Chris.'

'I want you on this one, Jo. Doing what you do best. If you're involved, the plod have more chance of catching whoever did this.'

'Look, Chris. The police call behavioural analysts in when there's a complex crime. A series of them, usually. They don't use people like me for a straightforward killing.'

I hated reducing Red's death to something that sounded mundane, but I had to reason with Chris. Make him realise that I couldn't help, not in the way I suspected he wanted me to.

'Callum won't call me in on this.'

'Well, you'd better make sure he does.'

'How?' It was my turn to raise my voice. 'And why do you need an insider anyway? Red's mum can keep you in the loop with whatever the police say.'

'She already has,' he cut across me. 'But whatever Red was doing at that site . . . he wasn't stealing diesel; I can tell you that for nothing.' I sensed from his voice that he was pacing. Imagined him prowling the small cell, like the caged animal he was. 'Someone killed one of mine and I want to know who!'

'You've got more resources than I have.'

'Sources on the street know nothing.' He carried on as if I hadn't spoken. 'If Red had been thieving I'd know about it. But he wasn't . . . had no need to. He was earning more working for me than he could ever make nicking poxy diesel.' His breathing was heavy as he became more worked up. 'Christ, we graduated from that kind of stuff before we left school. Not our game, Jo.'

My heart rate was beginning to descend from the heights of panic. 'OK,' I said more calmly. 'If you know what he *wasn't* doing there, then what do you think he *was* doing?'

'Not a clue. But I know what I *don't* want it to be.'

'What?'

'A hit . . . another gang. Taking out one of mine . . . someone close to me, to send a message. Make a move, while I'm stuck in here. Maybe a shot across our bows before they move in on my territory.'

And then I knew where this was coming from. The suspicion that it was the start of a turf war. The very thing that had put Chris behind bars for life.

It made perfect sense. Something like this was bound to trigger his paranoia. The same fear for Sarah and the boys that had led him to kill two rival gang leaders and got him banged up for consecutive life sentences.

'I can keep my ear to the ground—'

'I need more than that,' he snapped. 'Get inside this investigation and feed everything that's going on back to me. If my family's in danger, or another gang is about to make a move, I haven't got time to dick about. Make it happen, Jo, or your dirty little secret will be front page news.'

I stared at the phone in my hand as he hung up, leaving me sitting in the dark with just his threat for company.

Chapter Ten

Kingsberry Farm, Sunday, 2nd February

After the call from Chris, predictably, sleep eluded me. My mind raced at a million miles an hour as it ran around the problem, like a rabbit in a trap.

Did I think he would tell the police that I'd had something to do with a prisoner's death in the Monster Mansion?

There was no way I could know for sure. But he'd been right when he said it really wouldn't make much difference to his sentence.

We both knew the chances of him being freed before his young son became a middle-aged man were slim to none.

Would he ruin my life?

The thought of Callum knowing. What that would do to us.

Chris McGarry's affable charm and easy manner won people over, but I was under no illusions as to what lay beneath that friendly exterior. A character that could change in a heartbeat, with a ferocious capacity for violence that had put him at the top of an organised crime gang and held him there for decades. An organisation that thrived on fear and intimidation.

The same intimidation he was leveraging with me now.

I hadn't known Chris was going to kill someone in prison. But if I *had* would I have stopped it? Given who and what the intended victim was and how many innocent lives he'd destroyed?

Who knows?

Had it bothered me that a dangerous predator had died?

No.

I was just relieved that Chris had managed to get away with it. What did that say about me?

That I was the same as Chris?

That I'd done this job for too long and become desensitised to violence and death?

I didn't think so. But maybe I wasn't the right person to judge? To see it in myself?

All these thoughts had haunted my fitful attempts to rest, leaving me tossing and turning through the night. Until I'd fallen into a heavy and disturbed sleep in the early hours.

My heart suddenly leaped, and for a second, I lay – bathed in sweat – not knowing what had woken me. I squinted at the digital clock: 7.20 a.m. Then jumped when my phone rang again.

'Hello?' I mumbled.

'Jo?' Callum's voice, with an edge of urgency that made me sit bolt upright in bed. I leaned against the headboard, feeling my heart thud loudly against my ribs.

The irrational thought that he'd read my mind, that he knew.

'Sorry if I woke you,' he was saying. 'Waited until now . . . thought you'd be out walking Harvey.'

'I should be,' I mumbled, looking at the clock again as if it might say something different. 'Couldn't sleep last night . . . dozed off in the early hours.'

'Sorry.'

'Don't be.' I rubbed my eyes with my free hand. 'What's up?'

'Call came in this morning from North Yorkshire Police. Young girl, sexually assaulted and left for dead. Last night, on moorland, middle of nowhere.'

That woke me up.

'Oh my God.' I swung my legs out of bed, reaching for my dressing gown. '"Left for dead". So she survived?'

'Against all the odds.' His breath gusted down the phone.

I cradled the phone under my chin, slipping into my robe, as a thought occurred to me. 'Why did North Yorkshire call you? Surely, it's on their—'

'Because she was abducted on their patch, but she was attacked and left on a track near Wytch's Tarn, which is in our district. So, joint investigation.'

I could sense there was more coming.

'Once they could interview her, in hospital,' he added, 'she told them one of the people she spoke to before the attack was you.'

Chapter Eleven

Fordley Police Station, Sunday, 2nd February

'Rachel Taylor,' Callum said, as he poured strong black coffee from the percolator, which dripped an endless supply into the pot on the bookshelf in his office.

He gestured to me with the pot, but I shook my head, always preferring tea when I could.

'I didn't get her surname,' I said, thinking back to the young girl putting plasters on her blistered feet on the moorland track above my farmhouse.

'Came across her when I was walking Harvey. We only chatted for a few minutes.'

'Well, she remembers you.' He sat back down, shifting papers on the desk to make room for the mug. 'Which is why North Yorkshire Police need you to make a statement, seeing as you were among the last people she spoke to before being kidnapped and sexually assaulted.'

I shook my head in disbelief. Thinking about the pretty young girl with the happy smile I'd seen just forty-eight hours earlier.

'Unbelievable,' I muttered – wishing now that I'd accepted his offer of coffee.

'They need you to confirm the time and place you met. The route she says she was planning to take . . . you know the drill, Jo.'

Unfortunately, I did.

So many questions ran through my mind, all jostling for pole position. For a moment, I didn't speak.

'You OK?' Piercing blue eyes watched me over the rim of his mug as he took another mouthful of caffeine.

'Yes.' I rubbed my eyes, still gritty from a night of no sleep. 'Is she . . .? I mean, where is she now?'

'Airedale Hospital.'

'Is she badly hurt?' I almost didn't want to ask, but needed to know.

He shrugged. 'Bad enough. She was hit from behind – to disable her, so the attacker could throw her into the back of a vehicle. Came round in the boot, with a bag or sack over her head.'

'Bloody hell,' I breathed, struggling to even comprehend the horror of that.

'She thinks he must have taken her boots off when he bundled her into the back, because, when he stopped and dragged her out of the vehicle, she was barefoot.'

'That's when he raped her?'

'No,' Callum said. 'Threw her over his shoulder and carried her. She was in and out of consciousness, so not sure for how long. Finally put her on the ground, then sexually assaulted her.'

'Presumably still with the hood over her head?' I could hear myself describing the horror in a businesslike tone. But that's what this job was. Dealing with the most sordid, most inhumane acts. Reciting a litany of abuse with an emotional detachment that – I knew – was protection against the realities of it all.

'Hmm. During the assault, he tied a ligature round her neck and began strangling her.'

'Jesus.'

'Obviously intended to kill her, but, thankfully, was interrupted by a bloke coming down the track from the moor.'

'What was *he* doing up there in the middle of the night?' I asked.

'Ghost hunting,' he said, without missing a beat.

'What?'

He grinned. 'Looking for Tommy Earnshaw's corpse lights, or UFOs or whatever the hell they think they are.'

'Seriously?'

He nodded. 'He lives and works in Halifax. Runs a magazine.' He rummaged through the notes on his desk, reading from a sheet. '*The Third Eye*.' He dropped the paperwork back onto the pile. 'All about occult stuff – ghosts and ghouls.'

'Well, lucky for Rachel he was there.' That was all I could think to say to that.

'Daniel Dunglas.'

'Really?'

Callum frowned. 'What's wrong with that? It's the guy's name.'

'Nothing . . . except it's also the name of a Scottish psychic and medium, from the eighteen hundreds.'

He raised an eyebrow. 'I'm always amazed by how much random shit you know.' But he was smiling when he said it.

I shrugged. 'You should be thankful I do. Can't say it doesn't prove useful, can you?'

'Suppose not.'

'The Victorian Dunglas claimed to be able to speak with the dead. Conducted séances attended by the great and the good of the time. Even royalty.'

'Might be why he chose the name then.' Callum stretched back in his chair, rolling his shoulders. 'His real name's Terry Smith. He changed it by deed poll ten years ago.'

'He's probably hoping most people don't know as much random shit as me then.'

'How so?'

'Harry Houdini met Dunglas and denounced him as a fraud.'

'Well, good old Terry says he saw someone running away, down the track, and almost stumbled on Rachel. He thought she was dead. Managed to loosen the ligature and found a faint pulse. A farmer out late, checking on his sheep, came across both of them and helped Terry, or Daniel, carry Rachel to his vehicle. He'd left it on one of those rough tracks grouse shooters use during the season before walking up to the grouse moors. They drove her into Stanbury.'

I was thinking about her mother, who she phoned whenever she could. 'What about her family?'

'They live in London. On their way to the hospital as we speak. We're waiting for the doctor to call to let us know when we can question her.' He glanced at his watch. 'Got a briefing in ten minutes.' He glanced across at me. 'Appreciate you sitting in on this one once you've given your statement, if you're up for it?'

'Of course.'

If I'd known what was about to unfold, I might not have been so enthusiastic.

Chapter Twelve

Fordley Police Station, Sunday, 2nd February

During a major enquiry, there was no such thing as a Sunday morning; or a weekend; or holidays for that matter.

Things moved fast. Making the most of the 'golden hour'. As the name suggested, the first sixty minutes after an offence has been committed.

The more time that passes after that, the more chance of evidence being lost, witnesses' memories failing or crucial forensics being compromised.

In reality, most detectives extended that time, as it could take more than an hour for them to even become aware that a crime had been committed.

I knew Callum regarded the first two or three days as the critical period. When it would be all hands on deck, all leave cancelled and every resource called upon to track an offender.

The major incident room was already a hive of activity when I slipped in and grabbed a seat beside DC Beth Hastings. Every desk was occupied and it was standing room only.

'Who's the new girl?' I whispered to Beth, nodding to a young woman standing at the back.

She swivelled round to look. 'Brooke Samson. She's a DC. Some kind of whizz kid in Digital Forensics.'

'What happened to Charlie Thompson?' The young DS I'd been quite fond of, who'd been part of Callum's team.

'Just quit. Handed in his papers – out of the blue.'

'Really?' I was surprised. 'Thought he was one of the good ones.'

Beth shrugged. 'Couldn't stand the pace.'

'Where's he gone?'

'Hull.'

'Why on earth has he gone there?'

'God knows . . . daft sod.'

Callum took his place at the front of the room and turned to face his team.

'Thanks for coming in, at such short notice and on a Sunday morning,' he said, as everyone started to settle down, pulling out notebooks and cradling cups of coffee.

'To soften the blow,' he was saying, 'I've got a budget code for the overtime.'

There were noises of approval from around the room and half-sheepish smiles as the code was written down in notebooks.

Callum tapped Rachel's picture, already on the whiteboard. 'You've all seen the initial report. Rachel Taylor – twenty-two years old. Hiking the Pennine Way, on her own.' He walked over to a map of the route pinned to the wall. 'She was heading north, along this route.' He traced a red dotted line along the map. 'On Friday morning, she was here, near Kingsberry Farm.' He tapped the spot. 'And met Jo.'

All eyes turned to me. I took that as my cue.

'I was walking Harvey when we met on the track. She'd taken a wrong turn in the fog, showed me her map and we talked about the route she was going to take.'

'Which was?' It was Frank Heslopp, Callum's DI.

'Detour to visit Top Withens. Then take a loop into Hebden Bridge. From there she was doing the leg to Ickornshaw. Said she had a B & B booked there.'

'How far is that final leg?' DC Shah Akhtar.

'Six to eight hours' walk, depending on your pace,' I said, always finding it easier to judge a hiking distance in time, rather than miles.

'All this is in Jo's statement.' Callum referred to the notes. 'You all have copies.' He turned back to the map. 'After leaving Jo, Rachel carried on as planned. The weather slowed her down and visibility on the tops was pretty bad. Not wanting to take a wrong turn again, Rachel camped out on the moors on Friday night and picked up the route late on Saturday morning.'

'But she never got to Ickornshaw?' Beth asked, without looking up from her notes.

Callum shook his head, perching on the corner of a desk.

'She made it in to Hebden Bridge by mid-morning. I've got uniform out there checking the places she said she visited.' He turned to his DC. 'Shah?'

The young detective glanced at the notes on his iPad.

'Rachel visited the Innovation Café in Saint George's Square. Thinks she got there around ten thirty. I rang this morning and spoke with the manager. She doesn't remember Rachel specifically. They get a lot of backpackers. Rachel said she sat at a table outside. Had coffee and cake, then looked in a few of the local shops.' He glanced up at Callum. 'We're securing CCTV from local businesses. Hopefully be able to track Rachel through town. See if anyone stands out. Maybe the attacker followed her from there.'

Callum nodded. 'Pedestrians *and* vehicles. We need to cover all the bases. Whoever abducted her had transport.'

'According to her initial statement,' Beth said, 'Rachel left Hebden Bridge around twelve o'clock and picked up the moors trail.'

'She walked on her own for about an hour, then met up with a group of students on a hike.' Callum picked up the narrative. 'They walked together and got chatting. Rachel went with them to a pub.' He checked the map, tapping it with his finger. 'Here, Tarn Hill Tavern.'

He took a mouthful of coffee, and sat back on the corner of the desk. 'She left there around three o'clock. Shah and Beth – I want you to talk to the landlord at the pub. Secure any CCTV.'

'There isn't any,' I said, drawing everyone's attention. 'At least not inside the pub.'

'One of your regular haunts is it then, Jo?' Heslopp grinned.

I ignored the look Callum shot my way, neither of us keen to let the general workforce know we'd been there just a few days before.

'I'll speak to them anyway,' Beth said. 'You never know.'

'She wasn't going to make it to Ickornshaw before it got dark,' I said to no one in particular.

'Risky,' Beth muttered, chewing on the end of her pen.

'Sunset would be around five,' Callum said. 'She'd considered camping out again, but knew the B & B were expecting her, so decided to push on.'

He stared at the map for a moment, his gaze going between that and Rachel's picture.

'She nearly made it,' he said, almost to himself. 'She was on a track that dropped down from the moors and would have taken her onto the Keighley Road, at Cowling. It was dark by then. She was using her head torch.' He tapped the spot on the map. 'That's where she was abducted.'

'She'd done the remote bit.' I slowly shook my head. 'The last part of that route is some of the most desolate across the moorland. That's where you'd imagine you'd be most vulnerable. And then, almost within sight of civilisation, she gets attacked.'

'He had a vehicle,' Beth said quietly. 'So, she was actually more at risk on a road than she was on exposed moorland tracks.'

There was a lull as those thoughts percolated.

Callum broke the silence. 'OK – working hypotheses?'

'A random,' Frank Heslopp offered. 'Opportune attack. Guy sees a young girl hiking alone in the dark. Takes his chance.'

'Possibly,' Callum agreed.

'Someone who'd seen Rachel earlier,' Shah said. 'In Hebden Bridge, or the pub where she went with the other walkers maybe? Knew where she was headed and intercepted her.'

'But they'd need a vehicle,' Beth chipped in. 'Would have to leave the group and pick up their transport.'

'They need eliminating.' Callum made a note. 'ANPR cameras along the route into Cowling. Any CCTV needs securing – although there's probably not much out there.' Then he turned to me. 'Jo, any thoughts?'

I hated coming up with a scenario on the fly and said as much. 'Not really enough to go on yet.'

'Just ideas at this stage.' Callum wasn't letting me off the hook. 'You'll have initial thoughts on it?'

I took a long breath. 'Don't think you're dealing with an opportunist here.'

'OK.' Callum sat forward, resting his hands on his knees. 'Why not?'

'Whoever this is,' I said slowly, 'it isn't his first outing.' I tapped a pencil against my teeth. A habit I had when I was thinking and one that drove Jen nuts. 'He took off her boots and socks in the back of the vehicle, presumably to make sure she couldn't run away. He had a kidnap kit ready to go.' I glanced at the notes I'd made. 'Bindings . . . a hood and the ribbon he used as a ligature.'

'Could still be some weirdo driving round with all that in his car, just looking for a vulnerable victim.' Heslopp was reluctant to let it go. 'Peter Sutcliffe – the Yorkshire Ripper – did that.'

'True,' I conceded, although I still didn't think this was simply a case of Rachel being in the wrong place at the wrong time. 'But it's still indicative of an offender who's done this before. Whether he was on the prowl looking for a lone female after dark, or he'd seen Rachel earlier and followed her – this isn't his first rodeo.' I directed myself to Callum. 'This was too slick. Too practised.'

Callum nodded, his eyes never leaving mine. 'OK. Tony, once we have a HOLMES file opened on this, let's see if there's been any similar incidents or attacks nationwide.'

In a reference to that most famous of fictional detectives, Sherlock Holmes, the Home Office Large Major Enquiry System, was the national police computer system used to collect and collate information gathered during a major crime investigation. In conjunction with the Police National Computer, the team would be able to look for patterns of historic or ongoing investigations that had similar elements to this one.

'Another thing.' I was thinking aloud. 'Why drive her all those miles away before attacking her?'

'The moors near the tarn are pretty remote,' Beth said.

I shook my head. 'The kidnap site was remote enough.' I tapped my teeth again as I thought it through. 'Already dark . . . no houses around there.'

'Bit too close to the road, though,' Callum added.

I stared at the map.

'Lots of remote, lonely moorland between Cowling and where she was found above Stanbury. Her attacker could have stopped at a dozen places along that route.'

'We know offenders don't like to shit on their own doorstep,' Frank Heslopp said. 'Maybe he's driving her away from his home ground to somewhere less local.'

'Despite your eloquent turn of phrase,' Callum said, 'you've got a point, Frank. Maybe our man is from the Cowling or Ickornshaw area?' He looked at me. 'Jo?'

'Possibly.' Something about that long drive still didn't feel right to me, but Frank's theory was sound enough.

The team had consulted a geographical profiler in the past so I knew I was preaching to the converted.

'We know geographic or spatial profiling has shown in the past that offenders like to operate in a "safe zone". Somewhere they feel comfortable.'

'That would be the attack site rather than the kidnap site in this case?' Beth said to the room in general.

'Yes,' I agreed. 'The kidnap site wouldn't be ideal. Your man had to snatch Rachel from a location that presents itself. Near to where he can leave a vehicle. Even with a certain amount of planning there would be too many variables for him to feel safe committing the final act there. Unless you're dealing with a blitz attacker.'

'Which this isn't?' Callum added.

'No.' I shook my head. 'Definitely not. This is an organised offender.'

I got up and walked over to the map, tracing the route with my finger. 'Frank's right,' I murmured. 'Often, offenders avoid committing the crime too close to home. If they know another area well – especially if it's remote – then the likelihood is they'll take their victim from the kidnap site to another location. One they've prepared, or at least feel comfortable in.'

I stared at the red pin on the map, which marked the spot on the moor where Rachel had almost died.

'A location where they have multiple escape routes, should they be compromised.'

'Spoiled for choice on open moorland,' Heslopp muttered.

'So, we concentrate on the area around Cowling and Ickornshaw,' Callum said. 'If that's his home ground. All ANPR cameras in and around the area. Also, secure any CCTV or doorbell cameras from shops . . . and houses. See if any cross-reference to vehicles from any part of Rachel's route that day, in case our man was following her. If Jo's right and he's not an opportunist, then he saw her somewhere else, or knows her.'

I sat back down – still looking at the map – but my mind was on the attacker. 'The ribbon . . . used as a ligature.' I asked. 'Did that belong to Rachel? Or did the attacker bring that?'

'Not Rachel's,' Tony Morgan said.

Callum clicked some keys on his laptop and an image came up on the screen at the front of the room.

It was a picture taken by crime scene investigators, when they catalogued all the evidence – which included Rachel. She was a living, breathing crime scene.

Everything she had been wearing, including the ligature that doctors had removed from around her neck in A & E, had been carefully photographed, removed and bagged as evidence.

I knew, from bitter experience, that Rachel's hands and body would have been swabbed. Scrapings taken from beneath her fingernails and tape-lifts from her clothes and skin.

The extra invasion no doubt adding to the shock and humiliation of a sexual assault, but a necessary process if vital DNA evidence from her attacker was to be captured and preserved.

I looked at the image of a bright red, silky ribbon, splattered with dirt and mud. Creased where it had been tied. A ruler had been placed beside it, for scale, before it was photographed.

A thin line of brown discoloured the band along one edge. I knew, without asking, that it was blood. No doubt from where the unforgiving fabric had bitten into Rachel's skin.

'That's significant,' I said.

'What?' Callum asked, frowning at me.

'The ribbon.'

'In what way?'

'I don't know yet. But it's important . . . to him.'

I thought about the sequence of events. The way Rachel had been kidnapped, the practised nature of it all.

'If he hadn't been interrupted by Daniel *whatshisface*,' I said quietly, still looking at the image, 'Rachel would be dead.'

Callum nodded. 'She was pretty close to it. Hospital said she was lucky.'

'He's been luckier.' I looked at Callum, holding his gaze with mine. 'He's not been caught . . . and there's something else.'

'What?'

'I think he's killed before.'

Chapter Thirteen

Kingsberry Farm, Monday Morning

'Poor girl.' Jen shook her head, as she put a fresh mug of tea on my cluttered desk. 'And to think you'd seen her on Friday.'

I took a mouthful of tea. 'I know.' I glanced at my notes – the ones I'd made in the early hours of the morning. Unable to sleep as images of Rachel and the horrors she'd endured had scrolled through my mind, like an unrelenting newsflash.

'Bit too close to home,' Jen was saying as she sat at her own desk across the room. 'Up here, we always feel so far removed from what goes on in the city.' She scratched her grey curls with the end of her pencil, before pushing it behind her ear. 'Then something like this happens, and you realise, we're not immune to it, even out in the sticks.'

Whatever I was about to say was interrupted when the office phone rang.

'McCready,' I answered distractedly, still studying my notes.

'Jo.' Callum's voice pulled my attention back. 'You free today?'

I stared at the manuscript of my book, which had lain untouched for the last few weeks.

'I can be . . . depends what it is?'

'Rachel Taylor,' he said simply, as if that explained everything.

My stomach lurched at the thought that she'd taken a turn for the worse.

'Is she OK? I mean, has something else happened?'

'Doctors have said we can speak to her today. I'm sending Beth and Shah to Airedale Hospital, but I was wondering whether you'd go along too?'

'Yes,' I agreed without a second thought.

'She's in a fragile state . . .'

'I can imagine.'

'Thought having you along might help. You know – a psychologist? You might be able to pick up on something. Help her remember. She mentioned seeing you . . . obviously a friendly face being there, rather than just a couple of cops at the bedside.'

'Absolutely.'

* * *

Airedale Hospital was originally built among green fields on the edge of the Dales. Although bigger than the old cottage hospitals that served the villages and farming communities back in the day, this mainly two-storey seventies building still reminded me of those places.

Smaller and somehow more intimate, with the dubious accolade of having the largest single flat roof of any English hospital. Which unfortunately meant it also suffered from the most roof leaks of any functioning hospital in the country.

A fact I was reminded of as I stepped around a bucket, half-full of rainwater, which still plopped into it from some unseen spot, above a yellow sign warning me not to slip on the recently mopped floor. I navigated the corridors to the side ward where I'd arranged to meet Beth and Shah.

I spotted them standing outside a door halfway along the hallway, chatting quietly. Beth saw me over Shah's shoulder and smiled, nodding a greeting.

'You want a coffee?' Shah offered when I reached them.

'No, thanks.'

Then he remembered my preference. 'Machine does tea?'

I resisted the urge to visibly shudder as I politely declined.

He shrugged. 'Not a tea drinker, so wouldn't know.' He looked at the cardboard cup in his hand. 'I can suffer bad coffee though – need the caffeine.'

'Right.' Beth pulled her jacket straight. 'Let's get on.'

Shah tapped lightly at the door to the side room.

A female uniformed officer was sitting in the high-backed chair beside Rachel's bed. She stood up when we entered.

'You can take a break.' Beth smiled.

We waited until she'd left the room, closing the door behind her with a soft 'click'.

Rachel lay in a bed that somehow made her look small.

Propped on three pillows, her brunette hair splayed out across the white pillowcases. She looked even younger than her twenty-two years.

My eyes were immediately drawn to the wide adhesive dressing across her throat and the image of that silk ribbon flashed through my mind. The dark bloodstain along the edge where it had bitten into her pale skin.

Her head had been bandaged and there was a livid bruise across one cheekbone which was turning a sickly shade of yellow.

She looked at us with bloodshot eyes – caused by the bursting of blood vessels in the conjunctiva when she was strangled. What Elle would refer to as petechial haemorrhaging. Lucky for Rachel, in her case, not the typical result of fatal asphyxiation.

Dark rings like purple smudges beneath her eyes were testament to the trauma she'd gone through and the lack of sleep that, inevitably, went with it.

Beth made the introductions, producing her warrant card. But Rachel's eyes were on me.

'You're Jo,' she said, before Beth could get round to it.

'Yes.' I smiled, gently, thinking of the first time we'd met. Ignorant of what was about to happen. Wishing I could somehow have known and been able to prevent any of it.

But here we were.

'I told them I'd spoken to you.' Her voice was no more than a hoarse whisper. Another result of her near-fatal strangulation.

Applying such pressure to a person's throat could permanently damage the vocal cords, but only time would tell whether that would be the case for Rachel.

Even her words sounded brittle, fragile. 'When they asked whether I'd seen anyone on the trail . . . you know? Whether I'd told anyone where I was headed.'

I nodded, accepting Beth's gesture for me to take the seat next to the bed.

'Is that why you're here?' Rachel asked.

I glanced at Beth, who took her cue. 'Partly.' She smiled. 'But also, because Jo's worked with us before. She's a psychologist. Thought you might want someone to speak to . . . you know, after we leave. Might help?'

Rachel half nodded, her eyes suddenly becoming moist with unshed tears. Evidence of the raw emotions that lurked just beneath the surface of that fragile smile. The feelings that would spill down her cheeks if she blinked.

She reached out for a tissue from the bedside table, the movement making her wince in pain.

Shah stepped forward and grabbed the tissue for her.

'Thanks.' She sniffed, wiping her nose and dabbing at her eyelashes.

Beth pulled a plastic chair closer to the bed and got out her iPad, as Shah stood discreetly by the window, leaning on the sill. His figure partially blocking out the watery sunlight.

'I know you've been through a lot,' Beth began, 'but it's best to get your statement of events as soon as possible.' She smiled sympathetically. 'Memories fade quickly, you know? Details get lost the further away from an event we get.'

Rachel just nodded, swallowing hard.

'Of course, if you'd rather not do this now, we can come back later, but as I say . . .'

'No.' Rachel's eyes held firmly to Beth's. 'Now . . . let's do it now.'

'I've got the initial report from North Yorkshire Police,' Beth said, her eyes studying Rachel carefully. Wary of pushing too hard or moving too fast.

Walking that fine line between wanting to get to the information the police needed, while remaining sensitive to a vulnerable victim of a horrendous attack.

'Tell us what you remember, Rachel?' Beth said quietly. 'Anything at all . . . however small.'

Rachel's gaze went between the three of us. Then, taking a long breath, she closed her eyes. I watched the rhythmic rise and fall of her chest. She was taking deep breaths, trying to calm herself. The pulse point on her collarbone fluttered and I could imagine her heart rate increasing as she took herself back to the attack that nearly ended her life.

'I remember everything before . . . before it happened. But then it gets a bit fuzzy.'

Beth nodded, even though Rachel couldn't see the gesture with her eyes closed. 'That's OK, take your time. Go back to the bits you *can* remember – we'll start there.'

'Obviously, I met Jo on Friday.' Her lips curved into a thin half-smile. 'And Harvey. I went on to Top Withens.' The smile faded. She still had her eyes closed. 'The weather was awful so I didn't stay long. I camped out on Friday night. Could have pushed on, but was worried about getting lost in the bad weather.'

'Did you see anyone else that night?' Beth prompted.

A silent shake of her head. 'Weather broke in the morning. I packed up and went into Hebden Bridge.' Her story stopped as she began to cough. Her throat sounded raw – she was losing what little voice she had.

Shah stepped to the side of the bed and poured some water into a plastic cup. 'Here – take a drink.'

Rachel eased herself higher up the pillows, grimacing at the pain and took the cup in fingers that were trembling slightly.

Beth read from her iPad. 'Save your voice, Rachel. I'll read here what we've got – just nod if you agree with the account. Stop me if we've got anything wrong, OK?'

Rachel nodded, handing the cup to Shah and lying back against the pillows.

Beth went through the young girl's movements. Visiting the café in Hebden Bridge. Pausing, she looked up from the notes. 'Did you chat to anyone at the café? Strike up a conversation with another visitor?'

Rachel shook her head, pursing her lips in thought. 'Only to order coffee and cake. It was packed, so I sat outside. The sun had come out . . . it wasn't too cold.'

'And you didn't notice anyone watching you, or following you. Anyone that looked odd or was acting strangely?'

Again, a 'no' with a shake of her head.

'You looked in a few of the local shops.' Beth glanced up from her notes. 'Can you remember which ones?'

Rachel's brow drew down as she frowned. 'Err . . . the soap shop . . .'

'Yorkshire Soap Company?'

Rachel nodded. 'Bought some handmade soap for my mum.' Her voice cracked and a tear ran down her cheek. She sniffed and wiped at it with the back of her hand. 'Then got some bread from the bakery . . . oh and I got some cash from the machine at the Co-op.'

Shah made a note from his perch by the window. That was a new fact and maybe an important one.

'Then what?' Beth's tone was encouraging.

'Set off . . . back on the route.' Rachel opened her eyes, glancing from Beth to me. As if she wanted to be sure she was saying the right thing.

'To Ickornshaw?'

'Yes.'

'You said you walked across the moors for an hour and then met up with some students and that you went with them to the Tarn Hill Tavern?'

'Hmm.' She nodded, reaching for the water again.

'You gave some names.' Beth glanced at her notes. 'Mike and . . . Lucy? Do you remember any of the others?'

Rachel was finding it hard to swallow, even water. 'No, just the ones I was sitting with really.'

'Did you talk to them about where you'd be walking?'

She nodded. 'Of course, they were interested. Mike and his girlfriend said they'd always wanted to do the Pennine Way.'

I could see Shah out of the corner of my eye, making notes.

Beth asked all the usual questions about the people in the pub. Had Rachel noticed anyone acting strangely? Did the group talk to anyone else in there? Did anyone from the pub leave at the same time she did?

There was nothing out of the ordinary. No detail Rachel could remember that would raise any red flags. But I could see her body changing as the questions got closer to the attack.

A soft blush crept up her neck and into her cheeks and her breathing was becoming slightly more rapid as her blood pressure no doubt began to climb.

'Did any of the students mention having a vehicle, or driving at any point?'

'No. They'd come by train. They were going to camp up at Wytch's Tarn. It's been all over the socials – ghost sightings or something. They were going back to university next day, I think.'

She was getting restless – her legs moving under the bedsheet as she became more nervous. It wasn't lost on Beth, who shot me a quick look.

'Would you like to take a break, Rachel?' I gently touched her arm, but she shook her head.

'No, I'm fine.' Though she didn't sound convincing.

'Did you leave the pub on your own?' Beth pressed on.

'Yes. They were going up to the tarn. Asked me to go too, but I had to get back on the route. I knew I'd be losing the light.'

'What do you remember then?'

'I walked,' she said with a slight shrug. 'Didn't see anyone over the moors. The weather wasn't too bad and I made decent time.'

'You saw no one at all?' Beth asked.

Rachel turned her face towards the window, shaking her head in silence. She knew we were getting to the crucial moment in this timeline and she didn't want to go there. I couldn't blame her.

'You were headed for the B & B you had booked?'

'Hmm, but I knew I'd be arriving late.'

'Did you ring ahead – let them know you'd be late?' Even though Beth knew the answer – the police had checked with the guest house already.

'There was no signal on the moor, so I couldn't.'

'It would be getting dark by then?' Again, Beth already knew. But she was easing Rachel into the narrative, leading her slowly to where she needed her to be.

'Yes. I was using my headtorch by the time I got near Cowling.'

'Go on.'

'I remember checking the map, knowing I was almost there. That I'd be able to see the road soon . . .'

Her voice trailed off and she looked at me, with something close to an appeal in those large eyes. I gently squeezed her hand.

'I know that track.' I smiled reassuringly. 'I've walked it with Harvey.' She gave a weak smile at the mention of his name. 'Did you get as far as the road?'

The pillows rustled as she shook her head. 'Last thing I remember is coming down the last bit of the track. Must have been a few hundred yards away from the main road. I climbed over the stile.'

'Then what?' I asked, my eyes holding hers.

Her eyes were almost pleading with mine. Her chin quivered. 'Nothing after that . . . nothing . . .'

'You're doing really well, Rachel,' Beth said from over my shoulder.

The room was suddenly very still, as if the air had stopped moving. The only sound the soft ticking of the white-faced clock above the door.

'Take a breath, Rachel,' I said, lowering my voice to barely a whisper. Still looking into those pitifully bloodshot eyes. 'Close your eyes and take yourself back to that moment.'

A tear escaped from the corner of her eye and ran down the side of her nose. 'I can't,' she whispered.

'I know it's painful to go back there.' I kept my voice low and even – reassuring. The same tone I'd used during hypnotherapy sessions, when I'd had a therapy practice, many years ago.

'You're safe . . . you're here, with us. Just relax and see whether anything comes back to you . . . any tiny detail that can help us.' She took a deep breath. 'That's right . . . just breathe. If it gets too much, just open your eyes and you're back here with us.'

'It was dark . . .' she began, haltingly. 'I could only see the ground in front . . . in the beam of my headtorch.'

'What can you hear?' I said.

She rolled her head slightly on the pillow. 'The grass, rustling in the breeze.'

'Good. Go on.'

'It was cold . . . freezing. My boots were crunching on the track.'

'What else?'

She frowned. 'Something . . . I don't know . . . a step, someone was there.'

'Where was the sound coming from?'

'Behind . . . yes . . . then I started to turn and . . .' Her eyes flew open. 'No!'

The sudden, unexpected shout made us all jump.

Rachel began to cry. 'That was when he hit me.'

I pulled another tissue from the box and pressed it into her palm.

'It's OK, Rachel.' I tried to soothe her. 'It's OK, you're safe. You're here with us. He can't hurt you now.'

I turned to Beth, about to suggest we take a break. But Rachel carried on talking.

Beth gave me a half-nod. A silent gesture to let the narrative run for as long as we could. This was where we could get vital information. Capture elusive memories that might be lost if we stopped this flow of consciousness.

'I don't remember much.' She sobbed. 'Just fragmented bits . . . odd sounds. When I came round, I didn't know where I was. It took me a while to realise I was in the boot of a car. I could smell petrol, hear the engine. But I couldn't see anything. He'd put something over my head – a bag, hood, or something.'

'It's OK,' I said again.

'I kept drifting in and out. The pain in my head felt like it was going to explode. I tried to move . . . kick out . . . that's when I realised my feet were bare.'

'He'd removed your boots and your socks?' I asked.

She just nodded, sniffing and wiping her nose with the crumpled tissue. 'My arms . . . I couldn't move them. There was pain in my wrists, something biting into my skin.'

I could sense Beth looking at me, but I didn't want to take my attention from Rachel. We knew from the people who found her that her hands had been secured behind her back, with zip ties. The farmer had cut them off her when he got her to his vehicle.

'What's the next thing you remember?'

'When we stopped.'

Chapter Fourteen

Airedale Hospital, Monday Morning

The silence stretched out, as if we held a collective breath. No one wanting to break the delicate moment that settled around us.

The sound of Rachel's breathing and the rhythmic ticking of the clock – a metronome of anticipation.

The temptation to speak, to prompt what came next was almost unbearable.

Instead, I gave Rachel's fingers a gentle squeeze.

It was enough.

She took a breath, her croaky voice even more hoarse as she began to speak again.

'He . . . he opened the boot and dragged me out. I could feel cold air on my bare feet.' She squeezed her eyes closed, taking a ragged breath before she could continue.

'He picked me up, threw me over his shoulder and carried me.'

I looked at Beth, expecting her to pick up the questions. But she raised her chin in a gesture for me to take the lead.

'Did he speak to you at all?' I asked.

Rachel shook her head. 'Just grunted when he was walking – with the effort. My head was pressed against his back. The pain was worse, as the blood ran into my head. I was hanging upside down.'

She opened her eyes and looked into mine. The pain I saw there was almost unbearable to witness.

'I passed out, I think.'

'Did you have any idea where you were?' I probed, gently. Knowing we were approaching the most painful of memories.

'The moors.'

'How did you know that?' Beth asked quietly.

Rachel looked at her and frowned. As if she was having to think about that.

'The smell,' she said finally. 'I've walked the moors for so long, I know that smell.'

I knew what she meant. It was the same for me. Living there and walking those fells every day with Harvey. The unique scent of the earth and the heather.

An olfactory marker as unique as the land itself. One that changed subtly with the seasons. Purple heather and wild flowers in the summer. Damp moss and hard tussock grasses in the winter and the smell of peat underfoot.

Even the rocks had an aroma – when the drystone walls were warmed by the sun, or soaked with rain.

'I came round when he dumped me on the ground.' Rachel's brow furrowed with the memory and another tear rolled down her cheek. 'I was . . . I pleaded then.' A sob caught in her throat.

'Did he say anything?' I asked.

She shook her head, crying quietly now. Her painful throat making the sound of her sobbing even more raw.

'He pulled my jeans down, ripped my . . . my coat and my shirt open . . .' Her voice trailed away with a low moaning sound that was visceral. Like a wounded animal. 'He was groping me, feeling my body all over.'

Tears streamed down her face when she looked at me with anguished eyes. 'But he couldn't . . . he couldn't do it.'

It was my turn to frown. 'He stopped?' I asked.

'He lay on top of me . . . his weight. I thought he was going to crush me. Then he fumbled about . . . you know . . . but nothing happened.'

Beth cleared her throat. 'You mean he didn't penetrate you?'

Rachel's face burned with embarrassment and my heart ached for her. That she should have to go through this at all was bad enough, but to have to recount it to strangers just added to the humiliation and pain I knew she was already feeling.

Her chin quivered as she fought for self-control. 'I waited, knowing what he was going to do, but he didn't.' She reached for the water and I handed her the plastic cup.

She took a sip and grimaced. She was having trouble swallowing, after straining her voice to speak for so long.

'You thought he was going to rape you?' I pre-empted, not wanting her to have to spell this out. Although that's what Beth and Shah needed.

I avoided looking at either of them, knowing I was leading their witness, but watching her struggle to articulate the horror of what had happened to her was too much for me.

Unlike the police, I was in the business of healing trauma. Of lessening a person's emotional pain. To watch it bleed out, like a raw wound, went against every instinct.

Rachel nodded, her focus firmly on me now.

'But although he tried, he couldn't?' I said it for her, to save her the agony.

Again a nod.

'Then what did he do?'

'He got off me.' Her voice no more than a whisper. 'I felt him move away. I . . . I thought he was just going to leave me there. Prayed he was going to.'

'How long did he leave you like that, on the ground?'

'A few seconds. Then he knelt over me, straddling me with his knees, and I felt him tie something round my neck.'

The ribbon.

'He tightened it, cutting off my breath. I kept thinking, I can't believe I'm going to die like this. He was tightening it . . . until . . . until I blacked out.'

I squeezed her hand and turned to look at Beth, pleading with my eyes for this to stop.

The young DC nodded. 'OK, Rachel. You've done brilliantly. I think that's enough for now.'

Rachel sniffed into her tissue, dried the tears on her cheeks.

As I got up from the chair, Rachel caught my hand in hers. Her firm grip surprised me.

'You will catch him? Please?'

I couldn't speak for the lump in my throat. Just gave her a nod. But I knew then that I would do whatever it took to see this sick bastard behind bars.

Chapter Fifteen

Fordley Police Station, Monday Afternoon

'She has some memory of coming round, seeing a man leaning over her.' Callum was reading from his notes. Addressing the team from the front of the briefing room. 'But it's hazy. She can't identify who it was with any certainty.'

'We're pretty sure it was this guy.' Shah glanced at his iPad to check. 'Daniel Dunglas?'

Callum nodded. 'AKA Terry Smith. Says he was walking the track above Ponden reservoir. It was dark, but in the beam of his headtorch, he saw someone. Thinks it was a man, from the size and build of the figure. Saw him stand up from the ground beside the trail and take off. Then he almost stumbled on what he thought was a bundle of clothes, or a discarded sleeping bag. Turns out it was Rachel.'

'Apart from height and build.' Tony Morgan, Callum's DS. 'Could he say anything else about the attacker? Clothes, facial features? Anything?'

Callum shook his head. 'Too dark – just a silhouette in dark clothing.'

'So, what was Dunglas doing up there in the middle of the night?' Beth voiced what everyone else was thinking.

'He says,' Callum couldn't resist a smile, 'that he was looking for corpse lights.'

'What?' Beth was incredulous.

'It's in the notes.' Callum sounded as disbelieving as he had in the pub, when Tommy Earnshaw had been spinning his yarns. 'Or Jo can explain it during the break.' All eyes were on me. I just smiled and shrugged.

'Local folklore,' I said, by way of an explanation.

Frank Heslopp snorted. 'Bloody carrot crunchers, you lot. It's all that interbreeding in these remote villages on the moors – weird bunch.'

As everyone laughed, Callum slipped off the edge of the desk and took a chair. 'Dunglas edits a magazine about occult bollocks. He was up there to check out some sightings by a couple of scared kids that's gone viral.'

Tony Morgan was studying his notes and a map he had spread out on the table.

'The students Rachel hooked up with in the pub said they were going to camp by Wytch's Tarn . . . ghost spotting.' He looked up, chewing the end of his pen. 'Take it that's the same thing Dunglas was there for?' He grinned. 'Unless there's more than one ghost prowling the moors?'

'Yes,' I sighed. 'Same sightings. Same witch hunt.'

'Must've been a bit crowded up near the tarn this weekend,' Beth said without humour. 'Students, Dunglas and all these New Age hippies I keep seeing, posting on social media. Our attacker was taking a hell of a chance being there with all this activity going on.'

I'd been thinking the same thing, but my thoughts were interrupted when Callum began flipping through his notes.

'You've all got copies of the initial Forensics report,' he was saying. 'Obviously, the site on the moorland where Rachel was found has been cordoned off. Crime scene investigators are still working the scene.'

Outdoor scenes were notoriously difficult for crime scene officers, who had to contend with the weather, as well as all the other considerations in preserving fragile evidence. I knew that while the tent would cover the immediate area where Rachel had been found that was only a small piece of ground. The attacker could have left evidence as he ran away and the moors were an unforgiving place to work, even in summer.

The police and Forensics service would have their resources stretched to the limit to cover as much ground as possible in the hunt for potential evidence, before the wind and rain removed it.

'Dunglas had to loosen the ribbon around Rachel's neck,' Callum was saying, 'in order to remove the hood. So his finger-prints are all over those items. He's had his prints and DNA swabs taken for elimination purposes. So has the farmer who helped carry her to his truck and drove her into Stanbury.'

'What do we know about him?' Tony asked.

'Owns a farm in the valley,' Shah read from his notes. 'Keeps sheep on the hill. He was out looking for some strays that had been reported on the road earlier in the evening. He checks out.' Shah sat back and stretched aching shoulders. 'Says he didn't see the attacker running away so we've only got Dunglas's statement on that.'

'Forensic evidence is going to be compromised.' Beth said. 'From Dunglas; the farmer; his vehicle . . .'

She was right. It would be frustrating for the Forensic officers, to try to eliminate all the trace evidence Rachel would have picked up after being found, and try to isolate anything left by her attacker. But preservation of life was always the first priority in these cases – it was just another complication to be dealt with. One I was grateful for, because anything less would mean Rachel hadn't survived.

'Anything from CCTV in Hebden Bridge, Shah?' Callum turned to the young DC.

Shah sat straighter in his chair, reading from his notes. 'Got footage from local shops. We can track Rachel's movements pretty much the whole time she's in the village.'

He cued up the video and cast it to the screen at the front of the room. All eyes turned to the images.

Shah went to the screen, tapping Rachel's figure with his pen.

'Here she's at the coffee shop.' He fast-forwarded to the part where Rachel leaves, to the next bit of footage, taken from a different shop camera in the high street. His pen following the figure, easily identified, carrying a rucksack.

'We can see her looking in shop windows . . . going into the soap shop.' The image flickered and changed to a view from inside the shop.

I leaned forward to get a better view. Not looking at Rachel, but at the people around her. A couple of older women. A young girl. No men.

'This is the best footage we have of Rachel before she leaves the village.' Shah clicked some keys and we were looking at the view from above the cash machine at the Co-op.

There was a queue behind her. Two women and one man.

'He's looking away from the camera,' Tony said. 'Wearing a baseball cap with a hoodie pulled over the top. Can't make out his face.'

We all waited until he stepped up to the machine, where usually the camera could get a good look at a person's features. But the dark hood and peak of the cap made it impossible.

'Not necessarily suspicious,' Beth said. 'I mean, it's February – bloody freezing.'

'Get on to the bank,' Callum said. 'Get his details from the transaction at the ATM.'

'His line of sight . . .' I said to the room in general.

'What?' Tony asked.

'Shah, can you rewind to where he steps up to the machine?' I said, getting up to go to the front.

I stared at the image again, close up, as Shah slowly took it back frame by frame.

'Stop . . . there.' I put my finger on the screen. 'He's taking his card out of his back pocket, but he's looking to his left, not at the ATM.'

'The direction Rachel went.' Callum picked up.

'Hmmm. Can we go back to where Rachel's in shot?'

I wasn't sure exactly what I was looking for, but there was something . . .

'There.'

Shah froze the picture.

Rachel was standing at the machine. She'd put in her number and was presumably waiting for her money. In that second, she looked up, directly into the camera.

The eerie moment she stared directly at us had drawn everyone's attention to her. I looked along the queue – two people behind – to the man in the hoodie. He was staring intently at Rachel.

* * *

Callum had allocated actions to the team. Tony, who was a magician with video and CCTV, had been tasked with stitching together all the footage of Rachel, so it could be viewed in one continuous sequence.

Shah was looking for any footage of the guy in the hoodie – which meant trawling back over everything they already had for that day, in addition to contacting the bank to retrieve details from the cash machine.

Number plate recognition cameras and CCTV were being examined to see whether any vehicles stood out.

'Would be a gift from the gods if our man in the hoodie is seen getting into a vehicle with a nice, clear number plate,' Callum had said, as I followed him into his office after the briefing.

I knew what he meant, but it was never that easy.

'Got officers interviewing the students Rachel met. See if they can add anything useful.'

'Any hits on similar attacks historically?'

He was already shaking his head, as he poured a coffee from the percolator on his bookshelf. 'Early days, but so far nothing.' He turned back to me, gesturing with the coffee mug. 'You still feel our attacker has done this before?'

'Certain,' I said without hesitation.

'How certain?'

I shrugged. 'Can't put a percentage on it, if that's what you want. But it's too practiced, Cal. Too slick. He had everything with him that he needed, including the ribbon, which I'll bet all the money I haven't got is significant to him.'

He took a mouthful of coffee. 'OK. I've worked with you long enough to trust your instincts . . . for now.'

I watched his head of silver hair, bent over the mountain of paperwork. 'Speaking of instincts . . .' I wasn't sure how to broach the subject so as usual, just winged it. 'Any news on the murder at the landfill?'

'Think we've found the murder weapon.'

I felt the breath catch in my throat, and struggled not to make it obvious. 'That's massive.'

He glanced up at me – his blue eyes, perceptive as ever, boring into mine. It took every ounce of control to manage my body language and not give away any 'tells' that I was more interested than I should be.

'Waiting for Forensics to confirm but looks likely.'

'What was it?'

'A wrench,' he said simply, already going back to his paperwork. 'Found in one of the utility vehicles. Got what looks like traces of blood on it. Like I say, Forensics will say for sure.'

'Near Red's body?'

He looked up from the paperwork, studying me for an uncomfortable second before asking, 'The vehicle or the wrench?'

I shrugged, trying to make it look inconsequential. 'Either.'

He dropped his pen and sat back in his chair, considering me with the unnerving focus of a professional investigator. 'Why so interested?'

I took a breath, shrugging again. 'Because it's Red. Like you said, I knew him.' Keeping my tone neutral. 'Because I'm going to see his mother and the details matter to me on this one.'

'Really?'

I met his steady gaze with one of my own. 'Yes, really. You said yourself, he was murdered. Not everyday someone I know, someone whose family I'm fond of, gets murdered. If there's anything I can do to help, then I want to.'

He nodded slowly. 'Well, for what it's worth, the vehicle was parked a few hundred yards from where the body was found. The wrench had been wiped and put in the toolbox in the truck.'

I was silent as I thought about it.

'So, the killer hit Red, tried to clean the wrench, then hid it among other tools?'

'Looks like it.'

'Why not take it away with him?'

Callum shrugged. 'Maybe he got it from there in the first place and it would arouse suspicion if it had gone missing. I'm waiting for an answer from the site supervisor.'

'Fingerprints?' I asked, hopefully.

'With any luck, but I'm not holding my breath. As I say, waiting for results to come back.'

I couldn't push further without making him even more suspicious. But as I was leaving the office, his voice halted me with my hand on the doorknob.

'None of this goes any further.'

I raised my eyebrows. 'You need to tell me that?'

The thin smile didn't reach his eyes. 'Like you said, not every day you visit the grieving mother of a murder victim you knew personally. Just make sure information from this investigation stays inside the investigation.'

The way he looked at me sent a shudder down my spine. The same feeling I'd had as I sat in the dark, listening to Chris McGarry's threats.

It was almost as if he knew.

Chapter Sixteen

Fordley, Tuesday Afternoon

Audrey Wilcox was busy in the kitchen as I sat on the comfortable velour sofa in her neat semi-detached council house.

I listened to the sounds of her making a brew – the wheels of her wheelchair squeaking against the lino tiles.

'Need a hand, Audrey?' Although I could already predict the answer.

'No, sweetheart, I'm OK.'

Fiercely independent, Audrey had resisted any attempts by Red to move from the house where she'd lived all her married life. Or from the council estate where she'd been brought up by her parents, before moving here with Red's dad.

The estate had changed beyond all recognition since she'd brought up her son, become a widow and suffered her health problems.

I knew from speaking with Red during his time in Armley prison that he'd worried about his mother – now in her eighties – living in an area that had become run-down and crime-ridden. Wanting desperately to move her to a new house on the edge of town, which he could easily afford to buy outright and have adapted for her needs. But Audrey was having none of it.

This was where she belonged, she said. She knew everyone here and they knew her. Even the 'bad uns' as she called them. But they also knew Red and the man he worked for, which made this probably the safest place for a vulnerable, elderly lady like Audrey to live.

No one was ever going to give her any trouble.

Her neatly painted fence and gate weren't covered in graffiti like many of the others. She was never going to be the target of thieves or con men, or have rubbish dumped in her pristine little front garden, which had been kept neat and tidy by Red.

'Here we go, lovely.' Audrey appeared in the specially widened doorway, the teapot and cups on the tray on her knee.

I took the tray and put it on the table between us, as she settled her chair next to mine.

'How are you coping?' I smiled into pale blue eyes, rheumy with age, but as perceptive as ever, as I poured tea from the blue patterned China teapot into the delicate little cups.

'Oh . . . you know . . .' Her chin quivered slightly and she pulled a tissue from her cardigan sleeve and dabbed her nose.

I handed her a cup, which she took in a hand that trembled slightly.

'I'm so sorry, Audrey.'

Her eyes glistened with unshed tears. 'I know you are.' She put the cup on her knee and reached out, taking my hand. Her skin felt cool and parchment thin. 'I keep expecting him to walk through that door any minute . . . But he isn't going to, is he?'

I'd faced grieving families before. Spoken to those who'd lost loved ones. Seen people utterly broken by grief, and managed it all with a professional armour that shielded me from the rawness of their emotions. Prevented the visceral, intense blade of loss piercing through, to wound me too.

But this was different.

Audrey was someone I'd come to know. Her son too – for all that he was associated with criminals. They were both, at heart, good people.

Mother and son, devoted to one another. A genuine love and care that ran deep. Impressive and touching in its authenticity.

'Are you going to be all right, Audrey?'

She sniffed, trying to smile but failing. Her head of tight grey curls, nodding, as she looked down, a tear running off her chin, to plop onto her paisley-print apron.

'Some of Red's friends have been round.'

They would be people he worked with. People employed by Chris McGarry. Friends nevertheless, who were equally fond of Audrey. She'd known the ones who'd lived on the estate since they were kids.

'Are they taking care of everything for you?'

'Shopping and the like.' She nodded slowly.

I'd actually been thinking of funeral arrangements. Dealing with the coroner, the police, paperwork.

Then, as if she knew, she added, 'They won't give him to me . . . my boy.' A sob escaped her.

I squeezed her bony fingers in mine. 'I know, I'm sorry. It's just because of the way he passed, Audrey. They need to keep hold of him for a while, until they know what happened.'

'Passed?' Her lip curled and she snorted in disgust. 'He didn't pass, love, he was murdered.' She spat the word, the venom in her voice taking me by surprise. This gentle woman that I'd never heard speak like this before.

'I know.' It was all I could say.

'Chris . . . he's rung me, you know.'

I opened my mouth to ask how? When? Surely not on the burner phone in the middle of the night?

'I'm on his prison PIN number.'

'Oh . . . yes, of course.'

'He's taking care of the arrangements . . . once they let me have my boy back. Joshua's been visiting him, to help arrange things. He was the one who told Chris what had happened.' She sniffed and wiped her nose with the tissue. 'Do you think it'll be long . . . before I can lay him to rest properly?'

I thought of Callum, of Elle and all the work she would have to do. Of the post-mortem and the tests. Red's body was a crime scene. A vital piece of evidence.

'I can ask, if you'd like?'

'Yes.' She dabbed at her eyes. 'Yes, if you can.'

'You should have a family liaison officer, to let you know what's happening, take care of any questions you have.'

'I have.' She lifted her head, seeming to straighten up. 'A woman. From Fordley Police.'

'Have you spoken to her?'

A vigorous shake of the head. 'Won't have her in my house.' Those pale blue eyes took on a sudden sharpness. 'After what they did to my boy . . . putting him in prison. I won't speak to the police. I'm sure she's a very nice woman, but I don't trust any of that shower.'

I couldn't help but smile. 'I understand that.'

'They said he was thieving, at the landfill site.' Her tongue clucked. 'Nonsense. He was no thief.'

I took a sip of tea. 'Do you know what he might have been doing there?'

A shake of the head, but there was a shift. A sudden caution in her demeanour.

'Audrey?'

The tissue was twisting in her fingers. 'He'd been different, lately. There was something worrying him, but he wouldn't say what. He never wanted to burden me, but I knew something was up.'

'Something to do with his work?'

'Don't think so . . .'

'A friend?'

Audrey shifted slightly in her seat and her eyes slid away from mine.

'Did he have a girlfriend?'

'No!' The word sharp, brittle.

As far as I knew, Red had never had a girlfriend in the usual sense of the word. His neurodiversity made it difficult for him to navigate relationships with women beyond friendships. But his gentle nature and lack of guile were endearing and I could imagine the right person forging a closer bond with him.

The way his mother had answered was telling.

'Was he involved with a woman? Maybe someone you didn't approve of?'

Her lips paled as she pressed them in a tight line and looked over my shoulder, simply shaking her head.

'I might be able to help,' I prompted gently. 'If you'll let me?' I squeezed her hand again. 'I helped Red before.'

Her face softened then, and her eyes met mine. 'I know you did, sweetheart,' she said softly. 'And I'll always be grateful for that.' She pursed her lips in thought. Then took a breath. 'Not a girlfriend . . . just a friend. But he was different after she came along. I didn't like her.'

'Who is she?'

'Penny, he called her.'

'Her surname?'

'Don't know.'

'Know where I can find her?'

'A club. In town. That's all I know.'

'Do you remember the name of the club?'

She shook her head as she handed me her teacup – still full. I put it back on the tray. 'They were friends, that's all.' Her tone was insistent.

'OK.'

'But she was using him. He was running round for her . . . all hours of the night. I knew she called him, could hear them talking down here till the early hours. Then he'd just go out. Wouldn't tell me where he was going.' Her expression was pained. 'He always told me everything. Unless it was about *her*. She was making him keep secrets from me, and now look, he's gone.'

'Have you told the police any of this?'

'No! And you don't either. They never helped him before and they won't help him now. Just call him a thief. They don't care about the likes of us.'

Another set of secrets to keep.

'But if I find out something that might help the police catch whoever killed your son . . . I can tell them then? Surely, you want whoever did this to be caught?'

She nodded, sobbing quietly as I put my arms round her shoulders and held her.

Chapter Seventeen

Kingsberry Farm, Wednesday Morning

'Daniel Dunglas,' Callum was saying. 'He bothers me.'

'Can't think why.' I smiled, cradling the phone between my chin and my shoulder as I filled the kettle. 'Weird name, ghost-hunter and psychic.' I'd looked up his magazine and website. 'What on earth could bother you about him?'

'They say sarcasm is the lowest form of wit.'

'Taking it to new lows. It's a skill, what can I say?'

'Traffic have been going through ANPR cameras on the roads around the moor.'

'OK.'

'Any vehicles in the area from Friday night to early Sunday morning are being logged and the owners traced and interviewed.'

'I can feel good news coming.'

'Ran the plate of a Volvo and got a hit. It belongs to Dunglas.'

'Where does it put him?' I flipped the lid on the Aga and put the kettle on the hotplate, absently kicking a ball across the kitchen for Harvey.

'Tracked it from Keighley to Kingsberry village, as far as ANPR cameras go. Then nothing after he gets on to the moor road.'

I leaned my back against the Aga, enjoying the warmth, as I thought about the possible routes from there.

'So, he could have been going to Haworth, Stanbury or any of the areas around there.'

'Or parking up on the edge of the moors, where there's no camera coverage.'

I could hear Callum taking a drink – no doubt treacle-thick coffee from his eternal percolator.

'He never denied being on the moor on Saturday night.' I could hear myself playing devil's advocate. 'After all, he found Rachel. He had to have transport to get up there.'

'So far, so innocent,' Callum went on. 'Officers went to interview him, along with any other vehicle owners who were around in the right time frame . . .'

'And?'

'Says he left the car in the Tarn Hill Tavern car park.'

'Ahh.'

'You were right. No CCTV at the pub – inside or out – so we only have his word for the sequence of events and the times.'

'Which are?'

Harvey dropped the ball at my feet and I kicked it under the kitchen table, then watched him barrel the chairs out of the way as he went after it.

'What's all the noise?' Callum asked.

'Harvey – rearranging the furniture.'

'Dunglas says he dropped the car there, late afternoon. Doesn't remember the exact time. Says he just went in to use the loo then left to walk to Wytch's Tarn.'

'So, he could have been there at the same time Rachel was in the pub with the students?'

'Officers put that to him. He says the pub was busy and he wasn't paying any attention. Denies seeing Rachel or the students.'

'I sense a "but" coming.'

'I don't believe him,' he said simply. 'Shah went back to the hospital and showed Rachel a picture of Dunglas, taken from his website. Unfortunately, she doesn't remember him.'

'Not even from when he found her on the moor?'

I could sense him shaking his head. 'She was unconscious when he took the hood off and loosened the ligature from around her neck. In and out of consciousness all the way to the hospital. Doesn't remember being taken into Stanbury in the farmer's truck either.' He paused and I heard him take another drink. 'Might her memory come back?'

'Maybe.' The kettle whistled on the hotplate. I lifted it off. 'Strangulation effectively starves the brain of oxygen, causing cerebral hypoxia. How long the brain was deprived affects the degree of memory loss.'

'Could it be permanent?'

'Only time will tell. Victims of this type of attack often have memory problems. If her brain was deprived of oxygen for a long time, or at least until the ligature was loosened, Rachel might have ongoing problems, like forgetfulness or trouble concentrating. Sleep problems, memory issues.' I poured scalding water into the teapot. 'The list goes on. Her memory of the attack might never be clear or complete. It's to be hoped she doesn't have long-term damage.'

'Hmm. Well, I sent uniform to track down the students in the pub.' I could hear the shuffling of paperwork. 'She named two of them in particular.'

'Mike and Lucy?'

'Well remembered – yes. They were shown pictures of Dunglas and Mike remembered seeing him in the pub.'

'Why so memorable?'

'Because the place was packed. Mike and his girlfriend got the first round in and everyone was standing round the bar. After about half an hour, a man he identified as Dunglas got up from a window seat and they asked him if they could take the table.'

'Not just a quick visit to the loo like he said, then?'

'Exactly. Why lie about something like that?'

'In my experience, when people lie about something seemingly unimportant, it's because it's important.'

'I'm having him brought in for a formal interview this after-noon if you fancy observing?'

I glanced at the clock over the Aga. 'Fine – what time?'

'Two o'clock.'

'Great, yes.'

After everything I'd heard about our Mr Dunglas, I was intrigued to see him. If I'd known what I was letting myself in for, I might not have been so keen.

Chapter Eighteen

Fordley Police Station, Wednesday Afternoon

I sat in an observation room, watching on screen the interview taking place across the corridor.

When I'd checked out his website, the picture of Daniel Dunglas must have been at least ten years out of date.

The man on the screen was in his mid-fifties. He still had long hair but it was grey now, not dark, although still tied in a ponytail that reached to the middle of his back.

I smiled as I remembered one of my dad's sayings, from an older generation who couldn't understand why a man wouldn't have a traditional short back and sides.

Beneath every ponytail you'll always find a horse's arse.

This man was far from an arse though.

His unique look was completed by a long grey beard. All that was missing was a black pointy hat and he'd be really rocking the wizard vibe.

Shrewd green eyes, obviously weighing up his interviewers. Certainly not missing anything that was going on around him.

The 'energy' that surrounded him seemed insightful. That elusive thing that I'd always been able to see in others, but could never quite explain. What 'New Agers' would call an aura.

I'd come to understand it as a faint vibration of energy around a person.

For some reason, ever since I was a child, I was able to see it. Like the heat haze that rises from tarmac on a hot day. A shimmering margin around an individual. Not coloured – just there.

Something I didn't discuss or try to explain, in case people thought I was weird. Callum certainly would.

Invaluable in the work I did – often giving me an extra 'edge' when it came to reading people. But it was unpredictable. Sometimes more obvious, other times not really visible at all. I'd learned that when people were in a heightened state of emotion – stressed or afraid – I became more aware of it. Or it became stronger.

Daniel Dunglas's energy – his demeanour was so calm, it was almost translucent. He was obviously totally unfazed by his surroundings. Which was unusual for people who weren't used to being interviewed by the police.

'Has he got a criminal record?' I asked Callum, who was sitting next to me. Tipped back in his chair, arms folded as he watched his DS, Tony Morgan, leading the interview, with Beth taking notes.

'Nope. Not under Dunglas, or his real name, Terry Smith.'

I chewed the end of my pencil, leaning forward to get a closer look, as Tony continued with his line of questioning.

'You said you left your car in the car park, then just popped in to use the toilet at the pub. Is that right, Mr Dunglas?'

'Daniel . . . please.' He smiled, the pale skin around his eyes crinkling at the corners. 'Yes, as far as I remember.'

Tony pushed a photograph across the table. 'Do you remember seeing this girl in the pub?'

Dunglas looked at the picture, touching it lightly with a thin finger. I noticed his nails were a little too long and neatly filed.

'It's the young woman I found on the moor.' He glanced at Tony – an expression of regret creasing his features. 'Unfortunately, she didn't look like that when I found her.'

'Did you notice her in the pub?' Tony asked again.

The man pursed his lips, slowly shaking his head. 'No. I don't recall seeing her, until I came across her that night.'

Tony sent two more photographs across to join the first. 'What about these people?'

'The students,' Callum said, for my benefit. 'Mike and Lucy.'

Again, a shake of the head.

'You're saying you don't remember seeing them?' Tony asked for clarity.

'No.' His smile was thinner this time, caution creeping into his body language.

'You see, that's where we have a bit of a problem, Daniel.' Tony tapped the latest pictures. 'You said you didn't stay in the pub, just went to use the toilet?'

He didn't answer. Just gave a half-nod. Shifting in his seat and clasping his hands together on the table in front of him. Stilling any movement of his long fingers. Waiting to see what came next; letting Tony drive the narrative, rather than give anything away.

'But these two people remember *you*. They were with a group of students standing at the bar that lunchtime.'

It wasn't a question, but Tony paused, looking expectantly at the man opposite. Giving him the chance to fill the silence.

Dunglas looked at the photographs again, studying them more carefully. Then raised his eyebrows, as though light had dawned.

'Ahh, yes, I remember now. I had gone in to use the toilet, a communal-type loo, but it was occupied. So, I came to stand by the bar and wait. I felt a bit self-conscious, just standing there, not buying anything, and it occurred to me that some places don't like you to use the facilities, unless you're a customer.' He stopped, as if that explained everything.

'Go on,' Tony prompted.

'I ordered a lemonade while I was waiting. Then the loo came free and I went in. When I came out, a seat became available so I sat there while I finished my drink.' He tapped one of the photographs. 'Is this the young man who asked if he could have the table, as I was leaving?'

'You tell me.' Tony smiled, but there was an edge to the question.

'Yes,' Dunglas said finally. 'It must be. That's the only explanation.'

'Do you recognise him?' Tony pressed.

'I can't say I do, really. I mean, it was a fleeting exchange. But if they were with the group of students at the bar then that's the only explanation I can give for why they might remember me.'

'And you don't remember seeing Rachel?' Tony asked. 'She was with them when they came to your table.'

A slight hesitation, then: 'No. But then I didn't expect it to become so important at the time.'

'How long was your car in the Tarn Hill Tavern car park?'

Dunglas ran a fingertip across one eyebrow, frowning as he considered the question. 'Well, until the early hours of the morning, I suppose.'

'You're not sure of the time?'

He gave a thin smile. 'It had been a long night, Sergeant . . . eventful. I was tired after everything and when I got back to the car, no, I didn't look at the clock.'

Tony made a show of looking at his notes, though I knew he didn't need them. 'Take me through the sequence of events, after you found Rachel.'

Dunglas leaned back in his chair, sighing, as if bored at having to go through this all again. But I knew it was all part of the process. Checking the veracity of a story by its consistency. Roll events forward, then tell it again, in reverse. See if anything in the account changes.

'Just as I found her, almost as soon as I'd loosened the ribbon from around her neck and slipped off the hood, the farmer appeared.'

'What happened next?'

'Well, he was as shocked as me. To see a young girl laying there . . . like that. We checked to make sure she was breathing and I got my phone to try to make a call, but my battery had died. The farmer said there was no way emergency services would be able to get up there and it would be better if we carried Rachel down to his truck. So, that's what we did.'

'Then what?'

'As soon as we got to the truck, he drove and I called 999, using his phone. His farm was just five minutes away, in Stanbury. As soon as we got there, the paramedics and police turned up – we all arrived at the same time.' He sat back and spread his hands out, palms up. 'And you know the rest.'

'You gave a preliminary statement to the officers attending.' Tony was reading from his notes again. 'Then the farmer offered to take you back to your car?'

Dunglas nodded. 'His wife was in a bit of a state, seeing the young girl and hearing what had happened to her. I didn't want to drag him away from her. Besides, I didn't want to travel back in his vehicle.'

'Why not?' Tony frowned.

'The energy,' Dunglas said simply, as if the police officer should totally understand that.

'The what?'

'Energy.' Dunglas steepled his long fingers in front of him, tapping his lips with them. 'We'd carried that poor girl in the truck. The energy of the attack, of what she'd suffered, saturated the space.'

He paused, waiting for Tony to say something. When he didn't, Dunglas carried on.

'It polluted everything. I really didn't want to be around it any longer. It was toxic for my spirit. I needed to cleanse myself of it.'

'And how did you do that . . . exactly?' I was impressed at Tony's ability to keep his tone so non-judgemental.

'I needed to clear my head. Walking back.'

'Almost an hour . . . to walk that far.'

'An hour from Wytch's Tarn to the pub,' Dunglas corrected him. 'But from Stanbury, along the road and then a shortcut across the moors, coming from the opposite direction to the Tarn, it's about forty minutes or so.'

'And did it work?' Tony asked.

'Oh yes. I chanted healing mantras, deflected the negative energy as I walked.'

Beth dutifully made her notes. I could only imagine what she was thinking.

The rest of the interview was predictably unhelpful. Dunglas continued to say he didn't remember seeing Rachel before finding her on the moor.

He couldn't give a more detailed description of the figure he'd seen running away from the spot where he found Rachel.

'No', he didn't see anyone on his walk back to the car and 'no' there was no one around when he got back to the tavern, which was in darkness and locked up for the night.

Twenty minutes later, the interview was concluded. Callum went back to his office and called Frank Heslopp in. We both took seats in front of his desk.

'What do you think, Jo?' Callum watched me over the rim of his mug.

'He's difficult to read.' I could hear the caution in my voice.

Profilers had, in the past, been accused of derailing investigations with misleading analysis. There had even been a high-profile case, decades earlier, of a massive miscarriage of justice. With the wrong man jailed for a murder he didn't commit, blamed in large part on the opinion of a psychologist. Thankfully, not me.

Since then, psychological profiles were used sparingly by police. Just one tool in the box of investigative techniques. Never to be relied upon solely to drive the direction of a major enquiry. A fact I was ever mindful of when asked to give an opinion on the hoof, like this.

'If I didn't already know,' I said, 'I'd suspect he'd been interviewed before. He was too relaxed for an average member of the public brought in for questioning.'

'No record of prior arrests.' Frank repeated what Callum had said to me earlier.

'He's confident,' I went on. 'Sure of himself.' I thought back to the man I'd watched on the screen. 'Almost impassive.'

'Seemed to me,' Callum said, 'he thought it was all beneath him. Like he was observing Tony and Beth, rather than being at the centre of it.'

'Hmm,' I agreed. 'A dissociation with the severity of his situation. Unfazed.'

'Like a psychopath would be.' Frank dropped his opinion like a hand grenade, minus its pin.

I shot him a look. Sometimes a little knowledge could be a dangerous thing.

'Bit of a leap, Frank.' I raised my eyebrows. 'From unconcerned to psychopathic.'

'You're the expert, Doc,' the old DI conceded. 'You're supposed to be able to spot 'em.'

Callum turned to me. 'Well?'

I slowly shook my head. 'Not been exposed to him long enough to give a detailed psychological analysis. But from what I've seen so far, he's not displaying overtly psychopathic traits . . .'

'But?' Callum pressed.

I shrugged. 'Narcissistic, I'd say. I'd need to watch him more, be exposed to him more, before I'd commit.'

Callum's impatience was as legendary as my own, but this was too serious for me to speculate at such an early stage, and I said so.

'But,' I conceded, 'he's cool under pressure. Confident in his ability to withstand your questions and not be tripped up. He's more intelligent than he appears and I think that's a conscious deception on his part.'

'You mean he wants us to underestimate him?' Callum took another mouthful of caffeine.

I nodded. 'Probably.'

'We only have his word that he saw this shadowy figure, running away from Rachel on the moors,' Frank said. 'He could be her attacker.'

'Agreed.' Callum was already shuffling paperwork. 'Dunglas could have been tying the ligature, not loosening it, before the farmer stumbled across him.'

'And we only have his word that the Volvo was in the Tarn Hill car park, and not nearer to where Rachel was attacked. No CCTV to prove or disprove that,' Frank concluded.

Callum was already picking up the phone on his desk. 'I'm going to have his car brought in for forensic examination.' He began punching in a number he knew by heart. 'If there's the slightest trace of Rachel in the boot, they'll find it.'

* * *

Walking through reception, I was still mulling over everything I'd seen and heard in Callum's office. Heading for the double glass doors and distractedly rooting in my handbag for my car keys.

Head down, I walked straight into someone coming out of the lift, dropping my keys in the process.

'Oh, sorry.' My eyes travelled up the long, slim figure blocking my way, stopping when piercing green eyes looked down into mine.

It was Daniel Dunglas.

'My fault entirely.' He gave me a half-smile. 'Allow me.' He stooped down and picked up the keys that had skittered across the tiled floor.

His cold fingers brushed mine as he handed them to me. And then he stopped, frozen for a moment, still holding my fingers.

'You have a spirit with you.'

Automatically, I looked over my shoulder. Whatever I'd expected him to say, it wasn't that.

'What?'

'A spirit,' he said again, as if it was the most natural thing to say to a stranger.

I disentangled my fingers from his, studying his face for some sign of humour or guile. There was none.

'You see it?' It was an effort not to sound sceptical and I had to resist the urge to look behind me again.

His expression was deadly serious, as he nodded slightly. Glancing over my right shoulder.

'He looks over you.'

'He?'

I was acutely aware that we were standing in an open reception area, in a police station. Thankfully it wasn't busy. Only the civilian receptionist behind the desk, working at her computer, paying us no attention.

He studied me for a moment, as if debating whether to say more. I waited, curious but unconvinced.

What he said next shocked me to my core.

'Your father.'

Chapter Nineteen

Kingsberry Farm, Wednesday Night

'He said that?' Jen sounded incredulous over the phone. 'That he could see the spirit of your dad . . . looking over your shoulder?'

I reached for the kettle. 'Yep. My guardian angel.'

There was a snort of derision down the line. 'So, what did *you* say?'

'Didn't know what to say.' My mind went back to that moment – in a public space, when a stranger told me he could see the image of my father standing beside me.

The man I'd missed every minute of every day since he died almost six years before. My rock. The anchor in my life.

The loss of him made much more turbulent by Mamma. A seemingly fussy, Italian matriarch to the outside world, but a fierce critic behind closed doors. Employing a subtle mix of negative evaluation and disapproval, which, as a child, ate away at my fledgling self-esteem.

If it hadn't been for my father, my mother would have turned me into an anxiety-ridden, people-pleaser. Forever seeking her approval, which would have been soul-destroying, because, to this day, it had never been forthcoming.

'I just stared at him,' I said, putting the kettle back without filling it. After the day I'd had, tea wasn't going to cut it.

I went to the wine rack by the door and selected a bottle of Merlot. 'I mean, what can you say to that?'

How's he doing? Is he OK? These were all things that came to mind at the time, but none seemed appropriate.

'Then what?' Jen asked.

'He said: "Your father is worried about what you're getting into. He wants you to step away."'

'What the hell is that supposed to mean?'

Chris McGarry? Paying a debt to a gangster? Lying to Callum about what Chris held over me?

'No idea,' I lied. Starting to pour a small one, then making it larger.

'Sounds to me like he just talks in riddles. To throw you off guard and make you think he really *is* in touch with the other side.'

Jen's scepticism was the solid weight of reality pinning my feet to the ground. Which was exactly what I needed. Why I'd rung her.

But the stab of guilt I felt deep inside just heightened the pain of not being able to tell her about Chris McGarry. About the death at the Monster Mansion that he was blackmailing me with. A burden I had to carry alone. One of my own making. Ice-cold in the way it isolated me from the people I cared most about. The people I usually relied on when the chips were down.

'You know how this works better than anyone,' she was saying. 'Fake psychic mediums using cold reading techniques. Mentalists . . .'

I took a warming sip of the wine. 'I know. Behavioural analysis without the psychology degree.'

Jen was right. In a way, these people who claimed to 'know' things often used techniques not too dissimilar to the ones employed in my own field.

Reading body language, expressions, the demeanour of the 'sitter', to interpret their internal thought processes. But while I worked in a field of psychology, what Dunglas did fell into the category of mysticism, magic or just plain fakery.

'That doesn't explain the rest though.' I was choosing my words carefully.

'The "rest"?'

I sat at the kitchen table, Harvey curled up at my feet, and sipped more wine as I thought back to the bizarre conversation.

'Dunglas stared at me, studied me.' I ran my hand through my hair, trying to straighten out my thoughts. 'I made sure I didn't leak any "tells". Nothing he could "read". I was curious about what he might come up with.'

'And?'

'He said: "You see things too, don't you?"' I took another sip of wine, absently rubbing Harvey's side with my foot. '"You can see what others can't."'

There was a short silence, as Jen thought about it. 'Any chance he already knew who you were? I mean, could he have seen you upstairs, when he was coming out of the interview room?'

'No, I don't think so. But even if he had that wouldn't tell him who I was, or what I did for a living.'

'There hasn't been anything in the press about this case, either,' Jen murmured almost to herself. 'You're not officially involved in any police enquiries at the moment.' Then almost as an afterthought, 'Are you?'

'No.' I swirled the blood-red liquid round the glass, staring into its depths for answers it was never going to give me. 'Like you say, probably just bullshit. Taking a guess and hoping to hit the mark.'

'What did you make of him?'

I thought about that for a minute, taking a bigger sip of wine. 'It was strange,' I said quietly. 'In that moment, when he was standing in front of me, I couldn't see his energy . . . nothing at all.'

Jen was the only person who knew what I meant. The only one I'd confided in; about the emotional energy I could sometimes see in people.

'But everyone has it,' she said.

'I know, but I couldn't pick up on his at all.'

'Perhaps he's a vampire.' She laughed.

'Hmm.' But I couldn't raise a smile.

Chapter Twenty

Kingsberry Farm – Wednesday Night

Sleep eluded me. Despite a second glass of wine, sitting beside the fire in the lounge, trying to unwind, before finally going up to bed.

I punched my pillow into shape, wishing I could do the same with my subconscious, which insisted on running Dunglas's unsettling words through my brain, like an annoying song you hear on the radio and can't get out of your head.

Conflicting emotions battled for primacy, as I tossed around.

My logical mind refusing to believe that Daniel Dunglas was anything other than a New Age mystic, who, I had no doubt, believed in his own so-called psychic abilities, but which, in my world, could have no foundation in reality.

All of that vying with the powerful desire to believe that my father *could* still be a presence in my life. That he hadn't just ended with his last breath.

That the indomitable Irish-Yorkshire spirit and strong presence he'd had in this life had somehow found a way to hold on to the things he loved most. Tenaciously refusing to leave this physical plane, to leave me.

Love versus logic. Hope against reality. Longing and grief willing to squash scientific reasoning to find solace.

Those were the things people like Dunglas used to earn a living from the bereaved and the lost. Or in his case, to sell his magazine.

If a tantalising glimpse of being able to contact a lost loved one could have this effect on me, I could only imagine what it would do to someone like Audrey Wilcox. What kind of a hold could someone like Dunglas have over her?

My sore eyes felt gritty and I finally gave in to the urge to close them against the shadows flitting across my bedroom ceiling.

I jumped when my phone rang.

'McCready.'

'It's me.' No preamble, but this voice needed no introduction.

'Chris.' My heart hammered in my chest, as I propped myself up on one elbow.

'Any news?'

I took a breath, trying to slow my pulse and lower my blood pressure, which had just spiked off the scale.

'Why can't you call during business hours like a normal person?' I snapped.

'Yeah?' A short, humourless laugh. 'And use the phone on the landing when the screws record all my calls? You've come up with better suggestions, Jo.'

I sat up and leaned back against the headboard. 'I'm getting precious little sleep as it is without your midnight calls.'

'Sorry,' he said, unconvincingly. 'I haven't got long. Have you got anything for me?'

I took a long breath as I tried to put my thoughts into some kind of order.

'I spoke to Audrey. Went to pay my respects. Poor woman's in pieces.'

'I know. Which is why I need some answers. Find out who did this—'

'But it won't change anything, will it?' I cut across him. 'Won't bring Red back to his mother?'

'No!' The word exploded in my ear. 'But in *my* world, it sends a message, Jo. That no one can mess with my people, *my* business and not suffer the consequences.'

107

And there it was. In that one sentence. Chris McGarry's violent narcissism laid bare. As if I needed proof of something I already knew, but which Chris had always been careful to shield from me. Our previous interactions had been nothing but polite and professional.

But the façade had crumbled and he didn't care that I could see it.

This was all about *him*.

He could say it was revenge for the death of a man he regarded as a brother. A friend he'd had since childhood.

He could pretend it was to get justice for a grieving mother. But what it was *really* about was punishing those who had dared to take something away from Chris McGarry.

He regarded his business, his friends, even his family as just that – *his*.

Property. Territory. And someone had violated it. That, in his estimation, had to be punished.

'Audrey said you were taking care of her.'

'Of course.' His tone softened. 'She was like a mother to us kids growing up, 'course I'm going to look after her.'

'I'll try to find out when they can release Red's body. She wants to arrange a funeral.'

His breath gusted down the phone in frustration. 'I didn't ring for chit-chat, Jo,' he snapped. 'I can get all this from Audrey.'

'OK . . . OK.' I sat on the edge of the bed, staring into the dim half-light of my bedroom, as I ran through what I knew that might appease him.

'You were right – detectives believe Red was there to steal diesel. Or maybe scoping out some heavy machinery to be stolen later.'

'Couldn't detect their arses with both hands, that lot.'

'His vehicle was found on a track near the perimeter and they know he cut through the chain-link fence to get in there, on the night he was killed.'

'So far, you're not telling me anything I don't already know . . .'

I had to give him *something*. Anything to keep him at bay. But maybe nothing too vital.

'They think they've found the murder weapon.' As the words left my mouth, I knew I'd crossed a line.

Callum's voice came back to haunt me.

Just make sure information from this investigation stays inside the investigation.

'This is more like it. What was it?'

'A wrench. They're testing for forensics and fingerprints, and before you ask, no, the results aren't in yet.'

There was a moment's pause, and I could imagine Chris, pacing, as he mulled over what I'd said.

'Anything else?'

'Audrey mentioned a woman – Penny. I think she's significant.'

'How?'

'Not sure,' I admitted. 'But Audrey said Red's behaviour changed lately and she was certain it had something to do with this woman. Do you know her?'

I could sense him shaking his head even before he spoke. 'No. But I knew he was seeing someone. Some of the lads were ribbing him about it.'

'Girlfriend?'

'Doubt it. Red said she was a friend. Knowing him, that's probably all she was.'

'Know where I can find her?'

'He'd started spending a lot of time at a club in Fordley, by all accounts. That wasn't usual for Red, so maybe it's something to do with this bird?'

'Which club?'

'Dunno. I'll put you on to one of my lads who might know.'

'Why don't you just ask him yourself? Let him have the late-night calls.' I could hear the irritation in my voice. Dangerous to let it show, but I couldn't help it.

My legendary short fuse was being burned down to its limit.

Tired and strung out by being backed into a corner, when my usual response to being against the wall would be to come out swinging. But that wouldn't work with an opponent like Chris McGarry.

'Red was one of mine.' I could tell he was speaking through gritted teeth. 'A fact not lost on the police. If I ask any of my crew to go poking around this, they'll be all over them like a nasty rash and I don't need plod sniffing round my businesses.'

I kept quiet, knowing he was right.

'I want *you* to chase this down, Jo. I trust your instincts. If you think this Penny might have something to do with what happened to Red – or knows who does – then I want you to find out. My lads can help track her down, but I don't want them visible.'

'But I don't understand why—'

'Because if this is another group moving into my territory, well, then my lads getting involved will be the spark that'll set the whole damned thing off. My family are on the outside, Jo. Sarah and the kids. I don't want them caught up in the middle of a war. I can't afford to show my hand . . . not yet. Not until I know for sure what's going on.'

'I suppose—'

He cut across me, in no mood to listen now.

'But anything you find out, you give to me, understand? Don't go spilling it all to your boyfriend. If you do, I'll know.'

'I know you don't like it, but the police have all the resources. They could help, Chris. If you *really* want to find out who killed Red?'

'Oh, I do.' His tone sent a trickle of adrenaline down my spine. 'I just want to make sure I get to them first.'

Chapter Twenty-One

Hartshead, Thursday Afternoon

Freddie Harris – known affectionately to his friends as Hazza – was propping up the bar of the Gray Ox Inn when I arrived for our meeting.

Although I'd never met him, Chris McGarry's description meant there was no mistaking the well-dressed man he euphemistically called his 'lieutenant' the moment I entered the pub.

He was, unsurprisingly, facing the door and smiled as I came in – obviously recognising me as the woman his boss wanted him to speak to.

'You must be Jo?' I simply nodded. 'What you having?'

'Soda and lime, please.' Then, in answer to his raised eyebrow, 'I'm driving.'

''Course you are.' He grinned. 'Not the sort of place you can easily get to on foot, unless you're a local, eh?'

He took his pint from the bar and gestured to a corner with a jerk of his head. 'Got us a table – bit quieter over here.'

I took my drink and followed him to an empty alcove at the other side of the pub.

'The boss said you needed some info about Red?' He settled himself in the chair facing the door, taking a sip of beer.

'He was seeing someone . . . a woman?'

Hazza nodded, staring into his pint. 'Sorry business – old Red. Miss the soft git.' He looked up and sniffed.

'This woman?' I pressed.

'Penny.'

'Do you know her last name?'

He shook his head. 'Didn't get to that.'

'Did you meet her?'

'Not exactly.' He took another drink. 'Saw her once, when I dropped Red off at the club where she worked. She was having a fag outside. I stayed in the car – didn't meet her.'

'Which club was it?'

'Hades.' He laughed. 'About right for that hellhole.'

I'd heard of the place. Though 'nightclub' was a pretentious description for what was a faded pub with a late-night disco.

It had a reputation for fights in the early hours of the morning when the customers were chucked out, and a serious drugs problem at just about every other hour it was open.

'What do you know about her?' I wasn't holding out much hope, but he surprised me.

'Red said she was a friend.'

'Think it was anything more than that?'

He shook his head, moving the pint glass around on its beer mat. 'Red didn't have girlfriends, in the normal sense of the word. He had friends . . . you know?'

I nodded, staying silent. He seemed in a reflective mood, so I was happy to let him talk.

'He met her about a year ago – at the hospital.'

'Hospital?'

'Yeah, Audrey got taken in to A & E – middle of the night. She'd had a nasty fall at home. Red was with her, obviously. This Penny was in the next cubicle. Only separated by a curtain – so you can hear everything that's going on. Apparently, she'd been beaten up by some punter. Was in a pretty bad way. Police came during the night to talk to her.' He shrugged. 'After they left, the girl was on her own.' He looked at me and smiled. 'Red was soft as putty. Went to talk to her. Ask if she needed anything, and that's how he got to know her.'

'Attacked by a punter? She was a sex worker?'

His laugh was humourless. 'That's a nice way of phrasing it. Bit of a rough tart, by all accounts, but you could never say that to Red.'

'But he knew what she did for a living?'

'Oh yeah, he knew. Ignored it, I suppose. He just liked her, wouldn't hear anything bad about her.' A micro-expression flitted across his face, but not before I'd read it. Disapproval.

'I sense a "but" coming?' I prompted.

Another shrug. 'I thought she took the piss – you know?'

'In what way?' I smiled and sipped my own drink, trying to keep it more conversational and less like an interview.

'Took advantage of his good nature. The lads didn't like that.'

'Did any of the guys you work with get to know her . . . or more about her?'

'No. Red knew we thought she was taking him for a ride, so he kept her in the background. Didn't introduce her around.'

'Was she using him for money?'

Hazza nodded. 'He could afford it, I suppose. Living in that council house with Audrey. He never flashed the cash. Only expense he really had, after the house, was his vehicle. The fuck-off four-by-four that he drove round in.' He laughed. 'We used to say he looked like a farmer, driving that thing. But he loved it. He gave the tart money. Not lent it, gave it.'

'But she still worked? I mean, he wasn't paying her to come off the game?'

'Don't know how much she rinsed him for, but whatever it was, she didn't stop working.' He drained the last of his pint. 'After she was attacked, she didn't work the streets though. Just operated out of the club. Red called in through the week, would sit at the bar and chat to her. Seeing her with him sent a bit of a message. You know? That she was looked after by the

McGarrys. Or at least by Red. That was probably the best way he knew to keep her as safe as he could.'

'He was acting like her minder?' I instantly regretted saying it, as Hazza shot me a look.

'He wasn't her pimp, if that's what you're implying?' he snapped. 'Chris isn't into that game and no one who works for him would be either.'

'Sorry, I didn't mean it that way.'

Hazza frowned. 'Chris has a reputation . . . you know?'

Typically twisted standards.

The McGarry brothers in their time, and Chris's father and uncles before them, had built up a fearsome reputation as a powerful crime family. Providing protection for the pubs and clubs in Yorkshire – for a fee. Before graduating, under Chris's 'new management', into drugs and arms dealing.

Their rumoured connections with drug lords in Colombia and Miami made them a force to be reckoned with and secured their place as a major organised crime group.

Pushing drugs onto the streets, creating crime to fund a habit that ruined lives, was obviously acceptable to the likes of Hazza and his associates. Not to mention a trade that meant gun crime was on the rise on inner-city streets. But profiting from prostitution was something they regarded as beneath them. A line they wouldn't cross. A trade Chris McGarry wouldn't sanction.

Unbelievable.

'Why would Audrey think this Penny might be connected to what happened to Red?' I shifted away from my faux pas.

'I doubt she was the one who caved his head in at the landfill.' Was no real answer. I waited. Then he added, 'But he was bothered about something and shifty, lately. Kept going off grid and usually we'd find out he'd been with her on some goose chase.'

'Goose chase?'

'They were always going off in his car. She had him running round for her, but none of us knew what it was all about.'

The waitress walked past the table and he ordered another pint, gesturing to my glass, but I'd hardly touched it.

'This was lately?'

He nodded. 'The last few months. Spent more time together, after the business with the police. He was a shoulder to cry on, if you know what I mean?'

'Business with the police?'

'The attack – last year. She'd made a statement at the hospital and later, Red went with her to the station to be interviewed. But nothing came of it. It really screwed her up. She was leaning on Red a lot, because the anniversary of it was coming up. He was holding her together. She kept pushing the police to do more about it, said she was remembering more from that night, that might help but . . .' He shrugged.

Reading between the lines, I knew what he was hinting at. I took a not-so-wild guess.

'She didn't think the police were taking it seriously?'

'Neither of them did. Because she was on the game.'

I knew that for a lot of sex workers getting beaten up by their clients was almost an occupational hazard. Whatever they did for a living didn't make it right, but often the police wouldn't put as many man hours into it as they should.

'Is there any more you can tell me?'

'Not really.' The waitress came back with Hazza's pint. He waited until she was out of earshot, before adding, 'Far as I know, she's still at Hades. You could try her there.' He pushed a piece of paper, with a number scrawled on it, across the table. 'I was going to talk to her, but the boss doesn't want us getting involved. That's my number. Anything you find, let me know so I can keep the boss up to date. If you need anything, just bell me.'

Chapter Twenty-Two

Kingsberry Farm, Friday Morning

'You want me to go where, with you?' Geoff Perrett – my old university lecturer, mentor and, since his retirement, my friend – sounded as surprised as I'd expected when I'd phoned him.

'I know it's a strange request—'

'Strange?' He cut across me with his usual curmudgeonly directness. 'Knowing me as you do, I'd say it's positively ludicrous.'

'I know, but—'

'I'm a real ale man,' he said, exasperated. 'And the furthest I'm likely to go for a pint is the local pub in the village, not traipse all the way to Fordley, to go to some dive.'

I couldn't argue. Hades *was* a dive.

'I'm not asking you to go there for a drink.'

'That's even worse.'

'But I can't walk in there on my own,' I persisted.

'What, and you'll look even less conspicuous, walking in there with a grizzly academic, almost twice your age and crippled with arthritis? Talk about the odd couple. You couldn't attract more attention, if you tried.'

'It's not about being inconspicuous.' Although hearing him spell it out, I had to admit, he had a point. 'As a woman on my own, I'd be hassled every five minutes in that place. I need a man with me.'

'And any man will do?' He huffed his disapproval. 'I'm hardly bodyguard material, am I? What about that cop . . . Ferguson?'

'He can't know about it.'

'Ah, and there it is,' he said, triumphantly. 'The *real* reason you want to drag me out of my comfortable armchair and into some den of iniquity.'

'Oh God, you're *so* dramatic.' But I couldn't help smiling.

'I suppose I do qualify as your keeper of secrets so one more shouldn't make a difference.' I heard him take a drink, knowing his preference would be strong builders' tea. 'Want to tell me exactly *why* you're keeping this visit a secret from our illustrious constabulary?'

'I'm following a lead . . . for a friend.' I was choosing my words carefully. 'It's unofficial, but it blurs the boundaries into a live case that Callum's working.'

'And you don't think he'd be best pleased having you trampling all over his investigation?' Geoff concluded.

'I never "trample",' I said in disgust. 'But until I know what I've got, I'd rather not show my hand, that's all.'

'OK.' He sighed. 'Tonight then, but you're coming to Haworth to pick me up. I don't do public transport these days.'

* * *

In theory, the drive from the village of Haworth to Kirkgate Lane in Fordley should take just over thirty minutes. But with the freezing weather, traffic, as we neared the city, was moving at a crawl.

Geoff huffed his discontent, moaning at every driver who slowed us down and every red light that held us up.

'Now I remember why I don't leave the village these days,' he said, rubbing the condensation from the passenger window with the sleeve of his heavy overcoat. 'This city's changed beyond all recognition, and not for the better.'

I couldn't help smiling at his curmudgeonly manner, which I knew was only partly genuine.

At university, I'd always found his gruff nature amusing. While he intimidated the other students, I'd always seen the twinkle behind those heavy-rimmed glasses. A giveaway to the generous personality beneath the cantankerous exterior.

'Well, it was all horse-drawn carriages in your day, wasn't it?'

'Cheeky,' he said to his reflection in the passenger window. 'So, how do you want to play this, when we finally get there?'

'I thought you could create a distraction by starting a bar brawl, and I'll sneak up to the office and interrogate the manager.'

'Knowing you, I could almost believe you're serious.'

I navigated around a bus and accelerated up the hill from the centre of Fordley, towards a less salubrious area of the city.

Kirkgate Lane, as the name suggests, ran from the centre of Fordley to the spot halfway up the hill, where a gate to the original Anglo-Saxon church had stood, overlooking the ford that gave the city its name.

Like many of the older districts of the inner city, it was once a vibrant area, bustling with independent shops, selling everything from homewares to greengrocery.

Now, it seemed like row upon row of gaming arcades and vape or phone shops, interspersed with South Asian restaurants and an exotic-looking shisha lounge.

There were three pubs along the Lane. None of which were frequented by the upwardly mobile or more affluent residents of Fordley and all of which had shady reputations. The worst of all was Hades.

I drove past it, noting the two bouncers manning the doors.

A woman with long red hair, wearing a ragged-looking fur jacket and a bright red miniskirt and shiny PVC boots, was leaning against the wall, smoking a cigarette.

Further along the Lane, I could see two young women – wearing clothes that showed off far too much skin for a freezing February night – chatting and smoking. As I slowed the car, one of

118

them looked over, then, realising we weren't potential punters, went back to her friend.

We parked on a side street and I helped Geoff out.

'Bloody hell,' he complained as he unfolded himself from the seat. 'If this car was any lower, our arses would be on the ground.'

If the bouncers thought we were an unlikely couple, they didn't let it show. Nodding politely as we went through the dark-wood doors, into the dim interior.

Thumping bass from loud music reverberated in my ribcage and coloured lights strobed from a DJ stand in a dark corner.

At just after ten o'clock, it was already busy. Most of the tables were taken and groups were standing around the main bar. We wound our way through the crowd.

'My feet are sticking to the carpet,' Geoff muttered, only half under his breath.

'Stop moaning.' I hooked my arm through his and steered him towards the long mahogany bar. 'Come on, I'll buy you a drink.'

Geoff eyed the pumps suspiciously, but his face brightened at the sight of a beer he obviously approved of.

'What'll it be?' The barman had to almost shout above the din.

'A pint of Yorkshire Blonde.' Geoff shot me a sideways look. 'Seeing as I've been bullied here by one.'

I didn't order anything but stood by Geoff as he waited for his drink, leaning my back against the bar, to take in the place.

I'd been here a couple of times as a teenager, even though my parents would have had a fit if they'd known. To be honest, apart from music, it hadn't changed much. Even the carpet was the same one my feet had stuck to back then.

I gazed around the room, taking in the clientele. Noting who looked drunk – which was most people. Those who were there for a good time and oblivious to what was going on around them and, more importantly, those who weren't.

A big man stood at the other end of the bar. He was dressed casually, nothing marking him out as staff, but I could tell by his body language and demeanour that he wasn't a customer.

I let my eyes slide past him, looking around the bar generally, but keeping him in my peripheral vision.

Geoff was chatting about the virtues of pale ale and I nodded and smiled, but he didn't have my full attention.

The big man was chatting to a young waitress collecting glasses, but he wasn't looking directly at her. His eyes were scanning the place over her shoulder, aware of everything going on. Hyper-vigilant. Erect stance, feet firmly planted. Hands clasped lightly in front of him in the classic 'ready position'. Looking relaxed when he was anything but – he was working.

I had him pegged as ex-military or security service trained and I knew he would have marked me out too. So, no point waiting around, might as well go stick my head in the lion's mouth.

'You OK here for a minute?' I leaned close to Geoff's ear to be heard over the music.

He'd perched on a bar stool and was nursing his pint. 'Is this where you go put the thumb screws on someone?'

'Something like that. I'm only going to the end of the bar – keep an eye on me. If blokes start hassling, come over and buy me a drink . . . OK?'

He gave an exaggerated huff. 'I'll come over, but you can buy your own bloody drink.'

'Ever the gent.'

I went to the corner of the bar, standing next to the big man. He was at my elbow as I leaned on the counter, waiting to be noticed by the bar staff.

The queue was three deep – it could be a long wait. Though I needn't have worried. The arm beside me raised a fraction and the hassled barmaid noticed immediately and came straight over.

'Boss?'

'Serve this young lady next, Stacey, please.' His voice rumbled, like heavy wheels over gravel.

I glanced at him. 'Thanks.'

Perceptive blue eyes looked down at me, as he simply acknowledged with a slight nod.

Stacey took my order.

'So . . .' That low growling tone again. 'What can I do for you?'

Our eyes met and, in that look, one professional identified and acknowledged the other.

'Am I that obvious?' I smiled.

He gave a light shrug. 'Not at all.' He did a quick sweep of me, from head to toe. 'You'd pass to the untrained eye.'

I nodded and smiled, but said nothing.

'You a cop?' he asked, leaning both elbows on the bar, so our heads were close together and he could speak quietly.

'Nope. Doctor actually.'

He shot me a look, raising a sceptical eyebrow. 'But not the usual kind of doctor, am I right?'

'Maybe.' I returned the sweep – doing it deliberately slowly, head to toe. 'Ex-military . . . am I right?'

He grinned. 'Maybe.'

Stacey brought my drink over. Then, taking a nod from the man she called 'Boss', she refused my payment.

'Thanks.' I raised my glass to him. 'You the owner?'

'No,' he said quickly, as if the very thought was ludicrous. 'My friend's place. I just stepped up to manage it while he's . . . away.'

121

From his expression and tone, I took the sub-text for 'away' to be 'prison'.

'Not wanting to seem unfriendly,' he said slowly, 'but, if you *are* a cop then this might not be a healthy place to spend your Friday night.'

I turned to face him, leaning one elbow on the bar. 'Told you, I'm a doctor.'

''Course you did.' He smiled and this time it reached his eyes. 'I'm Luke, by the way.'

I took his extended hand. 'Jo.'

'Pleased to meet you, Jo. So, tell me, what's a, not-your-usual-kind-of-doctor, doing in here then?'

'I'm looking for Penny.' A statement more than a question. Deliberately vague, open-ended, so he could answer any way he chose.

He could have said he didn't know her – in which case, I was at a dead end. But he didn't.

Chapter Twenty-Three

Hades Club, Fordley

'Penny's not been in lately.' He didn't look at me as he spoke, his eyes scanning the room instead.

'Did she work here?'

He glanced at me then – those sharp eyes, scrutinising. 'Not in an official capacity.'

'But she worked *out* of here?'

He continued to study me, saying nothing but giving a half-nod. 'What's your interest?'

'She was a friend of a friend.'

'Which friend?'

I paused, considering whether using Red's name would help or hinder. Deciding it couldn't hurt.

'Red Wilcox.'

His eyes widened slightly. 'Wouldn't have you down as a mate of Red's.'

'I was his psychologist, when he was in Armley.' I pushed my card towards his elbow. He scooped it up and slipped it into his pocket. There was a slight shift in his manner that said my credentials were acceptable.

'Shame about Red. He seemed like a decent bloke.'

'He was.' I took a sip from my glass. 'Penny was a friend of his. I'm hoping she can shed some light on what might have happened to him?'

'Thought he was killed up at that tip site, at Keelham Hill?'

'He was. But I think Penny might know who or what he was involved with, that took him up there.'

'And you're not a cop . . . right?'

I smiled. 'I'm a friend of Red's mother.' I gave a shrug, as if to make light of my interest. 'I promised her I'd try to find out what I could. She doesn't trust the police. Doesn't think they'll give Red's death the time or resources, you know?'

He nodded then. Pursing his lips as he considered. Then he waved the barmaid over. 'Stacey was friendly with Penny – she might be able to help.'

He lifted the flap in the counter to let Stacey out and went behind the bar himself. 'Take your break, love. Go talk to Doctor Jo here. She's asking about Penny. Use the office.'

The young girl nodded, wiping her hands on a bar towel. I followed her to a door marked 'Private', up a flight of stairs to a dingy room at the top.

The 'office' consisted of an old desk, with a high-backed Chesterfield chair behind it. A matching sofa sat along the wall, facing a row of filing cabinets.

The place smelled of stale cigarettes and coffee.

Stacey plonked herself in the office chair. I took the sofa.

'You're a friend of Penny's?' I cut to the chase.

She nodded, her blonde ponytail swishing around her shoulders. 'Not massive . . . I mean not close. But she's in almost every night, and we chat at the bar, you know?'

'Know where I can find her?'

The girl frowned. 'No one's seen her in over a week. Not since what happened to Red.'

I thought about that as Stacey rummaged around the cluttered desk, finally uncovering a pack of cigarettes and helping herself.

'Think that's why she's not been here? Because of Red's death?'

She lit the cigarette, taking a deep draw, before blowing a column of smoke in my direction. 'Could be . . . I mean if a mate of mine got murdered, I might lay low for a bit too, wouldn't you?'

'Suppose so. Do you know her address?'

She gestured somewhere over her shoulder. 'On the Butter-field Estate, out of town. She's in one of the flats.'

'Know which one?'

She shook her head. 'Never went there.'

She pulled out her phone and started scrolling. For a minute, I thought she was looking up an address – something that could be useful – until it became apparent she was just absorbed in a world of her own that had nothing to do with our conversation.

'I know Red's mum,' I said, as a way to draw her attention back.

It didn't.

Stacey continued to smoke and scroll, her face illuminated in the blue glow of her screen.

'She said Penny and Red had become closer in the last few months.'

More scrolling . . .

Her indifference was starting to piss me off. 'You know who Red Wilcox worked for?'

She nodded without looking up from her phone.

'Well, *that* person wants to know what happened to Red. If Penny can help, I need to speak to her.'

Scrolling . . .

'If you can help, I'm sure Red's boss would be grateful.' I took a long breath, before hardening the tone. 'But if I tell him you had information but just couldn't give a shit, he might not be best pleased.'

She shot me a look, her thumb hovering over the phone. 'I . . . I didn't say that.' Some of the colour drained from her face.

'Then put the bloody phone down and talk to me,' I said quietly.

She did as she was told, taking another drag of the cigarette. But the cockiness was gone.

'Red was getting involved with something, probably for Penny. Do you know what it was?'

She hesitated for just a heartbeat. Long enough to consider her options. But the hint that I was here on behalf of Chris McGarry seemed to have the desired effect.

'She's been screwed up, ever since she got attacked last year. The anniversary of it was coming and it raked it all back up. She was a nervous wreck.'

'What did that have to do with Red?'

Stacey's knee started to bounce under the desk. Nervous energy that had nowhere to go.

'Penny didn't want to get the bus home late at night on her own. Red would come in and sit at the bar. Wait for her to finish, then give her a lift. That kind of stuff. Protection, I suppose.'

'What do you know about the attack . . . last year?'

She shrugged. 'Not a lot. But it changed her. Not just as a person, you know? Physically. Left her with memory problems. She was on antidepressants and she drank too much. Mixed with the pills, it didn't help.'

'Didn't stop her working though?' I wasn't being judgemental, but going by Stacey's reaction, that's how it must have sounded.

She sat forward, her eyes blazing with more emotion than she'd shown so far.

'What the fuck was she supposed to do? Get a job as a lawyer, or an accountant?' She sucked her teeth. 'Was off for a long time after that punter did what he did to her. Red paid her bills – I heard – until she was fit enough to work again. The Lane's all she knows so she came back. But Red was a friend – he did what he could to keep her safe.'

She angrily stubbed the cigarette out in the overflowing ashtray. 'So, that could be why she stopped coming here. After her protection got murdered. Don't you think?'

'When did you last see her?'

'What's today?'

'Friday . . . all day.'

She pulled a face. 'Then it'd be Tuesday.'

'*This* Tuesday?'

'No . . . last week.' She nodded, getting up from behind the desk. 'Yeah, over a week ago.' She glanced at the clock on the wall. 'That's my break done.'

I followed her back down the stairs.

Geoff was at the far end of the bar, where I'd left him. But he wasn't alone.

The tall redhead in the tattered fur jacket and miniskirt, who'd been leaning against the wall outside when we arrived, was perched on the stool next to him – their heads together in animated conversation. Amazingly, Geoff had a broad smile on his face.

I couldn't remember ever seeing him smile. It was transformational.

Stacey lifted the bar flap, following the direction of my eyes. 'That's Bren. She works the Lane. Knows everyone. Might be able to give you more info.'

My 'thank you' was cut off by the slamming of the countertop as she turned on her heel and walked away.

Chapter Twenty-Four

Hades Club, Fordley

Bren was already well on her way to being drunk. Geoff made the introductions, as his lady friend sipped the expensive vodka cocktail he'd bought her. Happily, not too drunk to make sense, or to share what she knew about her friend Penny.

'Really shook her up, that attack,' she was saying, as she leaned on Geoff's shoulder and took another sip of her drink. 'She were never the same after.'

'Did she report it to the police?' I already knew she had, but it was as good a place as any to start the conversation.

Bren snorted her disgust. 'Yeah, but you know what plod are like when it's one of us? Couldn't give a toss. Besides, she couldn't give a description then, so they didn't have owt to go on.' She laughed, and put her arm round Geoff's shoulder. 'Hardly going to call out the A Team to comb a country lane for evidence, are they?'

'A country lane?' I frowned. 'I thought she was attacked by a punter? I assumed she'd be in town, or in a car?'

Bren shook her head. 'He picked her up in his car, on the Lane. We was working together that night. I took his reg number.' Another sip of the cocktail, draining the glass. 'We did that for each other. Bit of extra security in case owt went wrong.'

'If you got his registration number, why didn't the police arrest him?'

'Cos it weren't him,' she said simply.

She twirled the stem of the empty cocktail glass between her finger and thumb, looking at Geoff expectantly.

I nodded to him. If another drink was what it took to keep the information flowing it was a small price to pay.

Geoff signalled to Stacey, who came over, taking the empty glass without a word.

'So, what happened that night?' I prompted.

'The guy she picked up drove her out of town. Said he didn't want to risk his car being clocked in the red-light district. Once they'd done the business, she wanted him to drive her back here, but he wouldn't. Just kicked her out of his car and drove off.'

'No gentleman,' Geoff said in disgust.

Bren nodded. 'Worse, they were up on the moor road – bloody middle of nowhere.'

Moor road.

That got my attention.

'No phone signal up there, so she started walking. After half an hour, she got a signal and called a taxi. They said they'd pick her up along the road, so she kept walking. That's when she got jumped.'

'Jumped?' I asked, offering my debit card to a sullen-faced Stacey when she replaced Bren's cocktail.

'Hit from behind.'

'Bloody hell,' Geoff breathed.

'She went down, but was too dazed to put up a fight. Bastard put a hood over her head.'

Her words hit me like a slap. 'What?'

'Yeah. He tried to move her, but she was coming round a bit then and put up a fight. She's a right feisty bitch when she wants to be, our Penny . . . clawing and kicking.'

'Did he tie her hands?'

'He tried to. Flipped her over – you know, face down and pinned her arms, but didn't manage to tie them. She was giving him trouble, so the bastard hit her again. Lucky the taxi showed up when it did.'

'Wait.' I was frantically piecing this together as Bren talked, trying to picture the sequence of events. 'She survived, because the attacker was disturbed?'

'Yeah. When he saw the headlights, he must have scarpered. Taxi driver took her straight to Fordley Royal Infirmary. Just as well – she wouldn't have been able to walk anymore.'

'Because of the head injury?' Geoff shook his head in disgust.

'No. Because the bastard had taken her shoes.'

Chapter Twenty-Five

Kingsberry Farm, Saturday Morning

I swivelled my chair round and stared out of the office window. It was one of those bright, frosty mornings that made winter feel glorious.

Cold painted the lawn with ice crystals that glinted in the slanting sunlight.

Blue tits and sparrows clustered around the hanging bird feeders, making the most of seeds to supplement their lean winter diet, and I watched Harvey patrolling his boundaries, sniffing the hedgerows and naked flowerbeds.

It would ordinarily have been one of those mornings where I would have been up and out early. Walking with Harvey in the blissful isolation of the moorland around my farmhouse.

But today, I couldn't feel the joy.

Bren had dropped a bombshell.

Her words had sent a thousand thoughts burning through my brain, like red-hot shrapnel.

The similarities between what she described happening to Penny and the attack on Rachel Taylor were seismic.

Rachel had been attacked by the same man – he'd been operating for over a year and, if my instincts were right, probably even longer than that.

I'd told Callum I thought this man had killed already. If he'd been out there, operating under the radar, hunting in the shadows all this time without being caught, how many other victims could there be?

The thought was terrifying.

We needed to find Penny – and fast.

She had vital information that connected her attacker to Rachel. Maybe even that crucial snippet, seemingly insignificant to her, but which could just hold the key to his identity.

I'd been trying to find her address. But with no surname to go on and just the vague suggestion that she lived in a flat, somewhere on the Butterfield Estate, it was a fruitless search.

There were dozens of tower blocks in the geographic area known as 'Butterfield'. The estate of the same name was only a portion of it and there were hundreds of flats in its tower blocks and maisonettes. Needles and haystacks were an understatement.

I'd already checked the electoral register with no success. Either Penny wasn't her real name, or she wasn't registered to vote.

Over the years, Jen had built up an impressive variety of ways to search for people. Gone were the days when we'd have used the Yellow Pages. Now, everything had gone digital and we had paid subscriptions to several online directories and databases, including Companies House and even some ancestry sites.

When it came to research, Jen was my secret weapon. But today was Saturday and I didn't want to disturb her valuable family time, which her husband, Henry, guarded jealously.

So, I'd done the preliminary searches myself. But so far, I was coming up empty.

The one source I knew would yield results, frustratingly, was the one I couldn't, or shouldn't, use.

Penny had reported the attack to the police. That would be on record. She'd be known by the cops who worked the area around the Lane, or by Vice officers.

But Chris McGarry's words kept scrolling through my mind . . .

Don't go spilling it all to your boyfriend. If you do, I'll know.

Somehow I had to get this information to the Major Enquiry Team, without letting Callum know about Hazza putting me on to Penny and the Hades Club. Callum's instincts would jump on any connection between me and Chris McGarry and that could mean endgame for me.

As if my thoughts had conjured him up, my phone rang. His name flashed on the caller ID.

'Hi,' I said too quickly. 'Just thinking about you.'

'All bad, probably.' But I could tell he was smiling.

'What's up?'

'Been thinking about Red Wilcox and the murder scene at the landfill.'

'Oh?'

'I want to go out there and see things for myself.'

'Thought you would have already.'

I could hear the shuffling of papers. 'Ordinarily. But once Rachel's attack landed, things got hectic. I've assigned it to Frank Heslopp, who's reporting to me. I'm SIO on Rachel's case – along with half a dozen others.'

I knew that real life was far removed from the image most people had of police investigations. On TV cop shows, the detectives handled one case at a time. In reality, HMET could have several major investigations running alongside each other. It was always a juggling act and one I was grateful I didn't have responsibility for.

'Thought you might want to come along?' he was saying.

That was a surprise.

'Didn't think you wanted me involved?'

His breath came down the phone in frustration. 'You already are, aren't you?'

'Meaning?'

'Red was a friend of yours—'

'How many times—'

'And as such, I know you won't have been able to leave it alone, despite my warning. In fact, knowing you, telling you to leave it would mean you'd go out of your way not to.'

'Thanks.' I tried to sound indignant, but he was right.

'I'm leaving in an hour. Want me to pick you up?'

'No, it's OK. I'll meet you there.'

I had places I needed to go later. People I wanted to talk to, as a theory was beginning to form in the back of my mind. Fledgling, but insistent.

I couldn't hold back on what I knew. However I framed it, whatever way I eventually told Callum, I knew I'd have to share this latest development. There was no easy way. So, I did what I always do – jumped in head first.

'I need to talk to you . . . about Red.'

'Just about to go into a meeting with the Chief Super. Can it wait until later?'

'Guess it'll have to.'

Chapter Twenty-Six

Keelham Hill Landfill Site, Saturday Afternoon

Keelham Hill was an area just a few miles from the village of Kingsberry, where I lived. And although I knew the landfill existed, I'd never been to it. But then, why would I?

It was also surprisingly well hidden from public view. So although the main route into Fordley ran past it, nothing was visible from the road.

As I followed the signs directing me on to a 'Private Road', which cut across the open moorland, I wasn't quite sure what to expect.

Like every other resident of Kingsberry and the larger city of Fordley, I'd read news articles about locals raising petitions, protesting against the planned expansion of the site. Complaining of the disruption of heavy vehicles and more importantly, the stench. But as I drove across the moors, I couldn't see any evidence of the eyesore I'd imagined. In fact, the scenery was stunning.

The village of Kingsberry was one of the highest in England, at 1,100 feet above sea level – on a clear day, it presented a view as far as the West Coast. Some said, if you looked hard enough, you could see the tiny outline of Blackpool Tower. Though I'd never been able to make it out myself and doubted the claim.

Towering wind turbines clustered along the top of a distant hill, one or two turning lazily in the breeze. The huge, white blades like giant ship's propellers, rotating across the horizon.

I picked up signs for 'Keelham Hill HWRC' – Household Waste Recycling Centre – advising me that all visitors had to stop at the gate and check in with the office.

I spotted the police vehicle before I reached the gate. Blue and white police tape, strung across the road and tied to bollards on the grass verge, marked the outer cordon of what was still a crime scene.

The uniformed officer checked my name and who I was there to see, but he already had my car registration listed. Callum had told them to expect me. After getting me to sign the scene log, he moved a bollard to one side to let me through.

A few hundred yards further down the road, I reached the single, heavy metal bar across the entrance to the site. It was unmanned and there didn't seem to be anyone around. I was just about to get out of my car when a guy in a hard hat and high-vis jacket came out of a Portakabin and walked towards me.

He swung the barrier open and waved me through, pointing to a black BMW that I instantly recognised, parked at the far corner of the car park.

Callum was leaning against the bonnet of his car. He was already wearing the white paper 'scene suit', required by Forensics, but even over his clothes it was providing precious little protection against the biting February wind.

I pulled my car next to his and climbed out. The cold hit me like a slap in the face.

'Bloody hell,' was his opener. 'Like the Arctic up here.'

'And you . . . from the Highlands of Scotland.' I laughed. 'Thought you'd be hardened to it by now.'

'Left Scotland when I was a kid, so it doesn't count.'

He handed me my scene suit, leaning against his car as he watched me struggle into it.

The cold was nipping the tops of my ears, and I pulled the paper hood up. Not that it made much difference.

'Dunglas's car has been impounded,' Callum said. 'Getting it tested for evidence of Rachel being in the boot.'

Anything I might have said was interrupted as Callum made a gesture that we should stop the conversation. The worker who'd opened the gate was walking towards us.

Callum made the introductions. 'Jo, this is Will Matheson, site supervisor.'

I took his extended hand. It was large and calloused, enveloping mine like a glove.

'Jo McCready.' I returned his ready smile.

'Police? Or are you with the Forensics lot?'

'Actually, I'm a psychologist.' I waited for him to ask more, but he didn't. Just acknowledged what I'd said with raised eyebrows.

'Your colleague here has already signed you in.' He indicated the Portakabin with a jerk of his head. 'So, if you're ready, I can take you up to the scene?'

He was already walking towards a dark-red Ford Ranger.

Callum fell in step beside me. 'Crime scene investigators are still here,' he explained. 'Might be a few days yet before they can release the scene. I'm meeting the crime scene manager.'

I watched as the supervisor climbed into the heavy four-by-four. The powerful engine growled into life.

'Is he allowed up there?' He wasn't wearing the same Forensic suits we were.

'Site regulations,' Callum muttered. 'Only way we can get access to their operational area is in an authorised vehicle. But Will stays in the truck and only takes us as far as the perimeter to the inner cordon.'

He opened the rear door. I had to use the grab handles to haul myself up and inside. 'Believe me,' Callum said as he pulled himself up behind me, 'you wouldn't want to walk it.'

As soon as we left the car park, I saw what he meant.

The hard surface gave way to a dirt track, created by heavy vehicles compacting the earth.

The Ford Ranger dropped a gear as it pulled up the steep incline, ridged with deep ruts. With the recent rain a lot of it had been churned into a muddy mess, which would have been a nightmare to navigate on foot.

I leaned forward between the front seats to get a better look.

'It isn't how I pictured it.'

Will shrugged, never taking his eyes from the track. 'What did you imagine?'

'Dirty . . . noisy.' I held on to the side of his seat as the truck swayed over the uneven surface. 'A cliff face of rubbish, I suppose. Covered in land gulls.'

'Well, it's quiet on a weekend – more so now, with you lot closing the site down.' I studied his profile for any sign that he was irritated or annoyed by the disruption the police investigation was causing. But there was none.

He was broad, but not overweight. Built like a rugby player. Older than me, but I couldn't determine his age – late fifties somewhere.

He reminded me of a rugged outdoorsman. The image completed by a thick beard, matching a mop of brown hair escaping from beneath the hard hat. He looked like a Canadian trapper from the eighteen hundreds. The only things missing were a rifle and animal furs.

'So, where's the rubbish going while this site is closed?' I was genuinely interested. Fascinated by an industry that I knew must exist, but never really thinking about the details of it.

One of those services we all take for granted. Like expecting water to come out of the tap, or electricity to be there when we flip a switch. Only realising how much we rely on it when something goes wrong and it's not there.

'Diverted to another centre for now. But it hasn't got the capacity we have. We don't just take waste from Fordley. It comes in from Halifax, Leeds . . . sometimes as far away as Manchester. They'll only be able to take the excess from us for a week or so.'

'Shouldn't be that long.' Callum's voice came over my shoulder. 'I'll get an idea from the crime scene manager today.'

Will nodded, still looking ahead. We were coming to a fork in the track. Another road joining from the left. He stopped the truck and picked up his radio from the dashboard.

'Checking haul road is clear? Four-by-four coming up.'

The radio crackled. 'All clear.'

'Thank you, weighbridge.'

He put his foot down and the Ranger's suspension swayed again over the rutted track.

He picked up on my earlier comment. 'I thought it would stink, and be organised chaos, when I came to work here. But it's not like that at all.'

'I can see.' I gazed out at neatly ordered fields of thick, black plastic sheeting, pinned down in tight squares and stretching over acres. Presumably covering the waste. Not a land gull in sight.

'This place is huge.' I was seriously impressed. 'How didn't I even know all this was here?'

'We're one of the biggest sites in England,' he explained. 'But we're as environmentally anonymous as we can be.'

'Activists are always in the press, complaining about it,' Callum said from the back.

'With no reason.' Will couldn't hide his frustration. 'Last time they complained about the smell coming from the site, the Environment Agency did an inspection. Gave us the all-clear.'

'So why the complaints?' Callum wasn't about to let it go.

Will shrugged. 'Activists love to protest about something. Turns out the ones making all the noise don't even live round here. Professional protestors. If they weren't here they'd be in London climbing the Houses of Parliament or something.'

We'd crested the top of the hill and the view unfolded in front of us.

Beyond the edge of the landfill site, in the far distance, the hills rolled on to the horizon. White with frost, like a patch-work quilt of fields, separated by thin-black seams of drystone walls.

'Wow,' Callum said.

'Not a bad office, is it?' Will said. 'This is as far as I go.' He looked across at me and smiled. 'I'd be a gent and help you down, but I'm not allowed out of the truck – you know, because of your forensics.'

I was aware of Callum opening the door on his side to jump down, until I put my hand on his arm, to hold him where he was.

'Just give me a minute.' I glanced at him. 'I need to get an overview. Get my bearings, before we go to the spot where Red was killed.'

Once – years ago – he might have questioned what I meant. But he'd worked with me long enough now to understand exactly what I was doing and why. He'd even learned to trust the process, despite it being a world away from the one he was used to.

I called it 'walking the scene'. A technique I used to get into the mind of an offender.

Letting myself think like them was never an easy part of the job, but for me it was the only way.

Physical evidence – forensics, CCTV, all the things the police used to piece together what had happened – could show us the sequence of events. But I needed to go beyond that.

Not only to know *what* had happened, but to answer the all-important *why*. Why this victim? Why kill them this way? Why here and why now? And, importantly for me, what motivated the killer?

By answering these questions, it could often give the police the answer to the million-dollar question – *who?*

For me that meant moving through the crime scene as the killer had done. Seeing the same things. Hearing the same sounds, breathing the same air.

Getting into his mindset until I could profile his thinking and understand what had brought him and his victim to this precise moment in time.

What were the motivations and drives that brought someone to this final scene of devastation, when they had committed the ultimate crime – murder?

Chapter Twenty-Seven

Keelham Hill Landfill Site, Saturday Afternoon

Will's eyes followed mine, as I looked through the window.

'Best vantage point – you can see the whole site from up here.'

I pointed to the fields of taut black plastic sheeting. I didn't even know what I needed to ask so I kept it vague.

'How does this work?'

'We keep a small area open for tipping. Called a "cell". Once it's full, we put a cap of plastic liner over it, to prevent scavenging pests and stop any smell.' He pointed to an uncovered area. 'That hole is the current operational waste cell. Eventually, it'll be capped – sealed forever.'

I looked out at the vastness of it. The crater beneath the industrial plastic liners must have taken the top off the whole hillside at one time. 'What was this? A quarry or something?'

'Used to be an open cast mine – last century,' Will said. 'Landfill company took it over in 2016. There are ten million tonnes of waste on the current site, but it's reaching capacity.'

'So, what happens when it's full?'

'It'll be landscaped and turned into a nature reserve.' He grinned. 'Then we'll all be out of a job.'

I studied him for a second. 'Have you always worked here?'

I expected the 'man and boy' line, but he surprised me.

'Nah – Merchant Navy before this. Been here now eight years.'

'Bit of a change.' It wasn't a question, just fishing to see what I caught.

Again, a shrug of wide shoulders. 'Young man's game at sea.'

'You seen enough?' Callum was getting impatient.

I nodded and opened the door then jumped down to the frozen, packed earth.

Will leaned out of his window as we began walking. 'I'll wait here,' he shouted. 'Take you back down when you're ready.'

* * *

Our boots crunched over the frozen tracks and I absently wondered whether the forensic paper overshoes we had to wear might tear on the rough earth.

Our breath plumed out in front of us, held suspended on the cold air. Mine more than Callum's as I was panting with the exertion.

I took a large lungful of air, breathing in through my nose to test for odour from the tip. But all I could smell was earth and grass and freezing-cold air.

As we rounded a bend, more police tape fluttered across the track, marking the inner cordon of the crime scene.

The PCSO guarding the barrier checked our IDs and we signed another log, before the tape was lifted to allow us in.

The crime scene manager – a young woman I recognised – was waiting for Callum just beyond the tape.

We both slipped the masks over our faces and Callum pulled up his hood, as she waved her arm to indicate the metal stepping plates that had been laid down to create a 'common approach path', preventing potential evidence being trampled.

We dutifully walked along the stepping stones of plates.

As Callum spoke to the manager, I watched the scene of crime investigators moving carefully around the scene.

A small white tent still stood over the spot where Red's body would have been. Thankfully long since removed to Elle's domain at the mortuary.

Anonymous white-suited figures, taking samples and photographs, of the last place Red would ever have seen.

I tried to imagine it as it would have been the previous Wednesday night. Pitch black, freezing.

I slowly turned through 360 degrees, taking in the ground, the skyline . . . the perimeter fence to my right.

In the distance, beyond the landfill, the outline of a stand of trees, where Red had hidden his vehicle.

My eyes traced the route along the edge of the adjoining farmer's field, from the trees to the fence, where a forensic officer was kneeling.

I could hear Elle's words . . .

Forensics found traces of blood and tissue on the sharp edges of the chain-link fencing. It's a match for Red.

'Why?' I murmured, almost to myself. 'Why did you break in here, Red?'

'Talking to yourself again?' Callum made me jump. I hadn't realised he was beside me.

'Not a place you'd want to end up, is it?' I said quietly, staring again at the little tent.

'Not sure I want to "*end up*" anywhere at all, least not for a while yet.' He was looking back the way we'd come. 'Being here certainly gives a better perspective.'

He pulled out an iPad and opened up the crime scene photographs. It was the first time I'd seen them.

The breath caught in my throat as I looked at the image of someone I'd known. A living, breathing person – with a grieving mother – reduced to a stiffened corpse, lying face down on a dirt track.

'Bloody hell,' I whispered.

'Sorry,' Callum said, not really sounding sorry at all.

I knew he had little sympathy for Red because of his association with the McGarry's. That was all Callum saw. All he needed or wanted to know.

144

To him, Red was a murder victim. But less deserving of his sympathy than someone he would consider an 'innocent' victim of crime.

I knew he would be thinking that Red's lifestyle – the people he associated with and the world he operated in – had led to his death.

Experience would suggest he was probably right.

Live by the sword, die by the sword.

But I couldn't be that dispassionate, or that removed.

For me, Red was Audrey's son. And she was an elderly woman, who didn't deserve to be burying her only child. Besides, I'd known the man. Callum hadn't. And I knew he wasn't the same as Chris McGarry and the criminals he worked with.

I kept my eyes glued to the image as I spoke.

'What was the orientation of his body in relation to the outside?'

He swiped to another photograph, taken before the tent had been erected.

'Head towards the fence,' he said, flicking through other images that I really didn't want to see.

I looked away.

'And the murder weapon . . . the wrench. It was found where?' I asked, taking a deep breath.

He pointed to an area where a huge vehicle was parked on the track to the tip face, a few hundred yards away. 'Toolbox in the compactor over there.'

I started walking towards the yellow monster-truck, with steel, spiked wheels. Looking like an overgrown Tonka toy.

I could sense Callum following me quietly.

He'd learned, long ago, to allow me to walk the area in silence. Gathering my thoughts as I tried to piece together the sequence of events.

It was only when I got near that the size of the compactor registered. The spiked wheels towered above my head, with steps leading up to the cab.

There were marks all over the yellow bodywork. Silver-grey smudges from the aluminium fingerprint powder that had been dusted everywhere.

Callum leaned against the metal wheel, looking through his iPad. He showed me the crime-scene photos.

One showed a spot beneath the passenger seat – holding a long, yellow toolbox.

'The compactor is usually parked in the compound with the other vehicles, but it wasn't that night,' Callum said. 'Will, the supervisor, said it had been a late shift and the driver left it here ready for the next morning. Wrench had been wiped, but not thoroughly enough. Blood and hair matching the victim was collected.' He flicked through some documents. 'Pathologist – your mate, Elle – has confirmed the wrench matches the pattern of the wound that killed Red. Obviously, everything's been removed for evidence.'

I studied the picture of a heavy metal wrench, about as long as my forearm, and could imagine the weight of it crashing down on to Red's skull. No wonder death was instantaneous.

I turned and looked back – towards the sad, little white tent – seeing, in my mind's eye, Red's attacker standing over his body. Having swung that fateful blow, killed a man. Then walking calmly over to this huge vehicle to replace the weapon that he'd taken from the toolbox.

'And Will confirmed that's where the wrench had come from? This vehicle?'

I felt Callum's nod.

I studied it all. Looking at the ground. The fence. The truck.

'How did the killer get into the truck in the first place?' I said, almost to myself.

'Door to the cab had been forced. Lock was broken.'

'Can you show me the pictures of Red again . . . where he was lying?'

Callum finger flicked across the screen, bringing up the sterile image. No smell – no body fluids in a picture. But I could imagine.

I found myself holding my breath. Just as I would if we'd been standing over Red's body for real. Thankfully I'd been spared that, this time.

'What's your working theory?' I asked quietly, still staring at the tent, as if by sheer force of will, I could bring Red back. Reverse events, hold the clock, so this wouldn't have happened at all.

'Attacker broke into the compactor. Red was part of this . . . whatever it was. They fight. Attacker grabs the wrench from the top of the toolbox and uses it as a weapon. Red ends up dead. Killer cleans the murder weapon, puts it back where it came from.'

'Any fingerprints on the weapon?' Although I could already guess the answer.

'No. Attacker wore gloves. No prints on the truck either.'

I thought back to the photos. 'Red wasn't wearing gloves – that's why he cut his hand on the fence.'

'Which is why we think the attacker broke into the cab and got hold of the wrench.'

'Any sign of the tool used to cut through the perimeter fence?'

'Found on the ground, where it had been used. Red's prints are on that.'

'So if that's how Red got in here, how did his killer get access to the site?'

'We think they came in here together,' Callum said. 'Red cuts the fence. Leaves the wire cutters on the ground, to collect when they leave. They both come onto the site. His partner, who's gloved up, breaks into the compactor. Whatever happens next, there's some sort of altercation between them and the killer hits Red with the wrench. Wipes it and puts it back, then exits through the fence same way they got in.'

I pursed my lips as I thought about it. 'Why break into the compactor?' I looked up at the behemoth above my head. 'If fuel theft is the reason you're going with, would they need to do that?'

'In the past they've smashed the fuel covers, but not always successfully. Easier to break into the cab and use the fuel release switch from in there.' He shrugged away from the side of the vehicle and looked up at it. 'Or maybe the aim was to steal the truck itself?'

I raised my eyebrows. 'For what? Joyriding?'

'Nothing would surprise me these days.' But I could tell he didn't believe that any more than I did.

He looked down at me. 'So, what do *you* think?'

I started slowly walking back towards the CSI tent. 'Whatever happened before the fight – altercation – I think Red was leaving when he was killed.'

'Go on.'

'He's facing the fence. I don't think he ended up in that position as the result of a fight. Elle said that apart from the graze from the fence, he had no fight or defence injuries on his hands or arms, but grazes to his knees.' I stopped and scuffed the hard earth with the toe of my boot. 'Don't suppose you could get any footprints?'

He shook his head. 'Earth was frozen.'

'I'll bet if you could, you'd get toe prints from Red's boots.'

'Why?'

'Because I think he was running towards the fence when he was hit from behind.'

We'd reached the tent.

I stopped and looked at the hole in the fence. The escape route Red had never reached in time.

'Rather than stand and fight, which he was more than capable of doing, he was running for his life. From something that scared him to death.'

Chapter Twenty-Eight

Fordley Police Station, Saturday Afternoon

As we'd travelled back from the landfill in separate cars, I hadn't had a chance to talk to Callum about Penny and what I'd found.

I'd tried to collar him before we'd left the car park at Keelham Hill, but he had to take a call from the incident room. I decided to try after the team briefing he'd asked me to attend back at the station.

The briefing room was full. Standing room only as everyone who wasn't out chasing up lines of enquiry attended.

Callum brought everyone up to speed with our visit to the landfill site and was talking them through what we'd learned from the supervisor when we'd gone back to his Portakabin office.

'I know it's in the notes from officers who attended the site when the body was discovered,' Callum was saying, 'but seeing it for myself gives us a different perspective on things . . . plus we got Jo's input.'

All eyes turned to me perched on a seat near the front. I raised my mug of tea in acknowledgement.

Callum turned to a large map of the site, which had been pinned up on the wall. It had been taken from the air and gave a good view of all the relevant areas. The site, the woods and farmers' fields that surrounded it and all the roads that dissected the moors to and from the landfill.

Yellow markers pinpointed where Red had left his truck in the woods. The hole in the fence and where his body was found. The vehicles and site office could be clearly seen.

'The site supervisor, Will Matheson, explained their security arrangements in more detail,' Callum was saying.

'Used to be a night watchman in a wood hut back in my day,' Frank Heslopp's voice growled from the front row.

'Technology is cheaper these days,' Tony Morgan chipped in. 'Doesn't drink tea or nod off listening to the cricket.'

Heslopp made some disgruntled reply, thankfully unintelligible.

'A security company patrol the perimeter. Walk round it twice during the night. They're not there full time. It's part of a wider round they cover for businesses in the area as part of rural crime prevention. Their last patrol was midnight and the fence was intact.'

Callum acknowledged Beth, who wanted to ask something.

'The site's been the target for fuel theft?'

He nodded. 'From the plant vehicles. Which is why, last year, the management made the decision to park them all in a utility area near the main gate.' He tapped the map, showing a level area at the edge of the haul road. 'Covered by CCTV cameras. Unfortunately for us, the compactor truck had been left at the tip face at the end of the previous shift. No CCTV up there.'

'What time do the first staff arrive?' Tony asked, making a note.

'The site isn't licensed to accept waste until after 6 a.m. Delivery trucks that arrive earlier are held at the weighbridge.' Callum was reading from the notes Will had given us, along with site plans and maps. 'Supervisor arrives first, about 5.30 a.m. Opens the site, turns the floodlights on, ready for the first deliveries.'

'And that's when Red's body was found?' I asked, trying to find it on my bundle of notes.

'No.' It was Frank Heslopp. 'That was 6.30 a.m. Apparently it was the driver of one of the first delivery trucks. Spotted the body by the fence as he came down the haul road from the tip face.'

I made a note. 'The fence was intact at midnight and I know Elle, the pathologist, can't get an exact time of death, as the body was outside on one of the coldest nights of the year. But putting this timeline together, we know Red was killed sometime between twelve and six thirty?'

'Yep – unless intelligence comes in that narrows that window.' Callum turned to DC Samson, a specialist in telephony. 'Speaking of which . . . anything on Red's phone, Brooke?'

The young detective shook her head, looking as frustrated as I knew she must be feeling.

'Last ping was from the mast at Kingsberry. I've triangulated it from the last time he used his phone. It puts him at Keelham.'

I knew from the case notes that Red's phone wasn't found with his body and was still missing.

'So, it's a fair assumption that the killer took Red's phone with them?' It was more of an observation than a question.

Brooke nodded. 'Search teams have combed the whole site, and the area between the landfill and Red's vehicle and his home. No sign of the phone. It's shown as deactivated. Last activity was midnight on Wednesday, when Red made a call to a number which wasn't answered. One of twenty calls to the same number over a twenty-four-hour period.'

'OK.' Callum was entering a note on his laptop. 'Get onto that number.'

'Already done it, Boss.' Brooke managed not to look too pleased. 'It belongs to a Penelope Lynch.'

My brain suddenly froze, and whatever Callum said in reply was lost on me as I stared at the young DS.

God bless you, Brooke Samson, I thought. *You've just saved my bacon.*

'I've applied to her phone provider for cell site data,' my saviour was saying. 'But we all know how slow they can be.'

'Then tell them to get their arses in gear,' Callum snapped. 'This is a murder investigation.'

'Done that, Boss.' The DC was unfazed. 'But what we do know is, over that period, none of Red's calls to Miss Lynch were answered.'

As the rest of the briefing ticked along, my brain was racing at a million miles an hour. Brooke had neatly introduced Penny's name, which meant I didn't have to.

Chris McGarry's threats – that I should feed anything I found directly to him – were a secondary consideration now. Her name had legitimately been introduced as evidence to the team, so I was out of the shit.

What happened when Penny was attacked the previous year put her front and centre into Rachel's case, and to withhold it would not only hamper that investigation, but make me guilty of perverting the course of justice, if ever it came out that I knew. I had to dovetail my information into the briefing.

While I was thinking of an elegant way to do that, Callum's mention of my name pulled my attention back into the room.

'Jo had some observations when we went to look at the scene.'

All eyes were on me.

I cleared my throat, glancing at the notes on the pad on my lap.

'I suppose,' I started hesitantly, still trying to juggle the contents in my mind of what I could and couldn't say, 'I have a different insight into this as I knew the victim.'

Everyone had notes on my previous contact with Red, as a client, so it didn't need lengthy explanation.

'Having assessed him while he was in Armley prison, I came to understand him as a person.' I glanced up at the sea of faces. 'I can tell you now that whatever Red was doing at that landfill, he wasn't there to steal machinery, or fuel.'

'With all due respect, Doc,' Frank Heslopp began, with a phrase I hated, because whatever came next was usually anything but respectful, 'understanding his psyche doesn't translate into whatever criminal activity he might get involved in.'

I held him with a steady gaze, just uncomfortable enough that he broke eye contact and fiddled with his notes.

'It can . . . actually,' I replied, keeping my tone even, non-confrontational. 'You see, whatever else you may think of the organisation Red was involved with as a person, he had an almost naive moral code. One instilled in him by his mother, whom he adored. He didn't deal in violence on behalf of the McGarrys despite having the physical presence and strength for it. He was never an enforcer.'

I could feel Callum's eyes on me and deliberately avoided looking his way.

'He was non-violent by nature—'

'That doesn't mean he wouldn't steal,' Heslopp cut across me.

'No . . . it doesn't,' I conceded. 'And we all know from his record that he had convictions for petty theft as a juvenile. But in later years, when he came out of prison, he became a driver for Chris McGarry. He made a promise to his mother that he'd go straight and he would never break that promise. He ran errands, took care of minor jobs for the firm. He wasn't involved in overt criminal activity.'

'And we all know you have an inside track on what goes on with Chris McGarry,' Callum muttered, just loud enough.

The room fell silent. People shifted uncomfortably.

The whole team knew that I had a working relationship with Chris and his solicitor, Joshua Weston. They also knew that Callum – as a senior police officer – didn't approve. But none of them felt comfortable having a ringside seat into our personal disagreements.

I made a point of ignoring the comment and carried on as if he'd never spoken.

'His moral code meant there were things he wouldn't get involved in, even if Chris asked him to.'

'But we've already established that theft wasn't one—'

It was my turn to cut across DI Heslopp.

'He was also fiercely loyal to the firm he regarded as family, and I know that what he would *never* do is go off on some unsanctioned venture of his own. Particularly one he knew would bring unwelcome attention to the McGarrys from the police.'

'How do you know it *wasn't* a sanctioned operation?' Callum's tone was level, but his eyes bored into me.

I'd long ago learned, from my clientele, that the best lie was one wrapped up in truth and I wasn't above using their tactics.

I looked him right in the eyes. 'Because I asked him.'

Callum raised one eyebrow. 'You've spoken to Chris McGarry about this?'

I nodded. 'You know I went to see his mother, Audrey? Well, Chris contacted me via Joshua to say he was grateful for that. I asked about Red. Chris is as keen to find out what happened to him as we are. They've been friends since school.'

I watched Callum's expression, almost able to hear the cogs turning. Before he even opened his mouth, I'd jumped ahead – I could predict the next question and was already coming up with my answer.

'He called you . . . from prison?'

If he had, the call would be logged on his prisoner's pin. Too easy to check and catch me out in a lie.

'No, but Joshua's been to visit him.' I knew that from Audrey. 'I asked him to pass on my question when they met.'

A prisoner's meetings with his solicitor were conducted in private. Unobserved and unrecorded. I made a mental note to give Joshua the heads-up, just in case Callum checked on that.

He slowly nodded, lips pursed in thought. I could tell that he accepted it – for now at least.

'Jo had a theory about the sequence of events when Red was killed.' Callum changed tack, making me do the same.

'Err, yes.' I got up and went to the map on the wall, giving myself valuable thinking time.

I tapped the spot marking the perimeter fence. 'I think Red was heading for the hole in the fence, leaving the scene, when he was hit from behind – the blow that killed him. I believe he probably knew his attacker, and they may have gone to the site together.'

'What about his attacker – can you tell us anything about him?' Callum directed his question to me.

I tapped my teeth with a fingernail as I considered what we had so far.

'Not much to go on yet.' I was choosing my words carefully. 'But what I can tell you is that the attack wasn't planned. Whatever happened that night, the killer acted on the spur of the moment.'

'How do you get that?' Heslopp asked.

'The murder weapon was on site, not something he brought with him. He'd broken into the vehicle – was wearing gloves, so there are no prints available. Red wasn't wearing gloves so we can eliminate him as the one who smashed the cab door. At some point, there's an altercation and the killer grabs the wrench from inside the vehicle. Afterwards, he wipes it. But he's rushing and doesn't do a thorough job, which suggests a certain amount of panic setting in. Again, that leads me to think this wasn't a coldly premeditated attack by an organised killer. He attacks Red from behind. If Red had anticipated the assault, he would have put up a fight. To me, this looks like a blitz attack. Unplanned and unexpected.'

'Doesn't change anything though, does it?' Heslopp asked. 'Still could be a falling-out among thieves.'

'Maybe. But it gives you some insight into the kind of person you're looking for. Admittedly, not as much as I'd like, but a start point.' I glanced at the post-mortem report from Elle.

'Pathologist says that from the angle of the blow to the head, the attacker wasn't as tall as the victim, but still around 1.8 metres.'

'That's six feet,' Heslopp chipped in. 'For those of us who still work in old money.'

I carried on. 'Taking that into account, I'd say you're looking for a male, physically fit. Probably aged between thirty and fifty-five. He might be in your system for other offences. Whoever this is, I don't see someone who's at ease with physical violence. He's certainly not calm and collected after the act.' I looked at the map again, putting myself in the attacker's shoes.

'This kind of offender is often compelled to return to the scene. To check on whether the murder weapon, for example, has been found. So, tell the scene guards to look out for someone hanging about – trying to engage police in conversation, or even inserting themselves into the investigation. Claiming to be a witness or to have information. He'll be wanting to get a handle on how the investigation is going and what you know.'

'Sounds like every journalist I've ever met.' Beth laughed.

'What's the situation with that?' I looked at Callum.

'Social media got ahead of us,' he said, pulling a face. 'Workers at the site posting that a body had been found up there. But that's all they know – for now.'

'So far, local press has agreed to keep a lid on things,' Heslopp added. 'At least until Forensics have released the scene. But it hasn't stopped the armchair detectives from speculating about what's happened or who the victim is.'

'It'll get out sooner or later,' Callum conceded. 'Press office are putting together a media release. They're not going to provide information about the cause of death or the type of weapon used. We can hold that back.'

I knew that in some cases, the police would keep certain aspects of the case away from the public and media. This could then be used as a 'control' or test to weed out false confessions or crank calls claiming to have insider information.

'Anything else?' Callum shifted gears again, trying to keep me off balance.

This was my chance to tell him what I knew.

'I said there was something I wanted to tell you, earlier . . .'

'Go on.'

'When I visited Red's mother, Audrey, she told me Red had been seeing a woman called Penny.'

'Penelope Lynch.' DC Brooke Samson didn't hide the triumph in her voice.

'Audrey didn't know her surname, but she didn't approve of her. Said that in the last few months, Red was getting more involved with her and his behaviour had changed. She believed this Penny might have had something to do with Red's death.'

Callum's eyes narrowed a fraction of a second before he opened his mouth – no doubt to ask me why this was the first he was hearing about it.

I held up my hand to halt the tirade. 'That's what I needed to speak to you about earlier, but we didn't get the chance to speak in private. And before you ask, I only found out the details last night.'

'Which were?' It was Frank Heslopp.

'Audrey knew Penny worked at the Hades Club in Fordley.'

An extension of the truth, but convenient enough for me to avoid telling them about Hazza.

Audrey had already told me she wouldn't speak to the family liaison officer, or the police in general. It meant I didn't have to admit I had a hotline directly into Chris McGarry's prison cell.

158

'I went to the Hades Club, to speak to Penny.'

Callum raised that enquiring eyebrow again, but said nothing, so I pressed on.

'I wanted to make sure it was significant, before I said anything to you. I mean, the fact that Audrey didn't like the company her son was keeping wasn't enough on its own.'

'OK . . .'

'Bren, one of the girls there, is a friend of hers. Apparently, Penny's a sex worker. Uses Hades Club as her base on the Lane. Bren says she hasn't been to the club since Red died. But she told me that Penny was attacked last year. She reported it to the police, but nothing came of it.'

'That'll be on the system,' Callum said to the room in general.

'On it, Boss.' Beth picked it up, without being asked.

'Here's the interesting bit though. During the assault, Penny's attacker put a hood over her head before attempting to strangle her. She survived because a taxi came along.'

'Similarities to Rachel,' Callum said.

'There's another connection.' I rode the silence for just a heartbeat. 'The attacker took Penny's shoes.'

Chapter Twenty-Nine

Kingsberry, Late Saturday Night

I'd left the briefing at Fordley nick, not long after dropping my bombshell.

Callum was allocating actions and the team were now working to find Penny Lynch as a matter of urgency.

I could only hope that it would simply be a matter of checking the records to get an address.

Beth had been tasked with getting the details of Penny's assault and any forensic evidence that might have been collected at the time. She was efficient and I knew if there was anything to find, she'd track it down.

After getting home, I packed the Land Rover for an extended walk with Harvey.

I'd inherited the old Defender from a farmer friend of mine, who'd passed away a few years before.

He'd had it since the late eighties, but it was still going strong. Although the no-frills interior made it a rough, if reliable, ride. Harvey loved it, as the rear was big enough for a padded mat and lots of dog towels for muddier walks.

It was the vehicle I used during the winter, when snow and ice would make my Roadster redundant. During the summer months, it lived in the barn beside my farmhouse, but at this time of year it came into its own.

Harvey danced around me as I slung an extra fleece and waterproofs into the back. He ran back towards the house, appearing a minute later carrying his favourite rubber ball in his mouth.

'We're not going out to play,' I said, wrestling the ball from his jowls. He barked at me, wagging his tail, and I relented and threw the ball into the boot. He jumped in after it and sat, eagerly looking out of the window, his long tail thudding noisily on the metal floor.

It was a twenty-five-minute drive from my farm at Kingsberry to Stanbury. From the files at the briefing, I'd taken the address of the farmer who'd helped Dunglas carry Rachel off the moor.

I parked the Land Rover just along the road from the entrance to his farm.

It was just after 7 p.m. Earlier than when they'd arrived here with Rachel exactly a week ago, but already dark.

I pictured the scene, as it would have been then. This dark road, alive with flashing blue and red lights of police and ambulances. A hive of activity.

Quiet now. Still and dark. Nothing to show that anything out of the ordinary had disturbed this peaceful village just a few days before.

I'd always felt as though places marred by trauma should look different somehow. That the horror and emotion of what happened should leave a mark on a place – just as it left an indelible scar on the people who'd been affected by it.

But they rarely did.

I'd visited more crime scenes than I cared to think about: bedsits, houses, parks, playgrounds and forests. All areas where someone had been beaten, raped, shot, stabbed or killed. Horrific events, soaked in emotion, and yet, days, or weeks later, those places returned to normal. Looking just the same as before.

The world turning and people going about their business as if nothing had happened.

Except for the victims and their families, for whom time stood still. Frozen in that moment when their lives had changed for ever and I knew, from my own personal experience, how strange that felt. That the world could just carry on, when for those people it would never be the same again.

Images of Rachel flickered across my mind.

Laughing as she sat on a rock near my home, playing with Harvey. Then fast-forward to her lying in a hospital bed – her face hollowed out by pain and shock. Eyes haunted by images I knew she would carry for the rest of her life.

I slowly drove past the farm and followed the road out of the village. Past the reservoir, which looked like a sheet of pewter, reflected in the thin moonlight.

The old engine growled, as it pulled up the hill, towards the moors.

There were no street lights here and in the pitch blackness, I had to slow down, peering into the disc of illumination created by the headlights, looking for the turn-off that marked a footpath away from the road.

I would have missed it, if it hadn't been for the wooden fingerpost-sign on the grass verge, declaring in English and, bizarrely, Japanese, that this was the public footpath onto the Pennine Way.

I drove a little way up the track – far enough from the road that, at this late hour, my vehicle couldn't be seen. This was the closest pull-in spot to the place where Rachel had been found.

I'd checked the map before we left and decided that if I'd been her abductor, this would probably be the spot I would choose to leave my car.

Cutting the engine was Harvey's signal that we'd arrived. He stretched up from his mat in the back and stuck his head between the front seats, resting a damp jowl on my shoulder.

I sat for a minute, staring into the blackness beyond the windscreen.

It was a week to the day since Rachel's attack and I knew that the outdoor scene on the moor had been released by Forensics.

I contemplated calling Callum, telling him that I was about to walk the scene. A routine he knew well. But I also knew, this time, he would tell me not to go.

He'd argue that it wasn't safe out on the moors at night, and then, when I was adamant that it was important I do this, he would insist on coming with me.

But I didn't want that. Not out of any foolhardy sense of bravado, but because I knew that if he was there beside me, the process wouldn't work.

I'd learned over the years that there was something about being alone when I walked a scene that allowed me to fully immerse myself in every aspect of the environment. Completely absorbing myself in the sounds, scents, feelings of a place.

My senses heightened to a pitch where I could almost feel what the offender had felt. See what he saw, hear what he heard. Enabling me, when it worked at its best, to think the way he thought.

If anyone else was there, it was a difficult state to achieve – sometimes impossible.

Harvey nuzzled my ear, impatient to be off on this unusual night hike. I ruffled his ears and slipped the mobile into my pocket.

'But I'm not alone, am I?' He panted in that way that made him look like he was grinning. 'I've got you.'

I let him out of the back and rummaged in my kitbag for the heavy Maglite torch Callum had given me. Only half joking when he'd said it could double as a blunt instrument, if required.

As I locked the Land Rover, the cold wind almost took my breath away.

I turned up the corduroy collar of my jacket and pulled on the leather gloves I kept in the pockets. Harvey was already heading up the track, in danger of disappearing into the darkness.

'Harvey – wait!'

He stopped, looking back impatiently as he waited for me to catch up.

My boots slipped on the uneven dirt and rock track, already hardening with a covering of ice that glittered in the torch beam.

We both knew this track well, had walked it often, although always in daylight and usually in warmer weather. But at least I didn't have to juggle a map as well as hold a torch and watch my footing.

The track was compacted earth and rock, which cut across the stiff tussock grass – easy to follow, even by torchlight. Helped by the white tip of Harvey's tail, which stuck up like a periscope, bobbing ahead of me in the inky blackness.

Trees along the way were crazy silhouettes – the branches, dark fingers disappearing into shades of grey. The rocky outcrops just vague outlines.

Even in summer this could be a desolate stretch of moors, valleys and hills. Described by William the Conqueror's surveyors in 1085 with a single word: 'wasteland'.

'Harvey . . . wait, boy.' He stood again, curbing the natural urge to run off into the frozen heather, chasing the scent of grouse or rabbit. Understanding this wasn't an ordinary ramble and that I needed him to stay close.

My breath plumed ahead of me, as I panted with the effort of the incline. It wasn't, by comparison to other parts of the trail, that steep. But I wasn't fit. A fact I was becoming more aware of these days.

The ache in my left thigh returned more often and faster than it used to whenever I exerted myself. My breath was more laboured. My fitness levels probably not helped by spells I'd had in hospital lately, after injuries sustained through the job.

Unbidden, my mother's voice seemed to echo out of the cold night. Her heavily accented Italian-English as cutting and demeaning as always.

Why you not get a proper job, Phina? This no life for a woman – chasing killers and rapists. Settle down with a husband . . . have babies . . .

'Think that ship's sailed,' I said aloud, causing Harvey to stop and stare at me. 'Sorry, boy, not talking to you.'

Reaching the top of the hill, I stopped, hands on my hips, to take in some deep lungfuls of ice-cold air and catch my breath.

Dutifully, Harvey came to sit beside me, leaning his five-stone weight against my leg.

I shone the torch beam ahead, checking we were still on the track that would lead to the spot where Rachel was found.

As we stood, motionless, I could make out the sounds of nocturnal animals, scurrying in the undergrowth. My breathing returned to normal and I drank in the stillness, sharpening my senses. Tuning in to what surrounded us.

A piercing scream split the air, making me jump, until I realised it was just a fox, when it was quickly followed by the bark of a vixen's mating call, carrying for miles down the valley.

We started walking again – the pace easier now as the path levelled out.

I'd checked before leaving the house and knew, from the files, where Rachel was found. But any concerns I had about missing the spot in the dark were quickly dispelled by a soft fluttering sound carried across the moorland.

Harvey barked and ran towards it. In the beam of the torch, I could make out the blue and white scrap of police tape, snagged on a bush beside the track.

Shining the torch on the ground, I carefully followed the common approach path created by crime scene investigators as they worked the area. Not to preserve evidence – anything remaining would have been found, photographed and bagged by now – but the worn route was simply easier to navigate than the frozen tussock grass. Hard and uneven under foot and responsible for many twisted or broken ankles of unwary hikers.

The last thing I needed now was to be incapacitated in this desolate place in the middle of the night.

Harvey had stopped – stock-still. His nose down, loudly sniffing a patch of earth. Probably where Rachel had been.

With olfactory senses a thousand times more sensitive than a human, I had no doubt that Harvey would be aware of smells left there – by Rachel, her attacker and the officers who had worked the scene.

Standing next to him, I shone the torch on the ground. Then snapped off the light and stood in darkness. Listening. Staring just above the horizon, until my night vision adjusted enough for me to make out our surroundings.

Could a man have carried Rachel, over his shoulder, from where I'd parked to this spot?

I knew I couldn't. But Rachel was slim and petite. It was easily doable, if our man was as fit as I suspected.

The path we'd just walked was intersected by another from my left.

The dark line of a drystone wall to my right sheltered this spot from harsh weather, or from sight.

The thrum of tuning in to what had happened here was real.

I could feel it in my veins, pulsing behind my eyes, as the adrenaline flowed through me, just as it had for Rachel's abductor.

This was how it worked . . . how it felt. To get inside the mind and see through the eyes of the person who had intended to kill, out on this lonely moor.

I knelt down beside the flattened grass, where he'd unceremoniously dumped his victim.

My heart began to hammer a little harder as I imagined what he would have been feeling. Having carried his prize to this spot. Now having her laid here – helpless. Isolated.

The exhilaration he would feel, knowing he'd come this far without being caught.

Nothing could stop him now from acting out the scenario he no doubt played and replayed in his mind. Until thinking about it wasn't enough and the urge climbed to unbearable heights. Until it finally drove him to act it out for real. The deviant ritual that somehow fuelled his fantasies.

Almost instinctively, I reached out and placed my hand, palm down, on the frozen grass, as if it could talk to me. Give up all its secrets, fill in the missing pieces.

My mind ran the sequence of events, like a film reel, spooling faster and faster.

Rachel crossing his path near Cowling. Him coming up behind her to deliver the blow that rendered her unconscious. Throwing her into the boot of a car. Putting a hood over her head and taking her boots and socks.

To deliver her here – to this spot.

I looked around, my hand still on the ground.

'Why here?' I whispered. 'Why bring her all the way back . . . almost the way she'd come, to this particular place?'

Because it means something, came the unbidden reply.

Because it's important to me . . . a vital part of my fantasy . . . my scenario.

'You dehumanise them, don't you?' I said quietly. 'That's why you use the hood. Not so they can't see you, but because you don't want to see *them*, do you?'

I studied the space again.

'Whoever you are,' I murmured quietly, 'I *will* find you.'

Suddenly Harvey began to growl. Softly, as if the warning was only for me to hear.

He stood, with his flanks at my shoulder. I squatted on my haunches, unwilling to stand and be silhouetted against the skyline.

Resting my arm along his broad back, I could feel his hackles rise beneath my hand. His ears pricked up and I followed the direction of his eyes.

There, just a few feet above the ground, an orb of light was moving steadily towards us.

Harvey growled a little louder, shifting his weight to plant his feet more firmly. I could feel the muscles in his shoulders bunching as he prepared to launch himself at whatever this thing was.

I felt for his collar, gripping it tightly, not wanting him to take off until I knew what we were facing.

I could hear Tommy Earnshaw's voice – in the pub.

Corpse lights . . . Omens of death . . . Evil on the moors, lass.

'Will-o'-the-wisp?' I whispered against Harvey's ear.

No. This light's not a flame . . . too solid.

As it got nearer, I heard another sound – the crunch of boots on the frozen grass – and realised that what I was seeing was the light from a torch, held low, against someone's side as they walked.

'Who's there?' I shouted.

No reply.

The light kept coming.

'Hello?' The plume from my breath hung, suspended in the air, almost as if holding my words. 'Talk to me . . . who's there?'

The crunching underfoot got louder, the light kept coming. But no reply.

Harvey had finally had enough. I felt his muscles flex a second before he propelled himself forward, breaking my hold on his collar, to run headlong at whoever was there.

'Harvey!' I called at the same time a man's voice screamed.

'Whoa! Call him off.'

I shone the Maglite in their direction, illuminating a tableau, frozen in the arena of light.

A man – his face obscured beneath the hood of a storm jacket and a scarf pulled over his face. Standing with both arms out, as if that could have stopped Harvey, who had obediently halted at my call. His snarling jaws an inch from the gloved hands stretched towards him.

I shone my torch into the eyes, which squinted painfully in my direction.

'Why didn't you answer me?' There was a slight tremor in my voice and I hated the unconscious display of weakness.

The figure continued to stare, but said nothing.

Kneeling put me at a disadvantage. I struggled on to my feet, my left thigh screaming in pain.

'Call the dog off.' The figure finally spoke, still not moving. His voice muffled by the scarf.

His eyes, visible in the slit between mask and hood, narrowed. Threateningly? Fearfully? I couldn't see enough to be sure.

'Not until I know who you are, and what you're doing here?'

'I could ask you the same thing?'

Despite the scarf, something about the voice sounded familiar.

But I was in no mood to play twenty questions.

'Pull the bloody scarf down so I can see your face or I'll let my dog have your bollocks!'

'OK . . . OK.' He snatched the scarf away.

Chapter Thirty

The Moors, Late Saturday Night

'Dunglas!'

His eyes widened. 'I saw you at the police station. But you have me at a disadvantage.'

'Harvey – stand.'

He reluctantly turned and trotted back, taking a stance at my side. Still growling low in his throat, his eyes fixed on this potential threat. Ready to launch if the man made one wrong move.

'I'm Doctor McCready, consultant for the police.'

He nodded to the patch of flattened grass at my feet. 'On this case?'

'Yes.'

Not entirely untrue.

'In the middle of the night?' The corners of his mouth twitched slightly, in something approximating a smile.

'What are *you* doing here?' I ignored his question.

He gestured to the moorland with the sweep of his arm. 'Walking.'

'In the middle of the night?' I volleyed his own words back.

'If you know who I am, then you know what I do.'

I brushed the grass from my knees, allowing vital time for my heart rate to return to normal.

'Supposedly.' My contempt was obvious.

He took a step towards me, but stopped as Harvey growled a low warning for him to keep his distance.

'You're not a believer?' he said simply.

I raised my eyebrows. 'In what? Ghosts? Spirit mediums, psychics?' It wasn't an answer, but all I was prepared to give him. Curious to see what he did with the statement.

'So, you dismiss everything I do. Everything I am, basically.'

I didn't reply, simply studied him in silence.

'McCready? I've read about you,' he finally said. 'Though I didn't realise who you were when I saw you at the station.'

'Didn't the spirits tell you?' I didn't try to hide the sarcasm.

He shifted his weight from one foot to another. A slight movement, but enough to cause Harvey's muscles to tense under my hand on his collar.

'Forensic psychologist, right?' That slight twitch of his lips again – more contemptuous than humorous. 'Not too dissimilar from my own field.'

A core tenet of my professional code was to treat people with 'unconditional positive regard'. But as I stood here, out on the moors, facing this man, I decided I had no positive regard for him, conditional or otherwise. In fact, I positively disliked him.

'Dissimilar in just about every way,' I said.

'You think I'm a fraud?'

I think you're a dickhead. Is what I thought.

'Like your namesake – Dunglas?' is what I actually said. 'Strange choice, if you want credibility.' I mimicked his quirk of the lips. 'Or are you banking on the fact that most people wouldn't know who Daniel Dunglas was?'

His eyes narrowed.

'You pride yourself on your intellect, don't you?' His words were quietly spoken, but the tone was cutting. 'Your father told me that.'

The mention of my deceased father brought my hackles up.

It felt insulting . . . disrespectful. That this man should try scoring points against me, by using someone he had never met, didn't know, in such a callous, calculating way.

171

'He's worried about you—'

'Enough.' I cut across him.

If he heard the warning in my voice, he chose to ignore it, pressing on with his half-baked 'spirit reading'.

'He tells me you're good at what you do, but you shouldn't take so many risks just to prove yourself in a man's world.'

The pulse behind my eyes betrayed the rise in my blood pressure as I listened to his sexist put-down, thinly disguised as a direct line to the dead.

'Or, he says . . . perhaps you just don't like men, doctor? Men like me.'

I'd heard enough.

I took a half-step forward. Harvey, whose collar I still held, moved with me. Dunglas wisely took a step back.

Not as confident as you'd like me to think, are you?

'I've heard enough of this bullshit. How about I share what your deceased relatives have to reveal about you . . . *Terry*?'

'Daniel.' A look flitted across his face, but not before I could read it. Annoyance. That I'd used his given name, the one he didn't want to be known by.

A chink in his psychological armour. One that, in a therapeutic setting, would be unethical to exploit.

But this wasn't therapy and right now I didn't give a shit.

'I'm getting a message from your grandmother.' I went for it. 'She's crossed over into spirit.'

Not too much of a stretch, given his age.

'She's telling me you were shy. Out of step with other kids at school. They bullied you because you were different, didn't they? Your grandmother was interested in the occult – she got you interested, but at school that just made you even weirder.'

Despite the cold air, a slight flush coloured his cheeks above the scarf, telling me I was right.

172

'Your brains got you into a good school, but your family weren't as well-off as your peers and you always felt inferior.'

I'd read in the police notes about his grammar school education and the fact that he'd been more or less brought up by his widowed grandmother, who was a member of a spiritualist church in Halifax.

I glanced at his long fingernails.

'You took up the guitar, to try to fit in, but it didn't work, did it? You still play, but now it goes with the image of the occult creative.'

'I don't think—'

'You told your school mates you could see spirits. It made them scared of you, so the bullies left you alone.'

'I—'

Go for his name.

Names are connected to our sense of self, it's who we are. To change it is a huge emotional step.

'Even your name was ordinary,' I goaded. '*Terry* – very working class. Boys in your school were called Marcus, or Lewis. Daniel was better. The name of someone you read about, in the field you were obsessed by as a kid. The occult . . . spiritualism.'

He shifted from one foot to another. Uncomfortable. I was getting to him.

'Your grandmother is upset that you wanted to leave your old identity behind. That you were ashamed of your family.'

He was breathing heavier now – I could hear it, see it.

'And as for me not liking men, Granny's telling me that's pure projection. That it's *you* who doesn't like women, *Daniel*. Or are you just afraid of them?'

He opened his mouth to say something, then clamped it shut again. Thinking better of it.

'But let's not go into your struggles with sex in adolescence and the mixed-up feelings about all the women who rejected you, *Daniel*.' I could hear the serrated edge to my tone, but I was beyond caring how much it cut. 'That could lead us into very dangerous ground, couldn't it?'

I stared pointedly at the spot at my feet, where Rachel had been dumped. All too aware that Daniel Dunglas was becoming a serious person of interest in Callum's enquiry.

'OK.' The volume went up an octave. 'You've made your point.'

'Good!' I let my eyes flash a warning I knew he couldn't miss. 'Then let's cut this misogynist bullshit, wrapped up as second sight, and you can tell me why you're coming back here, tonight of all nights?'

'I'm not . . . I mean I wasn't.'

I took perverse pleasure in the absence of his earlier arrogance. 'What then?'

'I was walking to Wytch's Tarn.' He indicated behind him. 'Follow this track far enough, it takes you there.'

My eyes followed the way he was pointing. 'This is the opposite direction.'

'I know. But I saw a light over here. Thought it might be a corpse light, so came over to take a look.' He glanced at the Maglite torch I was holding like a cudgel.

'Are we done now?' he finally said.

I nodded, reluctantly. Then clicked my fingers to Harvey, who began to follow as I got back on to the track.

Dunglas was watching as we walked away. But before he turned back towards the Tarn, he called out to me.

'Whether you believe, or not, I have a premonition. Something is coming, here . . . on the moor . . . soon.'

I stopped and turned to face the outline of his figure, lost in the darkness along the track.

'Secrets can't stay hidden . . . evil will show its face.' His disembodied voice came to me from the blackness.

'What does that mean?'

His next words were like ice-cold fingers clutching the back of my neck.

'A corpse.'

Chapter Thirty-One

Kingsberry Farm, Sunday Morning

Harvey's excited barking heralded Callum's arrival, long before I heard the crunch of car tyres on the gravel drive.

He'd phoned earlier to say he had news to share and was calling in for a coffee before going to the station.

I decided to wait until I saw him in person before telling him about my meeting with Dunglas, the previous night.

Harvey bounded over to him, as soon as he got out of the car, then followed him into the kitchen, to fuss around his legs in a happy tangle.

Callum sat at the kitchen table, ruffling Harvey's head, while I brought the cafetière, along with my teapot.

'Morning.' Callum finally managed to disengage himself from my dog, leaning across to give me a quick kiss. 'What a welcome.' He threw Harvey's ball into the corridor – more to give us a reprieve than in any serious attempt at playing.

'Anyone would think he hadn't seen you in a year.' I smiled, pouring myself a mug of tea. But my mind was distracted, preparing to tell him about Dunglas.

When it came to sharing news, he beat me to it.

'Got some info from Forensics,' he said, depressing the plunger on the coffee pot.

'Good news?'

'The hood and ribbon used on Rachel.' He poured himself a coffee. 'The hood's a black cotton drawstring bag – sold in sport shops as a gymsac.'

'Fancy name for what we used to call a "pump bag" in my day.'

'For your black elasticated plimsoles?' He grinned at me over the rim of his mug. 'That dates you.'

I ignored that. 'Can you find out where it was sold?'

He shook his head. 'Just about every sports outlet, in every major city. Not to mention online. Could have come from anywhere.'

Harvey padded back into the kitchen, dropping his ball at Callum's feet. He kicked it across the kitchen for him. 'Rachel's hair and DNA on the hood, as we'd expect, but no traces from her attacker.'

'And the ribbon?'

He sighed, stretching back in his chair. 'Odd one that. It was cut from a longer length – maybe a larger roll. And it's old.'

I frowned. 'Old?'

'It looks like silk, but it's actually a synthetic. Fabric composition puts it as being manufactured sometime during the seventies.'

I sipped my tea as I thought about that. 'I've always felt the ribbon is significant. An important item for the attacker.'

'It could be something he found . . . or inherited.'

'True. But however he came by it, he's kept it.' Even as I said it, I felt a certainty I'd learned to trust. 'It's become part of his signature.'

An offender's 'signature' was a behaviour they repeat, over and above what it takes to commit the crime.

Callum had worked with me long enough to know about psychological signatures without a lengthy explanation.

He pursed his lips as he thought about it, running a fingertip round the rim of his mug. 'Above and beyond his M.O., which can change over time as he gains experience?'

'Exactly. This attacker wants to kill by strangulation. He could do that with his bare hands. Or, if he uses a ligature, it could be anything.'

177

'The hood. The gymsac,' Callum said thoughtfully. 'Has a built-in drawstring . . . ideal for the job.'

'But he uses a length of ribbon that he brings along specifically for the task.' I stirred the teapot. 'Have you interviewed Penny Lynch yet, about her attack?' I was hoping there'd be mention of a ribbon there too. That would eliminate any doubt that her attacker and Rachel's were one and the same.

But Callum was already shaking his head. 'She's disappeared,' he said simply.

'Gone into hiding? Because of what happened to Red?'

Bren said Penny would have been terrified that her protector had been murdered. It wasn't a huge leap to think she might be lying low somewhere.

'Possibly, but when uniform went to her address the flat looked like she'd just got up and walked out. Last-known movements were over a week ago. She was seen leaving the flat. Neighbour thought she must have been going to work, but she never turned up at the Hades Club and no one has seen her since.'

'What about her phone?'

'Digital Forensics are working on that. But as far as we can tell, it was deactivated the same night.'

'What does that mean, exactly?'

He shrugged. 'Could be that the battery died, or it was switched off.'

'Maybe she's ditched her phone and left her address? Especially if she knows something about Red's death.'

'But if she's deliberately gone into hiding, she's not going to be found easily.' He took a mouthful of coffee. 'To be fair, we don't have the resources to launch a massive search for her. No one's even reported her as a missing person. She's over eighteen – entitled to relocate, if that's what she's done.'

'Beth was looking into the details of Penny's attack, last year?'

He nodded. 'Bren, the sex worker she teamed up with on the Lane, took the registration of the vehicle that picked Penny up, the night she was attacked. Officers visited the owner after the report.'

'Bren said it wasn't him.'

'It wasn't. He'd picked her up . . . took her onto the Moor Road for sex, but wouldn't drive her back into Fordley. They argued and he kicked her out of the car.'

'So, how was he eliminated?'

'His number plate was picked up by ANPR cameras in Halifax at the same time the taxi driver found Penny on the Moor Road. Plus, the reason he wouldn't drive her back into Fordley was because he had to pick his wife up from work. She was a nurse at Calderdale Hospital. She confirmed he was with her, in the car, at the time of the attack.'

'Would love to have been a fly on the wall when he explained why he needed an alibi.'

'Let's just say, they didn't celebrate their next anniversary.'

'Shame . . . not.'

'We got a break though. Penny still had the hood in her hand when the taxi driver found her.'

'Please tell me it's a match for the one used on Rachel?'

His broad smile was all the answer I needed.

'That means,' I said slowly, 'this attacker was active over a year ago, probably longer than that.'

'You were right – Rachel wasn't his first outing.'

Being right, in this, gave me no satisfaction at all.

We both sat in silence for a while, with Callum fussing Harvey.

'What are the odds of Rachel's attacker also attacking a friend of Red's?' I finally said.

'Long, I agree,' he said. 'But, without evidence that connects them all, they could just be coincidences.'

I raised my eyebrows at him. 'You believe in coincidences like that about as much as I do.'

'I'm a cop, Jo. Have to go where the evidence takes me. The hood used and the M.O. connect Rachel and Penny's attacks. But nothing links Red's murder to either of them apart from the fact that he was a friend of Penny's. There's nothing connecting him to Rachel either. The team have done a deep-dive into the background of all the victims. Rachel isn't linked in any way to Penny, or to Red. Plus, we haven't got anything that solidly connects these crimes to a suspect.'

'Hmm, well, speaking of which . . .'

Time to tell him about my meeting with Daniel Dunglas, the previous night.

Chapter Thirty-Two

Kingsberry Farm, Sunday Morning

'You went out on the moor, in the middle of the night . . . alone?'

If his voice had gone any higher, he'd have been singing soprano.

'I wasn't alone – I had Harvey.'

He glanced down at my dog, who was now lying across his feet, snoring contentedly.

'Not enough,' he murmured, even though he knew that Harvey had proved his worth more than once in the past. He was reluctant to let go of his annoyance.

'You know that walking the scene is what I do, Cal.'

'You could have done that in daylight.' His blue eyes darkened with barely supressed anger.

'You *also* know,' I cut across him, before he could work himself up into a full-blown tantrum, 'that, for it to be truly productive, it has to be as authentic as possible to the events as they happened.'

'And you couldn't have asked me to go with you?' The muscles bunched in his jaw as he tried to contain himself, knowing only too well that my own legendary temper would simply rise up to meet his and we'd end up having a row rather than a discussion.

'Works better when I'm alone.'

'Does it work better if our attacker is still out there? Prowling his hunting ground in the middle of the night, while you're "getting in the zone"?' He made air quotes with his fingers around that last bit, just to wind me up.

'I walk through the murder scene – literally. As close to the time it happened as possible and if that's the middle of the night then that's when I'll do it.' My eyes flashed an unmistakable warning, as I added, 'And I don't need your bloody permission to do my job the way I see fit.'

His expression was as hard as carved stone and his tone equally cold. 'You do if it's *my* investigation,' he said tightly. 'On *my* watch.'

'Do you want to carry on being pissed off with me or hear the interesting bit?'

He let out a slow breath, raking frustrated fingers through his hair in that 'tell' he had when he was getting to the end of his last remaining nerve. 'OK.'

I went through what had happened with Dunglas, playing down the menace I'd felt when he'd appeared, unexpectedly, out of the darkness.

When I finished, he stayed silent for what seemed like for ever, staring into his coffee mug, as if it had all the answers.

Finally, he took a breath. 'You believe the reason he gave for being there?'

I shrugged. 'I've researched him. His articles in this *Third Eye* magazine. I mean, it's what he does. Goes to locations where there's been reported sightings. Haunted houses, deserted hospitals . . .'

'Walking the scene . . . bit like you?'

I ignored the cutting tone. 'So, he could have been going up to Wytch's Tarn, like he said . . .'

'But?'

'I didn't believe him.'

'What then?'

I met his penetrating gaze. 'I think he was up there to visit the scene of the attack.'

He studied me for a heartbeat. 'Returning to the scene of his crime?'

'Maybe.'

I really wasn't certain about Dunglas. He was proving difficult for me to read and that made me uncomfortable.

'There's enough circumstantial evidence for him to be a serious person of interest already.' Callum said it quietly, as if he didn't want us to be overheard up here, wrapped in the solitary isolation of my farmhouse.

'I'm not saying I think he's our attacker, Cal. I haven't got enough to go on for that.' I pushed my teacup away, suddenly not wanting it. 'But, for what it's worth, I think he knows far more about these attacks than he's saying.'

'Maybe he's learning about it all from the spirits?' There was a glint in his eye as he said it.

'Yeah, right.'

'Forensics examined his car.'

I felt a surge of hope. 'And?'

He washed a hand across his face and I suddenly realised how exhausted he looked.

'Nothing.'

'What? At all?'

'Traces of soil and vegetation from the wheels and underneath his car prove it's been on the moor tracks. But he's never denied that. There's no unusual vegetation, where "X" marks the spot, so he could have collected those traces from the Tarn Hill Tavern car park, as he said. And, without CCTV, we can't prove whether his Volvo was actually in that car park on the night of Rachel's attack or not.'

'And the boot?' That was the crucial bit, but I already knew that if he wasn't leading with that, it hadn't proved conclusive.

'He has a rigid boot-liner in it . . . which he jet-washed the day after.'

I raised my eyebrows. 'Really?'

Callum nodded. 'Said it was muddy from his walking gear and that he always cleaned it after every outing. So, although it looks as suspicious as hell, it's done. Any trace of Rachel has probably gone down the drain . . . literally.'

'Surely, the boot floor isn't the only thing that could retain traces of her, if she was there?'

'No, and I'm getting Forensics to do another examination. It all costs money. You know how it works, Jo?'

Unfortunately, I did. Not like in the TV cop shows, where resources seemed endless – Forensics appeared to work for free and all test results came back in hours, rather than days or weeks.

'I'm having him brought in again, for questioning. You seeing him at the scene begs a few more questions, as well as valeting his car the day after the attack.' He glanced at his watch and drained the last of his coffee. 'Finding Penny Lynch is a priority now. I've got boots on the ground looking for her. Press office think it's time we enlist the media. Put out an appeal for her to come forward, or anyone who's seen her. Can't keep a lid on it much longer anyway.'

I was surprised they'd managed it this long and said so.

'And now that we have evidence that our offender has been active for at least a year—'

'Longer.' I was certain now.

'I'd like you to work up a preliminary profile. I'll get Beth to send you everything we've got on Penny's historic attack and on Rachel's.' He retrieved his jacket from the back of his chair.

'No problem.' I'd already started pulling something together from the information we had so far.

'Got to go.' He was patting pockets, searching for car keys. 'What do you make of Dunglas's last remark?'

'About a corpse on the moors?' I got up to walk him to the door. 'Dunno . . . Not as vague as his other pronouncements. Events will either bear him out or not.'

'Let's hope he's full of shite, then.' He pulled me to him and gave me a quick kiss on the lips, before opening the porch door, allowing an icy blast of wind into the house. The shiver it caused was almost a portent of the way his parting words made me feel.

'Last thing we need now is another body.'

Chapter Thirty-Three

Kingsberry Farm, Monday Morning

Apart from the mellow ticking of the grandfather clock that stood sentinel in the corner, my office was quiet.

None of the usual snoring from Harvey, who would normally have been sleeping on the Chinese rug in front of my desk. Or the clattering of computer keys from Jen's computer across the room.

Because, for the moment, it was just me in here. Sitting with my back to the distracting view, from the huge arched window that overlooked my garden and beyond to the moorland.

I'd been working on the preliminary profile Callum had asked for and become totally absorbed. Which was why Jen offered to take Harvey out for a long walk, knowing that I needed solitude at times like this.

My desk was strewn with files Callum had sent over the previous afternoon. Crime scene photographs were laid out on the floor, in a depressing collage of brutality and violence that, unfortunately, characterised these cases.

When I had a lot of information to take in, spreading it all out before me usually helped.

To the casual observer, it probably looked like total chaos, but each section represented a piece of the puzzle, as I saw it. Laid out in the same way I held the information in my brain. A total enigma to anyone else, but making perfect sense to me.

Having timelines laid out meant I could hover above and look down on things as a whole, rather than as fragmented separate cases.

It helped me to see the ever-illusive patterns I needed to uncover. The signatures of an offender – which, given time, could show me how his mind worked. How he planned. What drove him and which elements he needed to feed whatever fantasy was urging him on.

I read through the profile, glancing occasionally at the photographs around my feet.

Rachel's picture beamed up at me. Taken by proud parents at her graduation. She was animated in my mind, because I knew her as a person. Someone I'd met and spoken to. Mercifully, still alive.

Penny Lynch's photograph hadn't been taken in such happy times.

As a sex worker and drug user, she'd been in the Police National Computer, having committed various minor offences. The picture was taken from her file as there was no one who could provide anything more recent. Hopefully, once police tracked her down, or she came forward, I'd be able to speak to her too. Find out more about the attack on that lonely Moor Road.

I scanned the files giving height, weight, hair and eye colour.

Both girls were about the same height and build. Both brunettes. In the photographs, their hair was long and parted down the middle. Rachel's fell below her shoulders. Penny's not quite as long or lustrous, but the similarities were there.

I added a note to the profile: *Victim type?*

Sexual offenders often had an 'ideal type' of victim. They might select them based on gender, race or particular physical characteristics.

Two women with the same hair colour and style wasn't enough to definitively say this was our offender's type. But it was enough to mark it as a possibility and one that I couldn't ignore.

There was nothing else similar about their lives. Different demographics entirely. One a sex worker; the other a graduate about to take up a position as a corporate accountant. One from the south of England; the other, a local girl.

What marked them out was where they had crossed paths with their attacker.

Lonely locations along the Pennine Way.

His hunting ground.

I scanned the report I'd written, already developing a 'mind map' of this attacker. One that made me certain that if Callum and his team didn't catch him, he'd keep going. More worryingly, he'd keep escalating.

My mobile rang. The screen illuminated Callum's name.

'Hi.'

'You OK to speak?'

His voice was tense. He was ringing with bad news.

'What is it?'

'We've got another body.'

My stomach dropped. 'Oh God. Where?'

'In a drainage ditch along the Moor Road. Motorist pulled over to take a pee and saw a bone sticking out of the mud.'

'A bone?'

'From a skeleton. With a plastic bag over its head . . . tied with a ribbon.'

Chapter Thirty-Four

The Moor Road, Monday Morning

Pulsing blue lights of police cars blocking the route in both directions cast an eerie glow across an already surreal scene.

Forensics had arrived not long before and crime scene support vehicles lined the grass verges.

This was a desolate part of the moors. Dissected by a trans-Pennine route that ran parallel to the M62, linking Fordley to Manchester.

Rarely warm, even on the brightest summer days, it was bleak during winter months. Whipped by freezing wind and often lashed with rain and closed off by heavy snow. Thankfully we didn't have to contend with blizzards today. But the hills rising either side of us were dusted with white frost and the wind was arctic.

Where we stood was almost equidistant from my farmhouse at Kingsberry to Fordley centre. Used as a rat run from the city to the motorway, especially during morning or evening rush hour. I could only imagine the chaos closing this route would be causing to commuters today.

I studied Callum's profile as he watched the activity unfolding a few hundred yards away.

CSIs in white scene suits flitted in and out of a small white tent which had been erected over the drainage ditch where the body had been discovered.

Although what had been found, by an early morning motorist, could barely be described as a body.

I could hardly look at the grim, crime-scene photograph Callum had greeted me with, holding out his iPad.

We were standing a distance away, by fluttering blue and white tape tied to bollards that cordoned off the road, which was blocked by police vehicles. Traffic officers were waving down approaching vehicles and turning them around.

Callum was saying, 'This is as far as we go for now.'

'Thank God for that.' I handed the iPad back. 'The photograph is bad enough. Can't say I want to get any closer.'

He leaned against the side of the patrol car. 'First-responders, thought it might be animal bones. Usually is out here. But it was obviously a human arm.'

'Then they called in the cavalry?' I guessed.

He nodded, face grim. 'Would normally have to wait for a proper excavation. Get the experts to decide whether it's an ancient burial or something. You know? Anglo-Saxon or whatever.' He indicated the river of freezing water trickling across the road, forming sheets of ice against the verges of tussock grass.

'The drainage ditch is overflowing . . . all the rain we've had. By the time CSI arrived, the top half of the skeleton had come to the surface.'

I thought about the photograph Forensics had taken when they'd arrived.

'Hmm, don't suppose Anglo-Saxon burial rites involved tying Tesco carrier bags over the heads of the deceased.'

'Not usually.' He jammed his hands deeper into the pockets of his North Face jacket.

I followed his gaze to the hills on either side of the road, enclosing the ribbon of tarmac like the puckered edges of a wound.

'Shit, Jo,' he muttered through clenched teeth.

He didn't have to say anything else. I knew what he was thinking.

This made our offender a killer.

Rachel and Penny were the lucky ones. The ones who got away. But if he'd been going for years, how many more could there be?

We both turned as a figure in the anonymising white scene suit broke from the group by the tent and walked towards us, pulling the mask away from her face to greet Callum.

'You the SIO on this one, Callum?'

'Fraid so, Katie. This is Doctor Jo McCready, consultant forensic psychologist.'

I shook the proffered hand. 'Katie Brayzier, crime scene manager.' Katie smiled at me.

'Any idea how long the body's been there?' Callum cut to the chase.

Katie glanced back towards the forensics tent. 'The bones that are visible are pretty clean, but boggy soil can speed up decomposition, so that's not always a good indicator,' she said. 'Pathologist will be able to give you a better idea when they see the rest of it. What I can say though is that I don't think this is the original burial site.'

'Why not?' Callum frowned.

'This ditch is too shallow. If the body had been here for years, it would have been uncovered by now. I think it's been washed down here by the floods.' She stood with her hands on her hips, surveying the hills that enclosed the road. 'From up there some-where. The recent storms brought more rain than we've had in years. That's why this body got washed down here now. If it hadn't been for the biblical weather, it might never have been found.'

Biblical, I thought. *How appropriate. God's hand uncovering a murderer's work.*

'The Highways Authority maintain these ditches,' Katie was saying. 'They get cleaned out every so often. It can't have been here more than a day or so, I'd say.'

A shout from the tent caused her to turn away. 'Sorry, got to get back but I'll give you a call when I've got more.'

'Thanks.'

We both watched her go.

'I'm briefing the team later.' He looked down at me. 'You managed to get anywhere with the preliminary profile?'

I jerked my head towards the Land Rover. 'Brought it with me.'

'Good, then you can come along and present it to the team once I've told them about this. We're going to need all the help we can get.'

Chapter Thirty-Five

Fordley Police Station, Monday Afternoon

Every seat around the table in the briefing room was taken. Callum stood at the front and wasted no time getting down to the business at hand.

'You all know about development early this morning – when a body was found in a drainage ditch on the Moor Road. There are similarities with the attacks on Rachel Taylor and Penny Lynch.' He tapped keys on his laptop and the first crime scene photo flashed up on the large screen at the front of the room.

It showed the top half of a skeleton. One shoulder and arm, exposed to the elements. Poking through the surface water of the ditch. The skull, thankfully, was covered by what looked like a couple of supermarket carrier bags tied at the neck with a red ribbon.

One or two people shifted in their seats, some stared, fascinated. I looked away. I'd already seen what I needed to see.

'The remains have been collected and taken to the mortuary. Home Office pathologist, Dr Elle Richardson, has been appointed to undertake the post-mortem as this is an unnatural death.'

'Either that or it's the most bizarre suicide *I've* ever seen.' A young officer at the back laughed.

There were a few chuckles at the gallows humour. Common among those who dealt with horror on a daily basis. A coping mechanism. Never meant disrespectfully, though shocking to those not used to it.

Callum perched on the corner of the table, scrolling through notes on his iPad. 'We need to identify the body as a priority. We've got a Zoom call scheduled with Dr Richardson in half an hour. She might have more, to get that ball rolling.' He glanced up at the team. 'Beth, I want you to take that.'

'OK, Boss.'

'This is a murder enquiry – including the attempted murders of Penny Lynch and Rachel Taylor. But it goes without saying that we keep an open mind until we have confirmation from Dr Richardson, and Forensics.' Heads bobbed in agreement around the table. He looked at me. 'Does the body from this morning change anything in your initial profile, Jo?'

'No. In fact, it confirms initial theories I had about the offender.'

'Over to you then.'

I scanned my notes, before looking up at a sea of faces.

'I said earlier in the investigation that I thought Penny's attacker had killed before. If the body in the ditch *is* the same offender then you have a potential serial killer on your hands. One that's been operating for years without being caught.'

'Do we know how long the body could have been in the ditch?' DC Shah Akhtar asked.

Callum answered that one. 'Not long. CSI on scene don't think it's the original deposition site. It floods too often.'

'Suppose what I should have asked,' Shah clarified, 'is, do we know how old the remains are?'

Callum was already shaking his head. 'Hope the pathologist can tell us that. What we *do* know, though, is that Penny Lynch was attacked in a similar manner twelve months ago. So, if it is the same offender, as Jo says, he's been operating for at least a year. A date on the body will give us a better timeline.' He indicated me again. 'Jo?'

I read from my notes. 'The victims were incapacitated in a blitz attack. He doesn't engage them verbally, or lure them into his car. He comes up behind them and renders them unconscious with a blow to the back of the head. So, he may not have great social skills, or be comfortable talking to women in general. He may have an unstable history of relationships. Perhaps unable to sustain them. He could be in the system already, for violence against women – domestic abuse, that kind of thing. Research would suggest you're looking for a white male . . .'

'Age range?' Beth asked.

I pursed my lips as I thought about it. 'Difficult to be accurate until we know how many years he's been operating, but I'd say he's aged between thirty-five and fifty-five. You're not looking for a juvenile. Similarly, given the physicality of the crimes – the way he carried Rachel, for example – I doubt he'd be much older than mid-fifties.'

'Physically fit, then?' Tony Morgan offered.

I agreed. 'Either he has a hobby that keeps him fit – like the gym or sport – or his job fills that role.' I tapped my notes. 'He's of average IQ and will be in employment. More likely self-employed or manual work. Something that means he can move around with a certain amount of freedom, or unaccountability. Obviously has access to a vehicle. Either owns one, or can access one through work.'

'Could he drive for a job?' Tony asked.

'Possibly. But don't restrict your searches to lorry drivers or similar. It's more likely that driving is just one element of what he does.' I glanced at the map on the wall with pins indicating the attack sites.

'The moors are an area he feels comfortable in. He knows these locations well. Especially the Moor Road. I think he's local and has explored these moorland routes a lot.'

I got up and walked over to the map, tapping a public footpath marked in red.

'The Pennine Way connects all of these sites. Your man could be someone who hikes for a hobby. Either way, he's walked these paths and knows them intimately.' I perched on the edge of the table, letting one leg dangle, as I addressed the team.

'You've used geographic profiling before so you know that offenders conduct their crimes within comfort zones, which are often defined by an anchor point. The place they feel most secure operating from.'

Tony leaned back in his chair, chewing the end of his pen. 'Pennine Way goes all the way to Scotland. How do we find his anchor point over hundreds of miles?'

I stood in front of the map, tapping the village of Cowling where Rachel was abducted.

'This bothered me.' I said to no one in particular. 'Why abduct Rachel from here and then drive her all the way back to this spot on the moors? A distance of over eighteen miles to rape and murder her? Because make no mistake, that was his intention.'

No one spoke so I picked up a marker pen and drew a circle that enclosed all the pins on the board, including the most recent one of the body in the ditch.

'It didn't make sense. Unless his anchor point isn't where he abducts his victims, but where he kills them.'

Callum looked at the circle I'd drawn. 'That narrows it down.'

'This killer hunts along the Pennine Way. Most likely the area of it bounded by the Moor Road. But his killing ground is here.'

All eyes were on the map.

'Wytch's Tarn is almost in the middle of the circle.' Shah said.

'Where some local kids said they saw a skeletal hand coming out of the water, a week ago,' Callum said.

His eyes met mine and he held my gaze for just a heartbeat.

'Whaaat?' Beth was incredulous. 'Why wasn't it reported?'

196

'It was.' Callum slipped off the edge of the table and went back to his seat. 'Local police went up to take a look, next day, but couldn't find anything. Thought the kids had been under the influence.' He was making notes. 'I'll get a search team up to the Tarn. Get divers in there.'

I looked at Beth. 'You were right when you said our man was taking a hell of a risk carrying Rachel onto the moors that night. After the sighting at the Tarn, the area was crawling with ghost-hunters and thrill-seekers. That's what gave me the idea.'

'Idea?' Beth frowned.

I thought back to the night I'd walked up to the moors with Harvey. What I'd seen and felt as I tracked this killer's footsteps.

'It would have been safer for him to commit the crime near Cowling. So, why take the risk?' I tapped the map again. 'I think this spot was as close as he could get to the Tarn. The lake is important to him . . . it has to be *here*. But that night, he couldn't get there because of all the activity. So, he got as close as he could, without being seen.'

'Why not just go another night? Couple of weeks later, when the activity's died down?' It was Tony.

'Because not only does it have to be *this* specific location . . .' I went to my seat and opened Penny Lynch's file. 'It has to be on a specific date.'

Callum came to stand behind me, looking at the notes over my shoulder.

When I'd looked at the report Penny had filed the previous year, I'd seen it.

'Penny's attack was on the night of first of February, last year.' I rode the silence for just a second, before adding, 'Rachel was abducted on Saturday the first of February . . . *this* year.'

'Bloody hell.' Tony gave a low whistle.

I felt the warmth of Callum's breath against my ear as he whispered, 'Nice one.'

'These are theme-related crimes,' I said, as Callum went back to his place at the table. 'Your killer doesn't see his victims as individuals, but props in his scenario. Which *has* to be carried out at a specific place, on a specific date.'

'What about his signature behaviours?' Callum asked, making notes. 'What do they tell us?'

'He dehumanises these women,' I said. 'Evidenced by the initial blow from behind. He doesn't want to approach face to face and interact with them as individuals. Then, he hoods them. Not so they can't identify him, but because he doesn't want to see their faces. There's intense anger in these attacks. I think he has a deep hatred of women.'

'If he hates women,' Tony said, 'why does he want sex with them? Why not just kill them?'

'This isn't about sex in the normal sense. Sex for someone like him isn't about eroticism . . . or even arousal. It's about control . . . punishment. For this man, the sex act is an expression of violence and rage.'

'He couldn't perform,' Beth said. 'When he assaulted Rachel, she said he couldn't follow through with penetrative sex.'

I nodded. 'He's driven by a sexual motivator. Revenge, because he was cheated on by someone, maybe? Or because he was rejected. Jealousy . . . anger. All of those things can get mixed up with sex as a weapon. Strangulation is an expression of his anger too. As a method of killing, it's up close and personal. It takes a lot to literally squeeze the life out of someone.'

'What about the ribbon?' Callum asked. 'You said from the beginning, it was significant.'

'This theme has "props" that are important to him. Vital, in fact, for the whole fantasy to work. The ribbon *has* to be the ligature that he uses to kill his victims. He could use anything, but he brings that with him, specifically.'

Shah was looking at the image on his laptop, of the body in the ditch.

'What about the hood, then? I mean, it was the same type used for Penny and Rachel. So why use plastic bags on this victim?'

I'd been thinking about that, ever since I'd seen the photograph at the scene.

'I believe this person in the ditch was one of his early victims,' I said slowly. 'Before he perfected his "killing kit". Maybe even the very first one. That's where things aren't as practised, not as slick. Killers learn from their mistakes. They improve and refine their technique over time.'

It was a horrific concept, but a reality in the psyche of serial killers, which I'd come to know all too well.

'By studying the earlier killings,' I went on quietly, 'that's where we'll find his mistakes . . . see his learning curve. Be able to map his progress to becoming a professional hunter.'

Everyone had fallen silent. The room was eerily still.

Which was why we all jumped when the shriek of an incoming Zoom call shattered the moment.

Chapter Thirty-Six

Fordley Police Station, Monday Afternoon

Callum joined the call, then cast the image onto the TV screen, so everyone could see.

The familiar face of Elle Richardson appeared, larger than life, at the front of the room. She would be able to hear everyone in the room, but could only see Callum.

'Thanks for joining us, Doctor,' Callum said. 'Don't think we need introductions . . . you know the team – they're all here.'

Elle nodded, but her customary smile was absent. I knew her well enough to recognise when she was preoccupied and sombre. Today was one of those days. But given what she was dealing with, who could blame her?

'The bones from the drainage ditch were collected and sent to us earlier today.' She got straight down to business. 'They're currently being cleaned in the lab, but I wanted to bring you up to speed with what I've got so far – to get things moving.'

'Appreciate that.' Callum said, pen poised to make notes.

'What I can tell you is that it's the body of a female, who was somewhere between 165 and 170 centimetres tall.' She paused and glanced at the camera, with a half-smile. 'And if Doctor McCready's there that's between five foot five and five foot seven in old money, Jo.'

I laughed. 'Thanks, mate.'

Elle pushed fingers through her red curls, as she studied her notes.

'I won't bore you with the science, but basically, in humans, bones begin fusing from the age of sixteen. I can tell from the fusing of vertebrae and collarbone that our lady was somewhere between twenty-three and twenty-six years old when she died. There are signs of blunt-force trauma to the back of the skull. She was hit hard, from behind.'

'Was the blow sufficient to have killed her?' Callum asked.

Elle was already shaking her head. 'Slight linear fracture – I'd say that wasn't the cause of death. Given the state of the remains, we may never be able to say for sure how she died.'

'OK.' Callum made a note. 'Anything else?'

There was some hair – fairly long strands – still attached to the skull. Your victim was a brunette. No sign of dye or processing on the hair, so I'd say that was her natural colour.'

Callum was scribbling notes. 'That's useful.'

'The body was originally put in a sleeping bag, which was wrapped almost entirely in thick tape, like a mummy before presumably being disposed of. At some point, the top corner of the packaging has been torn – maybe as the remains shifted in soil or were exposed to water. That's why the shoulder and head were visible when the body was discovered. The good news for us is that the rest of the bag is intact.'

'Okaay.' Callum obviously wasn't quite sure why that was good news, but we were all about to find out.

'Which means some items buried with the body, which might have been washed away, have been retained in the bag.'

'Such as?' Callum spoke for us all.

Elle slipped the reading glasses from the top of her head back onto the bridge of her nose. 'Couple of coins and some fabric from the remains of clothing.'

'Elle,' I said, causing all eyes to turn to me. 'It's Jo,' I clarified, as I knew she couldn't see me. 'Can I ask, were there any shoes found in the sleeping bag?'

'Nothing to indicate she was wearing socks or tights, or at least, there's no trace of those on the bones of the feet or legs.

Also, no leather or canvas. But all the bones of both feet are intact, which leads me to think the body was buried with bare feet.'

Callum shot me a knowing look.

'I've charted all the bones that were brought in,' Elle was saying. 'And some are missing.'

'Which ones?' Callum asked.

'Right hand and right forearm, which were exposed by the tear in the bag. Other than that, your Jane Doe is pretty well preserved.'

'What about the fastening around the neck?'

Elle pulled some paperwork towards her. 'I'll be sending it for more tests, but I did a quick comparison to the ribbon recovered from Rachel Taylor's attack.' She glanced at the screen with a triumphant smile. 'Knew you'd be thinking about that.'

'And?' Callum asked.

'Even to the naked eye, it looks like a match. Nothing makes me think it'll be proved otherwise after more detailed tests. But you might be lucky, if there's any recoverable trace fibres or DNA on it.'

I took a long breath. All of this was just more proof that the woman in the ditch had been killed by our man. But what came next was more of a breakthrough than I could have hoped for.

'A necklace was trapped in the knot of the ribbon,' Elle said. 'Lucky, because otherwise it might have been lost.' She clicked some keys and a picture of a silver chain, with an ornate silver cross, appeared on screen. A ruler had been placed alongside it for comparison.

'I'll send the photos over by email, along with everything I've got so far.'

There was a pause as everyone absorbed the information before Callum asked the million-dollar question.

'Can you tell how long she's been dead?'

She frowned slightly and pursed her lips in an expression I knew only too well.

'Not easy at this early stage,' she said carefully. 'I've got a colleague at Northumbria University. I'm sending some samples to her. She's a specialist in analysing the decrease of proteins in bones after death.'

'Thought you weren't going to bore us with the science?' Tony quipped.

Elle pulled a face.

'I won't hold you to it,' Callum prompted. 'But ballpark?'

'Going by the condition of the bones and the wrappings and fabric left in the bag . . .'

It seemed as though the whole room was holding a collective breath.

'Probably decades.'

* * *

Everyone sat in stunned silence after the Zoom call ended.

'Bloody hell.' Tony was the first one to break the spell. 'Decades . . .'

Callum was looking at me, as if he expected me to pull a rabbit from a hat.

Elle's bombshell had surprised me as much as everyone else. Whatever I'd expected, it wasn't that.

I finally said, 'If Elle's right, your man's had a helluva long run.'

'Getting an ID on this body is paramount.' Callum was looking at Beth. He'd already allocated that line of enquiry to her.

'Decades though?' She held her hands out, palms up.

'Might get lucky with DNA, if she's in the system,' Tony supplied helpfully.

'And if she's not?' Beth swivelled her chair towards him.

'Missing persons,' Callum said simply. 'We've got gender, age, height, hair colour and a piece of jewellery. That's a start.'

'What about date range?' Beth was already making notes. 'How many decades do we go back . . . and location? She could have gone missing from anywhere.'

'If I'm right about the "themed" nature of these killings . . .' Everyone looked at me. 'You can narrow it down to females of that age, who went missing a day either side of February first.'

'Location could be anywhere in the country, though.' Beth sounded as harassed as she looked.

'No.' Even as I said it, I felt more certain than ever. 'If she was killed near the Tarn, she'll have been abducted from his hunting ground along the Pennine Way, where it's bordered by the Moor Road.'

I walked over to the map, and using the marker pen, drew a circle slightly larger than the first. 'Around here.'

Part of me dreaded being right – about the possibility of a serial killer who had been operating on my doorstep for decades. Hiding in plain sight.

'Jesus,' Callum muttered so quietly only I heard him. 'How many more?'

Chapter Thirty-Seven

Kingsberry Farm, Tuesday Morning

My eyes felt gritty and I had a splitting headache.

I leaned against the Aga, enjoying the warmth radiating from the hotplate, and poured myself another mug of tea.

I'd left the porch door open, so Harvey could run around in the garden. Not able to face walking this morning, after yet another dismal night with little sleep.

I cupped my hands around the mug and thought about my caller, the previous night.

Chris McGarry's late night phone-ins were wearing thin. A fact I wasn't slow to share with him, when I saw the time on my bedside clock.

'Fuck's sake, Chris! It's three a.m.'

'Morning, campers.' The grin in his voice wound me up even more.

'You're going to have to find another way to communicate,' I grizzled as I propped myself up on one elbow. 'Because this is seriously starting to piss me off.'

Outside of what he did for a living, he was handsome, charming and erudite. All the things that would ordinarily make him the ideal man. If it wasn't for the small matter of executing his rivals with a bullet to the back of the head.

He'd always treated me with respect. Something I'd put down to the fact that I wasn't from his world.

I wasn't a rival or a threat, but one of the professionals drawn into his orbit as a by-product of his lifestyle. Like his solicitor or the prison governor. To be treated differently, as, potentially, we could all make his passage through the prison system that little bit easier.

Maybe, because of that, I'd never felt afraid of Chris. Had never suffered from the automatic nervousness that seemed to afflict people whenever he walked into a room. They either showed utter deference, or tried to melt into the background, like grey men who didn't want to come to his attention.

But all that had changed after our first midnight call. When he'd threatened me and I'd seen that carefully cultivated mask drop away.

It should have made me more cautious.

Should have.

But I had a legendary short fuse, usually exacerbated by lack of sleep or stress – all of which Chris McGarry was delivering in spades right now.

Which contributed to a fractious call the night before, which the logical 'me' was beginning to regret in the cold light of day.

'Then give me something useful,' he'd said, tightly. 'And I won't need to keep calling.'

'There's nothing much I can add since our last call.'

'Not good enough.'

I sat upright, hugging my knees, in an attempt to ward off the cold. 'Chris . . . if I'd found anything, I'd let you know.'

'And how would you do that – unless I called you?' I could hear the sneer. 'You going to ring the governor and get him to put you through to my cell? Or maybe call me on my PIN number and let the screws record our conversation?'

My breath gusted down the phone as I swept my hair back and leaned against the headboard. Staring up into the darkness for some kind of divine intervention.

As alert as ever, Harvey must have heard my voice, and I heard his large paws padding up the stairs to see what all the fuss was about.

'I could always pass a message through Joshua, or your lieutenant Hazza? I'm sure he pays regular visits.'

'He does, but he can't come every day.' What little patience he had was wearing thin. 'I haven't got time for a fucking debate, Jo. Just tell me what's new and you can go back to sleep.'

My mind was racing through what we knew, and didn't know. Everything we'd learned since I'd last spoken to Chris. Sifting the details to come up with something I could tell him that wouldn't mean I revealed too much about the investigation. But even as those thoughts scrolled through my head I knew I'd long ago passed that point.

I absently stroked Harvey's head as he jumped up onto the bed and lay down next to me, nestling his nose into my side. Then, I just took a breath and told Chris everything I had on Red's case.

'The murder weapon – that wrench?' he said when I finally finished. 'Came from the site?'

I nodded, even though he was on the other end of the phone. 'No prints found.' I pre-empted his question. 'Killer wiped it, before putting it back in the truck.'

'What about Red's phone?'

'Wasn't found with his body. Looks like the killer took it.'

He muttered an expletive under his breath. 'And plod can't find this Penny Lynch either?' I knew it was a rhetorical question so stayed quiet.

'Bloody hell!' he finally exploded. 'What the fuck *do* they know?'

'Not a lot about Red's killing . . . so far,' I had to admit.

I could almost hear him thinking. 'After we last spoke, I put out some discreet feelers. Trying to find this Penny . . .'

'And?'

'Nothing. Which is unusual. If she's in Fordley, the people I contacted would know.'

'So, she's left town?'

'Probably. If she got a train or a coach, she could be anywhere. But wherever it is, she's not on my turf.'

'The police are planning a press conference,' I said, thoughtfully. 'Going to put out an appeal for her to come forward.'

'Good luck with that,' he snorted. 'The tart-with-a-heart only exists in the movies. If she's running scared, she's not going to stick her head above the parapet – even for Red.' The silence stretched out – then: 'Why a press conference? Penny Lynch isn't important enough – neither is Red, as far as plod are concerned.'

'Because it looks like she might be connected to a potential serial killer.'

'What? How?'

'The attack that brought her and Red together . . . over a year ago? It's been linked to a body they discovered on the moors yesterday. Similar M.O.'

'You said "serial killer".' His tone was matter-of-fact. 'One body isn't a series.'

Astute as ever.

'Method of attack on Penny was the same as another girl . . . attacked a week ago. Elements tie them both to the body found yesterday.'

'So?' He sounded as though he couldn't care less. 'Red's tart gets herself roughed up by some lunatic, who kills someone else.' He sucked his teeth, raising his voice as much as he dared. 'I don't give a shit about some ponce attacking prossies—'

'The last one wasn't a pr—'

'I want to know who killed Red and why!'

'You think you're the only one?' I shouted, not having to worry about being overheard. My raised voice had made Harvey jump. He'd lifted his head and growled softly, as he tried to work out where the potential threat was coming from.

'For Christ's sake, Chris, give me a break! If I knew, the police would know and the killer would be banged up by now. There's *nothing* else I can tell you.'

'I'm running out of patience, Jo. Find me something . . . fast.'

That was how our call had ended. Needless to say, I didn't get back to sleep, but spent what little was left of my night going over everything again and again.

The temptation to confide in Callum was overwhelming, but he would see through any thin attempt to give him half a story and hold back the rest.

But I knew I couldn't carry on ducking and diving. Trying to appease Chris McGarry and keep Callum's confidences at the same time. It was too exhausting, not to mention dangerous.

Harvey came bounding in, skittering across the kitchen floor, like a giddy kid and I went to shut out the freezing wind.

My phone rang, as I was attempting – and failing – to wipe Harvey's paws with a dog towel.

'Jo.' Callum sounded as though he been awake as long as I had, but less sluggish. 'Sorry for the early call.'

Glad someone is.

'What's up?'

'We're bringing Daniel Dunglas in, later today, for more questioning. I'd like you to observe the interview.'

'OK.' I was distracted, cradling my phone between my chin and my shoulder, as Harvey played tug-of-war with the corner of his towel.

'Forensics have found traces of fibres from Rachel's clothing and a strand of hair in his car.'

'That's brilliant news.' But he didn't sound as elated as he should. 'Isn't it?'

'They were found in the driver's side . . . the seat, to be exact.'

'So they could have been transferred from his clothes, after he'd had contact with Rachel, when he stumbled across her on the moor?' I joined the dots, as easily as any defence barrister would.

'Exactly. I suspect that's what he'll say.'

'Why do I feel a "but" coming?'

'They also found a minute flake of nail polish, on the inside of the boot lid.'

An image of Rachel sitting on the track above my house, stroking Harvey.

'Rachel didn't have painted fingernails,' I said.

'Not fingers . . . toes. Forensics got a scraping from her toenails at the hospital. It matches.'

Chapter Thirty-Eight

Fordley Police Station, Tuesday Afternoon

I sat in an observation room, watching on screen the interview of Daniel Dunglas taking place, just across the corridor.

Because of the forensics found in his car, the police had enough to arrest him. He'd been given the news when officers turned up at his home, before bringing him into Fordley police station. They'd secured his house and officers were there, waiting for a full Forensics search.

Personally, I wasn't sure they'd find much. Though I suspected the place would be filled with paraphernalia relating to his life in the occult world. We could only hope something more damning would turn up, but I wasn't holding my breath.

DS Tony Morgan was leading the interview, with Shah Akhtar as his support.

Tony had already gone through the basics, reminding Dunglas of his rights, and we were getting to the interesting part.

Dunglas had refused the offer of having a duty solicitor appointed for him, saying he had nothing to hide.

Callum sat beside me, nursing a mug of coffee. 'At least he's not going to be advised to go "no comment" on us,' he murmured.

I watched the man on screen. He seemed to have aged since I'd last seen him.

His cheekbones were more pronounced, and he looked to have lost some weight. The dark rings under his eyes hinted at broken sleep and the usually well-groomed beard looked straggly and unkempt.

They were asking him about his walk on the moors on Saturday night.

'You met Doctor McCready?' Tony said.

Dunglas simply nodded.

'Can you tell me what you were doing up there in the middle of the night?'

'Has Doctor McCready been asked the same question?'

'This isn't about her, Daniel. I'm interested in what *you* were doing there.'

A flicker of annoyance crossed his face. 'As I told the doctor, I was walking to Wytch's Tarn. I saw a light, bobbing about on the moor. I thought it might be one of these corpse lights I've heard so much about, so I went to look. But it turned out to be Doctor McCready's torch.'

'Why were you going to Wytch's Tarn in the middle of the night?'

He let out a long breath. 'It's what I do.' He sounded exasperated. 'How many times do I have to go over this?'

'One more time, Daniel.' Tony smiled.

'I investigate the paranormal, Detective, and I'm sure even you know that most activity of that kind happens at night, under cover of darkness.'

Tony nodded. 'Bit like criminal activity.'

'It's not a crime to go walking, anytime of the day or night.'

'You weren't there revisiting the spot where Rachel had been attacked?'

Dunglas sat up straighter. 'No.' His eyes flashed. 'I didn't even realise that was the spot until Doctor McCready pointed it out.'

I could see Tony didn't believe that any more than I did.

'As you were leaving, you said something interesting to Doctor McCready. Do you remember what that was?'

'No.'

'He's lying,' I muttered to Callum, who simply nodded.

Tony made a show of reading from his notes. 'You said . . . "Something is coming, here, on the moor". Do you remember saying that, Daniel?'

He shifted uncomfortably in his chair, shrugging. 'I possibly said something of the sort.'

Tony glanced at notes I knew he didn't need. 'You then said "Secrets can't stay hidden . . . evil will show its face."' Tony leaned forward slightly, his elbows on the table. 'What exactly did you mean by that?'

Everyone waited in the silence that followed. There was a shift in Dunglas's body language.

'He's leaking stress signals,' I said.

Callum leaned a little closer to the screen, as Dunglas seemed to pull himself together.

'I was right, wasn't I?' He couldn't keep the triumph out of his voice.

News about the skeleton on the moor had leaked and the press were all over it. The wife of the motorist who'd discovered the remains had posted it on social media and it spread fast.

There were grainy images of police and forensic activity on the moor – from walkers, trying to take photos, long distance on their phones. One news outlet had even put a drone up and footage from above was playing an endless loop on twenty-four-hour news channels.

'Press conference is scheduled for this afternoon.' Callum didn't sound happy about it. 'No choice now it's out there.'

I glanced at his profile. Tense in the glow of the screen.

'Might work in your favour.' I was trying to sound positive. 'To ID the remains. Someone out there must know who she is.'

Our attention was pulled back to events across the corridor.

'Yes, you were right,' Tony said. 'What I'm interested in is how did you know, Daniel? That the remains of a young woman were about to turn up on the moor?'

'I have second sight,' he said simply, as if that was a normal thing to say. 'Premonitions.' He opened his arms and spread his hands, palms up, like a magician revealing a trick. 'The spirits told me that the moors were about to give up their secrets in the form of a corpse.' His smile was thin. 'And they did . . . didn't they?'

Tony could have said what we were all thinking. That this was just so much bullshit. Or that Dunglas, like his Victorian namesake, was a charlatan and a fraud. But instead, he did what he was trained to do.

He went with the line he was being given. In a totally non-judgemental way and with a straight face. Because he knew that this might be leading up to a confession.

Daniel Dunglas wouldn't be the first murderer to claim he heard voices, telling him things only the killer would know. Or urging him to commit his crimes.

Some killers genuinely did suffer from psychotic episodes, but in my experience, they were in a minority. Those who genuinely suffered from such hallucinations tended to be caught fairly quickly after committing their crimes. Lacking the planning or guile to evade police for long.

Far more faked it, in an attempt to mitigate what they'd done or get a lighter sentence.

I'd heard it all. From Peter Sutcliffe, the Yorkshire Ripper claiming to hear voices coming from a headstone, when he was working as a gravedigger, to David Berkowitz, the 'Son of Sam' killer in America, claiming that he'd been told to commit his murders by a demon, inhabiting his neighbour's dog – called Harvey, as it happened.

A handy dissociation from the crimes they'd committed. Something that could also be used by the defence, to get a sentence in a secure psychiatric hospital. Regarded by many as a softer alternative to prison.

Even in the short time I'd spent with Dunglas, I didn't believe for one minute that he suffered from severe mental illness.

'He either genuinely believes he had psychic abilities,' I said, still watching the interview, 'or he's a fake.'

I felt, rather than saw, Callum turn to look at me. 'You're discounting the possibility that he really *does* talk to spirits?'

I shot him a look. 'Aren't you?'

He grinned at me. 'What do you think?'

We both turned back to the job at hand.

'Yes. You were right,' Tony was saying. 'Did the spirits tell you anything else about the corpse, Daniel? Like who she is?'

'No.'

'Do you know how she died?'

'Strangled.'

'Not damning that he knows that,' Callum was saying. 'Motorist saw the bag over her head, tied at the throat. It's in the public domain.'

But I knew the cause of death hadn't been ascertained. Until we had the final report from the pathologist – Elle Richardson – and I said as much.

Callum just nodded, his focus fixed on the drama unfolding, just a few feet away.

Tony nodded slowly. 'Do you know who strangled her, Daniel?'

'No.'

'The spirits haven't told you that?'

Dunglas's eyebrows rose, as he clicked his tongue. 'You're mocking me, Detective.'

'Not at all,' Tony replied. 'I believe you know things no one else could. If you say the spirits tell you then I'll accept that.'

'You're implying that I know because I had something to do with it.' Dunglas's tone hardened.

'Did you?'

'Of course not.' He shifted in his chair, half turning away from Tony. 'I'm getting tired of this.' He suddenly changed tack – maybe to shift the topic away from the corpse on the moor. 'When will I get my car back?'

'When Forensics have released it.'

'And how long will *that* be?' He wasn't even trying to hide his impatience.

Gone the affable, all-knowing, calm exterior he was so fond of projecting.

'The strain's telling on him,' I said, not looking away from the screen.

'Good.' Callum folded his arms and nodded towards the screen. 'If Gandalf here *is* our man, I want to put him under pressure and see what comes out when he cracks.'

'Forensics have found evidence of Rachel Taylor in your car, Daniel,' Tony said – his tone deliberately non-accusatory. 'How do you account for that?'

Dunglas's eyes open wider, in an instinctive look of surprise. 'I . . . er . . . I can't.'

Shah produced a photograph and pushed it across the table. I couldn't see what it was, but suspected it was an image of the traces of fibre Forensics had found.

Tony tapped the image. 'That's a picture of tape lifts taken from your Volvo, Daniel. It shows fibres from the fleece Rachel was wearing underneath her waterproof jacket.'

Dunglas pulled the picture closer and stared down at it, frowning. 'It can't be.' He looked up at Tony. 'She was never in my car.'

'There's no doubt the fibres are a match,' Tony said.

Shah passed another picture over, to join the first.

'And this is a strand of Rachel's hair. Also, a perfect match, and also found in your car.'

I looked at Callum, who was staring intently at the scene. 'Don't they have to tell him *where* in the car they were found?'

He pursed his lips, never looking away from the interview. Nodding slowly. 'Yes, but I wanted to see what reaction we got first. See if he reveals more before he knows that.'

If he'd had a solicitor sitting next to him, I knew they'd never have been allowed to get away with a tactic like that. But it had been Dunglas's choice not to have one appointed.

Dunglas sat in what seemed to be stunned silence.

Tony and Shah knew better than to break the pause with questions. They were going to let it stretch out painfully, until Dunglas filled it – hopefully with something incriminating.

He sat back in the hard plastic chair, smoothing his beard with one hand as he continued to stare at the photographs. Finally, he looked across the table at his inquisitors.

He moved the photos around with an index finger. 'Where *exactly* in my car were these found?'

'Shit,' Callum muttered under his breath.

Tony and Shah had to disclose the facts now.

'On the driver's seat,' Tony admitted.

I leaned closer to the screen to get a better look at Dunglas's face in this critical moment.

A smile tugged slightly at the corners of his mouth and his shoulders dropped as the tension left his body. Relief.

'I found Rachel,' he said quietly. 'I helped carry her down to the farmer's car. Obviously, these things could have transferred on to my clothing then.'

'He's relieved.' Callum didn't need me to read the body language for him.

'That's not evidence of guilt,' I added – just for the sake of balance.

He shot me a look. 'Don't sound so pleased.'

'Piss off.' The retort was out of my mouth automatically.

Callum raised an eyebrow.

'How can you say that?' I didn't hide the indignation. 'I'm here to give you feedback on his behaviour – body language. Don't shoot the messenger if it doesn't fit the narrative you'd like.'

His face was hard, muscles bunching in his jaw. 'I don't have a preferred narrative,' he said tightly.

I knew that wasn't true. Every cop on the team would have liked this to be tied up neatly with a bow.

But if Dunglas had confessed right then – when presented with the evidence – it would have felt far too tidy and we both knew it was rarely that easy.

But they hadn't played their ace yet. Tony was just coming to that.

Shah had produced a plastic evidence bag and a magnified image of what it contained.

'A flake of nail varnish,' Tony was saying. 'It matches the one Rachel used to paint her toes.' Tony watched Dunglas for a moment. When he said nothing, he added, 'Rachel's attacker removed her boots and socks. When she came round in the boot of the car, she was barefoot.'

Dunglas indulged in a slight smile, gesturing to the evidence with a jerk of his chin. 'As I said . . .' The calm tone was back in his voice. 'I carried her . . . this could have rubbed on to my clothing then, just like the fibres.'

Tony rode the moment for just a heartbeat, before adding, 'But you see, Daniel, we have a problem with that theory. Because this evidence wasn't found in the driver's side of your car, like the others.'

The wide brow furrowed again. 'Then where was it found?'

'On the *inside* of the boot lid.'

Dunglas's chest halted in its steady rise and fall as he held his breath for just a second before expelling it slowly.

'I'll have that solicitor now.'

Chapter Thirty-Nine

Wytch's Tarn, Wednesday Morning

It was early morning, and it was freezing.

I stood beside Callum on a ridge, looking down over Wytch's Tarn.

The ground rose around the lake, enclosing the Tarn in a natural hollow. Carved out by glacial ice that had scraped away the rock right down to the ancient slate layer underneath, preventing water from draining away.

The remnants of the night still clung to the frosty morning, its shadows slowly retreating as the sun began to climb. Though there was little warmth in the wintry light reflecting from the silver surface of the water.

Callum stamped his feet on the frozen ground, his breath pluming as he blew onto cupped hands.

'Should have brought gloves,' he said through gritted teeth.

Ordinarily, I'd have taken his hand and put it with mine, in my pocket, for warmth. But not today – in front of colleagues.

We watched as divers from the underwater search unit began walking into the still water.

'If it's any consolation—' I nodded towards them '—it'll be even colder in there.'

'Wouldn't do their job for a gold pig.' He glanced down at me. 'Anyway, want the bad news or the good news?'

He was keeping his face deliberately expressionless.

'Let's start with the bad.' I played along. 'Like medicine. Then the good can take the taste away.'

'Dunglas went "no comment" on us after he lawyered up yesterday.'

I'd left the previous day once Dunglas had requested a solicitor, knowing it could be hours before one turned up.

'Can't say I'm shocked,' I snorted. 'What's the good news?'

'We took advice from the CPS, last night. What we've got so far crosses the charging threshold.'

'You've charged him?' With what they'd found, I wasn't surprised.

'Yep.' Callum looked more pleased than I'd seen him in a while. 'Charged with the kidnap and attempted murder of Rachel Taylor. There's even enough to arrest him on suspicion of the attempted murder of Penny Lynch, given the similarities in the two attacks.'

I didn't know what to say to that so for a second, I said nothing. Just letting the information settle.

'He's been remanded in custody,' he was saying. 'In Armley prison until they can set a court date.'

'If the body in the ditch is connected,' I was thinking out loud, 'then Dunglas is in the frame for that one as well.'

Callum nodded, still watching the divers, who were now on their hands and knees, moving slowly forward into deeper water. Feeling their way.

'Explains how he knew there was another body on the moor,' he said. 'If he put it there.'

'What happens next?'

Broad shoulders shrugged beneath his jacket. 'We find Penny Lynch. Get as much evidence as we can from her attack and start building our case for the prosecution.'

'Saw your press conference, yesterday.'

I knew he hated doing them, but he'd come across well, as always.

'Already generated some calls,' he said. 'Officers are follow-ing up leads on her whereabouts.'

Whatever I was about to say to that was lost when Callum's phone rang. He fished it out of his jacket pocket and I listened to one half of a conversation.

'Hi, Beth.'

He was nodding to whatever she was saying. Then he shot me a look, his eyebrow raised. 'Bloody hell.'

I couldn't contain myself. 'What?'

He held the phone against his chest to cover the microphone. 'Beth's got an ID on the body.' He went back to her. 'OK. Great work, Beth. Thanks.'

I watched impatiently as he put the phone in his pocket, staring over the water in silence. I didn't want to rob him of thinking time, but the wait was excruciating.

I was just about to break the silence when a shout went up from the surface team in the dinghy.

The diver who was near the centre of the lake appeared at the surface. His arm was stretched above his head, holding the bleached-white skeletal bones of a forearm and hand.

Callum jogged down to the edge of the water to talk to the dive team leader and I stood and watched the animated exchange.

Eventually, after what seemed an eternity, Callum came jogging back up the slope.

He indicated the lake with a jerk of his head. 'Result. Let's just hope it's from our skeleton and not another body.'

'What's Beth got?'

'She thinks our Jane Doe is Lorraine Stevens. Reported as a missing person by her boyfriend. Photograph on file shows her wearing the silver necklace recovered from our skeleton. She had long brown hair and was twenty-five when she went missing – so age, height and hair colour all match what Elle Richardson gave us.'

He paused and I knew there was one crucial piece of information to come.

'Did she go missing on the first of February?' I asked.

He nodded.

'When?'

'In 1994.'

Chapter Forty

Kingsberry Farm, Wednesday Afternoon

Callum stayed at the Tarn, while I left to drive back to the farm.

I was still mulling over the fact that Daniel Dunglas had been charged with attempted murder.

Given the similarities with the remains found in the drainage ditch, could he be a serial killer? If our skeleton was Lorraine Stevens, we were looking at a murder that had remained unsolved for over thirty years.

Daniel Dunglas?

I now had to reframe my thinking about him. From weird pseudo-spiritualist to serial killer. But somehow, even though I disliked the man, I just couldn't make that leap.

He fitted the profile in so many ways. The age was right. His awkward social skills and misogynistic attitude. He'd been born and brought up in Halifax and knew the Pennine walks well.

No doubt Callum's team would be conducting a thorough trawl of his history and interviewing anyone who knew him or who'd ever been associated with him.

I'd always believed the offender had not only attacked other women, but had probably escalated to killing already.

Knowing I'd been right gave me a sick sense of dread. Not least because Lorraine Stevens had a family somewhere, who would soon be facing their worst nightmare.

The team wouldn't release the identity until they were certain it was her. Only then would they approach the family to identify the jewellery and any other belongings. The media would be the last to be told.

Or at least, that's how it should work. Though I knew from bitter past experience it didn't always go so smoothly. The advent of social media was both a blessing and a curse, where police investigations were concerned.

A great tool for connecting with the public and for investigators to do a deep-dive into the social life and background of victims and suspects alike. But also, the fastest means of leaking information that investigators didn't want in the public domain.

Every bystander and morbid onlooker was a mobile news outlet. Complete with camera or video footage that could travel around the world at the click of a button. Often devoid of crucial context and subject to the speculation of armchair sleuths, which was rarely helpful.

The press office was working hard to keep a lid on developments with the skeletal remains. The team, meanwhile, were waiting for more results from Elle and Forensics.

Callum had asked me to look at all the information they had on Lorraine Stevens and run an analysis of whether it added anything to the profile I'd drawn up – to be ahead of the curve, if it turned out to be her.

He wanted me to have it ready for that evening's team briefing.

Beth had emailed the initial missing person's report to me, along with any information she could find on the system relating to Lorraine or the initial investigation into her disappearance.

I was scrolling through the files on my laptop – sending pages to the printer, which whirred in the corner of the office, as it spewed out the relevant sheets.

I'd never been able to process detailed information from the screen. Maybe it was a legacy of being trained so many decades ago in the 'old school' methods of textbooks and printed psyche reports. Or maybe, as my son Alex was so fond of telling me, it was a sign I was getting old?

Jen scooped the latest sheets from the printer and brought them to my desk, adding them to the growing pile at my elbow.

'Brew?'

'Oh, you read my mind.'

'All part of the job.' She collected my mug and headed for the kitchen, Harvey at her heels, knowing a biscuit was often part of the tea-brewing process.

The missing persons – mispers – report included photographs of Lorraine provided by her family.

A pretty girl stared back at me. Her blue eyes full of life as she smiled for the camera. The note on the back said it had been taken at her twenty-first birthday party, in the summer of 1990.

I laid the photograph next to the ones I had of Penny Lynch and Rachel Taylor.

A line of three images. Three girls, all in their twenties. All slim and pretty. All with long, straight, dark hair, parted neatly down the middle.

I knew then that our predator hunted a certain type of prey.

Chapter Forty-One

Fordley Police Station, Wednesday Evening

When I'd arrived at the incident room, it wasn't as packed as before. Some desks were empty as officers were out following up lines of enquiry. But there was still a 'buzz' about the place. An urgency, like crackling electricity that ran through everyone involved.

Beth handed me the obligatory mug of tea, smiling as she sipped her coffee. 'Things are getting interesting,' she said. 'We need confirmation from dental records, but pretty sure our body is Lorraine Stevens.'

'Certainly interesting, but terrifying at the same time.'

'Because it means Dunglas has been doing this for three decades?'

I nodded, blowing the steam from my mug.

'Doesn't necessarily mean there are more victims, though.' She was trying to sound optimistic. 'He might not have been active all that time.'

'Oh, he has been.' My conviction in this killer's prolific nature was becoming more solid by the minute. The more I looked at the offences and his M.O., the more certain I was about his nature. But somehow I still couldn't shake the feeling that Daniel Dunglas wasn't it.

Before I could say any more, Callum walked out of his office and headed for the briefing room.

Beth gathered up her notes. 'Show-time.'

* * *

I listened as Callum brought everyone up to speed on the find at Wytch's Tarn. Most of the details washed over me as I contemplated what I was about to say. My attention pulled back to the job at hand as he added something I didn't know.

'Dr Elle Richardson is joining us via Zoom. She's got quite a bit of information to share.'

Right on cue, the chimes of an incoming call announced Elle's arrival. Everyone's attention turned to the big screen.

'Evening, Callum . . . team.' Elle sounded tired. I could only imagine the hours she'd been putting in.

'What've you got for us, Doctor?' Callum cut straight to business.

'Well, first of all, my colleague at Northumbria University has conducted tests on the samples I sent her. The decrease of proteins in the bones after death led her to estimate that your victim has been dead for approximately thirty years.'

'That fits with a potential ID we have,' Callum confirmed, still not revealing the name, even to Elle. It had to stay in this room until we knew for certain.

'Also, the coins found with the body are dated 1993 and 1994. Not that it's definitive, but it all helps.'

'Any idea of cause of death?' Callum asked.

'Because all the soft tissue has gone, it's almost impossible to establish the cause of death with complete certainty.' She glanced at the screen, flicking her hair back in that characteristic 'tell' she had, when she was going to reveal something significant. 'I *can* say the blow to the back of the head wouldn't have been fatal though.'

'I can feel a "but" coming.' Callum smiled at the screen.

'Very perceptive, Detective.' Elle smiled back.

One of these days, I thought, *you're going to slip up and call him Boy Scout to his face.*

'Your skeleton had a fracture of the hyoid bone, which is a U-shaped bone situated in the anterior midline of the neck. Between the chin and the thyroid cartilage.' Elle was indicating the spot on her throat in demonstration. 'I suppose you're not interested in what it does?'

'Not really,' Callum admitted. 'Unless it has some bearing on our case?'

'It's function in life not so much. But what this little bone does, when it's put under pressure, has a very important bearing on your case.' Elle went on, totally unfazed. Her style – even in situations like this – made me smile.

'In cases of death by hanging or strangulation, this bone can reveal evidence of peri-mortem trauma.'

'Er, want to translate that?'

'It tends to break.'

'So our victim was strangled?'

'Yes. It may still not have been the cause of death, as it can break even when the victim survives a strangulation attempt. But given all the other evidence, I'd say, there's a high probability strangulation was a contributing factor.'

Callum glanced at the team. Everyone was transfixed. All understanding the significance of Elle's findings.

'All of this will be in my report,' she was saying. 'Including some interesting findings regarding the deposition site.' She glanced at the screen. 'Want me to go on?'

'Yes . . . absolutely.' Callum was on the edge of his seat.

'There are traces of aquatic and semi-aquatic plants and insects in the wrappings from the body, and on the skeleton itself.' Elle adjusted her glasses as she read from her notes. 'I've sent the samples to a forensic botanist. They should be able to tell you where they originated. Identify the body of water where the victim's remains were originally deposited. I found similar samples on the hand and arm, recovered by the dive team today.'

'Do they belong to our skeleton?' Callum asked.

'Yes,' came the unequivocal reply.

I could feel the tension leave the room – everyone relieved that we weren't looking for another body.

'The question then is, how come they were found in separate locations?' It was Shah Akhtar.

'Either your murderer cut the arm off and deposited it elsewhere, although I can find no evidence of cut or saw marks on the bones to suggest that,' Elle said, removing her glasses and pinching the bridge of her nose. 'More likely, they became separated when the body was moved at some point. Either by your killer, or movement by water and land. As things shift, burial sites can move over years, or in this case, decades. The botanist can give you more information on that.'

As Elle's presentation came to an end, everyone breathed again.

Chapter Forty-Two

Fordley Police Station, Wednesday Evening

Beth was next up – giving the team everything she had found on the woman we believed to be our victim.

'Lorraine Stevens. Twenty-six years old. Lived in the village of Kingsberry with her boyfriend. Went missing on Tuesday, first of February 1994.'

Kingsberry – the village nearest to my farmhouse.

I didn't live there in 1994. I was just leaving university and totally absorbed in the trial of a notorious serial killer, which began that year. Jacob Malecki, accused of killing fifteen people over a thirteen-year period. It was big news at the time, and as a newly qualified forensic psychologist, fascinating to me.

I was ashamed to admit that news of a missing person in a village on the edge of Fordley had completely passed me by at the time.

The picture I'd seen in the file appeared on the screen.

'Her boyfriend . . .' Beth glanced at her notes '. . . Max Radcliffe, reported her missing the next day. Apparently, she was on her way to a party being thrown by some friends. He didn't want her to go and they'd rowed about it. He refused to drive her, so she set off to walk, at about 9 p.m. It should have taken her around twenty minutes but she never made it. He only knew something was wrong when she didn't return home the next day. He went round to the friend's house, where the party had been, and they said she'd never turned up the night before.'

'The boyfriend would be the last person to have seen her then.' Tony Morgan didn't need to say that would make Max

Radcliffe a person of interest. Everyone in the room knew that's how these things worked.

'He was interviewed and eliminated.' Beth read from the file. 'After Lorraine left, he went to the local pub. Landlord and one of his mates put him there until closing time. Then his friend went back to the house to stay with him. He was drunk by then and his mate wanted to make sure he didn't try to drive over to the party. When Lorraine left, she'd packed a few things, said she might stay over. He didn't call it in until the following afternoon, when he'd sobered up enough to drive over to pick her up.'

'What about the people at the party?' Shah asked.

'They all checked out too.' Beth frowned. 'Weird lot though, by all accounts.'

'Weird how?' I asked.

Beth shrugged. 'Bit of a hippy bunch. The house was a small-holding on the edge of Keelham village, just off Well Heads. Willow Farm.'

I knew the area well.

Though Keelham called itself a village, it was just a small community of terrace houses and cottages, clustered around a crossroads on the Brighouse and Denholme Road.

Well Heads was a short stretch of main road, between Keelham and the village of Thornton. Blink and you'd miss it. No post office or local shops – just terrace cottages that strad-dled the crossroads, and an amazing farm shop further along the road. The area was surrounded by fields and farmland.

'Any connection between Lorraine Stevens and Daniel Dunglas?' Callum spoke without looking up from his notes.

'Nothing I can find so far,' Beth said. 'But I'm still looking into the people who lived there. They were trying the original *Good Life*. Growing their own veg, keeping chickens and a goat for milk. There'd been a few complaints from locals about noise from some of the parties. Couple of them got busted for possession of cannabis, but nothing more serious than that.'

'Is that why the boyfriend disapproved?' Shah asked.

'It doesn't say in the records. But apparently Lorraine lived with them before she met Max. He wasn't up for the commune lifestyle, so she moved in with him when things got more serious between them.'

'OK.' Callum perched on the corner of the desk. 'We need a list of everyone living at Willow Farm at the time and everyone at the party that night. All to be traced, interviewed and eliminated . . . or not.'

Everyone scribbled notes as Beth continued, 'The boyfriend went on local radio, asking for Lorraine to get in touch. Organised a poster and flyer campaign around Fordley. Boots on the ground made house-to-house enquiries but came up empty.'

Callum picked up the narrative. 'Her parents, who lived in Fordley, offered a reward of ten thousand pounds. A lot of money in the nineties. But even that drew a blank, apart from cranks coming out of the woodwork. Sightings were reported all over the country. From London to Edinburgh – all false leads.'

Beth continued, 'Her lifestyle was called into question. She'd been a bit of a wild child in her day. Ran away from home at sixteen. Turned up at Greenham Common – the RAF base in Berkshire, where the women's peace camp was.'

'Studied that,' Shah piped up. 'Modern history in school.'

Callum rolled his eyes. 'OK, no need to rub in the age differences.'

'Lived on the camp for a year then moved on. Her parents said she had a nomadic lifestyle. Moving from one squat or camp to another, until she finally turned up at the hippy commune at the farm in Keelham.'

'So, when she disappeared with a bag packed in 1994,' Shah hazarded a guess, 'people thought she just moved on again?'

Beth nodded. 'Her bag and belongings were never found. She walked out of her home and vanished into thin air.'

'What about the boyfriend?' Shah asked.

'Max Radcliffe died of cancer five years ago,' Beth said.

'To this day,' Callum said, 'the family have never given up hope. The case remains open. Her case has now been upgraded from a missing person to murder.'

The room fell silent for a moment. Then Callum nodded to me.

'Jo's added to her original profile, in light of recent developments . . . Jo?'

I left my seat, going over to the whiteboard to add the printed photo of Lorraine Stevens to the other two of Rachel Taylor and Penny Lunch.

'These victims bear a striking resemblance to each other. All white females, around the same age. Slim, pretty, all brunettes.'

I turned to face the room. 'In my original profile, I said these were "theme-related killings".' I tapped the three photos. 'These victims have been chosen because they represent someone in our offender's fantasy or actual history.'

I perched on the edge of the table.

'These murders are part of a scenario. It's very specific, as we've already established. The killings have to take place on a certain date and in a certain place.' I indicated the pictures on the board. 'And his victims have to resemble a specific person. One that he's killing repeatedly.'

'A girlfriend?' Shah asked.

'Possibly.'

'Anything else about him, Jo?' Callum prompted.

'I believe Lorraine Stevens was his first victim. It wasn't as well planned as his attacks on Rachel and Penny. With Lorraine, he used plastic bags as a hood, because he didn't have a pre-pared "kill kit" back then.'

'Dunglas fits, so far,' Beth said.

I had to be cautious, and said so.

'Now that you've charged Dunglas, the profile should be set aside. There's a danger of confirmation bias. Looking to make him fit.'

'Agreed,' Callum said. 'But analysing the killer's behaviours still has value, if it leads us to more victims . . . potentially.'

'Helps build a case – for or against,' Shah added.

'Wytch's Tarn is significant.' Callum frowned. 'Like the date of the attacks; the hood; the ribbon. We can press Dunglas on those things. Find out what his connection is to the Tarn. There could be more bodies in there.'

Tony drew a long breath. 'We'll know soon enough. When the dive teams finish the search.'

'If we're right,' Shah said, cautiously, 'and he killed Lorraine in 1994, why would he go quiet, until last year – when he attacked Penny Lynch?'

'He wouldn't.' All eyes turned to me. 'Unless he's spent time in prison. Or moved to other parts of the country. He wouldn't stop.'

'Dunglas has no previous convictions,' Beth said. 'No prison time.'

'We keep looking into his background,' Callum said. 'Where was he and what was he doing in the nineties?' He paused for a second, before adding, 'And have there been any unsolved disappearances of young women, around the first of February for the past thirty-one years?'

Chapter Forty-Three

Fordley Police Station, Wednesday Evening

Before the briefing broke, the DS from Digital Forensics brought the team up to speed with her findings from the phone data for Penny Lynch.

As only one of two people who had survived a murder attempt, and could potentially give clues to the attacker's identity, the search for Penny had priority. So far, all leads were coming up empty.

'On Tuesday night when the neighbour last saw her,' Brooke was saying, 'Penny's phone pinged from the mast nearest her home on the Butterfield Estate, at 8.47 p.m.' She scrolled through the data on her laptop. 'CCTV puts her at a bus stop on Halifax Road. That's the bus she usually took to get to the Hades Club in Fordley. She made a call to a number from the bus stop at 8.50 p.m.'

'Do we know who she called?' Callum asked.

Brooke was nodding. 'Traced the number to Brenda Coles.'

'Bren,' I said. 'Her friend at the club.'

'Call lasted less than a minute.' Brooke clicked some keys and cast CCTV footage up on the screen.

Everyone swivelled round to look.

A figure in a fur jacket, over a tight skirt and boots, walking away from the bus stop. She looked like she was on the phone.

Brooke continued, 'Penny called to say she'd missed the bus, and was going to walk until the next one came along. Tony secured CCTV from shops along the route.'

The young DS had created a timeline of CCTV footage, showing Penny's progress.

We all watched the grainy image of a small figure walking along roads that were getting less populated. On a freezing January night, after nine o'clock, there weren't many passers-by and most of the shops were shut.

'At 9.04, she made another call. This time to Jimmy Wilcox's phone.'

'Red,' I said, to no one in particular.

Brooke nodded. 'Call lasted just over a minute.'

'With Red's phone missing,' Callum said. 'There's no way of knowing what that was about.'

'Think we can hazard a guess, boss,' Tony said, 'by what happened next.'

He fast-forwarded the images of Penny's progress, until the last few seconds.

'This was captured from CCTV in a pub car park. Time stamped at 9.14 p.m.,' he said. 'Keep watching . . .'

Everyone stared at the screen.

It had begun sleeting. The freezing rain causing horizontal lines to streak across the lens of the camera, affecting the clarity.

Penny pulled up the collar of her jacket and buried her head down. She really wasn't dressed for the weather.

She must have been freezing, I thought as I continued to watch.

A large four-by-four vehicle indicated and pulled in just ahead of her. Penny, head still down, quickened her pace, and as she got level the passenger door opened and she climbed inside.

'Can't see the reg number,' Callum muttered, moving nearer to the screen.

'I sent the images to the Forensic Science Service,' Tony said. 'They can't enhance it enough for a licence plate, but they've identified it as a Ford Ranger. The footage is black and white, but they can say it's a dark colour.'

'Red Wilcox's vehicle,' Beth said, 'is a dark blue Ford Ranger.'

'Could Penny's last call be to Red to ask for a lift?' Callum addressed the room in general.

'Red used to give Penny lifts home from the club,' I chipped in. 'Because, after her attack, she didn't like travelling on her own in the early hours.'

'That's the last image I can find,' Tony said. 'No sign of the vehicle in Fordley that night and Penny never arrived at the Hades Club.'

'Last ping from Penny's phone,' Brooke added, 'was 9.30 p.m. from the mast near Kingsberry village. After that the phone goes dark.'

Which I knew meant either it had been switched off, or Penny had taken the battery out of it and deactivated it. Or maybe dumped it, so she couldn't be traced.

'That's the opposite direction to the Hades Club,' Beth said.

Tony tapped his notes. 'The route from where she got in the vehicle, up to Kingsberry, takes the road across the moors. No CCTV – so, no idea where they went from there.'

'But here's another anomaly,' Brooke said, chewing the end of her pen. 'Red's phone records show that at nine forty-five that night, he called Penny's number. It went unanswered. He continued to call, every half hour or so, until after midnight. Why would he do that, if he'd just picked her up?'

'He obviously dropped her off somewhere,' Beth said. 'Then maybe was calling to make sure she'd arrived safely?'

'Or maybe they had a row in the car?' Tony said. 'She got out and stormed off?' He gave a short laugh. 'My missus has done that. Then you're calling every few minutes to see where she is . . . make sure she's OK.'

'The next day . . . Wednesday,' Tony was saying. 'Red continued to call Penny's number, until that evening.'

'The night he was killed,' I said.

'Her friends all assumed she went into hiding, because of Red's killing,' Callum said. 'But this shows she disappeared the day *before* he died.'

'What we know for sure,' Tony summarised. 'Red's left calling her for the next twenty-four hours, until he's killed at the landfill.'

I sat, silently staring at the information on the whiteboard. The photographs; the map, with its grim little pins; the frozen grainy images from CCTV.

'Red was looking for her,' I murmured. 'Right up until he was killed.'

'Which means she could be implicated in the murder,' Callum said. 'We need to trace her.'

Brooke was scrolling through the call data. 'There are other numbers from Penny's phone provider. I've identified most of them, but there are a couple that are burner phones. No idea who they're registered to. But I'll keep working on it.'

'Circulate those call lists to the team,' Callum said. 'Never know our luck – they may turn up somewhere.'

Chapter Forty-Four

The Moors, Thursday Morning

Harvey bounded ahead of me, across an open field of freshly fallen snow. I followed the deep holes left by his paws as he dug his muzzle into the frost, creating an ice-dome on his nose.

He loved the winter. The new smells and the sight of fresh snow gave him the 'zoomies'. He'd race around in a blur of crazy excitement, like a kid at Christmas.

But his antics were lost on me today. My mind was going over all the seemingly disparate elements of the cases Callum was dealing with. But the knots just seemed to be pulling even tighter.

Frank Heslopp was the DI on Red's murder and attended joint briefings, as that case was linked to Penny Lynch.

But I wasn't privy to everything and certainly not getting anything I could share with Chris McGarry – who, thankfully, had gone quiet for the last few nights. Not that I was sleeping any better.

The details of Rachel and Penny's attacks and the murder of Lorraine Stevens kept scrolling through my mind. I was so lost in thought, I jumped when my phone rang.

It was Callum.

'We've got a positive ID on dental records.'

My breath left me in a frosty plume. 'Lorraine?'

'Yeah.' I could hear him taking a drink, guessing it was his obligatory black coffee. 'I'm going to break the news to the family.'

I couldn't think of a worse job.

'Do you have to be the one to do it?'

'She's been found on my watch, Jo.' He sounded weary. 'I'm SIO on it. I want to speak to the father, in person. He's been waiting over thirty years for news of his daughter.'

'Don't envy you that.'

'Hmm. In other news, got the report back from the botanist.'

'OK.'

Harvey was dancing round my feet. I threw a snowball for him, watching his confusion as he pounced on the spot where it landed but just got a mouthful of snow.

'Want the whole eighteen pages, or just the edited highlights?'

'The short version.'

'The aquatic insects and plants on the skeletal remains are unique to Wytch's Tarn.'

'So, Lorraine's body was put in there . . . in 1994?'

'Looks like it. Apparently, because of all the rain we've had, the water table across that part of the moor has risen to the highest level in a decade. That's what disturbed the remains, which were probably buried in silt deposits at the bottom of the Tarn. As the body shifted, the right arm was detached.'

'But how did the rest of the body end up in the drainage ditch beside the road?'

'After the war, the uplands were drained for "agricultural improvement", which, in that area, meant sheep grazing. They dug hundreds of kilometres of channels.'

A distant memory suddenly came back to me. Conversations with my father as we hiked the moors when I was a teenager.

'Think the locals call them "grips",' I said.

'Clever sod. You could have saved me these eighteen pages.' But I could hear the smile in his voice. 'Yes . . . "grips". In the case of the Tarn, the ground level changed since the original channels were dug in the forties. Some are now under the existing moorland. When the water level rose, they carried the body into the drainage ditch where it was found.'

'Just as Dunglas said,' I recalled. 'The moor . . . giving up its secrets.'

*   *   *

After the call with Callum, I stayed on the moor, sitting on a drystone wall, thinking about everything he'd said.

There was something I was missing, like an itch at the back of my brain that I couldn't scratch. It had been niggling me for days and as I sat on the frozen wall, absently watching Harvey playing in the snow, I let my unconscious ramble along routes of its own.

It was there somewhere. A fact I'd come across or something I'd heard or seen during this investigation.

I replayed conversations from the various team briefings, but it wasn't that. Finally, as I was giving up, it came to me.

Something I'd seen.

I slid off the wall and turned towards the house. 'Harvey . . . come.'

He gave a disgruntled snort as he realised we were heading back and began following more slowly, never as enthusiastic on the return trip.

Chapter Forty-Five

Kingsberry Farm, Thursday Morning

After putting the kettle on the Aga, I hurried down to the office. Harvey followed and sat, sphinx-like on the Chinese rug in front of my desk, watching me boot up the laptop.

'Sorry for the short walk, boy. I'll make it up to you.'

He 'flumped' in disgust, dropping his jowls onto outstretched paws. Not looking impressed.

The kettle whistled on the Aga, and I went down the corridor, into the kitchen to make a pot of tea.

Harvey was already snoring when I returned.

I opened the file of crime scene photographs, looking for the one that had been bothering me.

The silver chain and cross that Lorraine Stevens had been wearing when she died. The one snagged in the ties of the carrier bags and ribbon around her neck, which Elle had removed during the post-mortem.

I enlarged the image as much as I could, without distorting the detail.

The chain was simple enough, but the cross itself had an intriguing design. It caught my attention when I'd first seen it. Something I'd seen before – years ago, when I was a kid.

The sound of the porch door slamming pulled me away from the photo. Harvey was on his feet, while he was still asleep, barking himself awake, as he made for the door.

'It's only Jen,' I called after him.

'Morning,' she called from the kitchen and I could hear the sounds of Harvey pouncing all over her, as if he hadn't seen her for years.

By the time Jen bustled through the door, with Harvey at her heels, I was halfway up the short library ladder, which leaned against my bookcase.

The whole left wall of my office was floor-to-ceiling shelves, with volumes covering every topic on murder, methods and the monsters who committed them. If a murder had been committed since documents had been kept, there would be some reference to it here.

There was something about an actual book that I found far more accessible than reading from a screen. I used the internet as a research tool, like most people. But for me, books were and always had been the foundations of my knowledge. My go-to when I needed a reference.

The information in my own personal archives, here in this room, was so familiar to me that I could usually lay my hand on whatever I needed faster than I could find it on the internet. With the happy bonus that I didn't fall down distracting rabbit holes.

'Careful up there, you,' Jen half-scolded, fussing as usual since my last accident.

Why was it that what I wanted was always on the highest shelf?

It was a thick volume – leather bound and beautiful. Looking like something from Harry Potter. I'd found it in an old bookshop when I was a student and probably hadn't looked at it in years. But I knew, if my hunch was right, I'd find what I needed in its musty-scented pages. I dumped it on my desk, scattering papers.

Jen was looking over my shoulder as I began flicking through.

'Anything I can help with?'

'Not sure.'

While Jen used search engines, I was delving into more ancient texts and it didn't take long before I found what I was looking for.

Chapter Forty-Six

Tarn Hill Tavern, Thursday Afternoon

Logs crackled in the grate, sending a shower of sparks up the chimney of the wide stone fireplace. The warmth was more than welcome as the temperature had plummeted overnight.

I'd parked my Land Rover in the pub car park and just that short walk had left me frozen. I huddled closer to the fire, nursing the warm mug of mulled wine that Stan, the landlord, had coaxed me to order.

'Need something to warm yer cockles, lass, on a day like today.'

He wasn't wrong. The first thick flurries of snow were just beginning to drift past the mullioned windows, heralding worse for later. The sky was heavy with snow and the weathermen were already issuing warnings for high ground. And it didn't get much higher than here, on the top of the Pennines.

The door banged as the person I was here to see made his entrance, accompanied by an almost theatrical howl of freezing wind.

'Usual, Stan,' Tommy Earnshaw called out by way of a greeting. Then came to sit opposite me, resting elbows on his knees as he leaned towards the fire.

'By 'eck, it's thin out there.' He grinned at me, displaying what my father would have called a row of 'tombstone teeth'.

'Want your pint on the bar, Tommy?' Stan called over.

'No, I'll take it here by the fire, with the lass, thanks.'

Stan brought the beer over and we waited until we were alone. The pub was almost empty today. Just a couple eating lunch at a corner table. Most sensible people probably staying away from such a remote place with bad weather forecast.

Tommy took a sip from his glass, wiping froth from his top lip. 'Not every day I get a phone call from a pretty girl, inviting me for a pint.'

'Thanks for coming, Tommy.'

'You know I'm here every day anyway, lass. What's to do?'

'You've worked these moors all your life. Know them like the back of your hand.'

'Aye.'

'You'd have been working thirty years ago?'

He grinned. 'Back when I was young and even more good-looking, aye.'

'Do you recall anything unusual going on around Wytch's Tarn in those days?'

He rubbed his bristly chin, his eyes going to the fire. 'I saw lots of strange stuff, all over the moors in them days.' His sharp eyes met and held mine. 'But you're looking for something specific, lass. Want to tell me what?'

Knowing how much Tommy loved a good story, I didn't want to lead him so he'd just spin some yarn to keep me happy.

'What kind of people were drawn to the Tarn?'

He shrugged. 'Same as today. Hippies and them that's interested in its history.'

I pulled a picture of Dunglas up on my phone. 'Do you know this man?'

He squinted at the small screen. 'Know *of* him. But don't *know* him, personally, like.'

'Know what, of him?'

The media had run the news that a fifty-five-year-old man had been arrested on suspicion of the kidnap and attempted murder of a female hiker. But his name and photograph hadn't been released – yet.

'He's the chap that runs that ghosty magazine. I've seen him around lately. Came in here once, to get warm before setting off over to Wytch's Tarn. But never spoken to him.'

I studied him for a moment, debating the best way to draw from him what I suspected he knew.

Finally, I pulled a sheet of paper from my pocket. I'd photocopied it from my old leather book before leaving the office.

It was an image of the same cross Lorraine Stevens had been wearing. But instead of being cast in silver, this one was woven from rushes. Four pointed arms, set at right angles from a diamond shaped centre, tied at the ends with string.

Tommy stared at it for a moment, then began nodding slowly. 'I've seen that.'

'At the Tarn?'

He simply nodded, taking another sip from his pint.

'Talk to me,' was all I said, leaving him to answer any way he wanted.

'Bit like Stonehenge.'

I frowned. 'What is?'

'The Tarn.' He was staring into the fire. 'Got a history. Draws them types. At certain times of year.'

'What types?'

He stayed silent.

This wasn't like Tommy.

Usually, it was hard to shut him up. Spinning his tales whether anyone wanted to listen or not. This reticence was so out of character, it was intriguing, and more than a little unnerving.

I was desperate to ask my questions, but realised silence was more powerful. So, I let it stretch out between us, until I could almost see its thread, like a tangible thing. Strained and quivering. Aching to be broken. Finally, Tommy did.

'Witches.' He said it so quietly, I almost missed it.

'What?'

He gazed into the fire, as if he was watching it play out in the flames, from all those years ago.

'Witches. As real as any from Old Ma Hewitt's day. Real as I'm sitting here.'

'They gathered at the Tarn?'

'Aye.' He sipped his pint. 'I'd seen fires round the Tarn for years, knew people went there. Thought it were harmless until they started taking my sheep.'

'What?'

'One year, I were missing a ewe. Went looking for her and found 'em at the Tarn. They were drinking her milk. Didn't harm her and when it were over, they let her go back to the flock. So, I let it pass. But I were watching out for them after that.'

'Did it happen again?'

'Not for another year.'

I tapped the picture in his hand. 'And this?'

'They all held them crosses. Dead of night and freezing cold. They'd have a big bonfire at the Tarn. All dressed in white robes. Dancing and chanting round the fire. They'd take a ewe and drink her milk. Then they'd throw them crosses onto the bonfire.'

'Doesn't sound too bad,' I said, quietly.

'Aye, if that'd been all.'

'What else?' I was almost whispering.

'One year, I went over to watch . . . hidden like.'

'Go on . . .'

'They had one lass in the middle of it all. In white robes. They chanted and whatnot, then took her to the edge of the Tarn and stripped her. Washed her in the freezing-cold water, kind of dunking her under. Thought they might do a Ma Hewitt on her. But then they brought her to the edge of the bonfire and laid her down. Then they all . . .' His voice trailed off and he couldn't meet my eyes.

'What?'

'Men and women . . . both.' He didn't want to say it, couldn't utter the words.

I took a guess. 'They had sex with her?'

He nodded. Dropping his head, as if ashamed at the very thought.

'Not proud that I watched it, lass.' He looked up, taking a long breath. 'But I were a young man then.'

I reached out and touched his arm. 'It's OK.'

'Well, I'm ashamed of it, lass. Wouldn't normally tell it, but can see it's important. For something you're working on?'

I nodded. 'Yes. It is important.' I produced a photograph of Lorraine Stevens. 'Have you ever seen this woman before?'

'Aye. She was the one on the ground.'

I was surprised and said so.

'How could you be so sure, Tommy? It was a long time ago, and dark that night.'

He was silent as we both sat, listening to the crackle of the fire. Then, he finished his pint, wiping his sleeve across his mouth.

'There was enough light from the bonfire to see her clear enough that night. But maybe I wouldn't have remembered after all these years if she hadn't gone missing a couple of years later.' He spoke quietly, shaking his head. 'Her picture were on posters all over. I recognised her from that night. I should've said summat. But what I'd seen were a long time before she disappeared. And truth be told, I didn't want to say I'd spied on 'em, like some peeping Tom – even though it's my name.' He tried a smile, but didn't quite pull it off.

'I understand.' I smiled back.

'They'd been there every year.' He stood up and began fastening his coat. 'I'd see the bonfire from across the moors, but I never went to watch again. Just stayed near, so I could check on my ewes.' He stopped, with a hand on the back of his chair.

'So, this ritual couldn't have anything to do with her going missing. That's how I figured it. So, it didn't matter if I said nowt.'

'Did you ever see them on the moor at any other time?'

He shook his head. 'Just around New Moon.'

He put his empty glass on the table.

'Do you want another pint, Tommy?'

'Nah, lass, no stomach for it now.'

'Sorry.'

He made to go, then turned back. 'Between us, lass . . . eh?'

I didn't reply, knowing I couldn't promise that – not really.

He waved to Stan behind the bar, but stopped with his hand on the door handle. Turning back to me.

'She's still alive – after a fashion.'

'Who?'

'The witch who ran it all. Lives in the same house in Keelham.'

'Who? Where?'

So many questions.

'Locals back then called it the "Hippy House". Willow Farm.'

Chapter Forty-Seven

Fordley Police Station, Thursday Evening

Callum was sitting in his office, studying the photos and notes I'd strewn across his desk.

'So, this is Saint Brigid's cross?' He was looking at the image of the silver cross from Lorraine Stevens' body.

'Yes . . . and no.'

He scraped his chair back. 'Can see I'm going to need caffeine for this one.'

He went to the percolator that dripped treacle-like coffee into a jug on his bookshelf.

'The original Brigid was a pagan goddess. In fact, she was considered one of the most powerful Celtic gods. Pre-dating Christianity by hundreds of years.'

That's what I'd been looking for in my tome back at the farm. Not the Christian version, but the Celtic Wiccan history I had vague memories of as a child.

'The Church pinched Brigid, transfiguring her into a Christian saint, to ease the conversion of Irish pagans to Christianity.'

He turned back with a mug, shifting papers to make room for it as he sat back down. 'OK.'

'Back in Ireland, you still find these crosses made out of rushes or straw. The superstitious hang them around the hearth or over doorways to protect their homes from evil. Traditionally, they keep them for a year and then burn them at "Imbolc", to destroy all the evil they've collected.'

'Imbolc?' He raised an eyebrow.

'Wiccans hold a festival in honour of the pagan goddess, Brigid, at the halfway point between the winter solstice and the spring equinox. "Imbolc". Some people call it "Candlemas".'

'What do you call it?'

I paused for just a second before the big reveal. 'First of February.'

'Right up Daniel Dunglas's street. Pagan, occult stuff. It's what he's into.'

Then I told him about my conversation earlier with Tommy Earnshaw.

'He called them witches,' I said. 'But I don't think they were. Not in the traditional sense anyway.'

'What other kind of sense is there, where witches are concerned?'

I ignored that. 'I've done some research and I think what he saw was a pagan circle. Whatever that ritual was, it was a corruption of the traditional Imbolc. Probably a hybrid of various rituals and beliefs they've come up with themselves . . . Or one that's evolved over the years.'

'Why did they steal the ewe?' He frowned.

'In Celtic folklore, the word "imbolc" means "in the belly of the mother". It's all about fertility and rebirth. Sheep are starting to get pregnant and produce milk. Life's milk is a part of the symbolic hope for spring.'

Callum pulled a face. 'Glad I'm C. of E.'

I tapped the map on his desk.

'I think Wytch's Tarn is important to them because of its association with the witch trials, but also, pagan myths about Brigid say she was born with a flame over her head. There have been a lot of sightings of "corpse lights" – will-o'-the-wisps – on the Tarn. Especially at this time of the year, when the vegetation at the bottom releases gas as it rots.'

'The sex, presumably, relates to the fertility part of the myth?'

I said nothing. Watching as he put all the pieces together. 'And Tommy Earnshaw's certain the woman in the ritual was Lorraine Stevens?'

I nodded. 'It's something he's never forgotten, even after thirty years. What he saw that night still bothers him.'

He took a long, weary breath. 'Went to see her father today.'

I suddenly felt ashamed that I'd forgotten about that.

'How did it go?'

He pursed his lips. 'Much as you'd expect. Even after three decades, he was still praying she'd come back home one day.'

Families of the lost. Never giving up on their loved ones. Holding on to the thinnest thread of hope. As fragile as spider's silk and just as easily broken.

I'd met so many in my work and it always affected me deeply. As a mother – wondering how I would feel if my son just disappeared one day. The unbearable pain of never knowing what happened. Refusing to relinquish the possibility that the person was out there . . . somewhere. Just a heartbeat away.

'He said he wanted to see her . . . his daughter.'

That thought made my stomach drop. Knowing his precious child was reduced to a skeleton.

'I can understand the need,' I said. 'But . . . God, he can't see her like that.'

'Tried to talk him out of it without being too graphic. Explained that she'd been dead for thirty years, that there were scant remains.'

'And?'

'It was the most heartbreaking argument I've ever lost.'

'Surely, no one's going to let him see her as she is?'

He shrugged. 'It's his right . . . if he insists.' He took a mouthful of coffee and pulled a face. 'When I left the house felt different.'

'Know what you mean.'

I'd experienced it before. A shift from hope to grief that seemed to change the very fabric of a place. Years of emotion invested, yearning for a happy ending, suddenly transformed into utter despair.

It changed people. Places. Lives. Forever.

There was a tap on the door and Beth stuck her head inside the office. 'Boss, you need to see this.'

He gestured for her to come in.

She was clutching a sheaf of papers.

'Got a list from the 1994 census. People living at the small-holding – Willow Farm, Keelham.'

The Hippy House.

I watched him scan the names.

'Alma Byrd,' Beth explained. 'Owned the house then and still does.'

'Tommy said the high priestess of the pagan circle owned the house,' I said to Callum.

'High priestess?' Beth raised her eyebrows. 'You're shitting me.'

'I'll call a briefing,' Callum said distractedly as he scanned the list. 'Explain it all then. Don't recognise any of the names on here.' He sounded disappointed.

'Me neither.' Beth was already overlaying the page in his hand with a second. 'But these are the names of everyone who'd been at the party the night Lorraine Stevens went missing.'

Callum raised his eyebrows and gave a thin smile as he held the list out to me. 'Recognise anyone?'

My eyes ran quickly down the names, missing it on the first pass. Then I read more slowly. Seeing it the second time.

'Terry Smith.'

Callum flicked the page with his finger.

'Before he changed his name to Daniel Dunglas.'

Chapter Forty-Eight

Well Heads, Keelham, Friday Morning

The forecast was for snow. Locals didn't need a TV meteorologist to tell them about it, though. They could smell it in the air. Feel it in the biting wind that was bringing a cold front down from the Arctic.

It was only a fifteen-minute drive from my farmhouse in Kingsberry to Keelham village, a fact I was thankful for in this weather.

My old Land Rover Defender felt like it was made out of iron girders. Even with the heater on full blast, it was like sitting in a meat locker. I could see my breath and had to keep wiping condensation from the windscreen with my sleeve.

Callum had asked me to meet him and Beth at the place we'd dubbed 'The Hippy House'.

He wanted to speak to Alma Byrd, the owner. Informally for now, but that was likely to change, depending on what she told us. Beth was to take notes of the whole conversation and I was there as an 'observer'.

Not the first time Callum had used me as a human tuning fork. Picking up the nuances of body language and vocal intonation. In short, people reading so that he could get my impressions after the meeting. See how they compared to his own.

As I turned off Brighouse Road into Well Heads, I spotted Callum's unmarked BMW parked on the right-hand side, by the open, wooden five-bar gate that marked the boundary of the smallholding.

The driver's door of the BMW opened, as I did an illegal U-turn in the empty road and pulled up behind him.

Callum climbed out, pulling the collar of his coat up around his ears. He came to the passenger side, then realised my old vehicle didn't have electric windows and tugged the door open.

'Follow us up the drive and park up.'

'Morning to you too.'

He pulled a face. 'Sorry.'

I laughed. 'It's OK. Does Mrs Byrd know we're coming?'

He glanced towards the farmhouse, which looked like it hadn't changed in a hundred years. 'Beth rang ahead this morning. A carer answered the phone and said he'd pass the message on.'

'Carer?'

'Apparently, Mrs Byrd had a stroke a few years ago.'

Before I could say anything to that he slammed the door and was already jogging to his car.

The driveway was more of an uneven track, which bounced me from side to side as I navigated ruts and potholes.

The fields, on either side, were overgrown and littered with bits of old farm machinery. A small rusty tractor, like something from the days of *The Larkins*, was parked at the edge of a meadow, as if someone had just walked away from it in the middle of harvesting.

Callum parked beside a new Nissan Micra, which looked incongruous amid all the decay.

I abandoned the Land Rover on the grass verge beside the track and joined Beth and Callum on the doorstep as he knocked.

The door was answered by a tall, well-built man I estimated to be in his fifties, wearing the blue tunic of a health care worker. Grey-streaked brown hair escaped in tangled fronds from a beaded headband that matched the bangle on his wrist.

'Zachary White?' Callum smiled, holding up his warrant card. 'DCI Callum Ferguson, West Yorkshire Police. My DC, Beth Hastings, called you earlier about visiting Mrs Byrd?'

'Please, call me Zac, everyone does.' He cast a curious glance towards me.

'This is Dr Jo McCready.' Callum made the introductions. 'Consultant Forensic Psychologist – she's assisting with our enquiries.'

Satisfied, he stepped to one side. 'You'd better come in.'

We all dutifully followed Zac down a dimly lit corridor, which ran the length of the old house.

There was a faint smell of disinfectant and bleach, which wasn't altogether unpleasant.

The corridor led to a huge lounge at the back of the house. Light streamed in from large sash windows that overlooked the fields at the back. An old woman sat in a high-backed chair beside the window – her face turned away from us, towards the view.

The room was what my mother would describe as 'faded'.

Furniture, once trendy in the seventies, now looked depressing and well past its best. Brown and mustard patterned curtains matched the worn carpet, sofa and armchairs. The whole gloomy space was barely illuminated by a centre light with a single bulb covered by a cream, paper ball-shade, which reminded me of the one I'd had in my bedroom, as a teenager.

Crackling coal cast an orange glow from a large stone fireplace, with framed photographs on the mantel. It looked cosy, but the heat and the glow only seemed to reach half the room. The large space on our right was dim and felt chilly. The furniture had been removed to make room for a hospital bed with a large hoist beside it.

'Alma.' Zac touched the old lady's arm. 'The police I told you about are here.'

We stood in a semicircle around the chair, as the woman slowly turned her face to us.

I wasn't sure what I expected the high priestess of a pagan circle to look like, but ask me to draw her and I'd probably come up with an approximation of the 75-year-old Alma Byrd. Apart from the huge hooked nose and obligatory hairy wart, everything else pretty much matched my imagination. Long unruly white hair, framing a heavily wrinkled face, with thin pale lips and the unhealthy yellow pallor of the sick, who rarely ventured into sunlight. The droop at the right corner of her mouth and slackened facial muscles, no doubt a result of the stroke, gave her an unfriendly expression.

But it was her eyes that struck me.

Dark and hard as marbles – staring at us with an intensity that bordered on uncomfortable.

Alma's right arm lay across her body – the hand, palm up in her lap.

'Mrs Byrd's stroke,' I spoke quietly to Zac. 'Was it left hemisphere of the cerebrum?'

He nodded, as Callum shot me a look. Zac saved me the trouble of explaining.

'It affected Alma's speech and she lost the use of her right side – arm and hand mainly,' he said, going to stand behind the old lady's chair. 'She can hear and understand everything you say. You can direct your questions to her. Some words, you'll understand. Those you don't, I'll interpret. Her speech is quite limited.'

Just how limited was made clear when Alma grunted, gesturing to us with a lift of her chin.

Callum understood. 'I'm Detective Chief Inspector Callum Ferguson. West Yorkshire Police.' He introduced Beth and then me.

Alma looked at each of us, but her eyes stayed unnervingly on me. Perhaps because he'd said I was a doctor.

'I'm a forensic psychologist.' I smiled.

If I thought an explanation of the *kind* of doctor might help, I was wrong.

Alma cleared her throat and attempted to spit in my direction. The weakened side of her mouth affected her aim – landing a dribble of spittle on her own chin.

Zac hastily pulled a tissue from a box on the chair-side table. 'I'm sorry,' he said, wiping the old lady's chin. 'Alma doesn't like doctors. Or police.'

Instinctively, Callum took a step back.

I didn't want my presence to antagonise her so went to stand with my back to the coal fire. From here, I had a good view of the room, especially Alma, while effectively taking myself out of the arena.

'Are you Mrs Byrd's full-time carer?' Callum asked Zac.

'I'm here every morning and I cover periods when Mark needs me. I have other clients, weekday afternoons.'

'Alma's son, Mark Byrd?' Callum knew who lived in the house from the council records.

'Yes.'

'Do you live in?'

'Not exactly. I have a room here, if any night-sitting is needed. If Mark's working late or he needs a break. But I have my own place in Cullingworth.'

Callum made a note, nodding slowly.

'What work does Mark do?'

'He's a courier, for a local company. Deliveries.'

'Is he working now?'

'No. He does the shopping and runs errands on Friday mornings. He shouldn't be long.'

'The car parked outside, whose is that?'

'Mine.' Zac smiled. 'Do a lot of miles in my job.'

Callum took the chair opposite the old lady, putting him at eye level, but hopefully out of spitting distance.

'Mrs Byrd, I'm here to ask about Lorraine Stevens.'

Alma glared at him, then her lips twisted. 'No.' That was clear enough.

258

Callum produced a photograph and held it up. 'You remember Lorraine?'

Alma turned her face to the window.

'Mrs Byrd, we know Lorraine lived here, with you in this house, for several years during the late eighties and early nineties, before moving in with her boyfriend, Max Radcliffe.'

Alma continued to stare out of the window in silence.

I watched her unaffected left hand, laid on the blanket covering her knees. Her whole body was still. But the emotional energy she was giving off was so antagonistic, it was almost tangible.

Zac broke the uncomfortable silence. 'I might be able to help.'

'You knew Lorraine?' Callum asked.

'Yes. I spent a lot of time here in those days.'

'Go on.'

He shifted, perching on the arm of the chair beside his patient.

'My family lived in the village. This was a cool place to hang out. I mean, my parents were that uptight, they even starched their underwear.' He gave a short laugh. 'I was the typical rebellious teenager, you know? Alma's place was so laidback. A drop-in . . . commune. It attracted a lot of the youth. I mean, let's face it, there was bugger all else to do round here.'

'How often were you here?'

'Most days.'

'Tell us about Lorraine.'

'She was a few years older than me. Pretty. Everyone liked her.'

'What about this man?' Callum showed Zac an image on his iPad. I could see it was Daniel Dunglas

The other man studied it for a minute, then his eyes widened. 'Oh, my God, is that Terry?'

'Terry Smith – yes.'

Zac squinted at the picture again. 'He looks different there. Hardly recognised him.'

259

'When was the last time you saw him?'

Zac pursed his lips. 'God knows . . . years ago. He certainly didn't look like that picture.'

Callum held the screen in front of Mrs Byrd. 'Do you remember Terry?' She nodded.

'How often was Terry here?'

Zac gave a light shrug. 'All the time. Like the rest of us.'

'How did you spend your time when you were here, Zac?' Callum made the question sound so innocent.

'We just flopped, you know? Drank booze. Smoked pot. There were no real rules here. Everyone chilled. Did their own thing.'

'Were you at the party, the night Lorraine disappeared?'

Beth was scanning her notes. 'Your name isn't among those who were questioned.'

'That's because I wasn't at the house when the police came next day.'

'You didn't come forward when they asked for witnesses that night.' Callum's tone was deliberately non-judgemental.

'Didn't need the hassle,' Zac said simply. 'Besides, I had nothing to tell. I'd arrived earlier in the day, to hang out. Everyone was waiting for Lorraine to arrive, but she never did.'

'Did you leave the party at any time?' Callum asked.

'It wasn't a—'

Alma made a guttural sound, gripping Zac's knee with her good hand. He glanced down at her and patted her hand.

'Wasn't a party?' Callum ventured.

Zac said nothing, just continued to stroke Alma's hand. Watching Callum carefully, like a mongoose in front of a snake.

'It was Imbolc that night, wasn't it?' Callum pressed. 'And you were gathering at the house before a ritual up at Wytch's Tarn. That's why everyone was waiting for Lorraine Stevens, wasn't it?'

For a moment, I thought Zac was going to tough it out and stay silent.

'We can do this here,' Callum said, 'or down at Fordley police station. It's up to you?'

Finally, the man took a breath, looking down at Alma. 'They obviously know about the circle, Alma,' he said gently. 'Might as well tell them. There's nothing to hide.'

'No!' Alma spat the word out, like broken glass. Then muttered something we couldn't make out.

'She said "it's sacred",' Zac translated helpfully.

The bony fingers of the old lady's left hand gripped the blanket, her knuckles showing white with the pressure.

'It's a corruption.' I couldn't bite my lip any longer. 'To keep referring to your rituals as Imbolc, and that they were somehow sacred, is offensive to true Wiccans.'

'What the hell would *you* know?' Zac rounded on me.

'Enough to see that what Alma here came up with was a debasement of true Celtic beliefs . . .'

Just then, the front door banged 'Hello?' a man's voice called from the hallway.

'That's Mark.' Zac sounded relieved.

A tall, broad-shouldered man pushed the lounge door open with his foot and struggled in with several shopping bags, bringing the scent of cold air in with him.

'Sorry I wasn't . . . here when you arrived.' He shrugged out of his jacket, which Zac helpfully took from him. 'There was a queue in the chemist. Had to wait . . . for Mother's meds.'

He had a disfluency in his speech. Pauses where they shouldn't be, which made me suspect he'd suffered from a stammer in the past.

Callum made the introductions again, as Zac picked up the shopping and made a hasty retreat into the kitchen.

Callum recapped why we were here, though I suspected Mark already knew. No doubt Zac had filled him in during their earlier phone call.

I stayed in front of the fire, half listening, taking my chance to study the room.

The walls were covered with framed watercolours and sketches depicting local scenes. I walked over to take a closer look at a sketch of Wytch's Tarn, aware that Alma was watching me. I could feel those hard eyes boring into my back.

I deliberately spent longer than I needed, examining the drawing, until I heard grunting from across the room.

Alma was waving her left arm in my direction. She obviously didn't like me taking an interest.

'These are good.' I gave her my most innocent smile. 'Who did them?'

'Zac,' she said – clear as a bell. Dropping her arm back in her lap, as she glowered at me.

This was a woman used to being in control. More than that, used to commanding the people around her.

Even though he spoke to her informally, there was a deference in the way Zac conducted himself around Alma Byrd. A respect, probably instilled in those early days, when he used this house as a refuge.

It was clear to me that, despite the limitations imposed by the stroke, Alma Byrd was still a force to be reckoned with.

Chapter Forty-Nine

Willow Farm, Keelham, Friday Morning

'I understand you want to ask about Lorraine Stevens?' Mark was saying to Callum. 'Can I ask why after all these years?'

Zac had come from the kitchen and perched on the edge of an armchair, listening to the exchange.

'Her body was discovered a few days ago.'

Mark slowly sat down on a hard-backed chair beside his mother. 'Oh,' was all he said. He put his hand over his mother's. Squeezing it, in a seemingly reassuring gesture. Alma's glassy eyes watched his profile, as if transfixed.

'Were you here, when Lorraine disappeared, in 1994?' Callum asked, as Beth made notes.

He glanced at his mother, as if she would say something. She just continued to stare, uncharacteristically quiet.

'No. I was . . . living in America. Emigrated the year before. When I was eighteen.'

'Quite a move, at that age.'

'I had a job over there . . . for a few months. Enjoyed the life. There was nothing for me here.'

'What brought you back to the UK?'

'My mother. Her health wasn't good. She . . . made us promise not to put her in a home. So, after the stroke, in 2020, I came back. Once everyone could travel again . . . to take care of her.'

'Quite a decision.' I spoke for the first time, drawing everyone's attention. 'Uprooting, after you've made a life for yourself in America.'

Mark's right hand was balled up, rubbing his right thigh, in an unconsciously nervous gesture.

'It was that . . . or put her in . . . residential care.'

Alma made a sound in her throat and pulled her good hand away from beneath her son's. Gesturing into open air. He absently patted her arm. 'It's OK, Mother.' Replacing her hand into her lap and giving it a squeeze.

'You have no family here who could have helped out?' I kept my tone light.

'I'm an only child,' he said simply.

'You could have arranged for carers,' I suggested.

'We did.'

'We?' It was Callum.

'The agency . . . I mean Zac.'

'Mark knew I worked for an agency,' Zac said. 'Alma had taken a few falls, and needed carers, so he contacted me from the States and I organised it. But after the stroke five years ago, she needed full-time.'

'I thought it best if Mother . . . had someone she knew.' Mark gave Zac a half-smile. 'She wouldn't have outsiders here.'

'Outsiders'. Interesting choice of word.

'Still,' I persisted, 'leaving family and friends in America?'

'No . . . family over there.' Mark absently rubbed his thigh.

I indicated the paintings and sketches on the walls. 'These yours, Zac?'

Zac nodded. 'That's how I relax. Sketching and painting outdoors.'

Callum cleared his throat – a sign he was getting impatient.

'Did you know Lorraine Stevens?' he asked Mark.

'Yes. She lived here.'

'How long for?'

Alma made a sound and Mark squeezed her hand. 'Moved in when I was . . . twelve or thirteen.'

Callum checked his notes. 'She'd be nineteen then?'

Mark nodded. 'I left in 1993. She . . . moved in with her boy-friend around the time I left.'

Callum pulled up the same image of Dunglas that he'd shown Zac.

'Do you remember this man?'

Mark stared at the iPad then I saw the moment of recogni-tion behind his eyes. 'Looks like Terry.'

Callum nodded. 'How did he get on with Lorraine?'

Mark shrugged and looked at Zac, who took his cue.

'Same as everyone, I suppose. They were friends.'

'No arguments between them, no bad feelings?' Callum prompted.

'Not that I remember.' Zac nodded towards the old lady, who was watching everyone intently. 'Alma wouldn't allow discord. If people didn't get along, they weren't allowed to stay. She preserved harmony.'

I waited, knowing what was coming. Interested to see what reaction the next tranche of questions would elicit.

'You mean, they weren't allowed into the pagan circle?' Callum dropped the question almost casually.

Mark became suddenly very still.

'They know,' Zac said to Mark. 'About the rituals up at the Tarn.'

Mark looked from Beth to Callum. 'Not everyone here . . . was part of the circle. Some of the kids just came here to . . . listen to music and get away from their parents. The circle was separate.'

His mother was staring at him, with a look I couldn't quite decipher. Anger? Fear? The stroke affected her facial muscles in a way that made reading her more difficult.

'My mother didn't force her beliefs on anyone. Some were involved, others weren't.'

'What about you?' Callum asked.

'He was just a kid,' Zac interrupted.

'I'm sure Mark can speak for himself,' Callum replied, more calmly.

'I . . . yes. I mean, I'd grown up with Mother's beliefs. Of course.' His eyes darted from Callum to Zac and back again, like a hunted animal.

'Did you witness what went on at Wytch's Tarn?'

Alma suddenly became more animated. Raising her left arm to point at Callum, her knees beneath the blanket moving with restless agitation. 'Out!' she shouted. 'Out!'

Callum said nothing. Just watched Mark, waiting for a response.

Alma's son ran a hand across his face. 'It's not . . . illegal to practise paganism.'

'No, it's not,' Callum agreed, with a thin smile that didn't reach his eyes. 'Until the woman at the centre of the circle ends up murdered.'

Mark suddenly got up and paced over to the window, looking like he'd rather crawl under the sofa than have to talk about any of this.

'My mother was a pagan, my father too. I accepted it as normal, growing up . . . but I didn't . . . was never really part of it. As soon as I was old enough, I stepped out of it all.'

'Where's your father now?' Callum carried on, as if we were talking about the weather, not sexual rites around a bonfire on the moors.

A low moan came from Alma, like the growl of a predatory animal. Her eyes bored into Callum, as if by sheer force of will she could eviscerate him.

I could only imagine what she was like before the stroke. It was a terrifying thought.

'I never knew him. There's no name on my birth certificate.'

I could feel the pent-up frustration emanating from Zac like a tangible thing. Finally, he couldn't stand any more.

'Mark wasn't even here when Lorraine Stevens disappeared. Why do you have to push him like this?'

Mark held up a hand, as if halting traffic. 'It's OK, Zac.' He turned to Callum. 'I don't think my mother ever knew for sure who my father was. The commune was very sexually . . . liberated. Does it matter?'

'He's right!' Zac exploded, getting to his feet to stand beside Alma, putting his arm around her shoulders. 'What the hell has any of this to do with Lorraine's disappearance?'

'Just establishing who's who and how everyone in this, er, commune, interacted together.'

Callum turned his attention to Alma. 'We know, Mrs Byrd, that on the first of February, every year, your circle engaged in rituals up at Wytch's Tarn. Fertility rites were practised. There was a bonfire, where these symbols were burned.'

He held his iPad out to her, with the image of the original Saint Brigid's cross, woven in rushes and tied with string.

I watched her eyes. They never moved from Callum. Never even glanced at the picture.

He swiped his finger across the screen, pulling up a second image. The silver cross taken from Lorraine Stevens' body.

'Lorraine was wearing this when she was killed. Do you recognise it?'

Again, Alma's icy stare didn't move. Didn't look.

'What about this?' He swiped to the image of the ribbon.

The old lady's breathing changed, though her eyes stayed firmly fixed on Callum. Her chest rose and fell more quickly and the breath left her in gusts, pushed through those pale lips.

'Enough!' Zac shouted.

He stood up, ripping open the front of his tunic and pulling down the neck of the T-shirt he wore underneath.

Around his neck was a silver chain, with the same Brigid's cross as Lorraine.

He leaned over his patient, gently opening her collar, looping his finger around the chain Alma wore. Holding it out for us all to see, the silver cross dangling through his fingers.

'We all wore them,' he snapped. 'Alma gave them to everyone who was initiated into the circle as a gift. A sign of acceptance. Of belonging.' His eyes blazed with anger. 'So what?'

'Do you have one?' Callum asked Mark, who was standing, as if frozen to the spot, watching in horror at what was going on.

'No.'

I watched Zac gently replace the chain inside Alma's clothing and fasten the buttons on her blouse.

'I didn't . . . share my mother's beliefs,' he said quietly. 'Was never part of the circle.'

'What about the ribbon?' I spoke to the room, interested to see what reaction my question would elicit.

Mark looked blank and just shook his head.

Zac glared at me, his eyes flashing an anger that bubbled just beneath his benign façade. 'I've never seen it before.'

Callum leaned forward in his chair, directing himself to Zac. 'Over the years, did you take part in the rituals at the Tarn?'

'Yes.' Zac's chin jutted defiantly. 'So what?'

'And Terry Smith?'

'Yes.'

'What about 1994? When Lorraine Stevens didn't turn up. Did the ritual still go ahead?'

'Yes.'

'Was Terry at the Tarn that night?'

He thought for a moment. 'No.'

'But he was at the house earlier in the day?'

'Yes. He left before we went up to the moor.'

'Did he say where he was going?'

Zac's breath left him in exasperation. 'I don't remember. It was thirty years ago, for Christ's sake.'

'So how come you remember he wasn't at the Tarn?'

'Because it was the only year I'd been, when Lorraine wasn't there.' Zac's lips twitched in a half-smile. 'I remember vividly who took part, because of her replacement during the fertility rites.'

'Who?' Callum asked, in the same even tone.

'Me.'

Chapter Fifty

Kingsberry Farm, Saturday Morning

There had been a blizzard overnight, covering the moorland in a pillowy white duvet of fresh snow. It drifted in smooth curves over the drystone walls, obliterating familiar boundaries and landmarks. Transforming the hills into an almost featureless landscape.

I gazed out across the glittering groundswells, as I pressed the phone to my ear with frozen fingers.

'We're having Dunglas produced from Armley prison. Brought in for further questioning,' Callum was saying.

I stood beside the track, knowing that if I kept moving, I'd lose the phone signal. Harvey stopped a few yards ahead of me and looked back, curiously.

'What did you think of *The Addams Family* yesterday?' Callum asked.

'Zac's hardly Uncle Fester,' I laughed.

'No – he's weirder. Can you imagine him, at the centre of fertility rites?'

Tommy Earnshaw's words came back to me.

'Men and women, both,' I muttered.

'Urghh, that mean's him and Alma . . .' There was an audible shudder down the phone. 'Enough to put me off sex for life.'

'He would have had sex with Lorraine – at previous ceremonies – before she went missing,' I murmured thoughtfully.

'They *all* did, by the sound of it.'

'And yet he never asked about her.'

'What?'

'When you said her body had been found. He never asked how she'd died, or where she'd been discovered.'

There was a silence as he thought about it. 'None of them did, now you mention it.'

'What do you make of the son?'

'Mark? Feel sorry for the poor sod, being brought up around that lot. No wonder he scarpered to the other side of the world.'

'Hmm,' I agreed. 'Alma Byrd doesn't strike me as the maternal type.'

'Anyway, doesn't matter what I think of him,' Callum went on. 'He's outside our timeline when Lorraine went missing.'

'He never said what his job was . . . in the States.'

'Can answer that one.' I heard him leafing through paperwork. 'Started work as a volunteer in the visitors' centre at North Cascades National Park, in Washington State. It was a summer job. He got on well, played nice with the others and eventually they offered him a full-time position. That's when he decided to stay. He even took out US citizenship. I'll email everything over.'

'OK.'

'Meanwhile, we're doing a deep-dive into Zac White's background.'

'He's alibied for the night Lorraine vanished.' I stated the obvious. 'At the house all that day and went with everyone to the Tarn that night.'

'Everyone involved with that commune, pagan circle or whatever they like to call it is a serious person of interest. All going to be looked at again.'

'Be interested to know what Dunglas has to say for himself when you re-interview him.'

I'd always felt he knew more than he was letting on. After yesterday, I was even more certain.

'None of them admitted to knowing anything about the ribbon,' Callum was saying.

'And no evidence that it formed part of their rituals,' I added. 'So, when Dunglas saw it around Rachel's neck it may not have meant anything to him.'

'Unless he put it there,' Callum said. 'And I want to hear what he has to say when we show him the silver cross found on Lorraine's body. He was part of Alma Byrd's weird little group so he must have been given one too.'

I took a lungful of cold air to clear my thoughts. 'He still doesn't fit, for me,' I said, almost to myself.

'What bit?' Callum snorted. 'Taking part in pagan rituals up at the Tarn, but conveniently forgot to mention it? Found leaning over the half-dead body of a girl on the moors, with only his word for the fact that someone else attacked her? Her DNA in the boot of his car? Or the fact that he knew Lorraine Stevens before she went missing? *Intimately* knew her, at that—'

'Yes, but—'

'*And*,' he cut across me, 'left the house at the crucial time Lorraine disappeared? Bloody hell, Jo, what more do you want?'

'I deal in behaviours, remember?'

The volume went up as he got more animated. 'But his behaviours are suspicious too. Like skulking round the moors at the dead of night. Returning to the scene of Rachel's attack. Which no one would have known about, if you hadn't been there.'

'That's just it.' I was trying to verbalise a hunch. An instinctive feeling I trusted. Something intuitive that preceded hard knowledge. 'The attacks.'

'What about them?'

'I see rage in them.'

'Dunglas doesn't like women. That much is obvious.'

'He's uncomfortable around females,' I conceded. 'But it's contempt, not hatred.'

'That kind of internal pressure can be enough,' Callum persisted.

'That man couldn't build up enough internal pressure for a decent fart, never mind murderous rage.'

'Zac White has a temper,' he said, thoughtfully.

'Certainly does. Easily triggered too.'

'Well, you follow your instincts, Jo, and I'll follow mine. Never know, they might lead to the same place.'

Chapter Fifty-One

Kingsberry Farm, Saturday Afternoon

I sat at my desk, absently doodling, as I thought about everything we knew.

So many disjointed pieces. Lines of enquiry that seemed to have no connection, and yet must have . . . somehow.

Frustrated, I swivelled my chair and gazed out of the window, at huge flakes of snow drifting lazily onto my frozen lawn, their gentle dance choreographed by a light breeze.

According to Callum, his DI, Frank Heslopp, wasn't making much headway with Red's murder and all searches to locate Penny Lynch had come to nothing.

Her bank account hadn't been accessed and her phone had gone dark. Meaning no activity on social media either.

Privately, Frank and the rest of the team believed her disappearance wasn't voluntary. I agreed she hadn't gone into hiding. Though none of those details had been released to the media, who were still running appeals for her to come forward.

If Chris McGarry's contacts had no clue as to her whereabouts, it was likely she'd come to some kind of harm

I turned back to my desk, to the sheets of call data DC Brooke Samson had put together, scanning them for the dozenth time.

Nothing.

I looked at the supplementary list of anonymous numbers Callum had circulated to the team. Still nothing.

I'd scrawled a circle around one number that kept repeating. It was all over Penny's call data, but Brooke said it was a burner phone they couldn't trace and which had been deactivated.

Finally, I gave up.

Tea . . . that's what I needed. My brain always worked better with tea.

From his warm spot on the rug in front of my desk, Harvey lifted his head from his paws and watched as I went to the kitchen, but couldn't be bothered following.

I'd just put the kettle on the Aga when my mobile rang. It was a number I didn't recognise.

'McCready?'

'The not-your-usual-kind-of-doctor, Jo McCready?' A familiar gravelly voice I instantly recognised, but hadn't expected to hear from.

Luke – temporary manager of the Hades Club.

'You kept my card.'

'Of course.' I could hear the grin in his voice.

'What can I do for you?'

'More a case of what I can do for you.'

I held the phone under my chin as I dropped tea into the teapot.

'Go on.'

'Police are still looking for Penny Lynch.' It was more of a statement than a question.

'Yes.'

'There's something Stacey, my barmaid, didn't tell you, which might have a bearing on things.'

'Which is?'

'Penny was seeing someone, besides your mate Red Wilcox.'

'Who?'

'Same person who was knocking off Stacey. Which is probably why she wasn't in a sharing mood when you spoke to her. She's more than a little pissed off about it.'

'Do I have to guess?'

The kettle whistled. I lifted it off the hotplate. All my attention now focused on the voice at the end of the phone.

'Doubt you'd know his name. He hardly runs in your circles.'

'Try me?'

'All I know is his first name. Stacey doesn't know I've called you, by the way. Appreciate it if you could keep it to yourself, or I'm likely to be one barmaid down.'

'What's his name?'

Once he told me, that was enough. I didn't need any more.

I knew who the anonymous phone number on the list belonged to.

More than that, I knew they'd been lying to me.

Chapter Fifty-Two

McNamara's Pub, Fordley, Sunday Afternoon

As soon as I'd ended the call with Luke the previous afternoon, I'd run into my office to check the list of burner numbers from Brooke. Pulling out my mobile to scan through my own call history.

And there it was.

The same number that was listed on Penny Lynch's call data. Contacting her several times a week, from as far back as six months before she'd gone missing.

The same number I'd been given by Chris McGarry to set up a meeting with his lieutenant, just over a week ago.

The number was disconnected now. Typical for burner phones that, by their very nature, never stayed active for long. But Freddie Harris had given me a new number to reach him on, when I'd met him in the Gray Ox.

Given the conversation we were about to have, I decided the location for this meeting would be one of my choosing. Somewhere I felt safe – on home ground.

Finn McNamara had greeted me with his customary booming welcome, offering me a seat in my usual quiet corner. He'd raised his eyebrows when I'd asked to sit at a table next to the bar.

'What's up, lass?' His volume dropped, conspiratorially.

'I'm meeting someone.'

'All the more reason for a quiet corner, then.' He grinned.

'Not that kind of someone.'

His brows drew down. 'Everything OK?'

'Hope so.' I tried to give him a reassuring smile, but missed. 'Just feel safer if I'm in a more public place for this one.'

Without a word, he pulled out a seat at the table next to the bar, taking my coat and hanging it on the back of the chair.

'Nuff said, lass. I'll be at this end of the bar, cleaning glasses and keeping an eye out. Just give me the nod if you need me.'

He took my order. Surprised when it wasn't my usual tea. It probably should have been, as I was driving, but I figured I could risk one. I felt I needed it.

'Small Merlot, please.'

He nodded and left me to it.

Right on cue, the door to the bar opened, with an accompanying gust of winter air, as Freddie Harris – Hazza – made his entrance.

He scanned the room, grinning as he spotted me, and weaved his way across the pub.

'What you having?' His large frame loomed over me, casting a shadow across the table.

'I've already ordered, thanks.'

Before he could go to the bar, Finn was there, discreetly sizing him up. 'What'll it be, young man?'

'Pint of bitter, ta.'

Finn left us, as Hazza pulled out the chair opposite.

He cut to the chase. 'You got something for me to pass on to the boss?'

'That's up to you.'

He frowned. 'What?'

I studied him for a second. Calibrating his demeanour. Body language. Getting a baseline for his behaviours so that I could read them when they changed. Which they were about to.

'You lied to me,' I said simply.

'What you on about?'

'Penny Lynch.'

278

I could see his mind beginning to race. Trying to work out what I knew and how I knew it.

'What about her?'

'You said you didn't know her. That you'd never met. Only seen her outside the club when you dropped Red off. But that's not true, is it?'

The tension he'd been holding ebbed away and he leaned back in his chair. Relaxing as he thought he'd got the measure of this.

'You've been talking to Stacey at the Hades, right? You can't believe a word that comes out of her mouth. She's pissed off because I finished it with her. Making up stories about me seeing other women.' He gave a short laugh. 'I mean, Penny Lynch? Really. Wouldn't be seen dead with a tart like that.'

'Interesting choice of words.'

We both fell silent as Finn came over with the drinks, waiting until he went back behind the bar.

Hazza took a sip of his pint. 'Is that all?' he asked.

'You tell me?'

His energy shifted. Not by much, but enough. He was slipping from curious to annoyed.

'If you've got something to say, just say it. I've got things to do.'

I matched his energy with my own. Telegraphing that I wasn't about to be messed around. Leaning forward slightly, resting my elbows on the table and looking him directly in the eyes.

'I know you were seeing her,' I said quietly. 'For months. Stacey found out and that's why she dumped you. Not the other way around.'

'Bollocks.' He glared at me.

'Did Red know too? Is that why he ended up dead?'

Hazza became suddenly very still. His eyes locked on mine. 'You need to be very careful about what you say next.'

I didn't even think about it.

'Did you kill Red Wilcox?'

'No,' he said through gritted teeth. 'And it could be very dangerous for you to repeat that in the wrong company.'

I raised my eyebrows. 'Dangerous for who, Hazza? Me, or you? Because from where I'm sitting, you're in deep shit.'

'On the word of a pissed-off ex?'

'Stacey never said anything to me about you and Penny. She doesn't even realise I know.'

'Then?'

'The police have Penny's phone data.' I let the sentence hang. Watching his face as he scrambled to put the pieces together.

'So?' He was still trying to bluff it out.

'There's a burner phone number all over it. For months leading up to her disappearance and Red's murder.' I paused for just a heartbeat. 'Your number.'

'The police can't prove whose number that is.'

I pulled my mobile out of my jeans pocket. 'I can.'

His breathing became shallower as his eyes narrowed. I watched his whole body tense.

'You threatening me, McCready?'

Over his shoulder, I saw Finn behind the bar, pause with a bar towel inside a glass. The tension at our table, obvious to him, even if everyone else was oblivious.

Finn's eyes met mine and I gave a slight shake of my head, which Hazza thought was for him.

'Then what?' He ground the words out.

'Tell me your version then I'll decide what to do with it – and if you lie to me,' I added quietly, 'I'll know.'

I was counting on the fact that he wasn't sure how much I knew. Or where my information was coming from and that if he deviated from the truth, I'd know enough to catch him in the lie.

280

He took a long breath, glaring at me with a hatred that was palpable. I could see he was weighing up his options. Calculating the odds.

'OK,' he said finally. 'I lied about knowing Penny, but only because of how it looks. If Chris found out, he'd assume I had something to do with Red's death.'

'But Red found out?'

Hazza took another mouthful of beer. 'I never made any secret of it . . . that was the whole point.'

'What does that mean?'

He washed a hand across his face, gusting out a frustrated breath. 'It means I was pissed off with Red, OK? Chris treated him like a brother, like family. He got paid more than the rest of us . . . to do what? Never got involved in the sharp end of the business. Never got his hands dirty, like we did. But Chris gave him all the perks. The money . . . the travel. Even that fuck-off four-by-four truck was paid for by the boss.'

'So, you slept with Penny, just to rub his nose in it?'

He shrugged, looking uncomfortable at the unpalatable truth. 'Yeah, if you like.'

'It's not about what I'd like to hear, Freddie,' I said evenly. 'It's about the truth, all of it. So, tell me. Why Penny? Like you say, she's not your type.'

He shook his head, looking down at the tabletop. 'When Chris got banged up, he handed the reins to me. I have to keep the whole thing running. Yeah, I got paid well, but not enough for the responsibility. For putting me and mine in the firing line as head of the organisation.'

'Were you making a play for the top job?' I asked. 'Get all of it, instead of the crumbs Chris is throwing you?'

Hazza's eyes widened in genuine shock. 'God, no!' He instinctively glanced back over his shoulder, as if he expected his boss to be standing behind him.

'Don't even go there,' he hissed. 'I wouldn't want that . . . not ever. This is a McGarry business. Always will be. He has the respect of the people we deal with overseas. Their deal is with him. They would cut ties if Chris wasn't at the head of it.'

'Even though he's inside? Probably forever?'

Hazza nodded. 'That's not stopped anything. Not even slowed things down. No, I'm happy as his lieutenant.'

'Why this game-playing with Red, then?'

'Because lately, he's been taking the piss. Even though he was paid the same as us, without any of the risks, at least he used to show up. Put in the hours.'

'And that changed?'

He nodded. 'Running Penny round, like a bloody chauffeur. Giving her lifts home. Standing stag in the club, like unpaid protection. Wasn't even doing the minimum for the firm. We're putting in the graft and he's getting paid to run round, playing the Equalizer.'

'What does that mean?'

'That attack on Penny.'

'What about it?'

'She started to remember more. Wouldn't go to the police with it this time. So, Red took it on. That's what he was doing, when he should have been working for me . . . Chris.'

'That doesn't explain you and Penny?'

'Part of me wanted to show him that despite throwing money at her, paying her bills and being her lackey, she wouldn't show him any loyalty. Thought if he could see what an unfaithful tart she was, he'd drop her and we could get back to normal.'

'But they weren't romantically involved? I mean, he wasn't her boyfriend so why would it bother him, if she was seeing someone else?'

'Even though they were just mates, most blokes would be pissed off if they were paying a woman's bills and another man was on the scene. I mean, Red wasn't the sharpest tool, but even he would feel used.'

'Did he?'

'Yeah – we had words about it.' He took a draught from his glass. 'But Red was more annoyed that he thought I was using her, just to wind him up.'

'Wasn't that daft then, was he?'

'I wanted to know what it was all about too. Thought she'd tell me about this guy who'd attacked her. Red wouldn't say anything. But I thought she might. Then we could deal with it.'

'Did she?'

'A bit. Said she'd started to remember more from that night. Could piece it together. She remembered seeing his face – leaning over her before the taxi turned up and scared him off.'

'She could identify him?'

He was distractedly pushing a beer mat around the table. 'Thought she knew who he was. Said she'd seen him around, but she needed to be sure it was really him. Until then, she was keeping schtum. Was scared that if he got wind that her memory was returning, he'd come back and finish the job.'

'Red was helping her gather the evidence she needed?'

'Yeah.'

'Do you know where she is now?'

He shook his head. 'Could be lying low?'

'No. She went missing before Red was killed.'

'Then maybe she was right . . . about the guy who attacked her coming to finish the job?' He couldn't have sounded less bothered, if he'd tried.

'I need to get this to the investigation team,' I murmured – more to myself than him.

'If you think I'm walking into Fordley nick with any of this, you're deluded.'

I shot him a look. 'Or I could just tell Chris that you were knocking off Red's girlfriend—'

'She wasn't his gir—'

'And the police have your burner phone number all over her call history. He's going to put two and two together . . .'

'And get five! I'll end up with a bullet in the back of my head.'

'Or, you could tell the police what you've just told me?'

'Chris would think I'm just getting my story in to the police to cover my own arse. Wouldn't prove to him that I didn't have something to do with it. He'd kill me anyway.'

'Then we've got a problem.'

Hazza drained his pint then leaned across the table, his face inches from mine.

'No. You're the one with the problem, lady. You can believe what you like – I didn't kill Red. But think long and hard, because if you go telling Chris or the cops what you've got, I'm a dead man.'

His chair scraped back noisily as he stood up abruptly, pointing his index finger at me and 'cocking' his thumb to imitate a handgun, before walking out.

Chapter Fifty-Three

Kingsberry Farm, Monday Morning

Across my office, Jen was busy at the computer. Her fingers flying over the keys as she researched Alma Byrd and her strange commune.

I wasn't sure exactly what I expected her to find, but knowing the bohemian lifestyle they'd all led in the eighties and nineties, there was bound to be something.

'After Lorraine Stevens disappeared, looks like the circle disbanded.' Jen paused in her typing, scratching her grey curls with the end of a pencil. 'The media attention, and the backlash they got, scared a lot of the group away.'

'And that was before the advent of social media.' I rested my chin on my hand. 'Trolls had to knock on your door in those days, or send a poison pen letter. Not as easy as keyboard warriors have it now.'

'Or as anonymous.' Jen was reading from the screen. 'People writing into the local paper. Calling for them to be driven out of the village. "No devil worshippers in our back yard". Corrupting our youth, etcetera.'

'Did they get their pitchforks and "angry mob supplies" from the local hardware shop?' I laughed.

'Wasn't far off that. Says here Alma Byrd was attacked by an old woman with an umbrella in the local Co-op. No wonder she became a bit of a recluse. Looks like she dropped out of view after the media interest. Stayed at the farm and kept to herself.'

'Anything on Mark?'

Jen scrolled through some pages. 'Callum sent over documents relating to him taking American citizenship. Some photos from that and a small article in a local Seattle paper, about the Brit working as a ranger in the mountains. I'll make us a brew and then keep on digging.'

'It's OK.' I stood up and collected our cups. 'I'll do it.'

Harvey lolloped down the corridor at my heels, hopeful of a walk, or at the very least, a biscuit.

I needed to move, to take a breath and think about my meeting with Freddie Harris the day before. I was still processing everything he'd told me, trying to decide what to do about it.

As soon as he'd left the pub, Finn had appeared, taking the seat he'd just vacated.

'Looks like that went well, then.' He didn't try to hide the sarcasm. 'And before you try spinnin' me some old guff, I know who that was. So, want to tell me why Chris McGarry's right-hand man is making gestures to shoot my goddaughter?'

I took a large drink, slowly shaking my head. 'It's complicated.'

'Never thought it'd be simple.' His calloused hand reached across the table, enveloping mine like a warm glove. 'What you involved in, lass?'

Finn McNamara and his pub had been part of the fabric of this city for decades. He'd known Chris McGarry's father and uncles in the days when Old Man McGarry had run the city. Providing protection for the pubs and clubs – for a price. One that undoubtedly Finn had paid, like everyone else. But he had the respect of the old firm and was a drinking pal of the Old Man, or so my father told me.

I was under no illusion that, given his connections to the 'Old Country', Finn and his Irish kinsmen hadn't been strangers to the odd dodgy deal or covert business in their time either. Though he was totally legitimate now.

Even though those days were long gone, Finn kept his finger on the pulse. To know the faces and names of those it paid to be wary of. It was no surprise that he'd clocked Freddie Harris – even if the gangster didn't know him.

'I can't tell you.'

He raised his eyebrows. 'That means you really *should*.'

I couldn't meet his eyes. Reaching into my bag, I pulled out my notepad and pen. He watched me silently across the table as I scribbled Penny Lynch's name and Hazza's now deactivated burner number.

'If anything happens to me, Finn,' I said, pressing the folded note into his hand, 'see this gets to Callum.'

'Now you've *really* got me worried.' The concern in his eyes nearly unravelled me. Making me wish my father was still alive. But I knew Finn loved me almost as much.

'If anything happens to you, lass, and it's down to Freddie Harris, I'll not rest till I've settled the score and that's a promise.'

I gazed at the earnest expression, knowing he meant every word. Knowing too that the very thought of him risking everything for me was more than I could bear.

I squeezed his hand. 'No need for that.'

I scribbled another note. 'Keep this one safe,' I said as I passed it across the polished tabletop. 'For your eyes only, OK?'

He glanced at the phone number I'd written. One that I'd memorised from years ago.

'If anything *does* happen, call that number and tell the person who answers about Freddie Harris. You won't have to settle any scores, Finn. It'll be taken care of.'

He scanned the note, frowning. 'What's "Edge"?'

'Not a what . . . a "who".'

'Who, then?'

'Doesn't matter. Just know he's an old friend and I trust him with my life. If I'm gone, he'll take care of it.'

'And this number . . . what code is that?'

'Panama.'

His head shot up and he gave me a look that asked a thousand questions I couldn't answer. I patted his hand. 'You won't need it, Finn. I'm just taking out insurance. When this is over, you give me that note back. I'll shred it and we'll both pretend you never saw it.'

He nodded slowly, looking uncertain and more than a little worried.

The whistling kettle dragged my attention back to the present. I went through the familiar routine of making the tea. Scalding the pot, arranging the cups. There was something comforting about the ritual. A soothing ceremony that calmed me almost as much as the brew itself. Far more unhurried than dropping a tea bag into a cup. A relaxing interlude that gave me breathing space and valuable thinking time.

Sharing Edge Brinks' contact number with Finn was a calculated risk. The ex-Special Forces sniper was an old and trusted friend. Living, these days, beyond the reach of UK extradition. Someone who had sworn to come if I ever called. But one who also knew I never would, unless my life depended on it. Or had already been ended. I didn't think this was likely to be that serious, but a little insurance never hurt and I would rather use my 'ace in the hole' than have Finn risk everything to exact his own brand of revenge.

Going into the porch, I pulled open the door, allowing Harvey to catapult into the garden. Leaping into the snow to run off some energy while I waited for the tea to steep in the pot – or to 'mash' as we prefer to say in Yorkshire.

Harvey bounded back into the kitchen at the same moment Jen did.

'Blimey, Jen, where's the fire?'

'Look at this.' She held a sheet of paper in front of me. A picture she'd just printed off.

'Newspaper – the *Lake Chelan Mirror*. Article about the National Park's service in Stehekin Valley.'

I followed her finger to the caption beneath the grainy black and white photo.

'*UK relative travels to the North Cascade Mountains to visit Local Ranger*'.

For a moment, I didn't recognise the man standing beside Mark Byrd, with his arm around the man's shoulder. And then I did.

'Bloody hell!'

Whatever she might have said was lost as my mobile rang.

'You'll never guess who Mark Byrd's uncle is?' Callum didn't waste any time.

'Will Matheson, site supervisor at the Keelham Hill site.'

'You're just showing off now, McCready.'

'Can't take the credit for this one.'

Standing beside me, Jen could hear the conversation. 'That'd be me.'

'Need that woman on my team,' Callum said.

'What you need,' I said, 'is another conversation with Will Matheson.'

Chapter Fifty-Four

Kingsberry Village, Monday Morning

Daniel Dunglas was being produced from prison and taken for interview to Fordley police station. So, Callum had arranged for his DI, on the Red Wilcox case, Frank Heslopp, to visit Will Matheson at his home in Kingsberry village.

I was more than a little surprised when Frank asked me to go with him. We hadn't always seen eye to eye, although in recent years, a grudging mutual respect had developed between us.

When I'd first worked with the team, he'd regarded what I did as voodoo, but not as scientific and made no bones about saying so. My results had eventually won him over, and we rubbed along as colleagues with less friction these days.

He was what Callum described as 'old school'. A euphemism for a dinosaur of the police service. Cutting his teeth in the eighties, in his time at the Met. When racism, misogyny and homophobia were accepted as the norm.

Since then, he'd been on all the diversity courses and paid lip service to political correctness, but his bullish prejudices still bubbled beneath the surface. Wrapped up as macho banter whenever he thought he could get away with it. Which he'd quickly learned was never in my company.

I'd agreed to meet him at Will Matheson's address in the village. Which, thankfully, given the weather, was just four miles from my farmhouse.

The last few days had seen heavy snowfall all across the county. Gritter trucks had kept the main roads clear and in the more remote villages, farmers had done their bit. Using tractors to clear the roads. Pushing dirt-spattered piles of snow along the edges of the pavements.

It was late morning, but the cloud-softened light made it feel like dusk already. The sky, heavy with unshed snow, felt low and oppressive as I pulled up outside the row of terraced cottages on the outskirts of the village.

Frank's car was already there. The driver's window cracked open half an inch to allow the cloud of blue smoke from his cigarette to escape, but not the ice-cold fresh air to get in. He climbed out of the car, grinding the cigarette butt under his boot, as he saw me park up.

'No wonder they call it the "Mountain" up here,' he said. 'Bloody brass-monkey weather. Who in their right mind would want to live at this altitude?'

I ignored the dig – he knew very well this area was where I called home. 'Southern softie.' I grinned. 'Thought even you would have become acclimatised by now?'

We fell in step, walking the few yards to the cottage.

'I'm still a stranger in these parts. Only lived here twenty years.' He pulled the gate open for me. 'Matheson's expecting us. Called him earlier. Said he'd rather meet here than at the site.'

Before he could knock, the oak-stained front door was pulled open by the man I recognised from our first meeting.

'Come in.' Will's face was more serious than when I'd last met him. His usual sparkling eyes now shuttered and cautious.

The door opened directly into a small front room. Typical of the workers' cottages in these villages. Hundreds of years old, with thick Yorkshire-stone walls and mullioned windows that protected against the harsh weather, but small rooms. Characteristically, two upstairs and two down. What was known locally as a 'through-terrace'.

I could see into the kitchen at the back of the house. Its windows overlooking a small garden, which had been paved over to create a parking space. The Ford Ranger we'd travelled in at the site was there. The huge vehicle, looking even darker and more hulking in the small garden, almost blocked the light into the kitchen.

It amazed me how anyone could bring up a family in these small houses. Never mind two hundred years ago, when the toilet would be a shed out in the garden and families of six or eight would have lived here.

It even had its limitations for the man who was showing us to the comfy armchairs either side of the crackling coal fire. Will had to duck his head as he walked beneath the low ceiling beams.

'I believe you've already met Doctor McCready?' Frank said. 'You and I met at the Keelham site, when Red Wilcox's body was discovered.'

Will nodded in my direction. His whole body language aching with discomfort. Not unusual, I reasoned, for someone unused to having police in their home.

If he'd struck me as a mountain man when we'd met at Keelham Hill, he looked even bigger in this space. Like Hagrid in a doll's house.

'Would you like a brew?'

I glanced at Frank, who was already shaking his head. 'We're fine, thanks.' Typically answering for both of us. 'This won't take long.'

Will took a seat on a small sofa between us. 'What's all this about?' He glanced at me. 'I told you and your colleague everything I knew.'

'We're here on another matter.' Frank got straight down to business. 'As you may be aware, the body of a young woman was discovered in a drainage ditch along the Moor Road?'

'Think I've seen something about it on the news.' Will frowned. 'What's that got to do with me?'

'We've identified the body as that of Lorraine Stevens.' Frank paused, watching the man before him. Waiting for his reaction.

I was doing the same.

Will's face remained impassive, and then, slowly, his eyes widened.

'Yes . . . I remember the name. But God, that was years ago.'

'Ninety ninety-four,' Frank supplied helpfully.

'I remember when she disappeared. It was all over the news . . . the village. Posters everywhere.' Then he shot Frank a confused look. 'But I still don't understand.'

'You're Alma Byrd's brother,' Frank said simply, not wanting to waste time dancing around the issue. He'd obviously decided to just hit the man with it and see what he had to say.

For a second, he said nothing.

Then slowly nodded. 'Yes.'

'You don't share the same surname.'

'Alma changed hers by deed poll.'

Frank made a note, frowning. 'Why would she do that?'

'She "married".' He drew quotation marks with his fingers. 'One of the hippies at the house. They had their own ceremony up at the Tarn. It wasn't a legal marriage, but she took his surname by deed poll.' He looked from me to Frank and back again. 'So, she's my sister . . . What of it?'

'Lorraine Stevens was associated with your sister's commune. Were you questioned at the time of her disappearance?'

Although Frank was asking the question, he must have known the answer. It would have been a matter of record.

Will took a long breath. 'I didn't know Lorraine. I'd never met her.'

'That's not what I asked.' Frank smiled, but it didn't reach his eyes.

'No. I wasn't involved in the investigation at the time. I think a female police officer spoke to me as part of the routine door knocks at the time. Everyone in the village was spoken to at some point. They must have known about my connection to Alma, but it never came up.'

'You didn't know about the "circle"?'

'Of course, I knew,' Will snapped. Becoming more agitated, which I thought was a departure for this mild-mannered man. 'That's why we were estranged. Had been for years.'

'Tell us about that,' was all Frank said.

Will blew out a breath, sitting forward, elbows on his knees. Head down as he spoke.

'Alma's fifteen years older than me. I was the annoying baby brother, saddled on her when Mum was working. Which was just about all the time. She babysat, when she'd rather be out doing teenage stuff.' He shrugged. 'She didn't feel like a sister because of the age difference. By the time I was old enough to know her, she was an adult, leading her own life.'

'Go on,' Frank said.

Will shrugged. 'When I was a teenager, she was involved in the whole occult thing at Willow Farm.'

'You didn't share that?' I asked.

'You've got to be joking.' Will snorted. 'Thought they were all a bunch of weirdos. She'd moved by then, so I hardly saw her. I never went over there – kept well away. Didn't want any part of it.'

'What about her son, Mark?' Frank asked. 'How did you get along with him?'

'I was ten when he was born.' Will's expression softened slightly. 'Can you imagine, becoming an uncle at ten?'

'You and he must have been more like brothers.' I smiled, aiming to prise open an obvious soft spot.

'A lot of people thought we were. Looked a bit alike. Same hair and build . . . and our ages.'

'You were close?'

'Yeah. I felt sorry for the kid.' He gave a sad smile. 'Alma dumped him on me and Mum a lot when he was a baby. She was so wrapped up in the circle. Had no time for Mark. Mum didn't mind. She doted on her only grandson, even if his dad was a feckless hippy.'

'Do you know who Mark's father was?' Frank asked, making a note.

'No. Don't even think Alma knows. Silly tart slept around. They all did – at the commune. Free love and all that bollocks.'

'Could it have been the man she married . . . Byrd?'

'She met him after Mark was born. So, no.'

'What happened to him – the husband?'

'Left. Predictably. Think he was only there for a summer. Heard he'd died a few years later. Heart attack, I think.'

'You have a good relationship with Mark?' I didn't want to move away from that – it felt important.

'Yeah . . . well, don't see as much of him as I'd like. Since he came back from the States to care for Alma. It's a pretty full-on job. Especially as he works in between, doing the deliveries. We catch up, when he needs a break. Go for a pint or whatever.'

'What happened to your mum?' I kept on the family line.

'Passed away, when I was in my twenties.'

'I'm sorry.'

'It's OK. A release really. She was constantly worried about Mark. You know, the lifestyle at the commune. But when she got cancer, it was too much. I was still living at home, so I helped look after him when he was growing up. Think he spent more time at ours than with his mother. These days, social services would probably get involved. But in those days . . .' His thoughts tailed off and there was a silence.

Frank let it run for a moment, then, 'You were in the Merchant Navy?'

'Yeah. Joined when I was twenty-two, after Mum died. Did five years. General deckhand.'

'What brought you back?' I chipped in. Frank shot me a look, which I ignored.

'A woman – what else? Met when we docked in Thailand. She was an English girl – backpacking. We wrote and had long-distance phone calls. Eventually, we decided to give it a proper chance. I came back, bought this place and she moved in.'

'That would be around 1992?' Frank was doing the maths.

'Yeah. Lasted all of six months, then she went back to London.'

'Have you been here ever since?' I asked. Knowing that Frank would have all those answers from the council records. But I wanted to keep our conversation on a more personal level. Somehow, I had the feeling that's where deeper answers were buried.

'No. I rented this place out and went back to sea, couple of years later. There was nothing for me here. Mum had passed away. There were no decent jobs going. Certainly nothing that matched what I could earn on the ships.'

'What about Mark?' I asked, bringing him back to a subject he obviously had deep feelings about.

'He wanted out too,' he said simply. 'Away from his mother and those weirdos at the house. If I'd stayed, he could have moved in with me, but he knew I was planning on going back to sea. I even suggested he join me, but he didn't fancy the life.'

'Were the States your idea?' I hazarded a guess.

Will nodded. 'I had some contacts. Put him in touch. Even paid for his flight and gave him some start-up money.'

'Very generous of you.'

The words triggered an expression. Regret.

'Felt bad.' Will gazed into the flickering fire – the orange glow making him look, somehow, even more forlorn.

'About what?' I asked quietly.

'Leaving him.'

'When you joined the Navy . . . the first time?'

He nodded slowly, still staring into the flames, and I knew he was replaying scenes from the past.

'When I left the first time, he was only twelve. Mum was gone and with me away, he had to stay in that bloody house, with that poor excuse of a mother.' He sat up straighter, taking in a deep breath, as if to shake off the thoughts.

'Felt it was the least I could do. Help the lad get a fresh start. Have some kind of normal existence . . . chance at a better life.'

'What year did he leave?' Frank was checking the dates. Corroborating what Mark had said.

'That'd be 1993.' Will pursed his lips as he thought about it. 'Yeah. Would have to be then, because that's when he turned eighteen.'

'Where were you when Lorraine Stevens disappeared in '94?' Frank dropped the question in, almost casually.

'Here. Well, I was getting ready to go away. You know, sorting things out to rent this place. Putting my stuff in storage. I remember the media coverage. Knew she had something to do with Alma's place, because of all the talk in the village. But like I said, I never knew her.'

'When did you leave?' Frank's head was down, over his notes.

'It'd be the spring that year. Can't remember the exact date. April sometime, because the first ship I could get was sailing for Australia then.'

'OK,' Frank said. 'We can check that.' Then he added, 'Zac White. Do you know him?'

'He's Alma's carer.'

Frank nodded. 'Did you know him before that? Back in the early days of the commune?'

Will's surprise couldn't be faked. 'No. Was he there then?'

We both nodded.

'There were so many randoms.' Will shook his head. 'People coming and going. Some stayed for a weekend or a season. Others more permanently. But, like I say, I didn't go there, so wouldn't have known any of them really.' Then he changed tack, as if his thoughts had just caught up. 'I thought you were coming to see me about the body at the site . . . that Wilcox guy.'

'Not this time.' Frank was putting his notes away. 'But while we're here . . . do you know Penny Lynch?'

Will hesitated for just a second – thinking. Then slowly shook his head. 'Name doesn't ring a bell. Who is she?'

'Woman from Fordley,' Frank said. 'Went missing around the time of Mr Wilcox's murder.'

Will stood, as Frank got up to leave. 'No, sorry. Don't know her.'

Frank shook his hand. 'OK. Thanks for your time, Mr Matheson.'

When Will shook my hand briefly, his fingers were trembling.

Chapter Fifty-Five

Fordley Police Station, Monday Afternoon

The incident room seemed quiet, even though lots of desks were occupied. The undercurrent hum of energy still present. Intense, as officers followed up lines of enquiry. Conscious that the clock was ticking and the further away we moved from the time of the offence, the more evidence could be lost.

Frank sat across his desk from me, nursing a mug of coffee. I'd refused the tea as the kitchen was out of milk and the vending machine offering was beyond disgusting.

'Why do you think Matheson was nervous?' he was asking me.

'Could be any number of reasons. Just being questioned by the police makes even innocent people nervous. Or maybe it was talking about his sister.'

'Hmm.' Frank took a large mouthful of coffee, swirling it around before swallowing, as if it were a fine wine. 'What's your reading of him?'

I thought back to Will Matheson. To both meetings. One at work, where he would be displaying more adaptive behaviours and one in his relaxed home environment.

'A private man,' I said simply. 'Which might be another reason he was nervous. He's not comfortable with self-disclosure. Talking about his nephew and sister. That's personal ground. One he probably tries not to think about too much himself, never mind reveal it to strangers.'

'He did say he felt guilty leaving Mark when he was just twelve,' Frank said thoughtfully. 'Suppose the kid used Will and his mum's house as a refuge away from the weirdos. Must have felt abandoned when he lost that.' He took another gulp of coffee. 'What else . . . on Matheson?'

'He's non-confrontational by nature. Happy to keep to himself. Quite a solitary person and comfortable in his own company. Likes working outside . . . practical. The sea; Keelham Hill. That kind of life suits him. Loyalty is important to him. Takes his time to build personal relationships, but once you're in his inner circle, he's with you for life.'

'So family would be important to him?' Frank asked.

I nodded. 'His nephew, certainly.'

'Then why not the sister?'

I considered the apparent contradiction.

'Because she cut across his value system,' I said. 'People with his kind of profile live by a strong set of values. Alma was everything he isn't. She didn't value her family. Played at marriage in a fake ceremony at the Tarn. Slept around. Wasn't maternal. And family is important to Will. Evidenced by the way he stayed to look after his mother. He only went to sea once she'd passed away. That's also why he felt so bad about leaving Mark behind. Why he helped set him up in America. And went to visit him over there, once he'd got the ranger's job.'

Frank's response was cut off as Callum walked over, pulling up a chair, to sit across it, with his arms resting across the back.

'Just comparing notes on Will Matheson,' Frank said. Then continued to bring him up to speed on what we'd found, and my thoughts on him.

'Put it in your report, Frank,' Callum said when he'd finished. 'We can fill the team in at the next briefing.'

Frank nodded. 'What happened with Dunglas this morning?'

'Once he was presented with the list of names from the party, the night Lorraine disappeared, he made no bones about the fact that he'd been there.'

'Is that pun intended?' Frank smirked.

Callum pulled a face and carried on, 'Said he'd been part of the circle in those days and he'd hung out at the commune. Said he was there on the night in question, but left before they all went up to the Tarn.'

'Did he say *why* he missed the ritual?' I asked.

'Most twenty-year-old blokes wouldn't have.' Frank snorted. 'I'd be there like a shot at that age. Group shag? Even if it was outside in February.'

Callum ignored the inappropriate remark. 'Said he'd done too much cannabis and alcohol and remembered not feeling well, so he'd gone home.'

'Is he alibied?' Frank asked.

Callum was already shaking his head. 'Lived alone then, just as he does now. No one to corroborate his story. Now, thirty years on, we only have his word.'

'He can't deny knowing Lorraine,' I said.

'He doesn't, but made light of it. He knew her. They were all part of the circle. According to him, they didn't have any more of a relationship than that.'

'Apart from shagging her in group sex sessions once a year?' Frank chipped in.

I shot him a look. 'You really can't get that out of your head, can you?'

'Oh come on, even you can't say the sex thing's not important here?'

'To some more than others, evidently.'

'Children,' Callum interrupted. 'Play nice.' He rolled his knotted shoulders. 'Dunglas says the reason he never mentioned the circle is because he knew how it would look. Yes, he knew Lorraine but denies having anything to do with her murder.'

'Did you ask him about the ribbon?' I was curious.

The ribbon didn't seem to be a part of the circle's hybrid 'Imbolc' ritual, but I was certain it had vital significance to the killer.

'Dunglas said he saw it when he removed the hood from Rachel. He thought it was the ligature.'

'How did he seem when he was talking about it?'

Callum just shrugged and shook his head. 'Didn't seem like it meant anything to him.'

'Could I have a look at the recording of the interview?'

Callum scribbled a note. 'I'll email a link to you.' Then, back to Dunglas. 'The fact remains, he "found" Rachel. Was leaning over her body when the farmer appears, but we have no witnesses to anyone else being on the moor that night. The forensics in his car are pretty damning and he knew Lorraine and was in her company the day she vanished. Plus, she was attacked in the same way as Rachel.'

'What about Penny Lynch?' Frank asked. 'Any connection to Dunglas?'

'Not so far.' Callum couldn't hide his disappointment. 'M.O. obviously the same. But we can't put Dunglas on the Moor Road that night, or find any connection to Penny. When he was questioned, he denied knowing her. Didn't recognise her picture when we showed him. We're working on it. If there's a link, we'll find it.'

Penny Lynch.

I opened my mouth to tell them about Penny and Freddie Harris. Then shut it just as quickly.

I couldn't tell them what I knew without dropping myself in it. Awkward questions about Chris McGarry and his right-hand man and how I'd come by the information that Penny believed she could identify her attacker.

As I was trying to think of a way around my dilemma, Shah came in, looking flushed and a little out of breath.

'Got cash card info, from the bank in Hebden Bridge, Boss.'

The stranger in the line for the cash machine. Hiding his face from CCTV.

'Let's have it.' Callum sat up straighter, focused on the sheet of paper in his DC's hand.

'The card belongs to—'

'Boss.' Tony Morgan almost fell into the room. 'You've got to see this.'

'Blimey,' Frank Heslopp exclaimed. 'Leads are like bloody buses around here. Wait for ages for nothing, then they all come at once.'

'You first, Shah.' Callum was all business.

'Cash card used by the guy in the cap and hoodie belongs to Alma Byrd.'

I hadn't expected that.

Even Callum looked surprised. 'Whoever it was in that queue, think we can safely say, it wasn't Alma Byrd.'

'Think this might help,' Tony said, thrusting a sheet of paper into Callum's hand. 'Got a hit on a vehicle on CCTV in Hebden Bridge.'

Callum scanned the information.

'Just before the cash card was used,' Callum said. We all waited in suspense, until finally, he looked up. 'Will Matheson's Ford Ranger.'

Chapter Fifty-Six

Keelham, Monday Evening

Callum had called Will Matheson before leaving the station. The site manager said he was out with his nephew, having a drink in the local pub. He'd offered to go back home, but Callum said we'd meet them there.

'Added bonus, getting them together,' he'd said as he shrugged on his jacket.

The Raggalds pub occupied an isolated corner on the Brighouse and Denholme Road, just a mile from Keelham village. Callum had suggested we go together. Then, uncharacteristically, asked if he could stay the night at my place.

'Feels like we haven't spent any quality time together for ages,' he'd said, as soon as we were out of the incident room. 'Be nice to get a takeaway and a bottle of wine and cosy up in front of your log fire.'

'Oh, so it's my log fire you're after really?' I'd joked

He rolled his eyes, pulling me into a bear hug as soon as we were safely out of sight of the police station. 'You don't give me an inch, do you?' he said, rubbing my nose with his.

'Only if the takeaway's on you.'

And so, here we were, travelling in convoy – me following Callum in my car, to go and see Will and Mark, before going to mine, for what I hoped might be a relaxing interlude. God knew we both needed the break.

We spotted both men as soon as we walked into the large main bar. Sitting at a table in a corner. Will had his back to us, but Mark's eyes were on us before we'd even crossed the floor.

He was already looking nervous, as Callum reached their table – his shadow falling across them causing Will to look up, with a pint halfway to his mouth.

'Evening,' Callum said cheerily, sidling round the edge of the table to sit down. I took the chair next to Will, giving him a thin smile that conveyed a silent 'hello' and 'sorry for the interruption', all at the same time.

I said nothing, as Callum told them why we were there. Ending with, 'The cash card used in the machine belongs to your mother, Mark.'

Mark took a sip of the orange juice in front of him. Replacing the glass on its mat, before replying. 'Well, her pension and benefits get paid into her account, so I kept it open. It's not . . . illegal. I have . . . power of attorney.'

'I'm not suggesting anything illegal.' Callum smiled. 'But what I would like to know is, who was using the card that day?'

Mark looked across the table at his Uncle Will, then back to Callum. 'What day was it?'

'Saturday,' Callum said, then added pointedly, 'The first of February.' Neither man said anything. Callum added, 'A significant day in your family . . . Imbolc.'

I was carefully watching both of them. That's why Callum had brought me along. Why he usually included me in these things. To watch. To observe those 'tells' and gestures that were easily missed.

At the word 'Imbolc', a micro-expression crossed Will Matheson's face. Gone in a second, but not before I caught it. Almost like an emotional flinch.

Mark just became suddenly very still, staring intently at the beer mat on the table. 'We . . . I . . . don't mark that date anymore,' he said quietly. 'Those days are gone.' He looked up at Callum. 'The circle and the . . . people my mother associated with, caused a lot of hurt. A lot of . . . trouble in the village. But that's all . . . over now.'

'It was me,' Will said, causing us all to look at him.

'What was?' Callum asked, for clarity.

'Using the cash card that day.' He took a sip of his pint. 'Mark asked me to get some cash from Alma's account. Zac wasn't there. It was Saturday, his day off. Mark was stuck at the house with my sister. I had to go into Hebden to run some errands, so I did it while I was there.'

Mark nodded. 'Yes . . . yes, I remember now.'

Callum produced his iPad, turning the screen so we could all see the images taken from CCTV above the cash machine. He put it on the table between us.

The picture showed the line of people waiting. Rachel at the front, in that eerie moment when she looked up directly into the camera, with the figure in the hoodie standing a few feet behind her.

Callum tapped the screen. 'Do you recognise the girl?'

Will stared at it for a second, then shook his head. 'No, why would I?'

'Can you see where you are in this image?'

Will leaned over the screen, studying the line-up for a moment, before pointing to the figure in the hoodie. 'There.'

'But you don't remember seeing this girl?'

He slowly shook his head, pursing his lips thoughtfully.

'You seemed to be watching her,' Callum pointed out.

'Might look like that, but I can't say I remember. Probably just staring into space. Bored of waiting in the queue.' He smiled.

'How much cash did you draw out?' Callum's tone was almost casual.

'A hundred,' Will said with certainty. Then looked at his nephew.

Mark nodded. 'Yes, it was.'

Callum studied both men for a second, as if debating his next question. But I knew him well enough to know that he didn't need the thinking time. He was giving them silence to see if either of them would fill it.

Neither did.

'Where did you park . . . in Hebden?' Callum asked Will.

'Market Place car park.'

Callum slowly nodded. 'OK.' I thought he was going to say more, but instead, he stood up to leave and I did the same. 'Thank you, gentlemen. If we need anything further, we know where to find you.'

Callum had parked his car at the back of the pub and I'd followed him. Now as we walked to our cars, we were totally alone. He stopped beside his car, leaning against the door as I caught up.

Without a word, he pulled me to him, hugging me against his chest. I felt his lips brushing the top of my head, as he murmured quietly, 'That's work done for now.'

I leaned into the reassuring warmth of him, resting my cheek against his neck. 'Can't wait to get you back to mine,' I whispered.

'Really?'

I looked up at him, my eyes twinkling with mischief. 'Only because I'm starving and the Chinese is on you.'

Chapter Fifty-Seven

Kingsberry Farm, Monday Night

A bell was sounding. An alarm causing my heart to race. I was running, but my feet wouldn't move. I was trapped somewhere dark; somewhere dangerous. I forced myself to sit up, and then I opened my eyes.

My mobile was ringing. The screen lighting up my half of the bedroom in a hazy-blue glow. I propped myself on one elbow and snatched up the phone, just to stop the noise.

'McCready.'

'It's me.'

Chris McGarry's voice blew away the last vestiges of sleep that were clouding my brain and I suddenly remembered where I was. Who I was with.

I looked over my shoulder to the man lying beside me. A jolt of panic sending adrenaline racing through my veins, feeling like electricity crackling beneath my skin.

Instinctively, I said nothing. Just ended the call. Then held down the button that switched the phone off.

Chris McGarry would be furious that I'd hung up on him. I could almost see him pacing his small cell, cursing me as he redialled. I couldn't risk the phone ringing again and waking Callum.

Too late.

He rolled over, throwing one arm across my waist, pulling me down beside him.

'Who was that?' he murmured, voice thick with sleep.

'Wrong number,' I whispered, laying my head on his chest, listening to the reassuring thud of his steady heartbeat. Eventually his breathing slowed, as he went back to sleep.

I lay, staring at the shadows playing across my ceiling. My thoughts drifting back to the previous evening.

The Chinese food we'd eaten from plates on our knees in front of the fire. The candles causing shadows to tremble around the room. One bottle of wine, becoming two.

Clothes strewn around the bedroom. His hard body and soft lips, washing away my loneliness; fleetingly making me question my self-imposed emotional isolation. Fooling myself that we could maintain this bubble and hide away from the reality of our lives, for a while at least.

This is how it was with us. An undeniable chemistry that continually pulled us together only for circumstances, or our combined stubbornness, or bloody-mindedness, to force us apart again.

I'd accepted long ago that my life was too complicated, carried too many risks of trauma, to share it with anyone on a permanent basis. Though Callum was probably the only one who could survive it. His was much the same. The job he did. The risks he took. Though the secrets I kept from him, the things I'd done in the past, cast a long shadow over any possibility of us having a life together.

So I just bathed in these purple patches of happiness where I found them and tried not to overthink it.

I dozed fitfully, until the night sky began to brighten. Pale fingers of winter daylight curling around the edges of my curtains.

I gently lifted Callum's arm and slipped from under it, trying not to wake him. But I should have known, he slept too lightly for that.

'You OK?' His eyes opened slowly, gazing into mine. Our noses almost touching.

'Yes. You?'

He nodded, his hair rustling against my cotton pillow cases. 'Stay a bit longer.'

I could taste his breath. Feel the warmth of his body down the length of mine. It took every ounce of willpower to move away from his touch.

'Can't,' I whispered. 'Got work to do.'

He grunted and rolled over. 'OK. I'll follow you down.'

* * *

Harvey was in the garden, playing in the fresh snow drifts that were almost as high as my walls. I stood in the doorway, hugging my dressing gown around me, and watched him for a while, revelling in the windswept landscape of wild moorland.

Going back inside when the kettle boiled on the hotplate, I made toast and pondered the problems being thrown up by this enquiry.

As I'd tossed and turned in the early hours, fretting about Chris McGarry and his aborted call, a thought had started to bubble in my subconscious.

Snippets of conversations I'd had. People I'd spoken to and things I'd heard, drifted back to me. Teasing at a possible way out of my dilemma over Penny Lynch and the information I had about her attack and how to get it to the enquiry team.

If Callum hadn't stayed the night, I'd probably have come down to my office in the early hours to work through it. But as it was, I'd have to wait until he went to work.

As if my thoughts conjured him up, he appeared in the kitchen doorway. His hair damp from the shower. Smelling of soap and minty mouthwash.

He came and stood behind me as I put the cafetière on a tray with my teapot. Slipping his arms round my waist and nuzzling the nape of my neck.

'Last night was wonderful,' he said into my hair.

'Hmm, it was.'

He stepped aside as I carried the tray over to my long kitchen table and we sat in companiable silence for a minute. Then he reached across and took my hand, rubbing my wrist with his thumb.

'I'd like more time together,' he said quietly. 'Proper time, like last night.'

I nodded, not trusting myself to speak. It had been a long road back to where we were now, since he'd cheated on me the previous year. I knew he wanted to put our relationship on a more permanent footing, but I simply wasn't ready for that. For all kinds of reasons that I could never share with him.

'I've lived on my own for so long now . . .' I started to say.

'I know.' He squeezed my hand. 'But, when we're alone, I get a glimpse of a vulnerability underneath all that independence and competence.' His soft, lopsided smile did something to my insides. 'It's addictive. Makes me want more.'

I squeezed his hand in return. Then looked busy, buttering toast.

'Although I could have done without the early morning call.' He looked at me over the edge of sliced wholemeal, as he took a bite. 'Who was that?'

I shrugged. 'Someone wanting a taxi.'

'Really?' His eyes were concerned as he studied my face. 'That's what kept you awake for so long afterwards? A wrong number?'

The professional inquisitor. One who knew me so well.

'Thought you'd gone back to sleep?'

'Sleeping with one ear and one eye open.' He smiled. 'Goes with the job.'

'Well, move along, Sherlock. Nothing to see here.' I took a sip of tea. 'Just couldn't get back to sleep once they'd woken me, that's all. Too much going on in my head.'

'Scary place, that.' He drained his coffee cup. 'The inside of your head.'

He started making a move to go. Standing up and grabbing his jacket. 'Got to get in early.' He picked up the last piece of toast, to eat in the car. 'Getting the team to check Market Place car park in Hebden Bridge. See if Will Matheson did park there on the first of February.'

'He didn't hesitate when you asked him about it.' I thought back. 'Though neither of them liked the mention of Imbolc.'

'We'll be checking out their stories. What've you got planned?'

'Just reviewing the case notes.'

'Let me know if you find anything?' was his parting shot, before he left.

Chapter Fifty-Eight

Fordley, Tuesday Morning

After Callum left, I'd walked Harvey and waited for Jen to arrive at the farm.

'Need you to work your magic,' I'd said, as soon as she settled at her desk with a brew at her elbow.

'OK.' She grabbed a pen and pad. 'Fire away.'

'Need you to research these names and dates.' I'd written a note with details on Will Matheson and his nephew, in addition to Lorraine Stevens.

'Mark left in 1993 for America. His uncle went back to sea the following year, a few months after Lorraine Stevens disappeared.'

'Am I looking for anything in particular?'

I didn't want to restrict Jen's search. If I left her to follow her own path, she usually found things I didn't even know I needed. Better to give her free rein.

'Do what you usually do, Jen. Go where your instincts lead you.'

'Okey-dokey.'

I'd left her to it. Spending the next half-hour defrosting the Land Rover in calf-deep snow. In-between throwing snowballs for Harvey, before leaving him with Jen, to drive into town.

* * *

It was almost lunchtime when I parked up in a side street off the main Kirkgate Lane. Traffic through town had cleared fresh snowfall from the roads, turning it to dingy-grey slush, which washed into the gutters with every passing car.

I picked my way across icy puddles pooling on the cracked pavements and turned into the main road. Opposite, the Hades Club was starting to come awake. A woman in a cloth coat, which was far too thin for the freezing weather, was wiping the glass panels in the pub doors. A bucket of water at her feet, her yellow Marigold gloves steaming in the cold air.

On my side of the street, a few doors down, was a greasy spoon café. The old-fashioned type that still existed in this part of town. Looking out of place next to the modern shisha bar. Like a shabby old man in well-worn slippers sitting next to a young entrepreneur in a sharp suit.

A place with wobbly Formica tables and mismatched chairs that served thick bacon butties and steaming mugs of tea to early shift-workers or taxi drivers between jobs.

A place Bren had mentioned, when she'd been chatting to Geoff. Telling him that's where she went for breakfast most mornings, before starting work on the Lane.

I spotted her post box-red hair, as soon as I went in. She was sitting at a seat by the window.

'Morning, Bren,' I said cheerily, pulling out the seat opposite.

She glanced up at the mention of her name and for a second, her face was blank. Then a spark of recognition. 'Oh . . . you were with that nice bloke the other night. Sorry, love, can't remember your name.'

I pushed my card across the damp tabletop. 'Jo McCready.'

She squinted at the card. 'Doctor.' Her pale eyes met mine. 'Not a cop, then?'

'No.' I gestured to her cup. 'Fancy another?'

'Yeah, why not? Coffee, please.'

'How do you take it?'

'With a sausage butty.'

I couldn't help but laugh. 'No problem.'

Fifteen minutes later, Bren was draining the dregs from her coffee cup and I'd exhausted the small talk and was ready to get to the real reason I'd come to find her. I waited while she wiped the grease from her chin with a napkin.

'I need to ask you about Penny Lynch.'

Bren shook her head. 'Still not seen her. She's not been around . . . told you.'

'It's about something you said, before.'

She laughed. 'I was half-cut before. Can't remember the half of what I said.'

'You said that Penny was starting to remember more about her attacker? What exactly did she tell you about that, Bren?'

The older woman shrugged, looking suddenly uncomfortable. 'Not my story to tell, is it?'

'We can't ask Penny, can we? You're all I've got.'

She was already starting to shake her head. 'I ain't saying nothing.'

I reached across the table and covered her hand in mine, making her look at me. 'Bren, you were her friend.' I chose the words carefully. 'If you want to help her, you need to talk to me.'

'"Were"?' Her eyes opened wider. 'Has summat happened? Have they found her?'

'No,' I admitted. 'But she's been missing for so long now, with no activity on her phone or bank.' I squeezed her hand. 'I'm not going to lie to you. I think Penny's in trouble. Either she's come to harm already, or she's in danger.'

'I dunno.' But I could see she was hesitating.

'I know she was seeing Freddie Harris.'

Her head shot up at the mention of his name and she glanced around us, as if she expected him to suddenly appear.

'Who told you that?'

'He did.'

She raised her eyebrows in amazement, opening her mouth, then shutting it again, like a goldfish.

'Come on, Bren. You and Penny were mates. You had each other's backs. She told you everything, so you'd know who she was seeing. Freddie Harris told me himself, so you're not spilling a secret to me that he hasn't already.'

'So, if he's told you, why do you need me to say the same?'

'Because I'm not sure how honest he's being. The things Penny told him about her attacker. Her suspicions.'

She hesitated, but I could see the uncertainty starting to ebb away. 'I'm only using what you tell me to verify what I already know. Just so I can check the facts, before I decide what to do. What you know can really help your friend.'

'Hazza didn't care about Penny – not really. I told her as much, but she wanted to believe he did. Wouldn't listen to me, where he were concerned.'

'And Red?' It wasn't really a question, but I wanted to see what she had to say about him and his relationship with Freddie Harris.

She shrugged. 'He hated it. Could see Hazza was just using her.'

'Why would he do that? Hazza, I mean?'

'To piss Red off.' She lifted the mug to her lips, then remembered it was empty. 'They hated each other, you know?'

That confirmed what I already believed. And strengthened all of the reasons Freddie Harris wouldn't want Chris McGarry to know about it.

'Do you know why they didn't get along?'

'Hazza was always moaning that Red wasn't pulling his weight on the firm. That he was spending too much time helping Penny look for this bloke . . .'

'The man who attacked her?'

Bren nodded. 'Then, when Hazza started seeing Penny, it got worse. Because Red knew Hazza was just using her to get to him.'

The woman behind the counter appeared with another mug of coffee for Bren. I smiled my thanks.

'He bullied Red about it.' Bren took a sip of scalding coffee.

'How so?'

'Saying he wasn't man enough to have a proper girlfriend. That Penny was just using Red as a mug to pay her bills and chauffeur her around.'

Hearing that upset me more than I'd expected. Red Wilcox had been such a gentle soul. A man-child. Affectionate and loyal to his friends and family. I could only imagine the toll Freddie Harris's bullying would have taken. The thought of Harris trying to poison one of the closest friendships Red had made me angry too.

'Did they ever come to blows over it?'

'Even Hazza's not that stupid.' Bren snorted. 'Red might have been a gentle giant, but everyone's got a limit. I reckon if it had come to a fight, Red would have flattened Hazza.'

Unless he hit him from behind, I thought.

'Have you heard anything on the grapevine, Bren, that might suggest Freddie Harris had anything to do with Red's death?'

She hesitated for a minute, taking a sip of coffee. 'There's rumours on the street.'

'Saying what?'

'That maybe him and Red finally had it out.' She shrugged. 'And poor Red ended up dead.' Then she shot me a look. 'But you didn't get that from me . . . OK?'

'Any idea why they might have been up at the landfill site?'

'Not for certain. But some say Hazza had some lads from the Butterfield Estate, nicking stuff from up there.'

'Diesel?'

'What?'

'Fuel . . . from the vehicles?'

'Dunno. Summat though. Making money on the side.'

317

'Who are the "some who say" that?'

She shrugged, unwilling to give a name.

I took a guess. 'Stacey?' It wasn't a huge leap. The barmaid had been sleeping with Freddie Harris. Chances are, if anyone knew what he was up to, it would be her.

'You didn't hear that from me, neither.'

That's a 'yes', then.

I changed tack.

'When we first spoke about Penny and her attacker, you said she was remembering more?'

'Did I?'

She was starting to close down. Becoming more cautious.

'Your exact words were, "Penny couldn't give a description, *then*." The word "then" implies that she could give a description now.'

I watched the conflict wash across her face. 'You're too clever for me. Tying me up in words. What I said or might have meant. And I was drunk that night.'

'Freddie Harris told me much the same thing. That Penny thought she knew who her attacker was, but she wanted to be sure before she did anything about it. That she didn't trust the police, because of the way they'd treated her before. Come on, Bren. Help me out here. If you know anything, please. You'll be helping your friend, in a way no one else can.'

She sipped her coffee, staring out of the café window. Every ounce of me ached to push her to say something. But I bit my tongue. Waiting.

'Said he lived just outside Kingsberry village.'

'I need a name, Bren?'

'Penny never said. That's all she told me.'

'Will you tell the police what you've told me?'

She spluttered on a mouthful of coffee. 'Fuck that! Hazza would slit my throat.'

'The police need to know, Bren.'

'You tell 'em then.' She pushed the coffee cup away. 'But if you say you got it from me, I'll deny we ever spoke.'

But there was someone else I needed to speak to. Someone I had far less loyalty to than Bren.

Chapter Fifty-Nine

Fordley Police Station, Tuesday Afternoon

I accepted the mug of tea from Callum as we sat in his office, after I'd told him about my conversation with Bren.

'I'd pushed her about as far as she was willing to go,' I was saying.

'She's not going to make a reliable witness.'

'But what she told me, about Freddie Harris running a side hustle in stolen fuel?'

Callum nodded, wiping a hand across his eyes. 'Ties him to the landfill. That, plus his relationship with Penny Lynch, gives him a motive for killing Red.'

'After I'd spoken to Bren, I went across to the Hades to see the barmaid, Stacey.'

I waited for some kind of lecture, but Callum simply raised his eyebrows and stayed quiet. So, I pressed on.

'She's pissed off that Freddie Harris was seeing Penny Lynch. She dumped him when she found out. She's the one who told Bren about him recruiting lads from the Butterfield Estate to steal diesel from the landfill.'

'Think she'd talk to us?'

I nodded. 'She confirmed everything Bren told me . . . and more.'

'Such as?'

'Apparently, a few nights before Red's murder, she heard him and Freddie Harris arguing, at the club.'

'About what?'

'Red was threatening to tell Chris McGarry about the diesel thefts.'

'That's more than enough.' Callum was already on his feet, yanking open the door to his office. 'Tony!' he called to his DS in the outer office. 'Where's Frank?'

The DI on Red's murder.

'Not seen him, Boss.'

'Find him for me, will you? Tell him it's urgent.'

'On it,' I heard the young officer call back.

'Time we pulled Freddie Harris in. See what he has to say.'

'What about Bren . . . and Stacey?'

'What about them?'

'Can't speak for Stacey, but Bren's scared for her life. If she gets questioned about Freddie Harris.'

'If Stacey gives us what we need, we might be able to keep Bren out of it. Either way, we can offer them protection.'

I thought about that, as I watched Callum gathering the troops, to deal with this latest raft of information. Exactly how much protection they could offer and how effective it might be, against an organised crime group like the McGarrys, I wasn't too sure.

'We're going to be tied up for the foreseeable,' Callum said as I followed him out of the office.

I was trotting to keep up with him, as we neared the lifts. 'There's something else . . .'

'Can't stop. We can talk later. Find a spare desk and get whatever you need from Beth. I'll catch up with you when I get back.'

* * *

Beth put a mug of tea by my elbow, as I settled down to review the recording of Daniel Dunglas's last interview.

'If you need anything else, just give me a shout.'

'Thanks.' I adjusted the computer screen to avoid the afternoon sunlight.

'Oh, and by the way.' She swivelled on her heel as she turned back. 'The boss asked me to let you know. I checked the car park where Will Matheson said he'd left the Ford Ranger, the Saturday Rachel was in Hebden Bridge?'

'And?'

'Checks out. Market Place.'

That gave me more to think about.

Could Will Matheson have attacked Rachel? The team couldn't find any connection between the two of them. But then, I didn't believe our killer had to know his victims.

His character didn't scream psychopathic killer to me and I'd met enough to know the feeling. But then, my sensory acuity wasn't infallible. Especially if the person in question was adept at masking their true selves and if my time with them was limited, which it had been with Will.

'I was trying to tell Callum something, before he dashed off,' I said. 'Bren said Penny Lynch was remembering more about her attacker. She didn't trust the police to do much with it, so Red was helping her, trying to track him down.'

Beth perched on the corner of my borrowed desk. 'Go on.'

'Said she thought she could identify him. Didn't give Bren a name, but said he lived on the outskirts of Kingsberry village.'

'Keelham's on the edge of the village. Willow Farm too. The occult lot all live or have lived there.'

I nodded. 'Will Matheson's cottage is on the boundary between Keelham and Kingsberry.'

'I'll tell the boss.' She nodded to the computer screen. 'Meanwhile, I'll leave you with Daniel Dunglas.'

* * *

I trawled through the opening seconds of the interview. The introductions of Dunglas's solicitor and a recap of why they were there.

I skipped to the part where DS Tony Morgan was asking Daniel about the night Lorraine disappeared, back in 1994.

'I left, just before they went to the Tarn,' he was saying.

I calibrated his body language. Breathing. Skin tone. All the sensory clues that might change if he lied or began getting stressed by the questions.

Tony asked him why he left.

'I'd been there all afternoon,' he said, crossing his legs and shifting slightly, to present a sideways profile. A way to distance himself from the interview, even though there was nowhere to go.

'I'd been drinking and smoking cannabis. I wasn't feeling well. When the time came, I decided not to go.'

'But the ceremony was an important one,' Tony was saying. 'It only happened once a year. A key date in the circle's calendar.'

Dunglas shifted in his seat again. He really wasn't comfortable talking about Imbolc – or their corrupted version of it.

'Earlier, I'd gone out into the garden to get some air, trying to shake it off,' he said. 'It actually made me feel worse. I knew I wouldn't even be able to make the walk up to the Tarn, never mind take part in the ritual.'

Tony pretended to check his notes, though I knew he wouldn't have needed to. 'They didn't walk all the way from Keelham, though, did they?' he said with a slight smile. 'You took vehicles up to the tracks on the grouse moors. Left them there and walked to the Tarn.'

'I knew I wouldn't be able to do it,' he repeated. 'I went home.'

The interview rolled on. Descriptions of times and places. The fact that Dunglas didn't have an alibi as he lived alone.

All of this I knew from Callum's account of the questioning. I'd needed to see this for myself, to get a feeling for the way Dunglas had behaved. His demeanour. What his 'energy' looked like when the questions were put to him.

When Tony asked again, directly, whether he had anything to do with Lorraine's murder, he was stressed, certainly. Agitated and even annoyed. But I didn't think he'd lied outright when he gave an emphatic 'no'.

Finally, they reached the part I was most interested in.

Tony showed Dunglas the forensic photo of the red ribbon that had been around Rachel's neck when he found her.

He said he'd never seen it before.

I leaned in closer to the screen, slowing the tape to one frame at a time, so I could get a close-up of his face.

He barely glanced at the photograph. His eyes sliding away. Looking down and to one side. A head and eye position that indicated he was recalling feelings. Emotions attached to that image and I knew in that moment, the ribbon *did* mean something to him.

It wasn't disgust or revulsion at seeing something he'd first seen on a traumatic night, when he'd stumbled over an injured girl on the moors.

Daniel Dunglas attached significant emotion to that ribbon.

I'd stake all the money I didn't have on the fact that he'd seen it before and he knew what it meant.

Chapter Sixty

Fordley Police Station, Tuesday Evening

The incident room was half empty. Callum had returned and gone straight into his office with barely a word. The expression on his face was one I knew well. He was under pressure. Hardly surprising.

All the additional lines of enquiry coming in had been collated and put into HOLMES 2 – the Home Office Large Major Enquiry System. Sherlock's computerised namesake processed all the information to make sure vital links and clues weren't overlooked and generated dozens of actions for the team. Most of whom were out, following them up.

I knew, from the conversations going on around me, that uniform and CID officers were out, trying to locate Freddie Harris, to bring him in for questioning.

Stacey, the barmaid from Hades, was already in one of the interview rooms along the corridor and, according to Beth, was only too eager to drop her former lover in the shit. Telling them everything she knew, guessed or had overheard about Harris's activities both for Chris McGarry and, more importantly for this investigation, his sideline activities, involving thefts from Keelham Hill landfill site. That and his 'relationship' with Penny Lynch gave him more than enough motive for killing Red.

I'd finished writing up my report on the Daniel Dunglas interview and sent the electronic pages to print. But it was obvious, Callum and the team had bigger things to deal with.

However significant I believed it to be, Dunglas was safely banged up in Armley prison on remand and Beth and Shah were busy preparing the case for the Crown Prosecution Service, against Dunglas, for the attempted murders of Rachel Taylor and Penny Lynch, and the murder of Lorraine Stevens. While still keeping open minds about any new leads that came in – like Bren's comment about the attacker, possibly living on the outskirts of Kingsberry.

I chewed the end of my pen and stared at my notes. Penny Lynch overlapped both cases. The serial attacks and Red's killing. There was something I was missing. Something that, once I got hold of it, would seem obvious. But for now, eluded me.

The drab, functional clock above the door said it was after seven. My eyes were gritty and I couldn't remember the last time I'd eaten more than a digestive biscuit, dunked into endless cups of tea.

Time to call it a day. I gathered up my things, scooping my notes from the printer on the way to Callum's office. He saw me through the glass and gestured for me to go in, before I needed to knock.

'My notes on Dunglas's interview.' I dropped the file on his overflowing in-tray. 'I've saved the electronic version on your system.'

'Sorry we haven't had time to talk properly,' he said, leaning back and stretching. 'Beth told me what Bren said about Penny's memory of her attacker.'

I leaned against his desk. 'Shame she didn't get a name.'

He pulled a face. 'That would just make things too easy, wouldn't it? Saying he lived on the edge of the village, though . . . Could be anyone. Hardly narrows things down.'

'I know.' I barely stifled a yawn.

Callum tapped my notes with his finger. 'Before you go, give me the edited highlights. What's your take on Dunglas?'

'He lied about the ribbon,' I said simply. 'He's definitely seen it, or one like it. I think he knows the significance of it.'

Callum shrugged. 'We can put it to him again, but I doubt we'll get a different answer.'

'Boss.' Shah knocked, then poked his head round the door, making us both jump.

'What's up?' Callum asked.

'Just secured more CCTV from around Hebden Bridge, for the Saturday Rachel was there.' He held out his iPad, turning the screen so we could both see.

'CCTV from a building opposite the Innovation Café.'

There was the unmistakable image of Rachel, sitting at an outside table, the rucksack propped against her chair. My eyes scanned the other customers. An old couple. Young woman with a child in a buggy . . .

'What am I—'

Shah cut across my question, tapping the screen.

Callum and I both saw it at the same time. A figure, outside the pub across the road. Looking towards the café.

I squinted to get a better look. 'Is that . . . ?'

'Zachary White,' Callum supplied helpfully.

I stared at the image. 'Can we be sure he's watching Rachel?'

Callum shot me a look. 'Can't be sure he isn't.' He handed the device back to his DC. 'Pay him a visit, Shah. There could be a totally innocent reason he's there, and he might not have any connection to Rachel, but he needs to be interviewed and eliminated.'

We both watched Shah as he half jogged down the corridor.

'Right, that's me, done,' I said. 'I need food, a hot bath and a good night's sleep.'

Chapter Sixty-One

Kingsberry Farm, Tuesday Night

Getting the food and a hot bath had been the easy bit. A good night's sleep was more elusive. The large brandy I sipped, as I'd soaked in the bath, helped me relax, but I still lay awake for what seemed like hours, before finally drifting off. If only I'd had the sense to put my phone on silent so it's shrieking wouldn't have jolted me awake in the early hours.

'I don't appreciate people hanging up on me.' These were the first words I heard.

I rolled onto my back, with the phone to my ear, unwilling to open my eyes.

'I couldn't speak to you when you called, Chris. I wasn't alone.'

'Oh, coitus interruptus?' He laughed. 'You'll forgive me if I couldn't give a fuck . . . and yes, the pun is intended.'

I was about to tell him, he *would* have cared if he'd known who was lying next to me, but it really wasn't worth the fallout.

'I hope you've got something worth my time?'

'I *can* tell you, Red's death has nothing to do with a rival gang, so you can tell your paranoia to stand down.'

'You're sure about that?' he said tightly.

'Sure as I can be.'

'Either you are, or you're not?'

My legendary thin tolerance was exhausted.

'For fuck's sake, Chris!' I exploded down the phone. '*YOU* came to me, to find out what I could. If you don't trust my judgement, then piss off and hassle some other poor sod, who doesn't need the sleep.'

'OK ... OK, calm down.' I could hear him pacing. 'What makes them think this isn't a move from another group?'

'It's connected to Penny Lynch. The girl Red was seeing.' I was choosing my words carefully, trying not to drop Freddie Harris in it. Though I didn't owe him a damn thing, especially after the way he'd treated Red. But I also didn't want his death on my conscience, if Chris went off the deep end.

'Connected how?'

'Her attacker, from last year. I'm certain the same man attacked the latest victim and murdered Lorraine Stevens in 1994.'

'What's that got to do with Red?'

'Penny was on the point of being able to identify her attacker. Red was helping her gather more evidence, before they went to the police with it. I think Red got too close. Touched a nerve and that's what got him killed.'

The phone went silent for so long, I thought we'd been cut off. 'Chris?'

'Still here.' Another pause, then, 'If we find this sicko, then we find the person responsible for Red's death.'

'I think so.'

'Is there anything I can do?'

'I'd say get your contacts to try to locate Penny Lynch. But to be honest, the police are assuming she's dead.'

'Even so,' he said, 'anything I can pick up, could be helpful.'

'And, Chris . . .'

'What?'

'Letting me get a full night's sleep would be bloody helpful too.'

Chapter Sixty-Two

Kingsberry Farm, Wednesday Morning

After my call with Chris McGarry, I dozed, toying with the idea of giving up on sleep and gong downstairs to make a brew. At some point, I became vaguely aware of the sounds of a raging storm in the early hours of the morning, but then I must have slipped into a deep sleep, only cranking one eye open when Harvey stuck his wet nose against mine to wake me up.

'Sorry, boy.' I ruffled his ears, then quickly pulled my arm back beneath the duvet. It was bloody freezing, despite my central heating.

I lay there, unwilling to move out into the cold world. Preferring, for a while, to hide in my warm bubble and let my thoughts drift.

Harvey jumped onto the bed and snuggled next to me – a reminder that I would have to go downstairs soon and let him out. I squinted at the bedside clock: 9.20 a.m. I never slept this late, but felt justified, given Chris McGarry's nocturnal interruptions.

I began thinking about the cases that HMET were running. Like the rest of the team, I was fairly certain that Penny Lynch was dead. An inevitable conclusion, given the lack of sightings or electronic activity that is almost unavoidable these days.

Had Freddie Harris killed Red? He was certainly capable of it and I suspected that, to get to the rank he had, in one of the most powerful and feared organised crime groups in the country, he'd be no stranger to extreme violence. If not killing. Just like his boss.

Had he dispatched both Penny and Red, to avoid them telling Chris about his unauthorised activities? All possibilities that I knew the team would be considering.

As if I'd conjured him up, Callum's name lit up the screen of my mobile, a second before it rang.

'Hi,' I said, trying not to sound half asleep.

'Morning. You at the farm?'

'Yes. No need to ask where you are.' I pictured him at his desk.

'Feels like I live here. Anyway, I'm calling with an update.'

'OK.'

'Daniel Dunglas wants to see you.'

Hadn't expected that one. 'What?'

'Thought you'd already have seen the email.'

'Er . . . no. Late getting into the office this morning.' I swung my legs out of bed, holding the phone under my chin, as I pulled on a dressing gown.

'Prison liaison officer at Armley nick gave us the heads-up. Dunglas has sent you a V.O.'

A visiting order. From the last person I expected.

Harvey ran down the stairs ahead of me, into the kitchen, which was the warmest place in the house on a winter's morning. Thanks to the constant heat from the Aga.

I unbolted the porch door to let Harvey out and was almost rocked back on my heels by a blast of arctic air.

The weather outside was truly appalling, even by Yorkshire standards. Thick, heavy snow, falling in dense white sheets, twisted by a howling wind. I had to lean against the door to close it, before going back to the comfort of the Aga.

'Why would he want to see me?'

'Only one way to find out.'

I filled the kettle and flipped the lid on the hotplate. 'You happy for me to go?'

I could visualise him shrugging. 'If you're up for it. He might have something useful.'

Harvey began barking and I went to let him in. He shook himself, covering me in globs of freezing snow.

'What's all the noise?' Callum said.

'Harvey.' I grabbed his dog towel. 'Bringing in half the Arctic Circle.'

I was trying to rub down an uncooperative dog, while holding the mobile with my other hand. 'Did you speak to Zac White? About him being in Hebden, same time as Rachel?'

'Shah and Beth did.'

'And?'

'That Saturday was his day off. That's why Mark was at home, looking after his mother that day.'

'Which is why he couldn't go out to get cash and asked Will to go for him.'

'Yes. Zac said he went into Hebden to do some shopping. Then was going on a walk, to paint. We showed him the CCTV images. Agrees it was him standing outside the pub, looking towards the café, but says he wasn't watching Rachel. Doesn't remember seeing her that day and says he doesn't know her.'

I thought back to the framed watercolours in the living room at Alma Byrd's house.

'He paints on the moors.'

'Which puts him there at the same time as Rachel.'

'Large area, though. Possible for them to be on different routes and not see each other.'

'Equally possible that their paths *did* cross.'

I considered it all for a minute. 'If he *is* guilty of attacking Rachel, why would he tell you he was on the moors? Could have simply admitted being in Hebden and left it at that.'

Callum's reply stuttered – then I lost him altogether. I stared accusingly at the phone in my hand, as if glaring at it might do some good. Then he rang back.

'Was it something I said?'

'Phone cut off. It'll be the weather. You know what it's like up here.'

'Not just up there,' he said. 'There's been power outages all over the city. Amber weather warnings being issued.'

Harvey finally wriggled out of the towel and I followed him into the kitchen, just as the kettle whistled. I took it off the hotplate.

'There's been a development in our enquiries into Penny's attack last year.' Callum was saying. 'On the same night, Will Matheson's truck triggered a speed camera. Got issued a fixed penalty fine and points. He paid the fine online.'

'Where was the camera?'

'On the Brighouse and Denholm Road. Twenty minutes after the attack.'

I considered the route. 'It's what . . . about six or seven miles from the crime scene?'

'Easily doable in the time. That's not all.'

'Oh?'

'Remember the CCTV Tony secured, alongside Brooke's telephone data, that gave us Penny's route from home the night she disappeared?'

I thought back to the grainy images, blurred by snow across the lens. 'When she called Red for a lift, after she missed her bus?'

'Yeah. Well, the forensic science service have been doing more work on the images. The vehicle she got into wasn't Red's.'

'What?'

'Red's Ford Ranger has a sticker in the back window. We've checked it, in the compound. It's only small. In one corner. They've enhanced the CCTV enough to see the Ranger on the footage doesn't have it.'

'How can that be?' I knew I was being slow, but consoled myself that I'd only just woken up.

'She got into the wrong vehicle.'

I pondered on that as I poured water into the waiting teapot.

'She had her head down, walking into the snow,' he was saying. 'I've watched the footage again. She's got her face buried in her scarf. Hurrying. Not really looking. When she gets to the Ranger, the driver pushes the door open and she gets in. On the enhanced images, you can see that the passenger door isn't even properly closed when the car takes off.'

'Will Matheson has the same make and model,' I said. 'Red's Ford is dark blue . . . Will's is dark red. Easy to just see a dark-coloured Ranger.'

'Not a common vehicle, either. Easy mistake to make on a dark night, in poor visibility. We can't prove definitively, yet, that the vehicle belongs to Matheson, but they're working on it.'

'That explains why Red was calling her all night,' I said. 'Because he hadn't dropped her off, as we'd thought. He never collected her in the first place.'

'Which is why we're bringing Will Matheson in for questioning.'

Chapter Sixty-Three

Armley Prison, Leeds, Wednesday, Late Afternoon

As the crow flies, my journey to the prison should have taken about thirty minutes. But due to the weather conditions, it took over an hour.

On the drive in, I was thinking about everything Callum had told me – which put Will Matheson front and centre in the disappearance of Penny Lynch. Was he the man she remembered from her attack the year before? If so, had her fears been realised, that he'd come back to finish the job?

If Will Matheson was Penny's attacker then he was also responsible for Rachel Taylor's assault and the murder of Lorraine Stevens.

He'd left for sea just a few weeks after Lorraine's disappearance. Was that why? To flee the country after committing a murder?

It was too much to think about right now. I had to concentrate on the job at hand and have my focus squarely on my meeting with Dunglas.

I parked the Land Rover and before locking it up, I tried calling Jen at our office at the farm. It went straight to voicemail – which meant there was no signal up there. The weather had a lot to answer for.

Instead, I accessed emails on my phone, realising that the battery was getting low. I'd forgotten to charge it before leaving. I sent her a quick message, telling her about Callum's findings regarding Will Matheson. While I was tied up with Dunglas, she could be checking something I needed. Depending on what she found, I could talk to Callum later, when I'd had more time to consider the implications.

I left the comparative warmth of the Land Rover and trudged to the ominous-looking turreted prison, arriving wet and cold despite being dressed for the snow.

By the time I'd cleared security and been shown into the room we'd been allocated, I was still wet, but now I was hot as well and my clothes were clinging to me in uncomfortably damp folds.

Callum had told the prison that I was part of the investigation team, so we'd been allocated a private room. A courtesy usually offered to prisoners meeting their solicitors. No less dreary or depressing for that.

I'd lost count of the number of hours I'd spent in rooms just like this. The monotony of stark magnolia walls, only broken by a red metal strip that ran round the room at waist height, the panic button I hoped I wouldn't need. Typically, uncomfortable plastic chairs either side of a small, square table which was bolted to the floor and the distinctive scent of body odour and stale coffee.

The door finally opened and Daniel Dunglas was ushered in by a prison officer, who made sure his prisoner was seated before leaving us to stand guard outside the door.

'I wasn't sure you'd come.'

I considered the man opposite me. His hair and beard both looked slightly longer and streaked with more grey. Even this short amount of time in the prison system had taken its toll. For someone like Dunglas, unused to the environment, it must have been a terrifying place.

I'd seen it before with offenders on remand for the first time. Struggling to deal with the regime. The sounds; the smells. The constant clanging of metal doors and rattling of

336

keys. Accompanied by the endless shouts of prisoners and the long, long nights. People told me the nights were the worst. Hearing men screaming in their sleep. Alarms constantly going off, as prison officers ran to assist colleagues or inmates.

Even if remand prisoners were found innocent and released, the long weeks or months spent in these places would leave a lasting legacy – not usually for the better.

'I wasn't sure I'd come either,' I admitted.

He stretched his long legs beneath the table and flexed those thin bony fingers, his eyes never leaving mine.

'Your police friends are determined to keep me here,' he said, almost too quietly.

'Maybe because they think you're guilty.' Although the conversation I'd just had with Callum could throw doubt on that in due course. But I couldn't reveal that.

He raised one eyebrow. 'Is that what *you* think?'

I took a long breath. Unwilling to play games. There was no way I was going to share with him what I thought or believed.

'Let's not waste time, Dunglas.' I wasn't inclined to use his first name. 'You wanted to see me . . . what about?'

His brow furrowed in a deep frown, as he picked at his thumbnail.

'I'm here because of forensic evidence they found in my car.'

'I know that.'

'Crucially, the victim's toe polish in the boot.'

'I know that too.'

His eyes locked on mine, with an intensity that demanded attention.

'My solicitor had the clothing I was wearing that night tested by a private lab. They found flakes of the same nail polish on my waterproof over-trousers.' His voice had an uncharacteristic tremor to it.

He was scared and I couldn't blame him.

337

'I told the police, when I got back to my car at the pub car park, I stripped off my waterproofs and slung them in the boot. I didn't want to drive home in soaking-wet pants and jacket.' He glanced down at the tabletop. His hands were shaking. 'The nail polish was transferred to the boot from those clothes.' He looked back at me. 'I *know* that's how it got there, because that girl was never in my car. I swear to you.'

'Then tell the police that.'

'I have.' The volume got slightly louder with frustration. 'My solicitor has. He's tried to get me released on bail, on the basis of the new findings.' His eyes narrowed slightly, as his attitude shifted from fear to anger. 'But they're *still* going to run with the evidence they have. They're going to keep me here . . . in custody.'

'I'm sorry, but you need to take this up with your solicitor, not me.'

'You have input into this investigation, don't you?'

'Some, but not enough. And not the kind you need to get released.'

'I don't trust the police. They're not going to look for anyone else.' His tone was pleading. 'They think I did it and they won't listen to my solicitor. They want this to go to court.'

'Your legal team will be able to present their evidence then.' I tried to make it sound like it wasn't a bad option.

'I can't.' His voice cracked and he sobbed. 'I can't stay here until then. That could be a year . . . I can't.' He wiped his nose on the sleeve of his prison-issue grey sweatshirt. Finally sniffing and pulling himself together. We sat, facing each other in silence, for a long minute.

I was the one to break the stalemate.

'It didn't help that you lied about your involvement with the pagan circle,' I finally said. 'That you knew Lorraine Stevens.'

'They weren't asking me about that.' His voice was almost a wail. 'I didn't lie. I told them I didn't know the girl I found on the moors. That was the truth. I wasn't the one who attacked her, either. Finding that girl had nothing to do with the rest. Why would I mention something I was involved in decades ago, before that girl was even born?'

'Because you saw the ribbon around her neck,' was all I said.

He stared at me. 'Yes.'

'And when you saw that . . . you *knew* what it meant, didn't you?'

He simply nodded.

'It's connected to the circle?'

Again, a silent nod, looking down now. Unable to meet my eyes.

'All that stuff you said, about my father.' I had to know. 'Saying he wanted me to step back from this case. That was just to get me to leave this alone, wasn't it?'

He nodded slowly. 'I was worried you'd work it out. Connect me to the circle. I didn't want that to come out, because it would look bad. After Lorraine's disappearance. I didn't want the police connecting me to that, after finding that girl on the moors. I knew how it would look.'

'I was no more a threat to you than the police.'

His look was intense. 'Yes, you were. Because I know you *do* see things other people can't, don't you?'

I kept my face expressionless.

'Reading people is my job.'

'It's more than that,' he said quietly.

'I'm a psychologist, not a psychic.' That was all he was going to get.

'I was trying to scare you away, but the rest was true.'

'What was?'

'I did . . . can see your father. He stands beside—'

I held up my hand to halt him right there. Unprepared to listen.

339

'When I saw you on the moors, you were going to revisit the spot where Rachel was found, weren't you?'

'Yes.'

'Why?'

'I thought he might be there.'

'Who?'

And then he told me, and it was truly terrifying.

Chapter Sixty-Four

Leeds, Wednesday Evening

After leaving the prison, I sat in my Land Rover for a while, staring out at the blizzard engulfing the city, stunned by what I'd just heard.

Daniel Dunglas was on remand for murder and attempted murder. What he'd told me could simply be the desperate story of a man fighting for his life. But I didn't think so. It tied up most of the loose ends and made sense of everything else.

If it was true, it changed everything. But before I could present it to anyone, I had to be sure of my facts. Too many lives would be destroyed if I was wrong.

I turned the key, relieved when the old engine fired first time. Putting on the heater to get some warmth, I started to defrost the inside of the windscreen as well as the outside. The old Defender might not have all the mod cons, but in weather like this it was the most practical thing I could be driving, apart from maybe a tractor.

As I wiped the inside of the glass with my glove, I let my mind scroll through the pieces.

Penny Lynch and her connection to Red.

Will Matheson and his possible links to Penny's attack, from last year.

Rachel Taylor's abduction and attempted murder and how that was inextricably linked to Lorraine Stevens and the events of over thirty years ago.

I picked up my phone and looked at the screen. The battery was getting low and in this old vehicle, I didn't have a charger. Great – no phone signal either. I opened my emails, just on the off chance that something had come through while my phone had been in the prison security office's locker.

A reply from Jen.

I opened it and read quickly. Then to be sure, read it again, my heart hammering just a little faster as the repercussions hit home. I quickly forwarded it to the enquiry team.

A 'ping' alerted me to a voicemail that had been left while I was with Dunglas. It was from Callum.

Know you won't have your phone in the prison, but when you get this, go straight home and stay there. A call came in to the incident room from Zac White. It was broken up by bad signal. He's up at mountain . . . weather's bad – it scrambled his phone message, but you'll get the gist. I've attached it after this. We're going to Will Matheson's home to arrest him. I'll call you later.

I scrolled to the link and Zac White's voice filled my car.

He sounded panicked.

'*After you questioned me about the ribbon, I knew. Saw him driving through the village in the four-by-four . . .*' Something unintelligible followed, then, '*Got to talk to him. I know what he's doing . . . Alma. Tell Ferguson . . . meet at Will Matheson's place.*'

Then the message dropped out, along with my phone signal.

I needed to get back. I couldn't do anything sitting here. I began driving with my mobile on the seat next to me, so I could keep my eye on the reception. If it came back to life, I'd call Callum and tell him the name of the person who'd tried to kill Penny and Rachel. The same person, I knew now, had murdered Lorraine Stevens in 1994.

* * *

The route to Kingsberry was barely passable. For the last hour the Land Rover hadn't been able to go more than twenty miles an hour.

Whatever grit and salt had been spread by the council grit-ters was long buried under packed snow, which, as night fell, was turning to deadly patches of ice.

The windscreen on the Defender kept fogging up and I was constantly wiping it with my sleeve. I could see my own breath suspended on the cold air, which was barely above the tempera-tures outside, despite the old heater doing its best.

As I climbed higher and left the city behind, there were fewer cars and by the time I pulled on to the Brighouse and Denholme Road, it felt as though I was alone in a world of white.

Buses had long ago stopped running up to the higher villages and cars were abandoned at the sides of the road – some of them at crazy angles, blocking the way for tractors and gritters, which might otherwise have been able to clear the roads.

There was no one around. Hardly surprising as the wind on these high moors was turning the snowfall into a blizzard. Anyone with any sense was safely indoors.

I carefully wound my way between two empty cars that were almost in the middle of the road and as I slowed, took the chance to glance at my phone. The bars had slowly crept up and it looked like I had some signal, but the battery was dangerously low.

I stopped the Land Rover, pulling off one glove with my teeth, so I could use the phone and dialled Callum.

'Where are you?' were his first words.

'About a mile from Keelham.'

'Sorry . . . you're breaking up.'

'Keelham,' I shouted at my mobile.

'Zac White . . . house—' The dialogue was breaking up along with the unstable signal.

'What?' There was so much static on the line, I could barely hear him. 'Have you arrested Will Matheson?'

'Zac,' he shouted. 'He's dead.'

I stared at the mobile in my hand, trying to take in what he'd just said.

'How?' was all I came up with.

'Murdered. When we got to Matheson's . . . to meet him. You still there?'

'Yes—'

'Matheson . . . on the run. Get home . . . safe . . .'

'Cal, you need to know—'

'Say again. Can barely hear you.'

The line went dead as we were cut off.

I quickly tapped out a message and sent a text as well as a WhatsApp in the hope he'd get that, just as the screen faded to black and the battery died.

'Shit!' I threw my phone onto the passenger seat.

I was four miles from home, but I already knew I wasn't going there. If I was right, Alma Byrd's life was in danger.

I had to get to her before the killer did.

Chapter Sixty-Five

Keelham, Wednesday Night

As I drove, the street lights on either side started to go out, like dominoes falling, one after the other. The whole row tripping a runway of darkness ahead of me. A brightly lit farm on the hill suddenly disappeared into the white-out as the power cut hit it.

All I could see was the triangular wedge of glittering track in my headlights, as I crawled through the dead traffic lights at the crossroads and turned right into Well Heads.

I parked the Land Rover on the road by the gate to the farm and cut the engine. Retrieving the heavy Maglite torch, I climbed out of the Defender and gently clicked the door closed.

I stood and looked around me. As if on cue, the wind suddenly dropped, leaving an empty silence in the void. All I could hear was my own breathing and the thudding of my heartbeat.

The torch felt reassuringly heavy as I hefted it in my hand and turned towards the imposing farmhouse at the top of the track.

The place was in total darkness. The black façade on the hard-white ground seemed lifeless. Empty windows stared at me with blank eyes as I approached. The crunch of my boots on frozen ground sounded deafening in the snow-muffled landscape.

I had the unnerving feeling I was being watched and suddenly felt totally exposed and alone. But nothing was moving.

A direct approach through the front door would be reckless. Framing myself against the white snow as I entered. A perfect target for anyone who might be waiting inside.

Instead, I skirted around the side of the house, carefully avoiding the mounds of snow that I suspected were covering rusting farm machinery and debris I'd seen when we'd first visited.

The lounge and kitchen were both at the back. Beneath the lounge window, the snow was splashed by a flickering orange glow – light cast from the fireplace.

I got down on my knees and crawled beneath the level of the windowsill towards the kitchen door, biting my lip at the pain that shot through my left thigh. I could hear a man's voice coming from the room, above my head.

I reached the door and slowly stood up.

Please let this door be unlocked.

The door swung open easily as I turned the handle and I offered up a silent prayer of thanks to whichever Wiccan gods were looking down on this place.

The kitchen felt as cold as the garden. I stood, quiet and still for a moment, allowing my eyes to adjust to the dark, until I could make out a wooden kitchen table and chairs. An old-fashioned dresser against the wall to my left, and an open door straight in front – across the room. Gaping into the blackness of the hallway beyond.

The linoleum flooring felt precarious under my wet boots, slippery and untrustworthy. I walked on the toes of my boots, resisting the temptation to switch on the torch. Holding its comforting weight against my thigh as I gripped it in my right hand.

The thrumming of blood in my ears drowned out almost everything else, as I crossed what felt like an endless no-man's-land of hallway.

The lounge door was ajar. I put my eye to the gap. Across the room, I could just see Alma's hospital bed. Any view of her was blocked by the figure leaning over her.

I almost hesitated – unsure of my next move – and then I heard her high-pitched cry. Less than a scream. A keening sound, feeble and choking.

I pushed the door fully open and ran into the room.

The figure standing over the bed, with his hands around Alma's throat, half turned, twisting his upper body to look round, his right hand still gripping her neck.

'It's over, Mark.'

I hadn't intended to shout, but any attempt at calm control was drowned by the massive wave of adrenaline thundering through my system.

'Fucking bitch!' he shouted.

I wasn't sure whether he meant me or Alma. Not that it mattered – at least he'd released the grip on his mother's throat.

'It's finished,' I said.

My voice sounded calmer than I felt. I held the Maglite in front of me like a shield. What use was it? None, but it was all I had.

'Not yet,' he said.

His eyes glinted in the flickering light from the fire. He looked different. Harder. More confident. Gone the stutter and the uncertain demeanour. He even looked taller – was standing straighter. No longer hunched and cowering in the presence of the mother I knew he hated. The person in his life that he'd been symbolically killing with every victim he'd hunted and squeezed the life out of.

The figure on the bed wasn't moving. Was I too late? Was his mother dead already?

He took a step towards me and I instinctively took a step back. Even though we had the whole room between us, I didn't want him any closer. But the move backfired when I saw his thin smile.

'You're frightened,' he said quietly.

'That feeds something inside you, doesn't it, Mark?' I spoke calmy, quietly, despite every nerve and synapse screaming at me to run.

If Alma wasn't dead I couldn't leave her with him. I had to stay. Had to keep him engaged, long enough for Callum to get the message I'd sent.

God, I hope that message got through.

That thin smile again. It made him look suddenly feral and I knew in that instant, if I'd ever doubted it, that I was in the presence of true evil.

My skin began to crawl – adrenaline making the hairs stand up along my arms and prickle across my scalp. Nature's instinctive and unconscious response to the presence of a dangerous predator.

'I know what she did to you, Mark.' I indicated the prone body on the bed, trying not to let my tone reflect the revulsion that rose in my throat like bile.

'When you were just a child. The things you witnessed during the fertility rituals.'

'Really?' he spat, his eyes flashing with an anger he no longer needed to hide. 'If you know the half of what this bitch did to me, then you know why she has to die.'

I nodded, injecting as much empathy as possible into my demeanour. Not for the man, but for the child I knew had been so cruelly treated.

'Dunglas – Terry Smith – told me about the ribbon.'

Mark visibly flinched.

'I tried to hide it,' he said – his voice cracking with emotion. 'But when the circle met, she'd humiliate me, all over again. Make me take off my shirt so everyone could see it, around my neck. Like a brand.' His face twisted into a paroxysm of hatred. 'That's what the bitch did to me . . . fucking branded me.'

Dunglas had told me. When Mark was just twelve years old, his mother had initiated him into the fertility rites at Wytch's Tarn. A young boy, naked and shivering, presented to the coven. Lorraine Stevens, the older woman assigned to take his virginity.

348

Terrified and embarrassed, he couldn't perform, and so Alma Byrd had put the ribbon round his neck. As an emblem of failure.

'She sewed it on,' he said, curling his lip. 'Fucking sewed it, so I couldn't get it off, without cutting it, and then she'd know and I'd get a beating. I had to hide it under my shirt, under my school uniform.'

He took another step towards me as he spoke. This time I stood my ground, but he was too consumed by his story to notice.

'Can you imagine what that was like?'

'I'm so sorry, Mark. You didn't deserve that.'

'I couldn't have friends – in case they found out.' He was barely registering anything I said, lost in his own tortuous memories. 'Had to skip school whenever it was P.E. lessons. Couldn't go swimming, or even take my shirt off in the hot weather.'

He pointed behind him to the bed. 'And that bitch would laugh.' A droplet of spittle appeared at the corner of his mouth. I watched, transfixed, as it ran down his chin. He seemed oblivious. 'Said if I wanted to be free of it, all I had to do was be a man. Then she would change the ribbon for that cross they all wore. The one they got, once they'd been initiated.'

I could only imagine what his mother's cruelty had done to his fledgling personality. I wonder whether she'd known, or even cared, that her malice had buried a spark of smouldering anger and hate that would eventually ignite, destroying everything in its path. Costing innocent women their lives.

'She made me watch,' he was saying, 'while she had sex with a parade of dropouts and lowlifes who came through our lives. Thought it would teach me. Prepare me. I hated her and everything she believed. The others too.'

'Lorraine Stevens, especially?' I asked, quietly.

'She taunted me. After that night at the Tarn. Would touch me and laugh.' He began pacing. 'I was like a pet animal in this house. Everyone treating me with pity or amusement. Some tried to be kind, but never openly, because *she* wouldn't allow it. Like a dog that wasn't allowed treats. Five years of it.' He ground the words out through clenched teeth. 'It only stopped when I was seventeen, because she couldn't bully me anymore.'

That's when he moved in with his uncle. A year before going to America.

'I found the roll of ribbon in her sewing box,' he was saying. 'Took it with me when I left. Kept it so she could never use it again.'

But you used it instead, I thought. *On all the victims who came later.*

He turned, going back to the bed. I had to distract him.

'Tell me.' I raised my voice – just enough to pierce through his fury. 'What happened with Lorraine?'

He glared at me. 'Why? So, you can gloat, like all the other women in my life? Pick over the bones of my childhood, laugh at my humiliation? Call me less than a man? Or is your interest purely professional? Are you going to offer mitigation? Blame my dysfunctional sexuality in your psyche reports to get leniency?'

'Maybe it would help people to understand,' I said, 'if they knew what drove you to kill her.'

'I was in America when she went missing,' he said.

'But a year after you left . . . you came back, didn't you?'

That's what Jen's email had been about. The one I picked up as I left the prison.

As soon as I read the immigration records she'd found, I knew Mark had killed Lorraine Stevens.

Daniel Dunglas's revelations gave Mark Byrd all the motive anyone could need. His return to the UK, the day before Lorraine Stevens disappeared, provided the opportunity no one suspected he'd had.

Why else would his uncle, Will Matheson, neglect to say that his nephew had been back in the country during that crucial period? And returned to the USA the next day, before the police had even begun to suspect that Lorraine was more than just a missing person.

Mark became very still, and then started talking. Like a dam bursting. As if everything he'd held back all these years had to finally come out.

'I'd had a year to think, in America. It felt like I'd run away . . . like they'd won. I wanted to tell her.' He jerked his head towards the bed. 'What she'd done . . . the damage. So I came back. Didn't tell anyone . . . not even Uncle Will. Just got on a plane. Turned up at his door and asked to stay. The day before Imbolc. It had to be then.'

'Why?' I knew, but I was playing for time.

'They'd be together All the people who'd humiliated me. They'd be in this house, on that night. I told Will I needed to have it out with them. He wanted to come with me, but I needed to do it on my own. He lent me his car and I drove here. If she hadn't been walking . . . she'd still be alive.'

'Lorraine?'

'I didn't know why she was walking, but there she was, carrying an overnight bag. I pulled over. Said I'd flown back to visit my mother. Offered to give her a lift to the house.'

It was that easy, I thought. *Wrong place, wrong time and she simply got in the car with her killer.*

'You didn't intend to kill her, did you?'

He had a faraway look as he spoke. Almost on autopilot as he recalled the night that had changed so many lives.

'No. I was going to bring her here. Have it out with all of them.' His short laugh was devoid of humour. 'But having her next to me. Seeing her again, smelling her perfume. She was laughing at something, like she didn't have a care. The rage came back,' he said simply. 'I hit her. She slumped against the door and I felt . . . powerful. For the first time since she'd

351

mocked me all those years ago. I wasn't humiliated. I was in control.'

'What happened?'

'I drove to the moors. Parked on the grouse track and carried her to the Tarn.'

'Was she dead?' I needed to hear him say it.

'Not then.' His lips pulled into a thin smile. 'But soon. I finished it, where it had started. I had the ribbon with me. I'd taken it with me to throw in my mother's face. Instead, I tied it around that bitch's neck. Let it take her life, like it had robbed me of mine.'

'The circle went up there that night. The ritual went ahead. Why didn't they find her body?'

He laughed – the unexpected burst of sound making me jump. 'Hidden, in the bushes, just a few yards away. Imagine . . . they didn't even know. That amused me.'

'Did you stay, to watch?'

He shook his head. 'Couldn't. Didn't want to. Had to move the car anyway. I went back the next night and we wrapped her body and dumped her in the Tarn. I thought that was karma. Putting a witch in Wytch's Tarn.'

'We?'

He stared at me in silence.

'Your uncle. He helped you. He's been helping you ever since, hasn't he?'

'Leave him out of it.' He spat the words.

'It'll come out, Mark—'

But I never got to finish. Whatever mood of confession had descended on him evaporated as quickly as it had come. He'd purged enough and the time for talking was over.

I had a split second's notice that he was going to move as his whole body tensed. Then, making a guttural sound deep in his throat, he launched himself at me.

352

I turned and ran back through the hall, feeling the air move behind me as he closed the distance between us. Expecting at any second his hand to grab my hair or my clothes and pull me back.

My feet didn't seem to be moving fast enough. My legs pumping hard, but it felt as though I was running through a dream. The adrenaline and cortisol rush revving my brain and my responses to a level that made everything else seem like slow motion.

I barged the kitchen door with my shoulder as I hurtled through it. On the dresser to my right there was a wooden knife block. I dropped the Maglite so I could reach for it, my fingers touched the resin handle of the carving knife, just as I slipped on a puddle of melted snow. I went down, screaming in pain as my knee smashed against the floor. The carving knife clattering beneath the kitchen table – out of reach.

The next second, his whole body slammed into mine, pushing me face down. He grabbed my hair and jerked my head up, then snapped his forearm across my throat.

I couldn't move. He was straddling my back, my arms pinned uselessly beneath my own body. The squeezing across my throat was unbearable. My head felt like it was going to explode. I could hear his heavy breathing, feel the warmth of his breath against my face. I opened my mouth, but the only sound was my own choking.

My God, I'm going to die.

Dots appeared in front of my eyes and a loud buzzing in my head made other sounds recede. Distant, like slipping beneath the surface of deep water.

Then nothing.

Chapter Sixty-Six

Keelham, Wednesday Night

Someone was slapping my face. My head rolled from one side to the other with each blow, the hard surface beneath me hurting the back of my head.

'Doctor.' A voice, coming from a long way. 'Come on ... you can't die on me.' Another slap, harder this time.

'Stop,' I managed to croak. 'Fuck's sake!'

I opened my eyes. Will Matheson's face loomed just inches over mine. He was on his knees beside me. The Maglite torch was on the kitchen table, creating a pool of white light around us.

'Oh, thank God,' he breathed.

I tried to sit up. Pain shot behind my eyes, my neck felt dislocated. He pushed me back down with a hand on my shoulder.

'Best not move, until I can get an ambulance or something.'

My tongue felt swollen and I could taste blood in my mouth. 'Where ... ?' was all I could manage through my restricted throat.

He nodded to his nephew's prone body at my feet. 'I hit him with the torch,' he said simply.

A million questions raced through my mind, but I couldn't speak.

The police were looking for Will Matheson, to arrest him for murder.

How safe am I, right now?

My thoughts must have registered on my face.

'Don't worry,' he said quickly. 'I'm not going to hurt you.'

A movement caught my eye. The shadows seemed to shift behind him. It took a second for my mind to register what it was.

A face.

A figure.

The hand raised high. Torch light glinting on the blade of the knife.

I tried to scream a warning, but only a strangled croak came out as the blade swept down to land a heavy blow between Will's shoulders.

He screamed, twisting away from his attacker, then collapsed next to me. His eyes, glazed as he stared up at the ceiling, writhing for just a second before becoming still. Blood seeped from beneath him and I was vaguely aware of the warmth of it, seeping into my hair. But my attention was focused on the person now standing over me, still holding the knife.

Piercing black eyes peered at me through a tangle of white hair. Alma Byrd – swaying unsteadily. Her white nightgown splattered with blood. Mouth gaping open in a silent scream.

Then she moved. Her bony, bare feet shuffling towards me, as she held the knife in both hands, raised above her head. Her lunge towards me galvanised me out of my shock.

I swung both my legs across hers, sweeping her feet from under her. She fell backwards, with an ear-splitting scream that made my heart jump. Her head hit the floor with a sickening crack.

I sat up, expecting to see her unconscious, or worse. But defying the odds, she suddenly sat bolt upright, still clutching the knife.

My boots slid on the lino as I scrabbled backwards, trying to create distance between us. Reaching for the edge of the table above my head to pull myself onto my feet. But I had no strength in my arms.

Then everywhere was noise. The front door crashing off its hinges. Men shouting. Glass shattering all around me. Boots running down the hallway; at the same time, people burst through the kitchen door from outside.

So many people. Legs and boots around me and over me.

Two uniformed officers grabbed the old woman and hauled her to her feet. Taking the knife from her, they dragged her, screaming from the room.

I was dimly aware of a figure moving quickly through the back door, coming to kneel beside me. Arms around my shoulders – Callum, squeezing me against his chest.

'It's OK, Jo. You're going to be OK.'

Chapter Sixty-Seven

Fordley Royal Infirmary, A Week Later

Will Matheson's surgery had gone well and he'd been moved from the Intensive Care unit into a side room off the main surgical ward.

He'd been cautioned while lying in his hospital bed and charged with suspicion of the murder of Zac White. A uniformed police officer stood guard around the clock and for good measure, Will's left wrist was handcuffed to the bed rail.

'I thought you were dead,' I said, from my chair beside his bed.

'I was lucky.' He shifted gingerly, restricted by the wrap of bandages across his chest and shoulders.

'If it hadn't been for you, Mark would have killed me.'

He gave a thin smile, but his focus wasn't on me. It was Callum, sitting in the chair opposite, who had his full attention.

'I'm here to ask you about the night Zachary White was murdered – in your home.' Callum had the notes open on his iPad and was recording the conversation, after reminding Will of his rights.

'I've already given a statement to your colleagues,' Will said.

'I need you to tell it to me,' Callum said.

'What's Mark said?'

I knew that his nephew hadn't spoken a word since he'd been arrested and remanded to Strangeways prison.

Callum sidestepped the question. 'I want to hear your version of events.'

'I'd been working at our other site, in Scunthorpe. It was late when I got back. Zac had phoned me and asked if we could meet at mine that night, to talk. My front door was standing open. I thought I'd been burgled. But when I went in, I found him dead. I knew Mark had killed him.'

'Why didn't you call the police?'

'I don't have a landline. The mobile signal is patchy there at the best of times, but it was even worse because of the weather.' He looked from Callum to me and back again. 'Besides, he was dead. There was nothing I could do for him, but I needed to get to Alma's. I knew Mark was unravelling and I was scared of what he'd do next.'

'So you drove to Willow Farm?'

'Yes. But the main road was blocked by an abandoned truck. I had to go the long way round, along uncleared back roads. It seemed to take forever. I was in the truck, but even that struggled.' He looked at me. 'When I got there, Mark was attacking you . . . in the kitchen.'

Callum asked, 'What made you think your nephew killed Zac?'

'I've known about Mark for a long time,' Will said quietly.

'You admitted covering for him, in your earlier statement?'

Will nodded.

'When we questioned you and Mark about the use of Alma's cash card, in Hebden Bridge, you said it was you. Why did you lie?'

'Because Mark was supposed to be home, looking after Alma. It was Zac's day off. That girl had been abducted and Mark was there, caught on CCTV, watching her. If I hadn't covered for him, you would have suspected something.'

'Just so we're clear,' Callum said. 'You thought your nephew was involved in the attempted murder of Rachel Taylor . . . yet you lied for him?'

He dropped his head. 'Yes.'

'Why would he kill Zac?' Callum asked.

'You showed Zac a picture of the ribbon, when you went to question everyone at the house. He lied and said he'd never seen it before, but he knew the significance of it. Once he knew that ribbon was used in the attack on that girl on the moor, Zac made the connection to Mark and what had happened to him during the days of the circle.'

'Did he confront Mark about it?' Callum asked.

'He couldn't be certain at first, so he didn't say anything. But Zac had gone into Hebden on his day off. And after being questioned by your lot, about being on CCTV, he remembered seeing my four-by-four driving through town. Except it wasn't me driving, it was Mark. He knew then that Mark had lied about being home looking after Alma that day.'

That tallied with the garbled message Zac left for the enquiry team.

'Go on,' Callum prompted.

'He called me from Alma's house earlier on the day he died. He was waiting for Mark to get back from work, then he could leave. He told me he'd worked it out. That he suspected Mark had attacked Rachel and said we needed to go to the police together. I told him I'd meet him at my place that night. I knew then it was over and I'd have to tell you everything.'

'Is that why you killed him?' Callum asked. 'To stop him coming to us about your nephew?'

'No!' Will's shock wasn't faked. 'I was going to tell you everything, but Zac was dead when I got back. Mark must have come home while Zac was on the phone to me and overheard the call. Mark has keys to my house. Has for years. I think he went to my house and waited for Zac.'

'You're convinced Mark knew Zac was on to him?' I asked.

'As soon as Zac said he'd never seen the ribbon before, Mark knew. We talked about it when we were in the pub, before you came there the other night to question us. I told Mark to hold his nerve – stay calm and we'd sort it. But when I found Zac's body, I knew Mark had lost it.'

'You drove to your sister's house, because you thought Mark was going to harm her next?' Callum concluded.

Will nodded, tipping his head back against the pillows to stop the tears spilling down his face.

'Why did you keep lying for him?' I asked.

'The first time . . . Lorraine Stevens? Because I felt guilty about leaving him when he was just a kid. I wasn't here to protect him.'

'He was nineteen when he killed Lorraine. Not a kid.' Callum's tone held no empathy.

'I felt I owed him. When I came back from sea the first time, to settle down, he was seventeen. After my girlfriend left, he moved in with me. That's when I found out what had been going on.'

'Why didn't you report the abuse?' I asked.

'Mark begged me not to. He was embarrassed. Ashamed. He was just glad it was over. I confronted Alma, though. Bitch just laughed in my face.' He shook his head. 'You know, I don't even think she believed she'd done anything wrong. God knows how she became so twisted.'

'Don't think God had a lot to do with it,' I said grimly.

'When you left for sea the final time,' Callum went on, 'that's when you paid for Mark to go to America?'

'Least I could do. We were both leaving the country. It was over. Everything was behind him. He should never have come back. If he'd stayed there, he could have got on with his life and Lorraine Stevens would still be alive.'

'But she's not,' Callum snapped. 'He came back, killed her and you helped him dispose of her body.'

'I didn't know what was going to happen when he went out that night. When I found out, it was done. She was dead.' Will's voice rose. 'To be honest, after everything they did to him, I couldn't blame him. What good would it have done for

360

me to shop him to the police then? He was the victim. Why should he be banged up for life, after what they did? He was barely nineteen. His whole life in front of him.'

'So instead, you got him on the next flight out,' Callum said.

'Yes.' His chin jutted defiantly. 'I thought that was the end of the whole sordid mess and Mark was safe. No one would ever know he'd been back, not after thirty years. Didn't think they kept records that long.'

'They don't,' I admitted. 'At least not on computer. But immigration still have paper-based records.'

Jen had played a blinder. As always.

Because of the nature of the work we were involved in, she had built up an impressive list of useful contacts over the years. Individuals in agencies – both UK and overseas. An invaluable network that she nurtured and shared information with, in a mutual spirit of cooperation, which had proved useful to us on more than one occasion.

Information that might have taken weeks or months to retrieve through official channels, Jen could conjure up in a few phone calls. Usually followed by a bouquet of flowers or a bottle of favoured tipple, with a note of gratitude.

Will Matheson looked pale. The skin drawn tight across his cheekbones, eyelids heavy with a mixture of pain and exhaustion.

'If her body hadn't floated up from the Tarn,' he said, 'no one would have known.'

'But it did,' Callum said with cold finality. 'So you don't have to keep lying. You don't owe him a damn thing.'

'It's too late.' Will began to sob.

'What is?' Callum asked.

'Will?' I reached out and squeezed his arm. 'Apart from lying for him, what else have you done?'

'Killed for him.'

Chapter Sixty-Eight

Fordley Police Station, Thursday Morning

The key members of both investigation teams were in the briefing room. Callum and Frank Heslopp, as senior investigating officers, were bringing everyone up to speed with recent developments.

As part of his investigation into the murders of Penny Lynch and Red, Frank had questioned Will Matheson in hospital, the day before Callum and I had visited.

Frank had presented his suspect with evidence of his vehicle being clocked by a speed camera on the night of Penny's attack the previous year, in addition to the footage of Penny getting into his vehicle on the night she disappeared.

'All he said then,' Frank was saying, 'was that, in both cases, it hadn't been him driving the Ford Ranger. He claimed his nephew borrowed the vehicle last year and on the twenty-eighth of January this year. Apparently, he uses it all the time.'

'Why?' It was DC Shah Akhtar. 'When Mark has the delivery van?'

'Not allowed for personal use,' Frank said. 'Except to drive from home to the depot. It's got a tracker on it. But beyond saying it wasn't him driving that night, he clammed up.'

'Mark's not registered as a user for the Ranger,' Callum said. 'So, his name didn't come up.'

'Well, if all else fails, we can always do him for driving without insurance,' Shah laughed.

'Very funny,' Callum said. 'Getting back to business, seems like after Frank's visit, he had time to think overnight and when Jo and I spoke to Matheson yesterday, he was more talkative. He confessed to helping Mark dispose of Lorraine Stevens' body in Wytch's Tarn. You've got transcripts in the notes. But then, he went on to talk about Penny Lynch.'

Callum produced his iPad. 'Probably easier at this point to play the recording.'

Everyone settled down, sipping coffee or taking notes, as Callum pressed 'play'.

Will Matheson's familiar voice filled the room.

A few months ago, Mark told me about some trouble he was having, with a woman and her boyfriend.

What kind of trouble? Callum asked.

She accused him of attacking her the year before. Mark denied it. Said she was mistaken, but it made me think about the previous Imbolc, when he'd taken the truck. I asked if that's when she'd been attacked. He said he didn't know. But it made me nervous that he'd done something.

Callum paused the recording. 'The time he's referring to is February first, last year.'

'When Penny Lynch was attacked on the Moor Road,' Frank supplied helpfully.

Callum picked up the narrative. 'Matheson said, since Mark's return from the States to look after his mother, he'd made a point of spending that night every year with his nephew. Because it was a time of bad memories. He said they'd go to the pub, then watch movies at his place. Mark would stay at Will's house that night.'

'So, who looked after the old lady?' Beth asked.

'Zac White would stay over,' Frank said.

'And have their own little celebration of Imbolc?' Shah pulled a face and gave a mock shudder.

'If they did,' I said, 'they never said. But knowing those two, I wouldn't be surprised.'

'Last year was no different. They'd been out and Mark stayed over at Matheson's. But a few weeks later, Matheson received the fixed penalty notice through the post. That's the first he knew that his vehicle had been used that night without his knowledge.'

'Mark had taken it, while Will was asleep,' Frank said. 'He only fessed up when the speeding fine came through. Told his uncle he'd just gone for a drive because he couldn't sleep. At the time, Matheson accepted that. Nothing came of it, apart from the ticket, so he forgot about the incident. Until Mark told him about Penny Lynch's accusation.'

'The recording explains the rest,' Callum said, resuming the tape.

How had the woman identified Mark as her attacker?

She'd seen him making deliveries on the estate where she lived. Said she recognised him. Then this boyfriend got involved, Will was saying.

Red Wilcox? Callum asked.

Yeah. He followed Mark when he was on deliveries. So he knew where he worked and where he lived. Mark only told me about it because this Wilcox guy confronted him a few weeks ago and said they were going to the police.

Typical of Red to be naive enough to show his hand.

The other cop . . . Heslopp, Will was saying, *showed me CCTV of her getting into my truck. It was the twenty-eighth of January, this year. It was my truck, but I wasn't driving it. Mark had asked to borrow it.*

Did he say why he wanted it?

To go try talk to this woman.

Penny Lynch?' Callum clarified.

Yeah. He said the boyfriend wouldn't listen. He wanted to get her on her own – try to reason with her. When he drove onto the estate, he saw her walking and followed her in the truck. He was going to pick her up at the bus stop. Offer her a lift, so they could talk. But she got on her phone, so he waited. Then she started walking again. The snow got really bad. That's when he stopped and offered her a lift.

As I listened, I recalled watching the CCTV footage of that dreadful, snowy night. I didn't believe for one minute that Mark Byrd had thrown open the door of the truck and spoken to Penny. If he had, she would never have willingly climbed into his vehicle.

I was convinced, from what I'd seen, that he'd thrown open the door and pulled her in. I knew the team thought the same.

But this was the sanitised version that Mark had undoubtedly given his uncle. The one Will Matheson, with blind faith in his nephew, was convinced was the truth.

What happened when Mark brought the truck back? Callum was asking on the tape.

He . . . Mark was in a bit of a state, Will said. *He broke down. Told me she'd freaked out. Started screaming at him while he was driving. Hitting him. Getting hysterical. He was trying to calm her down, when she opened the door and threw herself out of the truck.*

I glanced round the room at the faces of the team and could see that they believed this about as much as I did.

Mark said he stopped and went back to where she was on the road. She'd cracked her head on the kerb and . . . was dead. He didn't know what to do, so he put her in the boot and drove back home.

Shah snorted his disbelief, but shut up when Callum gave him a look.

His home, or yours? Callum was asking on the tape.

His. He took her down into the basement and wrapped her up in plastic. He broke her phone and put the pieces in the wrapping with her. Then left her down in the cellar. He brought my truck back because he knew I needed it the next day. He told me it was an accident and asked if I could help him get rid of the body.

And you agreed?

I was amazed at the lack of judgement in Callum's tone. But that was all part of the job. The dispassionate acceptance of what was being said. No doubt, I displayed the same clinical detachment in my job, when people told me the most horrific things.

I thought about the gruesome scenario Will Matheson was describing. The fact that his nephew had taken the body of a woman to his home. A place he shared with his mother, and carried her down to the basement. Spending the night, while his mother no doubt slept upstairs, wrapping the corpse in plastic. It was like something out of a late-night horror movie.

The next morning, Will's voice echoed from the tape, *I drove to Willow Farm. Me and Mark brought the body up from the basement – through the kitchen to the back door and into my truck. I covered it with a tarpaulin in the back and went to the site. It was 4.30 in the morning,* Will said quietly. *I get to the waste site first, to open up. There was no one around.*

What did you do with the body? Callum was asking.

Drove my truck up the haul road to the tip face. Dropped the body in the current tipping cell. It was wrapped in black plastic. The drop was a good thirty feet. Once it was down there, you could hardly see it. But no one goes to the edge of the cell on foot, to look down. There was a pause and I remember Will taking a sip of water. Then the grim narrative went on.

I turned on the floodlights as usual. Opened up the site. The first delivery came in at 6 a.m. I made sure the load was tipped over the same spot. Same for all the deliveries for the rest of that morning.

Callum clicked off the recording.

Everyone sat in silence, until Frank Heslopp cleared his throat.

'The body's going to be more than thirty feet down, by now,' he said.

'No sign,' I added. 'No smell. Perfect place to dispose of a body.'

'What about Red Wilcox?' Beth asked. 'Did he say anything about what happened to him?'

Brooke Samson, the young DC from Digital Forensics, spoke for the first time.

'We know that Penny Lynch called Red from the bus stop on the night she went missing. I've tracked his phone from when he went to pick her up. Obviously, she wasn't there. His phone pings from masts around the Hades Club and various other locations in Fordley, as he looks for her. Last ping on the twenty-eighth of January puts him at Well Heads and later at Keelham.'

'Matheson said Red knew where Mark lived and worked,' I said to no one in particular.

'It's possible that Red went looking for Mark Byrd,' Frank said. 'Sees him driving the Ford Ranger to his house. Then later, taking it back to his uncle's.'

'If he followed Matheson the next morning,' Beth said, 'or even staked out Mark's house, he could have seen the four-by-four coming and going from Alma's.'

Callum stretched and ran a hand over his eyes. 'We'll never know for sure what he saw – unless he starts to talk. But what we *do* know is he was on to Mark Byrd. Not inconceivable that he followed him when Penny disappeared.'

'The next day, Wednesday,' Brooke said, 'Red's phone pings from the mast nearest Keelham Hill landfill. Where his truck was found. But there was no sign of the phone when Forensics secured the vehicle.'

'Working hypothesis . . . before I play the rest of the tape and give any spoilers.' Callum said, with a half-smile.

'Red's gone to Mark Byrd's house looking for Penny. Sees the four-by-four there that night. Follows it back to Matheson's place,'

Shah says. 'Presumably after seeing it go back to Mark Byrd's home, in the early hours, which is suspicious, he follows Matheson up to the tip site. Then stakes the place out during the day.'

'Waits until everyone leaves at night,' Beth continues. 'Breaks in through the perimeter fence . . .' She shrugs her shoulders at that point and looks round the room for inspiration.

'Get a gold star,' Callum says, as he presses the button to resume the recording.

I stayed until everyone had gone that night, Will Matheson continued. *Drove to the tip face in the truck, and looked over the cell, to make sure it was well covered. There'd been fifteen-hundred tons tipped that day. She was never going to be found.*

Did you see anyone else that night? Callum had asked.

As I was walking back – a big guy appeared from the direction of the perimeter fence. He didn't see me. I ducked behind the Compactor. I guessed, from Mark's description, it was the boyfriend. I watched him as he went to check out my Ranger. It wasn't locked. He searched it. When he came out of the back, he had something in his hand. Then he went over to the tip face. He stood, staring down into the cell for a long time. Will's voice cracked, and he took a ragged breath. *I could tell – Oh God . . . he knew she was in there.*

The compactor was unlocked. I got the wrench out of the toolbox and waited for him to walk back. He took me by surprise, because as he turned away from the cell, he started to run. I didn't have time to plan what I was going to do. As he came past, I just hit him.

You intended to kill him? Callum asked, as if it was an everyday question.

No . . . I don't know what I intended . . . Will wept as he spoke. *Or what I was thinking. Just that Mark said, her and the boyfriend were going to the police. If I'd let him go, he would have brought them to the site . . . searched it. Found her.*

Was he dead? Callum asked again. Although we knew the answer.

Yes. In his hand, he had a piece of her broken phone case. Mark must have missed it when he moved her body. I threw it into the waste cell. Found the boyfriend's phone, broke it up and threw that in as well.

Why didn't you put his body in there too?

A long pause, when I recalled Will sniffing, shaking his head, trying to collect his thoughts.

I was going to. I went to find some plastic to wrap his body. If I just dropped him into the waste cell, he might have been spotted. But wrapped in black plastic, a body just becomes another refuse sack, thirty feet down.

I cringed, listening to him speak about Red like that. Incredulous that a man like Will Matheson had become almost numb to what he'd been doing. A reminder, if I needed one, of how quickly the human mind can normalise the most horrific things.

But as I went down the haul road, the recording ground on, *I saw headlights outside the fence. I thought it might be the security company, coming to do a spot check. They sometimes do. They might have seen the cut fence and raised the alarm. I didn't have time to do what I planned. So I just wiped the wrench and put it back. Then broke the lock on the compactor door and made it look like a break-in.* Another sob. *I wanted to get out of there. I just left him . . . lying beside the haul road.*

The recording clicked off. Everyone sat in silence. No quips. No bad jokes or banter for once. And having listened, for the second time in two days, to the story of how Red had died, I was grateful for that.

Chapter Sixty-Nine

Kingsberry Farm, Two Weeks Later

Mark Byrd had been moved from Strangeways to a high-security psychiatric hospital, while independent tests were carried out to determine whether or not he was fit to stand trial.

Thankfully, it wasn't my job to make that determination, but I suspected he would appear in court when the time came.

I knew that his defence team – whoever drew that short straw – would be seeking independent psychiatric reports. Hopefully to prove that their client was either mad not bad, or had sufficient mitigation in the abuse he had suffered growing up at the hands of his mother, to warrant a more lenient sentence.

Alma had been sent to a secure psychiatric facility. Despite her condition, the police had still charged her with attempted murder of her brother. Diminished mental and physical capacity didn't give anyone a free pass to avoid prosecution.

I thought about the assessment of Mark that Callum had asked me to prepare for the Crown Prosecution Service.

Going back over everything I had seen and heard had been more painful than usual. I knew that was because it involved the death of someone I'd been fond of.

My thoughts turned to Red's mother, Audrey. She'd invited me to attend her son's funeral and I knew that I'd probably go. Much to Callum's annoyance.

'You do know it'll be attended by every scrote and gangster in Yorkshire?' he'd said in an attempt to dissuade me.

'At least I'll know everyone there then.' My reply, accompanied by my sweetest smile, just pissed him off even more, which I regarded as a happy bonus.

One person I knew would *not* be attending was Chris McGarry. Joshua Weston, his solicitor, had already told me that Chris had applied for permission to attend and the request had been refused.

He had rung me, though. Another late-night call, after the news had broken in the media that a man had been charged with Red's murder. Though no names had been released officially by the press.

I'd kept Freddie Harris's name out of it, as I gave Chris the details. Not because I liked the guy – quite the opposite. But because I didn't need a guilty conscience if Chris decided to punish his lieutenant for running a side hustle in stolen fuel and whatever else his fledgling gangsters were into.

If the CPS agreed the evidence against him, supplied by Stacey, crossed the charging threshold, Chris would find out, but at least I wouldn't be the one to have told him. Callum wasn't hopeful though that Stacey's statement was enough on its own to charge. So maybe Hazza would get away with it this time.

Despite threats and tantrums, I resisted Chris's demands for Will Matheson's name. He'd find out soon enough when Will came to court, charged with Red's murder. In addition to charges of assisting an offender by disposing of two bodies.

No need to put a bounty on the man's head while he served time on remand awaiting a court date. It would be tough enough to persuade Chris not to take revenge once Will was assigned whichever prison he was going to start his sentence. Though I would try, along with Joshua Weston, to persuade Chris to let this one go.

I leaned against the frozen trunk of the tree in my garden as I waited for Harvey to come back from his sniffing expedition. Jamming my hands deeper into the pockets of my jacket against the cold.

My thoughts turned again to Daniel Dunglas, who'd been released from prison following the recent arrests. I'd been thinking about him a lot lately. Less about him the man and more about the things he'd said about my father.

For that brief moment in the police station, when Dunglas had taken me completely by surprise by claiming he could see my father standing at my shoulder. I had to admit, I'd taken comfort in the thought that he might be there. To believe that he wasn't gone forever. That a silver thread of . . . something could still connect us.

I caught a movement out of the corner of my eye. A robin had come to perch on the end of the branch beside me.

I smiled, as I remembered something my mother always said. About robins being a sign of a lost loved one coming to visit when you missed them the most.

I watched the small bird, until it flew over the wall and out on to the moor. It left me with a sudden feeling – beyond the senses. A certainty that my father *was* watching over me. It was a comforting reassurance. Blind faith overriding cold logic. But why not?

My thoughts were interrupted by Harvey's thundering return. We went back inside and I returned to my desk and to the paperwork that seemed never-ending.

Chapter Seventy

Kingsberry Farm

Jen came in, carrying two mugs of tea. 'How's it going?'

'Just finished.' I dropped my pen on the blotter, taking a grateful sip of caffeine.

'Any news on the search at Keelham Hill landfill?' she asked.

I gave a weary nod. 'They found Penny Lynch.'

'That's good. No place to end up for eternity, is it?'

'Elle's done a preliminary examination.'

'Urghh.'

'No blow to the head. Looks like she was strangled – like the others.'

'That proves Mark Byrd was lying when he said she died throwing herself out of the truck.'

'Sometimes, Jen, I hate this job.'

'Thinking about Will Matheson?' she asked gently.

'Mind-reader.'

'Nah.' She smiled. 'That's your job title.' She blew the steam off her mug. 'But I know you. You feel sorry for him – even after what he did to Red.'

'That's the bit I struggle with,' I admitted. 'Covering for his nephew . . . that was driven by guilt. I can get that – to a point. Guilt is a powerful motivator. Especially as he felt responsible that Mark's abuse started as soon as he went off to sea. To feel that he owed him a protection now, that he hadn't given him then. But Red . . .' I shook my head, staring into my tea as if it had the answers. 'He didn't need to kill him.'

'He'd crossed the line, hadn't he?' Jen murmured. 'From protecting his nephew to enabling what he was doing.'

Neither of us spoke and for a minute, I listened to Harvey snoring on the rug in front of my desk.

'Sliding doors,' I said, thinking out loud.

'What?'

'You know, those "sliding doors" moments in life. When a simple, mundane decision has a massive impact. Like Mark deciding to come back from America to have that final showdown with his mother. Ending with Lorraine Stevens being murdered.'

'Why do you think he came back, all those years later?' Jen rested her chin on the palm of her hand. 'I mean, after the way he was treated as a kid, you wouldn't have thought he'd give a toss when his mother had the stroke.'

Callum had asked me the same question and my answer was echoed in the report I'd just completed.

'He told his uncle he felt duty bound, but that was bullshit. He wasn't coming back to care for her, it was all about revenge.'

'On her, you mean?'

'Yes. Because you're right, he didn't give a toss. I think he tormented her every hour of every day he was with her. Not physically. But verbally, emotionally. Which can be even worse.'

'But what about Zac? Why take him on? Someone who *did* care for Alma.'

'Because he needed periods of time when he could get out of the house,' I said simply. 'He wouldn't want to be imprisoned with the old woman, twenty-four-seven. And Zac was one of the few people who actually liked Alma and could put up with her. Anyone else would have quit the job after the first day.'

'But if Mark was emotionally abusing his mother, why didn't she tell Zac?'

'She was terrified of Mark. He would have punished her for saying anything. I suspected it when I'd seen them together at

374

the house. It all looked very caring,' I said, 'but their dynamic was "off".'

I thought back to our meeting in the lounge of that cold house. The way Mark held his mother's hand. Squeezing it in what seemed to be a reassuring way, but at the time, felt to me like he was warning her to keep quiet. More controlling than caring. And Alma, a woman I knew had been a domineering force before her stroke, appearing quiet in her son's presence. Transfixed when he spoke, but not out of pride, out of fear.

'Suppose he needed Zac to stay with her while he went to work, too?' Jen said. 'He had to earn money. Needed a job that was flexible.'

'And would leave him free to indulge in his extracurricular activities,' I said.

'The other attacks?'

I nodded. 'He didn't bank on good old Uncle Will being a self-appointed chaperone on the anniversary of Imbolc, every year. I believe he always intended to carry on. Lorraine wasn't a one-off. After he killed her, it was never going to be over.'

'Is that what this is about?' Jen waved a yellow Post-it note at me. 'Finding out about Mark Byrd's time as a ranger in the North Cascade mountains?'

'It's one of the most remote and least-travelled areas in the USA.' I took a sip of tea. 'Perfect place for a novice serial killer to hone his craft. Especially if his preferred prey are hikers and backpackers.'

'Only eighty or so permanent residents in the valley.' Jen had already started her research. 'The place is only accessible by plane, boat or on foot. In summer, the population increases when vacationers go to explore the remote hiking trails. Mark Byrd lived there year-round, which is unusual unless you're one of the town residents.'

'And he wasn't?'

She shook her head, never looking up from the screen. 'I emailed the National Parks Service. Out of season, Mark lived in a remote log cabin. Off-grid in an area of the Cascades that's almost cut off in winter. Real "Grizzly Adams" stuff.'

As I listened, I felt a cold fear gripping my stomach. 'Keep looking,' I said, dreading, but already suspecting what she might find.

Chapter Seventy-One

Haworth Village, Two Months Later

The evenings were becoming milder, now that spring was just around the corner. Callum had taken a rare Friday off work and joined me and Harvey for a walk on the moors above Haworth, one of my favourite places in the world.

The picturesque village, just a few miles from Fordley, was set in stunning countryside. Surrounded by wild moorlands of purple heather, made famous in *Wuthering Heights*. A novel, written by one of its iconic literary residents, Emily Brontë.

Now, we were sitting in the Hawthorn. A Georgian building that had originally been the village watchmaker's shop, but now was one of the best gastropubs in the area.

'They do great espresso martinis,' I said, handing my menu back to the waitress.

'Two of those then, please.' Callum smiled at her.

Harvey was under the table, already snoring. The heat of the log fire was soporific – another reason I needed the espresso.

'How did you know?' Callum was holding my hand across the table.

'About Mark Byrd's time in the Cascades?'

He nodded.

'That kind of ritualistic killing doesn't just stop. I knew, once he'd felt the freedom he described, after murdering Lorraine Stevens, he'd go on to do more. That if we went back over previous locations where he'd lived or worked, there'd be other victims.'

'That area was the perfect killing ground.'

Callum had put in a request to the Chelan County Sheriff's office, asking for a search to be conducted in the area where Mark Byrd lived, off-grid in his log cabin during the winter and the trails he worked during the summer.

It was a tall order. The mountain area around there was vast. But the universe seemed to be on our side and while a search team was combing the hiking trails, a wildlife photographer, there for the spring season, stumbled across a human skull in dense woodland.

That led the search team to bring in dogs and specialist officers from the FBI. At present count, the partial remains of five individual victims had been recovered. It appeared they'd been buried in the same wood, close to hiking trails. But being the Cascades, rather than the Pennines, wild animals had uncovered the remains and devoured or scattered them further afield.

'Don't know how many more,' Callum said, after the waitress had brought out martinis, 'but the FBI will keep going for as long as it takes.'

'He worked in those mountains for over twenty years.' I took a welcome sip of my drink, creamy and ice-cold. 'Unless Byrd starts talking, we may never know.'

'The FBI searched his cabin,' Callum added. 'In a cavity under the floor, they found dozens of pairs of hiking boots. Male and female.'

'Jesus,' I breathed.

It was a chilling thought. One that kept me awake at night. One that I was tired of having in my head.

Callum shifted in his seat. Something about his demeanour, his 'energy', suddenly put me on alert.

'There's something I wanted to ask you,' he said quietly. His eyes never leaving mine.

Here it comes.

I held his gaze, feeling my heart beat just a little harder.

'When we had the briefing about Red's murder, at the station . . .'

'Which one?' I went for a smile. Not sure I pulled it off. 'There were quite a few.'

'The one when you said you'd asked Chris McGarry whether Red was stealing fuel from the landfill. He told you it was an unsanctioned operation that Red wouldn't have been involved with?'

I could feel myself becoming suddenly very still. 'That's right.'

'Remind me again . . . how did Chris tell you that?'

I knew damn well that Callum didn't need reminding. He'd remember every detail. He was testing whether I remembered equally as well. Which meant he thought I'd been lying.

'I passed the question to him via his solicitor, Joshua Weston, why?'

I broke the uncomfortable eye contact by taking a sip of martini.

'They've found a burner phone in McGarry's cell.' He said it matter-of-factly, even though it was a bombshell to me.

Had Chris followed the operational security measures he insisted his gang use? Had he deleted the numbers he'd dialled after every call?

If he hadn't, my phone number would be all over his call history. Including the one that came in while Callum slept next to me. The one he hadn't believed was a wrong number that night.

Had he just caught me out in a lie that would spell the end of everything for me?

I resorted to a tactic that I'd always believed in. When my back was against the wall, when it looked like I had nowhere to go. Put my head right in the lion's mouth.

'Why?' My voice sounded stronger than I felt. 'Are you suggesting Chris was calling me from his cell? On an illegal phone that I didn't report?'

He watched me for what seemed like forever, but was probably a pause of only a second, before giving a slight shrug and a half-smile.

'Of course not. I know you wouldn't do that.' He took a sip of his drink. 'Besides, he deleted the numbers. Just thought I'd ask. You know? Cover all the bases. I've got Brooke Samson digging into it. We might not know *who* he was calling, but she can see *when* the phone was active. Seems it was red-hot during the investigation.'

I tried to look suitably offended.

'That shouldn't come as a surprise,' I said. 'Chris wanted to find out who killed Red. He was probably calling his crew. Contacts on the street. Putting out feelers to get any leads he could.'

'Hmm. That's my thinking. We're questioning Freddie Harris . . . he might know who he called during that time.'

My mind was racing a million miles an hour at the implications. I was trying to look like I was still 'in the moment' but I was more than distracted. He took my hand across the table, stroking my wrist with his thumb.

'When the court case is over, we need a break.'

'We?'

He nodded. 'Just the two of us. Somewhere warm.'

'But not remote.' I gave a shudder. 'No hiking mountain trails, if that's OK?'

I felt weary. Too tired to think.

'Is that a "yes"?' he asked.

I gave a weak smile. 'Maybe.'

Author's Note

For this novel, I confess I've played fast and loose with the geography of the Yorkshire Dales and the Pennine Way, for which I must apologise.

For the sake of the story, I invented locations that do not exist and situated them around places that do. Wytch's Tarn and the Tarn Hill Tavern are completely made up.

Keelham is a real place and it does have an amazing farm shop, which I can highly recommend, but Keelham Hill is fictitious and there is no landfill site in the area. Well Heads is also real, but the site of the fictional Willow Farm is open farmland.

I have, though, tried to capture the real beauty and awesome scenery around the Yorkshire Moors, which is a place I love. The landscape, which forms the backdrop to Jo McCready's world, is a living character for me and I hope I have done it justice.

The Gaelic ritual of Imbolc was altered for the purposes of the book. The Imbolc practices described in this story bear no resemblance to the actual festival, or those who celebrate it. This was purely done for dramatic effect and is not meant as a true representation, as Jo McCready is quick to point out.

Acknowledgements

As always, my thanks go to everyone at RCW Literary Agency. In particular, my agent, Jon Wood, who is finally convincing me to have as much faith in myself as he has. Also, to the team at Zaffre, especially my editor, Ben Willis, for his hard work and patience.

For my friend, Hayley Mortimer, and her husband, Lee Padget. I promised to put you in a Jo McCready story one day. I hope you like the result.

To Lorraine Stevens, for donating her name to a skeleton. I never intended to give your fictional namesake such a 'colourful' backstory, but she just evolved that way.

I'm so grateful for a chance meeting with Amanda Stevens. Our conversation over dinner one night gave me the inspiration for this book. Thank you, Amanda, for all your subsequent help with the inner workings of a landfill site. Your knowledge and experience proved invaluable.

I am always thankful for the help given to me by experts, in an attempt to get things right.

To the site manager and supervisor of a certain waste recycling centre, who wish to remain anonymous – huge thanks for arranging a private tour and giving your time so generously. I could never have nailed the details without your help.

To Dr Zoe Enstone, York St John University, for her information on witchcraft and Wiccans. You gave me the idea for Wytch's Tarn and your suggestion for its history with the swim tests in the witch trials was a fabulous addition. Your knowledge and expertise were invaluable. I can't thank you enough. I hope you'll forgive the liberties I took with Imbolc and the details of the festival? They are all my own invention.

Massive thanks, as always, to former Detective Superintendent Stu Spencer, for help and advice with the police procedural aspects of the book. Any errors in that regard are entirely mine. Thank you, Stu, for your time and patience when answering my endless questions.

Thank you to the people I share my words with, before they 'go public'. My Beta readers and good friends, Sharon Beddoes Alison Barnes and Katie Brayzier. Your feedback is very much appreciated.

My family are a huge support along the way. Especially my sons, Adam and Kyle, who are always on hand to help their technophobe mother with the technical stuff – both practical and fictional.

And finally, to my husband and best friend, Ian. You give me time, space and constant encouragement. I simply couldn't achieve any of this without your love and support. Thank you for being you and for looking after me the way you do.

Read on for an exclusive extract
from Lesley's next book

The Killer Inside

Chapter One

Fordley Police Station, July 2015

The incident room was unusually quiet considering there was a full-scale man-hunt under way. Every available officer was out chasing hundreds of lines of enquiry and tip-offs that had been generated by recent TV news coverage on a brutal, cold-blooded murder during an armed robbery.

Detective Sergeant Callum Ferguson glanced at the white-faced clock on the wall. It was almost 1am and he'd been on duty for the last three days straight.

He stretched aching shoulders, rolling his neck and pulled a face at the smell coming from his shirt. Levering himself out of the chair he'd been glued to for the last few hours, he went to the kitchen at the end of the corridor in search of caffeine. Strong, black coffee was the order of the day . . . or was it still night?

As he waited for the kettle to boil, his thoughts turned to the men the press had dubbed "Britain's most wanted". For once, it was no exaggeration.

Eddie Frazer and his older brother Duncan. Britain's most prolific armed robbers. On the run after the late-night robbery of a high-end jewellers in Fordley city centre had ended in the killing of the security guard.

Armed robbery – one of the most serious crimes in the statute books – was only topped by murder. In one fell swoop, the Frazers had gone to the top of the offences league table. Something that would earn them both more than one lifetime behind bars.

Callum poured boiling water onto cheap coffee granules and carried his mug back to the office, wishing the department could afford a proper coffee percolator.

He'd been trawling hours of CCTV footage from premises around the jewellers, as they'd pieced together the movements of the Frazer brothers prior to the robbery.

Predictably, the vital piece of film – from the shop itself – was missing. But that was all part of the Frazers' M.O. Their Modus Operandi. To take the flash drive from whatever cameras were operating in or outside the building and dispose of it, along with any other incriminating evidence. A strategy they'd perfected in the commission of high risk jobs that, over the years, had netted them millions of pounds in cash and jewellery. The kind of wealth they would never earn through legitimate employment open to two working class lads from impoverished backgrounds.

Not that such a route had ever been likely, given that their father, Freddie Frazer, was regarded as the best safe cracker in the business. An old-school, East End villain, employed by gangs whenever blowing a safe or an explosive entry into premises was required.

In the years before he died, Old Man Frazer helped his sons hone their craft. Passing on the trade he'd learned during his service with the Royal Engineers in World War II, making Europe safe by neutralizing unexploded ordnance. Returning home at the end of the war to a London that offered a man like him few opportunities and even less of a living wage. He'd gone on to use his skills in a less honourable, but far more lucrative, trade.

Callum took a mouthful of coffee without tasting it as he scanned the footage of the brothers. Parking a van and a motorbike in different side streets near the jewellers and walking separately to their target.

Both were dressed in black cargo pants and dark coloured jackets. Both wearing baseball caps pulled down low and bandanas covering the lower half of their faces. Less conspicuous than balaclavas.

Callum watched as the two figures, masked and anonymous, walked to the target, as if they had all the time in the world.

They certainly were 'surveillance savvy' as his boss, Detective Chief Inspector Ron Brennan, had said when he'd briefed the team.

'These men know what they're doing.' He'd addressed the room in the hours after the robbery. 'They steal the vehicles they're going to use weeks before the offence. Then stash them out of sight. Probably in a lockup somewhere, until the day of the job.'

The stout DCI tapped the whiteboard that had a map of the city stuck on it.

'They arrive separately, sometimes a few hours apart. Driving round to make sure there's no police presence. If the slightest thing smells 'off' they abandon the job and walk away. It might just be a feeling. An instinct that makes them uneasy. The villains equivalent of a "coppers nose".'

Brennan perched on the edge of a desk, his large stomach straining the buttons of his shirt.

'They've always gone armed,' he went on. 'When they've done bank jobs or travel agents, they fire shots over the heads of guards or members of the public. To intimidate . . .make them compliant.' He paused to look at the photo of the guard who'd been killed.

'People have been injured before trying to catch these bastards . . .' His words trailed off.

Callum knew Brennan was thinking about his closest friend. A cop who'd been injured in a car accident during a high-speed pursuit of the Frazers fifteen years earlier.

Brennan had been a DI in the Met then and his partner had sustained injuries that ended his police career. Brennan's team arrested the brothers and sent them both down for that offence. Unfortunately, it seemed, not for long enough. Brennan had moved to West Yorkshire to take up a promotion as DCI and here he was, by a twist of fate, hunting the Frazers again.

'This time,' Ron Brennan was saying. 'Someone's been killed.' He turned back to the sea of faces hanging on his every word.

'So, this is a murder enquiry and these two bastards are in the wind.' He stood in front of the team, legs slightly apart, as though bracing himself on the deck of a tilting ship.

'We've got Authorised Firearms Officers deployed with instructions to take whatever action they deem necessary to keep the public safe. These men are armed and dangerous and have shown they won't hesitate to shoot a police officer – or anyone else who gets in their way.'

Brennan's bitterness was palpable and Callum wondered whether his boss's involvement was strictly ethical, given that he had a personal investment in this. But as SIO – Senior Investigating Officer – on call when the robbery had gone down, Brennan had picked up the case and things were moving so fast there wasn't time to think about alternatives.

Callum gestured that he had a question. His boss acknowledged him with a nod.

'Callum?'

'You know these two better than anyone.'

'Unfortunately, yes.'

'In your opinion, will they stay together . . .or split up? Now they're on the run?'

The DCI took a long breath, blowing his cheeks out as he thought about it.

'Although they've always stuck together in the past, my gut tells me that this time they'll go their separate ways.'

'Why's that?' One of the young DCs at the back asked.

'Because they've crossed a line.' He moved from the corner of the desk and went to the board, standing for a long moment to stare at the mug shots of the Frazer brothers.

'One of them . . .' he tapped the pictures with a nicotine-stained finger, 'murdered that guard. Killing someone is a first for these two and that's going to shake them up. If I was the one who *didn't* pull the trigger, I'd want to distance myself from the one who did.' He turned to face his team. 'Wouldn't you?'

Callum listened to the murmur of voices around the room, uncertain about his own opinion on the matter.

He didn't have a brother. Didn't have any siblings for that matter. But if he had, and if they'd been as close as the Frazers, would he abandon his brother after something like this? He really wasn't sure. But he envied his boss's certainty.

He was determined to learn as much from Brennan as he could while serving as a DS on his team with the Regional Crime Squad. The man had an enviable reputation. Not just within West Yorkshire police, but across other forces too.

Known as a good thief taker. Someone who got results and the only officer in London's Metropolitan Force to have secured the arrest and conviction of both Frazer brothers.

As if his thoughts had conjured him up, Ron Brennan came into the incident room. He looked flushed and was slightly out of breath.

'Callum?' he called as he went into his glass-walled office.

'Boss?' The DS was already on his feet.

'Duncan Frazer's been shot dead by the firearms team.'

'Bloody hell! Where?'

Callum went into his boss's office, standing in front of the desk as DCI Brennan went through desk drawers, looking for something.

'Traffic got intelligence on a stolen car. Forced a stop on the M62. When officers approached, he pointed a sawn-off shotgun at them. They had no choice.'

Callum didn't think his boss sounded particularly cut up about it.

'And Eddie Frazer?'

Brennan fished a packet of cigarettes from one of the drawers and lit up, blowing a stream of smoke in the direction of the "No Smoking" sign.

'He wasn't in the car . . . unfortunately.'

Whatever Callum was going to say was cut short by his boss's desk phone ring.

'Brennan.'

Callum was standing close enough to hear the other side of the conversation.

'Eddie Frazer just made a call to the information hotline, sir. I've been asked to contact you as the SIO, so you can hear the recording.'

Brennan punched the handsfree button so they could both listen. 'OK . . . Go ahead.'

There was a hiss over the airwaves and then the voice of the man they were hunting filled the office.

'This is Eddie Frazer. You bastards just murdered my brother.'

The call handler chipped in.

'Sorry sir, who's murdered your brother?'

'You have!' Frazer shouted. *"Armed police shot him dead. When you stopped his car . . . We were talking on the phone. You bastards! I listened . . . heard it all, when you killed him . . .'*

Callum leaned closer to the phone. There were unintelligible sounds. He thought maybe the man was sobbing but couldn't tell for sure. Then the calmer voice of the call handler came through.

'What's your brother's name?'

'Duncan . . . Duncan Frazer.'

'OK. Can I ask–'

'No!' Eddie exploded down the phone. *'You can't ask any fucking thing. What you can do is listen, right?'*

'OK, I'm listening.'

'I know you're looking for me. You're hunting both of us. Well, you've got what you wanted. One of the Frazers in a fucking body bag and I know you want me next.'

'We don't want to hurt you–'

'I'm telling you now that I wasn't in on this robbery. I wasn't involved in killing that guard. But that won't matter to you lot . . . never has.'

'I'm sorry, can I–'

'You're not sorry!' He screamed down the phone, his voice cracking with rage. 'Now he's dead, it's just me. You lot will go to court and lie. Get me fitted up for this latest bit of work and throw away the key now it's murder. You're going to try to get me finished one way or the other. But I can prove I wasn't on this job. Can prove I didn't shoot that guard.'

'Okay.'

'So here it is . . . I'm going to call back in fifteen minutes and I want to speak to DCI Ron Brennan on the Regional Crime Squad – got that?'

'Yes.'

'Make sure it's Brennan. No one else. I'm not talking to some high-ranking monkey with braid on his cap trying to get the glory. It's got to be Brennan. He knows us. He'll know when I show him the evidence that it's right . . . Who it is. Brennan's been in this from the start, so he's got to be the one that hears me out.'

'Yes, got that.'

'Tell him I'll give him the proof once and for all. Not just this . . . all of it.'

'Right, and where are you?'

'I'm not telling you where I am.'

'OK.'

'Fifteen minutes.'

The line snapped off and Eddie Frazer was gone.